I0621665

DOORS OF DARKNESS

III

The Mall

EDITED BY
CALEB J. PECUE

INTRODUCTION BY
DUNCAN RALSTON

TERRORCORE
PUBLISHING

"Glamour Magique" copyright © 2025 by Nadine Stewart;
"Unnatural Wonders" copyright © 2025 by AJ Danna;
"Big Break" copyright © 2025 by Austin Hinderliter;
"Jilly's" copyright © 2025 by John Martin;
"Skin Deep" copyright © 2025 by Reece G. Donnell;
"Tangerine Blue" copyright © 2025 by Billie Karras;
"The Great Communicator" copyright © 2025 by Adrian DeLeon;
"Ballif's Boo-doir" copyright © 2025 by Liam Ray III;
"Bleed for Me" copyright © 2025 by G.D. Bowlin;
"Beneath Still Water" copyright © 2025 by Jason Harlow;
"Tandemonium" copyright © 2025 by AudraKate Gonzalez;
"A Simple Act of Kindness" copyright © 2025 by Vincent St. Claire;
"Little King" copyright © 2025 by William MacFarland;
"Parrish Photos" copyright © 2025 by Vanessa Leonardo;
"Waste Not, Want Not" copyright © 2025 by Fionna Cosgrove;
"Banana Split" copyright © 2025 by Elisabeth Tuttle;

All of the characters in this book are fictitious, and any resemblance to actual person, living or dead, is purely coincidental.

DOORS OF DARKNESS III: THE MALL

A Terrorcore Publishing LLC book / published by arrangement with Caleb J. Pecue

PRINTING HISTORY
Terrorcore edition published 2025

All rights reserved.
Copyright © 2025 by Caleb James Pecue.
Cover Design by Austin Hinderliter at Creepy Carves Design.
This book may not be reproduced in whole or in part,
by mimeograph or any other means, without permission.
For information email: Terrorcore Publishing,
terrorcorepublishing@gmail.com

Paperback Edition: 979-8-9889138-7-0,
Hardback Edition: 979-8-9889138-8-7,

Terrorcore Books are published by Terrorcore Publishing LLC
2501 Chatham Rd, Suite N
Springfield, IL 62704

Editor's Note

The following stories take place during the July 4th festivities at Sherwood Mall, a fictional mall in California, in 1986.

Doors of Darkness III: The Mall is the third volume in the *Doors of Darkness* series; however, it is not a continuation of any of the stories from the first or second volumes. One does not have to have read the first two volumes in order to enjoy this one.

Sherwood MALL

CLOTHING & FASHION

New Wave Threads	A1
Super Skates	A13
Denim Dream	A15
Sole Sensation	A18
Metro Menswear	A19
Retro Glam	B1
Rad Rags	B2
Little King Clothing *(p. 245)*	B5
Sharper Look	B6
Fit For You	B9
The Velvet Hanger	C1
Flex Appeal	C2
Something Blue	C3
Huwell's Fine Leathers *(p. 227)*	C11
High Tide Swim & Surf	C14
Tickled Pink	C15
Timberline Outfitters	D1
Charmed Life	E10
Draped in Velvet	E11
Street Style	F1
Crimson Kiss	F2
Beyond Basics	F8
Time Warp Tees	F10
The Ivy League	F12
Wild Wonders	F13

SHOES & ACCESSORIES

The Glitter Box	A5
The Satin Rose	A20
Bag Lady	A22
Tread Lightly	B3
Prestige Eyewear	C7
Sole Envy	E3
Mad Hatters	E5
Signature Scents	E9
The Fashion Vault	F6
Luxe Locks	F7
Adorned	G2
Frill Seeker	G3
Varsity Club	G5
Majective Frames	G7

Silken Dreams	G8

JEWELRY & LUXE

The Perfume Stop	A9
Gilded Age	B4
The Gold Mine	C4
Jeweler's Palace	E1
Gilded & Glitzy	F11

FOOD

Sweet Surrender	B12
Pizza Paradise	H1
Sizzle & Stack	H2
Orange Julius	H3
Banana Split *(p. 295)*	H4
Dog House Delights	H5

BEAUTY & GROOMING

Glam Slam	A2
Betty's Salon *(p. 89)*	A4
Sunkissed Styles	A21
Lush Lashes	B7
Funky Fingers	C9
The Classic Cut	D2

SPECIALTY STORES

All-Star Sports	A3
Grace's Lace	A8
Stich & Style	A11
Snap & Go	B8
Timeless Timepieces	B11
The Crafters' Nook	B13
Grand Expressions	D5
Victory Lane	E2
Ernie's Electronics *(p. 277)*	E4
Sherwood Pets	E8
Memento	F5
Parrish Photos *(p. 263)*	F14

HOBBIES

Puzzle Palace	A14
Ballif's Boo-doir *(p. 161)*	B14
Jack's Toy Box *(p. 141)*	C6

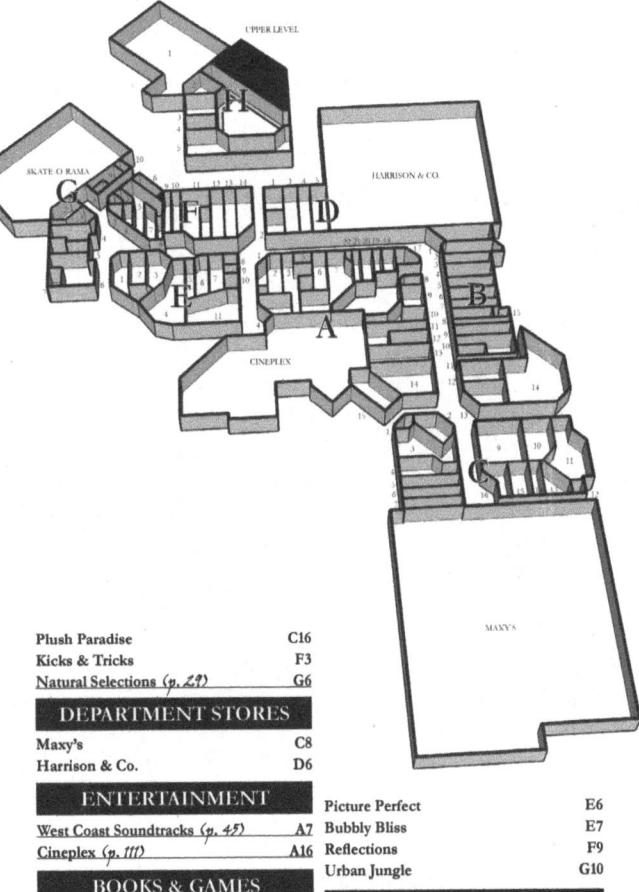

UPPER LEVEL

SKATE O RAMA

HARRISON & CO.

CINEPLEX

MAXY'S

WHAT CAN YOU SAY ABOUT shopping malls that hasn't already been said? Judging by the stories you're about to delve in to, quite a lot, apparently. If you've ever lived in any sort of urban center, malls will have been a ubiquitous part of your life whether you like it or not. Being able to buy everything in one place, your "one-stop shop," as they used to say, can be a difficult convenience to pass up. Malls aren't just shopping centers either, but also act as social hubs, where people convene to browse, have a quick bite to eat, watch a movie, or hang out with friends.

So what is it that makes the mall so innately disturbing? When—and *why*—did our love affair with malls become tainted by dread and outright horror?

Though the genesis of this change may have come decades earlier, the ultra-consumerism and mega-inflation of the late-1970s and early '80s in particular seemed to have warped our view of malls, inspiring such classic horror films as *Dawn of the Dead, Chopping Mall, Gremlins, Gremlins 2,* and the climax of *Prom Night II: Hello, Mary Lou.*

Since the late-twentieth century—a phrase which pains my Gen X heart to use—modern society has taken a different perspective on blind consumerism. Most of us no longer "shop 'til we drop"—a phrase in itself laced with unintentional horror—and though we may still consume just as much as we did then, these days, that consumption is likelier to be done at a big-box store, or from the comfort and convenience of our own homes via the internet.

With those big-box and online stores came the death knell for the shopping mall itself. In the 1980s, there were as many as twenty-five hundred malls in the continental United States. Now, upwards of four hundred are considered "dead" or "dying" by realtors. Is it a coincidence we call these abandoned centers of commerce "*dead* malls" or "*ghost* malls," terms both synonymous with horror?

I don't think so.

Inherently, we all feel the almost uncanny discomfort of the shopping mall. The *alienness*. I have this recurring dream. I'm walking in an empty mall after hours. It's at once familiar and strangely *un*familiar. I don't know why I'm there, but I know I went there because I needed… *something* (and isn't there always a *something* we need?). As I wander the familiar promenades and mezzanines, the ordinary begins to deform into an M.C. Escher nightmare. Escalators to nowhere. Stairwells that become catwalks with glass railings.

Picture yourself in one of these massive, brightly lit spaces. Maybe the mall you used to hang out in as a teen, or the one your parents took you to as a child. You're locked inside and you're alone—or at least you *think* you are. Maybe it's even the last *living* mall in the world.

The escalators stand still, silent. You wander through a food court lacking the comforting scents of greasy, fried foods, with empty tables and cold seats, with faint outlines of spills that won't quite come clean. (Is that *blood* there? No—it's just ketchup. *Got* to be.)

Storefronts are cloaked in half-light, filled with darkened aisles and rows upon rows of goods held behind glass, just out of reach. Mannequins frozen in unnatural poses, as if caught in mid-movement. The smell of sterile cleaning products, like a hospital. Or a morgue.

Everything too clean, too quiet.

As you quicken your pace, your footsteps echo off the glass atrium ceiling, down halls that seem to stretch much longer than they had a moment before. There's no canned music over the P.A., no shopper announcements. No buzz of conversation or the chaotic chatter of crowds. There's no children's laughter, no teens loitering outside a noisy arcade.

It's just you and you alone, left with a cold dread that the Mall itself might be listening to you. *Watching* you.

You begin to feel like if you keep going, the exits themselves might vanish. That the escalators might start moving again, though not in any direction you'd want to go. That some *thing* might be following a few steps behind you, always just out of sight.

Behind closed doors and down shadowy, silent aisles lurks a thousand liminal spaces, and you can't be certain that any of them are exactly empty.

You could lose your sanity quite easily here. Lose your *self*.

And if you wander too long, if you don't *hurry*, something else might find you.

Beware: from the horrifying to the bizarrely macabre, the tales within this anthology—within t*his mall*, Sherwood Mall—are guaranteed to disturb. The next time you visit the mall, you'll wonder if there might not be a bizarre alien creature within a hidden storeroom, or worse, a hidden room in which children disappear. Is that haunted attraction in the Boo-doir more than just plastic skeletons and rubber bats? What's that knocking behind the door in Jilly's? And what really happens when the lids close on the tanning bed in Tandemonium?

You will discover the chilling answers to these questions and more between the covers of this book or, more likely these days, on your e-reader screen.

Just be sure you make it out of Sherwood Mall before night falls . . . and enjoy your shopping experience while you still can.

Duncan Ralston
June 28th, 2025

1

GLAMOUR MAGIQUE
Nadine Stewart

H EY, KATIE-CAT! GIVE YOUR OLD man a hand here, would ya?" her Appa shouted from the side employee-only entrance near the back of the store. Kate peered down the last aisle and saw Appa struggling to hold the door open while maneuvering a dolly over the threshold.

"Hold on, hold on, before you break something, I'm coming." Kate dropped the price gun on the table and rushed to hold the door for her dad. "Appa, I thought the whole point of the sale this weekend was to thin out the inventory. The store is already so crowded. Where are we going to put all that?" She gestured to the five black boxes stacked on the dolly.

"Oh, don't you worry your pretty little head about that, my worrisome daughter, I have a feeling these products won't be hanging around very long. If I'm right, they are going to fly off the shelves."

It took every ounce of willpower she had not to roll her eyes and audibly groan. She had heard this same phrase more times than she could count, but she must not have done a good job at hiding her obvious doubts because when her Appa had finished offloading the boxes, he took her by the shoulders and looked her dead in the eyes, "This is different, Katie-Cat. This is going to change everything. Now, help me clear off the end of the aisle closest to the cash register. This is going to be a big display."

~

Earlier that morning, Kate was nearly finished marking down the last item for the Fourth of July sale when her dad received a phone call. Minutes later, his car keys jingled in his hand as he hurried towards the door, "Be back in a jiffy, Katie-Cat. Hold down the fort."

A few days ago, Kate went through the store, pulling any items off the shelves that could be considered summer-related. Now, she was arranging them on the table up front that she used for the books they sold (after reading them all herself, of course). She pushed aside the horror paperbacks by authors like Stephen King, Dean Koontz, and Anne Rice and stacked up the VC Andrews collections she'd scoured thrift shops to find. Those were unusually popular with teenage girls and housewives.

She had found a good variety of merchandise for the summer sale: novelty beach towels featuring surfers and geometric patterns, several 12-piece tabletop picnic and barbecue condiment sets, wooden-handled BBQ tongs, inflatable beach balls, and some miscellaneous outdoor kids toys, including a couple of Skip-Its, a Pogo-Ball, a few off-brand water guns, and even a couple of lawn dart sets—although Kate still wondered how safe those were for kids to play with.

Taking a break from hanging decorative bunting around the shop, Kate squirmed on the tall stool behind the counter, trying to get comfortable. Its worn leather cushion dug into the underside of her bare thighs, exposed from her jean shorts which did little to protect the sensitive skin. The silver duct tape that her Appa used to mend the rips and tears made her itch, leaving red welts that would look hideous if she even attempted to wear a bathing suit in the stifling July heat. Just another one of the many excuses she would use to cover up her body as much as possible if she was forced into some terrible, embarrassing social scenario. Kate hunched over the counter with her elbows resting on the glass display case that housed their fanciest costume jewelry, pushing her glasses up on the bridge of her nose and blowing out a poof of air to blow her hopelessly straight bangs out of her eyes. It housed everything from mood rings and best friend necklaces to gold chains and bangle-style bracelets. She thumbed through the pages of an issue of *Tales From the Crypt*. She could hear her Appa's voice in her head—*Don't lean on the glass, Katie-Cat. If you break it, we'll be up shit's creek.*

Their novelty bargain store—BARGAIN GIFTS & NOVELTIES—was tucked away at the far end of the eastern corridor of Sherwood Mall. It would be nearly impossible to find a smaller, more out-of-the-way spot, but Appa couldn't afford the rent on one of the bigger retail spaces with higher foot traffic. Sure, customers meandered in and out every day, but mostly in passing. Usually, while lost looking for the restrooms. Turning those "just browsing" customers into sales was a bit more difficult. Their store was . . . how would you say it nicely . . . eclectic? It was stocked with items that could draw a crowd, but that few needed or wanted.

Appa tried to stay on top of trends, but he was always either just too late as the popularity of something was dying down, or he found the knock-off version to sell. Which all ended up collecting dust for eternity while remaining on the shelves. No lie. Kate looked around at the crowded little store, wondering what Appa would grace their aisles with next. "Aisles" made their store sound larger and fancier than it was really. In truth, you walked through the entrance and were greeted by a mirrored wall of—blink and you'd miss them—back-lit glass shelves to the right across from the register where she sat now. These displayed what her Appa called the *fancy* collectibles. The top two shelves were dedicated to Blue Mountain Pottery pieces. These distinctive blue-green items from Canada used to be wildly popular and were often purchased as wedding gifts, but the fad seemed to be a tad outdated now, so various dishes, vases, ducks, dolphins, poodles, and swans remained untouched and forgotten. Below that were two shelves of Boyd's Bears and two shelves of Precious Moments ornaments. They sold more of these around certain holidays like Mother's Day or Christmas. Children and husbands returned each year like clockwork to pick out another figurine for their loved ones to add to their collections; a purchase that required little thought or effort.

To the left of the entrance near the register, Appa stocked discounted candy bars, chips, and other snacks. This was probably their highest turnaround and the most foot traffic they got, especially on weekends. Appa knew very well how much everything was marked up at the snack bar at the Cineplex and made sure to carry the same candy and chocolate but at much lower prices so that customers would buy from his store and then sneak their snacks into the movie theater. How their store made enough money to stay in business was a mystery to her, but it was probably because of this alone.

The remainder of the store was divided into three congested aisles by two rows of end-to-end mismatched wooden shelving units. The white brick walls were lined with shelves as well. A rack selling strange apparel, typically featuring misprinted logos or other illegally imported t-shirt designs of well-known cartoons and television series, was located in the open area in front of the store, right in front of the entrance, close to Kate's book table.

No matter how slow the inventory moved or how cramped the store got, Kate's dad still couldn't bring himself to let anything go. She suspected this was from his time in Korea. He didn't talk about his childhood very often. He preferred to focus on his new life in America, where he had met Kate's mother, but he still found value in teaching Kate about her culture through language and food. There were probably a dozen faux Korean mink blankets from ten years ago, pristine in their plastic zippered bags lining the tops of the back shelves. She was certain that the tops of them must have been covered in an inch-thick layer of dust. She and Appa didn't keep the shop as clean and organized as her Umma had, always flitting around with her rainbow feather duster like it was a magic wand ready to eradicate every dust mite in sight. When something wasn't selling, she'd be the first to notice and come up with the best strategy to move each item. Appa often said Kate's Umma could "sell sand to tourists at the beach." However, she didn't visit the store very often after becoming ill. Kate was left to take over her father's evening and weekend shifts after school, and they were both simply too busy to give dusting much thought.

Kate's thoughts were interrupted by a frantic-looking woman approaching the counter.

"Excuse me, miss . . ." her eyes darting around the store. She continued as she looked up and down each aisle. "Have you seen my son . . . he's eighteen, only about five-foot-one . . . has bad acne. His name is Tony and he's missing . . ." She showed Kate a photo and looked at her with wide eyes, half full of tears and hope.

"I'm terribly sorry, ma'am. It hasn't been very busy yet today, and no one matching that description has come in or wandered by that I've noticed, but I'll keep an eye out. Tony, short, with bad acne you said?" Though she wasn't sure she would need it, he was probably a run away or something. Kate wrote the young man's description on the receipt pad next to the register.

"Thank you, miss, I really appreciate that."

Kate watched as the woman did a half-shuffle run across the mall's white tiled floor into Maxy's department store across the way, her head cranking this way and that, looking for any signs of her son. If this was any indication of how this day was going to go, she was not looking forward to it. Kate was already dreading this weekend. Every store was required to participate in the annual *July 4ᵗʰ Red, White, and Blue Extravaganza Sale* at the mall, which meant hanging festive patriotic decorations and putting up sale signs. Her Appa loved it. He was proud of his American citizenship, but it just felt like a whole lot of work for such little payoff. Sure, they'd see a few more customers than usual and be able to clear out some old stock, but she'd rather just sit and read like usual.

~

Now Kate stood over the elegant black boxes her Appa had mysteriously acquired. With his silver boxcutter, Appa carefully opened them. She had to admit she was more than a little curious. These boxes looked fancier than anything they had ever stocked in the store. They were matte black with just two words embossed in gold in the middle of each box:

Glamour Magique

A cardboard display folded in thirds was inside the flatter box at the very top of the pile. The brand name was stamped below in the distinctive gold cursive font, and it fit around the end cap of the aisle with the faces of several celebrities at the top. Pictures of different cosmetics, including lipstick, eyeshadow, mascara, blush, and foundation, were displayed along the sides of the exhibit. The fact that they had never sold makeup before piqued Kate's interest even more. Kate didn't wear a lot of makeup, so she didn't know much about it or how to apply it properly. She felt self-conscious most of the time and felt like makeup only enhanced the areas of her face she already didn't like. Her hooded eyes never allowed her to wear eyeliner quite like the other girls, and she had small, thin lips she never even paid attention to until one mean girl in school pointed them out.

"Kate, you have bunny lips," Marissa had said, standing next to her, applying bright pink lipstick in front of the mirror in the girl's bathroom. At first, Kate thought she was being nice, after all, bunnies were cute, but it wouldn't be the first time her lack of understanding of social cues would bite her in the ass.

"Oh thanks, but do bunnies even have lips?" Kate had naively asked.

"That's my point!" Marissa snickered as she and the rest of her mean-girl posse giggled and flipped their pretty, perfectly crimped hair back out into the hallway.

This was pretty much the story of Kate's life. Now a senior in high school, she was still miserable every day and dreaded going to school, feeling like she didn't fit in. It was either because of her ethnicity or being a little chubbier than the other kids. One of her earliest and only memories from kindergarten was sitting on the ground outside at recess by the swings, alone and crying because one of her new friends had called her fat. Bullies would reiterate this phrase in one form or another, some more creative than others, for the rest of her years in school. So began a lifetime of low self-esteem punctuated by fad diets, Jane Fonda workout videos (a few of which were still on a shelf for sale somewhere here at the store), crying into her pillow late at night, and slowly developing such extreme social anxiety that Kate would rather stay home or work at the store than hang out with the few friends she did have. All to avoid any uncomfortable social situations where all she did was worry if her clothes were cool enough to fit in or if her outfit made her look fat. When a guy was nice to her, Kate would spend the entire night overthinking their conversation and intentions. Would any boy ever like her or kiss her? She would dejectedly realize, probably not. Why would they when they could pick any other skinny, pretty blonde girl from their friend group?

Kate's focus was drawn back to the boxes in front of her as the temperature in the store seemed to drop just then, the air conditioning rarely worked, and for one of the hottest weekends all year, Kate was confused when goosebumps erupted on her bare arms as an unexpected chilly breeze ruffled her shirt and blew through her hair as Appa opened the next box. Nestled into their own individual slots were several rows of black lipstick tubes. She and Appa each pulled one out. The tube itself was black with the gold *Glamour Magique* font. Turning it in her hand, she saw more words in gold cursive that said *"Naomi-Plum Kiss."* She showed her dad, and he handed her his. This one said *"Kelly-Berry Pink."*

"Appa, are these the only two colors?"

"Well, ya, Katie-Cat," he said, trying to sound confident, "like I . . . ah . . . said I got a great deal, and these are overstock items, so we aren't going to have the whole line, but this brand has been flying off the shelves in Europe. We are lucky I even got my hands on these."

"How *did* you come to *'get your hands on these'*?" Kate air quoted at her dad suspiciously.

Her Appa rubbed the back of his neck nervously, beads of sweat forming on his forehead.

"Appa?" He looked at her without saying anything as he lifted the lipstick, and its display stand out of the box. *"Appa?* What aren't you telling me?"

"It's nothing, really, Katie-Cat, my usual supplier, got a call from a guy who said he had some overstock that would go pretty fast. If he knew anyone interested, it needed to be picked up right away and to bring cash. But when I got there, John wasn't around, and the guy seemed desperate to unload everything on the back of the truck, along with a bunch of other items. He was twitchy, glancing over his shoulder, all amped up, rubbing his hands together, just acting all jittery like he was in a hurry. My first instinct was *Oh hell no*, I don't usually do business like that, Kate, you know that. I was ready to turn around and leave, thinking it was too risky. But when he uncovered these boxes, the sun hit the gold embossed lettering just right, sparkling in the morning light. The words *Glamour Magique* swam before my eyes, and something just said this was too good to be true. A deal like this doesn't come around very often, and I felt compelled to take the risk for some reason. Before I knew it, I had handed over the cash, was all loaded up, and on my way back to the mall."

"Appa, what if this is —" Kate looked around to make sure they were still alone, and no one had wandered in from the mall, " —*stolen* merchandise?" she whispered.

"It'll be fine, Katie-Cat. They can't be stolen. Not from around here, at least. I don't think this brand has even made it to stores in the States yet. Pretty sure we will be the only store around selling it, and that's another reason I had to jump at the chance. What perfect timing! With the Fourth of July Sale this weekend, we could surely bring in a crowd if we can figure out how to get the word out quickly. I wish we had some fliers or something to hand out."

Something wasn't sitting right with Kate. Her Appa was usually very by the book. He never took big risks like this. He avoided anything shady that could paint him, the family, or their business negatively. It was important to maintain one's honor and the honor of their family. That had been drilled into her since she was a child. Kate's grandparents had immigrated to America after the Korean War, wanting to believe in the ideas of American democracy and freedom . . . only to discover a country full of its own shameful history of racial oppression of immigrants and other people of color. They would not fall into any stereotypes placed on them. Her grandparents worked tirelessly to provide the best opportunities and a better future for their son, sending her dad to college and university. Yet, he still ended up having to be self-employed like so many other Korean-American men. It didn't make a difference that her dad spoke perfect English and considered himself as American as apple pie. His patriotism was not enough to break through the racial barriers in the workforce. She knew this hurt him deeply, but it was also why he worked hard to provide for their family honestly.

"Katie-Cat! Look, the company actually included some brochures. We can hand these out in the food court or outside the department stores. I bet when people see what we have, we will make a killing by the end of the weekend." Appa handed her the fliers out of the next box as he finished stocking the shelves with various cosmetics. Kate couldn't deny his enthusiasm. She enjoyed seeing her dad excited. *Lighter.* With her Umma sick, her Appa hadn't been his usual fun-loving self as often. She would keep the rest of her reservations to herself, hoping to hold onto this version of her Appa a little while longer.

Kate flipped through the pamphlet. It looked like all the products were named after celebrities or supermodels. Each page of the trifold leaflet featured a different celebrity or two matched up to a makeup product under banners that stated things like *Beauty Unveiled, Confidence Revealed* or *Makeup to Allure,* and even *Why Be You When You Could be Someone Else?* Glamour Magique promised you could have Naomi Campbell's lips, Cindy Crawford's cheekbones, Madonna's perfect skin, Grace Jones's eyes, or Brook Shields' brows, amongst others. Kate rolled her eyes at this, but oddly, she wondered if this lipstick could *genuinely* make her thin, little bunny lips look "Plump & Pouty" like Kelly LeBrock's. *Hmmm . . . maybe I should take one to try . . . it couldn't hurt, right?* Without realizing it, Kate had grabbed a handful of lipstick tubes from the shelf.

"Kate, what are you up to?" Her Appa looked at her strangely.

Interrupted from a trance-like state, Kate froze with a handful of lipstick. More tubes were sticking out of her pocket. "Ummm . . . I just ah . . . thought that maybe people would like to see the product while I handed out the fliers . . . ya. I figure it's just about lunchtime, so I could go hit the lunch crowd at the food court while you finish setting up the display."

Her Appa gave her a big smile, "That's my Katie-Cat, always thinking."

Grabbing another stack of brochures and waving a little salute, Kate headed towards the mall entrance. "That's me, always thinking!"

What was I thinking? I hate lipstick, and why was I grabbing handfuls of it? Kate made her way through the mall, past the area that housed the Cineplex. Looking up, she was reminded why she loved the neon lights that zig-zagged around the ceiling. The pink, blue, and purple lasers were mesmerizing. They helped distract her from the anxiety and claustrophobia she felt amongst the throngs of teenagers and families with screeching children closing in around her as she followed the wave of bodies through the concourse. She saw a bit of commotion as she neared the south escalators. A few people were huddled together with a security guard. *Probably shoplifters,* she thought to herself. They were always about but even more brazen during busy sale weekends when they were less likely to be caught.

The food court was directly above the opposite end of the mall from where Bargain Gifts & Novelties was located. As Kate slowly made her way up the escalator to the upper level of the mall, her stomach rumbled immediately as her nostrils were overwhelmed with the smell of greasy burgers, pizza, and the sickly sweet smell of waffle cones, all competing for attention. You'd think the onslaught of all the different food smells wafting from the food court would make you sick rather than beckon you in to spend half an hour trying to decide what you wanted to eat, but the loud whirring blenders from the Orange Julius stand both grated on Kate's nerves and made her crave a Triple Berry smoothie.

She ignored her stomach for the time being and parked herself at the top of one of the down escalators. As shoppers were heading back down after lunch, she handed them a brochure and told them to head to Bargain Gifts & Novelties for an exclusive chance to get their hands on the popular cosmetic line that wasn't yet available in any other store in the country. Some people looked genuinely intrigued, while others had never heard of it but said they'd check it out. However, Kate watched over the railing as most of them just threw the pamphlet in the garbage can at the bottom of the escalator.

"Oh my gosh, did you see what Becky was wearing? Like how did she think that looked good on her. I don't know what Billy sees in her. He could do so much better."

Oh crap, oh crap. Kate looked around frantically for a place to hide as the cackling, catty girls got closer, but it was too late. She knew there was always a possibility she could run into kids from school at the mall. Still, it rarely happened unless they came in to buy snacks for the movies. She was usually pretty stealthy at dodging anyone she wanted to avoid. If Kate saw them walking through the crowds, she could easily duck into a store until they walked by, but she'd have to face Marissa and her entourage full-on today. Kate tugged down her t-shirt to make sure her butt and tummy were covered while one hand went to her hair to see if it had any volume left at all, but she already knew it was more than likely bone straight. Why she let these girls get to her, she had no idea, but around them, she all of a sudden felt less than human, and the lipstick in her pocket seemed to be calling her name again. *You can be like them.*

"What are *you* doing here, Kate? Shouldn't you be stocking shelves or something in that dusty old store of your parents?" Marissa laughed, looking around at the other girls as if she had just made the funniest joke ever, and they burst into a fit of giggles right on cue.

Give them the lipstick . . . "Here, I have some ah—samples for you girls."

"Why would we want samples from . . . wait . . ." Marissa snatched the *Kelly-Berry Pink* lipstick out of Kate's hand. "You can't be serious. Where did you get these?" she asked, looking at Kate with utter disbelief.

"What? This?" She handed Marissa one of the *Glamour Magique* brochures. "It just so happens our store has received the only shipment in the country. Kind of like a . . . trial run . . . ya. If these overstock products do well, then they will consider opening to a wider market. We have a small exclusive sampling of products from the whole line." Kate clenched her jaw and gave a fake smile. *Why did I just make all that up?*

"Hold on, let me see that." Marissa and the bobblehead girls flipped through the brochure, trying to hold back their excitement. "How do we know this is the real stuff?"

"Try it on. Who else wants a free sample?" her voice, now an octave higher, sang out. Kate handed out the last of her pocket lipstick to a chorus of 'Me! Me! Me's!'"

Marissa unzipped her purple, leather fanny pack, pulling out a clamshell compact makeup mirror. Pursing her pouty mouth, she applied the frosty pink shade to her already perfect lips. "Whoa, far out." She turned her head sideways, then blew fake kisses at the mirror. "This is rad. My lips look so much plumper, wow. This stuff is like magic. Here, you girls try." She passed her mirror to the other girls, and they all took turns right there, standing in a semicircle at the top of the escalators, applying their shades. When they were all done, they stood *oohing* and *ahhing* at one another's lips.

Kate didn't get it. She didn't see any difference whatsoever in how these girls looked from five minutes ago. The only difference was the color of their lips. It was as if the lipstick itself made the wearer see an illusion of a transformation, but wasn't that what all makeup did? Transform you into someone you weren't? Kate shook off the odd feeling she was having again and chalked it up to the power of suggestion. "Remember, if you like what you see, then tell your friends to come check out *Glamour Magique* at Bargain Gifts & Novelties. We have limited stock, and it's going fast this weekend." Feeling weirdly confident, she turned her back and rode the escalator back to the bottom level of the mall.

~

By the time Kate arrived back at the store, her dad had finished the display. "Appa?" She had to admit it was pretty eye-catching. When you walked in the front entrance, your eyes were instantly drawn to the set-up. All the sparkly gold accents against the matte black background and packaging made the whole area thrum like a neon sign beckoning you to come closer. Kate stepped closer. *You know you could have it all . . .* Kate's head felt fuzzy, and her vision focused as she reached for the mascara—

"Katie-Cat! How did it go?"

Kate stumbled back, her Appa's hand on her shoulder, startling her. *What was she doing?* "Oh, you scared me." Kate laughed nervously. "It went okay. I kind of gave out some of the lipsticks as free samples, but before you get mad, hear me out. I was reading that brochure, and I think *Glamour Magique* is a product that has to be tried to be experienced. People won't believe it's any different than any other makeup product if they can't sample it first. If they do and they like it, then they will tell their friends about it, and then we can drum up some business through word of mouth."

"That's my Katie-Cat always —"

" —always thinking, I know." She rolled her eyes. Kate was starting to think she overthought everything.

"Well, Kate, do you think you can handle things here until closing tonight? I want to go home and check on your Umma. I'll take the opening shift tomorrow if you like."

"Ya that's fine, Appa. Tell Umma to save me some of her kong-guksu for dinner when I get home later." Kong-guksu, a cold noodle soup, was her favorite meal on hot summer days. As a child, Kate was frequently mocked and made fun of for bringing Korean lunches to school. She wished she could just eat a peanut butter and jelly sandwich like everyone else, but at home, she cherished the traditional Korean food that Umma had learned to cook from Kate's grandparents.

~

Kate secretly hated this time of night. Even on a busy holiday weekend, the mall was eerily quiet, especially at this end of the mall about half an hour before closing. It was different than the mornings. Mornings were a peaceful quiet, a time when she could just relax. Nights like this were just spooky. She always worried about creeps hanging around after hours. She had to make sure no one was hiding anywhere in the store as she locked up or that she wasn't followed to her car by anyone. In the winter when it was dark in the evenings, she would often call the security office and see if one of the guys could walk her through the dark parking lot. Even though it was still light out tonight, she felt anxious as she tidied up the backroom, preparing to close up.

It wasn't just the normal eeriness of the mall after hours that was getting to her. Kate couldn't stop thinking about Marissa and the desperate wannabes. They had hurried into the store earlier after their encounter at the escalators, but something wasn't right. They made a beeline towards the *Glamour Magique* display, practically tripping over one another. Kate watched with mild fascination and a little concern for their merchandise, but it was when they rushed the counter that she was taken aback. All the girls were licking and chewing their lips frantically. Some had bloody, cracked sores peeking out through heavily applied lipstick. They must have had ten coats caked on their mouths. It made them look like deranged beauty queens.

"Yo, Kate, like wow. This stuff is fantabulous! We have had so many looks. Guys can't keep from checking us out. We have to have one of everything in every color." A long, slimy, blood-tinged ribbon of drool dropped from her mouth onto the counter as she thrust a handful of items into Kate's hands. "Ring us up. Quick."

Kate, speechless, just stood and stared at them while punching in the prices on the register. Each of the girls now had matching clamshell mirrors and was pulling them out of their fanny packs, reapplying another coat of lipstick to their already gooey, crusty lips. She finished ringing them all up, handed them their bags, and they left as quickly as they came. *What the fuck!?*

Now she was alone at the far end of a creepy mall corridor and couldn't wait to close up and get the hell out of there. She had just flicked the switch on the storeroom wall to dim the main store lights when she heard the familiar *KA-DING KA-DING* of the sensor alerting them when someone entered the store. *Oh, what fresh hell is this* . . . she thought as she shut the storeroom door behind her. *KA-DING KA-DING.* Someone else had entered. *KA-DING KA-DING KA-DING KA-DING More customers?*

At this time of night? "Hey, we are just closing up, I'm sorry you're going to have to come back tom —"

Kate rounded the aisle in the dim light of the store, she cringed, shivering at what she saw. The mean-girl posse, standing three in a row just inside the store entrance, backlit by the mall lights. Only the girls looked more like melting plastic Barbie dolls now, as if someone had taken a blow torch to them. Lipstick and foundation oozed from their faces as skin slid off in shreds. Before Kate could take in the whole gruesome scene in front of her, her eyes fell to the floor where long smears of red painted the white tiles. Her eyes followed two bloody trails from the three girls in the entranceway across to the aisle with the end cap housing the *Glamour Magique* cosmetics.

There, lying on the floor in front of the display, was Marissa, who was almost completely unrecognizable if not for the purple fanny pack still strapped around her waist and her massively teased-out brunette bangs that were now matted to her forehead from a mixture of what appeared to be makeup, blood, and sweat. The worst part was her face looked like a peeled tomato, no skin left, just pulpy flesh. Her lips were gone, exposing her stark white teeth, smeared with frosty pink lipstick. Eyes bulging and bleeding, Marissa looked at Kate, guttural noises rising from her throat.

" . . . gggllleeeedddd gggwwoorrrrrre . . . kkkggh-helllpp . . . ggkkllleeed kkggllloorre." Marissa lifted a weak arm from the floor towards the shelf in front of her as blood spewed from her mouth. Half her tongue lay in a puddle of blood below her face.

Kate backed towards the front counter, covering her mouth as she gagged at what had become of Marissa. Things One, Two, and Three were now toppling over one another, trying to get to the makeup display. In better light now, she could see the girls' faces were peeled just like Marissa's. One girl's lips were missing completely, and the other two had chunks missing or dangling from their mouths. But their eyes . . . bulging like Marissa's, their eyes were black as ink, and bleeding dark inky trails down their faces—*SHPLOP! SHPLOP!* Kate, too much in shock to say or do anything until now, screamed— *SHPLOP! SHPLOP!* She ran for the phone as the eyeballs ruptured and popped out of the sockets of each of the now-mutilated beauty queens. *SHPLOP! SHPLOP!*

Fumbling, Kate's shaky fingers managed to press the buttons to dial 911.

"What's your emergency?"

"I . . . uh . . . there's . . ." the words caught in her throat. Kate struggled to think.

"Miss, Miss can you . . ." The voice on the phone was distorted, disconnected. The words spun in Kate's addled mind as nausea swept through her. She felt dizzy and unsteady on her feet, her hands trembling.

"The m-mall . . . bargain store . . ."

"Are you injured, Miss?"

"Th-these g-girls . . . th-they . . ." Kate shrieked as Marissa spasmed on the floor, gurgling moans bubbling from her throat. Kate swallowed. It tasted sour, vile . . . but no words came. Her head swirled, vaguely aware of the weight of the phone from her hand hitting the ground with a thud. Staring at it dumbfounded, Kate knew she had to do something, *anything,* as Marissa grew more still, her breathing less than a whisper.

A pulse . . . Kate thought. *I should check their pulse.* Kate turned her attention to the pile of girls, looking for any signs of life, with no rise or fall of their chests visible in the shadows, she bent towards one of the blonds when a gory hand reached up and grasped Kate's wrist. Long, bloodied fingernails dug into her arm. Kate screamed, watching the flesh from the fingers wrapped tightly around her melt and reduce to skeletal bones.

Just then, a flashlight beam swept across the storefront, the gold sparkle from the display caught Kate's attention out of the corner of her eye. *You, too, can be beautiful, just like them.* The signature gold cursive *Glamour Magique* danced across her vision. She stepped over Marissa's body as the commotion of security invading her store faded from her ears. She reached for the tube of frosted pink lipstick with all of its promises of allure and intrigue. She could be the skinny girl, the one with flawless skin and long lashes. The one who all the boys adored and the girls envied.

Kate took handfuls of product off the shelves and ripped off the caps, squeezing them out onto the floor. She twisted up tubes of lipstick, breaking off the waxy paste and squishing it under her white high-top sneakers. Kate continued to destroy product after product until she felt herself being pulled away from the display. Her stomach turned, and she thought she would vomit as she caught sight of the oozing mounds of flesh and goo in the middle of the store. It was all fake. None of it was real. Whatever *this* was, it only created an illusion of what the wearer desired to look like before turning them into monsters, desperate to live up to the unattainable beauty standards society thrusts upon them. It was all . . . a lie.

2
UNNATURAL WONDERS
AJ Danna

Earth, 66 MYA

E XPERTS SELDOM PERPETUATE the subjective belief that
seventy-five percent of Earth's life deserved to die
by mass extinction — but even experts can be wrong.

The impact was sudden, but the aftermath was slow
and excruciatingly painful. Triceratops and ankylosaurus
on land choked through thick, hot air as they lumbered
toward shelter. Between the ashen soil and sky, the tender
wings of flying pterosaurs were punctured by burning
projectiles. Chunks of fiery rock, fragments of Earth
first blown to the Heavens before crashing back down
with the fires of Hell, pummeled scales and skulls alike.
Even thriving plant life may have been scorched within
minutes of the extreme heat's domination of planet Earth.
It is unlikely that any living creature was instinctually
prepared for the cataclysmic effects brought upon by
the arrival of one rogue object. Leaving behind a crater
measured at twelve miles deep and ninety-three miles
wide, the carbonaceous chondrite asteroid exploded
on impact with a force equivalent to billions of nuclear
bombs simultaneously detonating.

The ensuing electrical storms and earthquakes certainly contributed to the fate that followed — though further study has pinpointed an even more lethal weapon in dust from the impact. Upon examining samples of rock extracted from a well-known fossil site nearly two thousand miles away from the crater, scientists observed a high concentration of fine silicate matter less than 8 micrometers across. This dust is hypothesized to have stayed suspended in the air for up to fifteen years, following a particularly bleak period during which the sun was blacked out for nearly two years, contributing to a fall in temperatures and the slow extermination of ecosystems. Exposed geological layers within the crater itself also reveal the sudden appearance of iridium, a rare metal more common in meteorites than in Earth's crust. Iridium-rich sediment is believed to have covered the Earth's surface well beyond the impact site following the collision.

Regardless of whether or not an extinction event of this magnitude was deserved, many experts agree that the Earth has been overdue for another.

Sherwood Mall, July 1986

Cliff tried to suppress his eye roll as pan flutes drowned out the common area's pop music. The mall security officer was all at once reminded of why he rarely stepped foot in Natural Selections; with high-end electronics and jewelry stores nearby, the hokey nature shop tucked away in a downstairs corner of Sherwood Mall had nothing worth stealing. A faux tree commanded the small shop, complete with a squishy rubber dinosaur resting beneath the branches. A meticulous Aztec stone carving was mounted on the wall behind the cash register. In each corner of the room, glistening geodes and skulls carved from crystal created an uncomfortable sense of being watched. Cases of fossils, mineral samples, and scientific equipment stood just out of reach from the drooling young dorks below. Cliff was at least glad he wouldn't have to field a shoplifting call from the two percent of retarded kids who preferred to touch a rain stick instead of a joystick.

The shopkeeper was even more insufferable than her clientele. They called her Mother Nature; very few people knew her real name, and even fewer could pronounce it. Cliff read her as an old Mexican hippie who looked like she'd stepped out of a crusty old *National Geographic* magazine, cracked and wrinkled with the stains of a reader who enjoyed naked African girls a little too much. After hobbling along for the whole of ten minutes just to light fresh incense in the store, Mother Nature's ancient lips were about to croak out the biggest embarrassment of all: the reason she interrupted Cliff's afternoon patrol. While President Reagan proudly commemorated Liberty Weekend in Washington, D.C., and Sherwood Mall lit up the summer sky with a patriotic fireworks spectacular, Natural Selections would be celebrating America's independence with . . . a rock.

"Quiero que entiendas por qué esto es muy importante. Entregar esta piedra es clave para lograr una venta explosiva."

Cliff couldn't hide his annoyance any longer. He sniffled loudly and raised a finger to the shopkeeper.

"No, no . . . English, por favor."

Mother Nature stared with an unchanged expression. Cliff, keeping his upright finger in Mother Nature's face, turned his head to bark at the other officer assigned to patrol his section. In a real law enforcement agency, Dan would likely be referred to as Cliff's partner—but here, Cliff thought, Dan was just the extra fat that someone forgot to trim before taking a regretfully chewy bite. Dan was busy poking the squishy dinosaur centerpiece when he heard Cliff's voice call him forward. The tubby officer pushed past a group of kids carrying buckets of sand and digging tools, bouncing off of him as they parted.

Mother Nature continued, "Soy demasiado débil para llevar la piedra y venderla, pero tú eres un hombre fuerte. Necesito tu ayuda esta misma noche."

Dan nodded with wide eyes, feigning understanding. Cliff anxiously bit down on his lip and hoped the fact that Dan had finished high school would benefit them for once. Dan understood enough of Mother Nature's native tongue to catch the basics.

Dan asked in English, "You need help moving a rock for the sale?"

"Sí. El iridio es muy pesado y valioso."

Dan paused before responding, shooting a glance at Cliff to see if he understood. Cliff was stone-faced, and White, as ever.

"¿Iridio?"

"Sí." Mother Nature lowered her voice and spoke directly to Dan. Peeved, Cliff moved forward to listen in—as though it would make any difference.

"¿Cuánto pagarías por ver el meteorito que cayó en México y mató a los dinosaurios?"

Dan laughed. He looked to Cliff, still serious and non-laughing, then back to Mother Nature. The amusement in their eyes was palpable. Mother Nature smirked with pride.

Dan translated, "She says it's a meteorite from Mexico that killed the dinosaurs."

My mistake, Cliff mused. *Even the Fourth of July rock is Mexican.*

Mother Nature beckoned them further into the store, continuing, "Se entregará esta noche. Llévalo a esta zona."

Passing a child-sized shelf of huggable plush dinosaurs, Mother Nature led the men to the store's main attraction. Situated along the store's back wall was an interactive fossil dig site, piled high with sand and littered with children. A dust cloud hung around the area, where children nestled on all fours to carry out their simulated excavations. The nearby glass windows granting passersby a view into Natural Selections projected the common area's artificial neon glow onto the fossil pit, helping the floating dust appear quite dense. Cliff sniffed and rubbed his nose; to his untrained eye, there was no reason for the glorified sandbox to be as popular with the kids as it was. Ironically, this was the one commodity that seemed to be holding their attention quite well, as they hypnotically and ferociously dug around the display's circular footprint.

Spanning the entirety of the back wall above the pit was a mural showcasing multicolored layers of exposed earth, embedded with fossilized remains. Mother Nature gestured to a primitive inscription in the mural, which Cliff had to squint to read:

"The soil of our ancestors . . . Mother Nature's gift . . . yours now to hold." *Yawn*.

Pointing a bony finger to the perimeter of the fossil pit, Mother Nature called attention to a large crate tucked in the corner opposite the shop's windows. The old woman pantomimed lifting something heavy from below and placing it on a tall driftwood shelf at the edge of the mural. She nodded to the men with an unblinking look of expectation. If her silent request meant what he thought it meant, Cliff could already imagine the rock toppling back down to Earth and shattering the skull of some unlucky kid in the sand crater, unaware he was about to join the dinosaurs in extinction. Dan, meanwhile, was practically sweating just looking at the size of the crate.

Before the officers could respond, a stern female voice called out behind them.

"Officer Daniel?"

Dan, saved by the bell, was delighted to see Deidre Montague standing just outside the glass doors of Natural Selections. The elderly woman came marching forward in a crocheted granny square vest, crossing only a few feet from Jeweler's Palace, the store she operated directly across from Natural Selections. Cliff was once again left alone with Mother Nature, much to his dismay. Dan strode confidently toward the stuffy jewelry store owner, who was holding a dejected young teen by the arm. Ms. Montague spoke quickly and with great aggravation.

"Officer Daniel, this young man was fondling my jewels."

Dan waited a moment before responding. The pimple-faced, leather-clad teen jumped to his defense.

"I was just looking at them!" he squeaked out.

"Our eyes are for looking . . . not our hands!" Ms. Montague mustered with frustration, peering down through her thick glasses.

Overhearing the escalating confrontation, Cliff once again raised a finger to Mother Nature.

"Uno second-o."

The remaining officer turned his back and strode to the doorway. Mother Nature's eyes narrowed, deepening the wrinkles at the gateway to her temples.

Cliff, with much bravado, bellowed, "Someone's got sticky fingers?"

Cliff grabbed the punky teen rather aggressively, reaching for his jacket pockets. With a gravelly chuckle, Cliff withdrew a heavy handful of gold necklaces. Allowing himself a moment of disbelieving amusement, playing with the necklaces like a Slinky, Cliff planted his full hands on his hips and shook his head.

"Woo-wee . . . you went right for the big guns. Ripping off quarters from Pac-Man ain't good enough for you, kid?" Cliff continued.

The dejected teen was already dreading a visit to Mall Jail, the second place in Sherwood Mall that a cool kid wouldn't want to be caught dead (with the first place being Natural Selections). He turned his oily face down to the pink neon reflections of the slick white tile floor, where his gaze would remain for the rest of his walk of shame.

Cliff reached his hand, still full of stolen loot, to the back of his uniform.

"We've gotta take you in. You'll be nice and cozy with Officer Daniel."

Cliff patted Dan on the butt, quite reverberantly, to Ms. Montague's visible shock.

Cliff continued, "Thanks for being a hero, Ms. Montague. Keep him out here for just a minute more, and we'll handle it from there." Cliff passed a handful of golden necklaces to the owner.

"Be quick, officers. I'm not comfortable being alone with a criminal." Ms. Montague quivered and adjusted her vest for even greater coverage of her frail body. Dan and Cliff smiled back, unsure how to respond to the mousy woman. Glancing back at Natural Selections, the two security officers tucked themselves around the corner from the doorway. Cliff growled out a hoarse whisper.

"That little son-of-a-gun went right for the gold. Not bad."

"Not bad at all."

Cliff rubbed his behind, tracing the outline of a stolen gold necklace he had slipped into his uniform pocket. Dan did the same, gently patting another necklace that Cliff had planted on his partner's rear end. Mother Nature peered through the glass windows of the store and saw the two men caressing their buttocks.

Dan whispered to Cliff, "If you thought these were nice, wait until you see the payout from the dinosaur rock. The old hag said it's loaded with iridium."

Cliff imagined a meteorite glittering with rich, crystallized colors, much like the other geodes in the store, sparkling so brightly the men would need to wear their favorite aviator sunglasses indoors. He replied, "No kidding . . . it's *our* Independence Day."

Dan nodded before saluting, "With liberty and justice for all."

Dan strode back to Ms. Montague and her hostage, now confined to a bench near Jeweler's Palace, and began the field trip to Mall Jail. Before joining them, Cliff turned back to Mother Nature, now appearing to mind her own business in Natural Selections. She locked eyes with Cliff, who smiled through his yellow teeth.

"We'll take good care of it, ma'am . . . hasta luego."

~

Mother Nature stood beneath the faux tree, peering up through the simulated leaves, imagining the warmth of sunlight. She wished for a natural golden hue that would be remarkable enough to drown out the hideous neon glow of Sherwood's common areas. She followed the branches with her gaze, beyond the fossil pit and the mural, toward the glass windows that separated Natural Selections from everything wrong with the modern world. Beyond the translucent border, teenagers with shaggy hair and baggy clothes carried out mating rituals in public. They could also occasionally be seen scratching out names and phrases along the mall's white walls. Today's graffiti would someday be proof of existence, the cave drawings of modern neanderthals.

Within Natural Selections, children played in the fossil pit, blissfully unaware of what form the dust burrowing under their fingernails once took. Dust was never just dust, especially in Mother Nature's eyes; the old world was still here, buried beneath the immaculate tile floors outside the glass windows. In here, however, children couldn't tell the difference. They couldn't fathom that there would someday be another child playing with their ashes, building sand castles and shopping malls with what remained of their short lives. When their dust covered the Earth, they'd never know it was their classmates and families who now slipped through gold-ringed fingers. When their house pets were reduced to grains for fattening hamburger cows, it may finally occur to them that the dust we walk upon today had once walked upon the layers of dust beneath.

Focusing on the mural of fossils embedded in layers of earth, Mother Nature's eyes reviewed the inscription. *"The soil of our ancestors . . . Mother Nature's gift . . . yours now to hold."* Mother Nature had taken great care in gathering natural wonders from Yucatán.

Suddenly, a clump of sand exploded upon the mural, as two rambunctious children began throwing handfuls of dust at each other. The hiss of sand rolling off their nylon parachute pants signaled mischief. The shopkeeper silently observed her customers at play; their laughter brought her joy, short-lived as it may be. Unsupervised children left alone with Mother Nature's gifts had often learned lessons quickly. She knew what would inevitably come. At first, it sounded like the coughing brought upon by a common cold; their laughter still rang through every few seconds, though in shorter bursts. Eventually, other young paleontologists were rubbernecking, turning away from the pursuit of buried fossils to locate the source of the coughing. The afflicted child put his hands up to cover his mouth, unaware the dust left upon his hands would only make the situation worse. As he doubled over with each fierce exhale, Mother Nature could hear the change from a dry heave to a wet cough. This, too, brought her joy.

Soon, the boy's colorful clothing was speckled with blood, as the surrounding bits of dry sand clumped together to make wet maroon mud. Mother Nature smiled, deepening her wrinkles once again. The boy's tears further dampened the dust below his feet, no longer used as a weapon in their childish game. From across the store, a frizzy-haired woman dripping with plastic bracelets and dangly earrings ran toward the pit, urgently passing Mother Nature with a rackety *jing, jing, jing* and a frantic *click, click, click*. The gaudy woman reached for the crying child, who climbed upon her shoulder like an orangutan. Mama bear used her free hand to retrieve an asthma inhaler from her neon vinyl fanny pack. She nursed the boy in her arms as he sucked his inhaler like an artificial teat, crying all the way out of Natural Selections.

Mother Nature watched as the bloody sand absorbed out of sight into the fossil pit.

~

Cliff wiped the white dust from his upper lip. He didn't want Dan to see where his share had been going. *Then again*, Cliff smirked, *maybe a line or two could help Dan shed a few pounds*. The larger officer swung open the bathroom door, struggling to zip up his uniform pants as he reunited with Cliff in the neon concourse. The lights eerily stayed on past closing time, casting the mall's common areas in abstract pink and purple shadows.

The men returned to Natural Selections to find the store locked up, with no Mother Nature in sight. Had she gone out to watch the fireworks the night before her big, patriotic rock reveal? *There's no way it's going to be that easy,* Cliff thought. He looked over his shoulder at an empty mall before sniffing so hard he coughed. He wasn't going to miss this place when they cashed out once and for all.

"Everyone's out front for the show. We'll take it out back through the loading dock."

Cliff reached for his key ring and bent down toward his boots to unlock the glass doors at Natural Selections. Dan kept watch from eye level, enjoying the task that didn't require bending down. Within seconds, the disbelieving guards walked right in, without a hippie or nerd to see them close the door on their grand entrance. The store was a futuristic rainforest in the murky darkness, leaves and rocks aglow with neon hues creeping in from the mall-facing glass. The squishy dinosaur looked even more lifelike in the eerie evening glow.

"Cut the cameras," Cliff chattered to Dan as they moved toward the crate containing the valuable rock.

Dan crossed to the retail counter under the watchful stone eyes of Tlaltecuhtli, carved Aztec goddess and de facto cash register protector. The flesh-and-blood guard below carefully shuffled through papers and lifted colorful Mexican ponchos on display to find any technology buried underneath. It was no surprise that Mother Nature hardly touched the Commodore 64 beside the register; the unit was covered in dust and hidden beneath layers of handwritten receipts. Dan carefully unplugged every cable that snaked through the clutter like plastic-coated tree roots. Meanwhile, Cliff tried his hand at moving the oversized crate, but the box's awkward length proved too difficult for one man to lift on his own. Cliff estimated it was about the size of a motorcycle; how Mother Nature managed to get the crate in the shop without their help was beyond him. *In which case, why did she need them to . . . ? Whatever.*

"Dan, I need you . . ." Cliff choked as he tried to finish the painful request. "I need your help."

Dan bent down with a huff, grabbing the other end of the crate. It was clear that Dan was doing most of the literal and metaphorical heavy lifting, however straining it may be.

"We'll set it down outside, lock the door, and then move to the back." Cliff confidently commanded as he struggled to keep the box upright.

Dan flatly responded, "Whatever you say."

Passing through the shadows, the men moved toward the pink glow of their sweet escape. They would be lucky if plush dinosaurs and crystal skulls were their only witnesses. Cliff sniffled with impatience before setting the box down at the glass doors that stood between them and freedom. As he opened the door, he heard the sweet sound of keys jingling. But these keys . . . echoed across the concourse.

Deidre Montague stood outside Jeweler's Palace, keys in hand, in the process of locking up the neighboring shop for the night. She was now face-to-face with Cliff. *Oh, shit. Shit, shit, shit.*

Cliff raised a friendly hand to greet her, without saying a word. Steps away, Dan was slumped over the crate and breathing heavily. Ms. Montague looked between the two men; not even her thick glasses could hide the suspicion in her eyes. Cliff continued smiling and offered Dan a hand to stand. Grabbing onto Cliff, who was nearly pulled to the ground, Dan regained his footing. Ms. Montague watched for a moment more before turning back to her shop and double-checking the locks. She then marched off into the shadows, letting her neon-tinted gaze toward Natural Selections linger just a bit longer than usual.

Dan panicked, "Do you think she saw us?"

Cliff sniffled, then replied, "With those glasses . . ."

"What do we do now?"

"We open it."

Dan wasn't so sure. "Why's that?"

"She saw the box. We have to leave it here. We'll just . . . break the thing into smaller pieces, and carry them out."

Dan stared in disbelief. "Cliff . . . I think. . ."

Cliff's frustration was heightened by his anxiety. He sniffled again. "What? You think what?"

Dan pointed a finger at Cliff's face, gaping in horror. Cliff wiped his calloused hand against his scruffy face, soaking his dried skin with blood. A thick stream trickled from his nose, pitter-pattering down to the shiny tile beneath his boots. His frantic attempt to wipe it clean with his boot only further smeared the liquid across the floor. Grabbing his nose tighter, he nasally yelped, "Inside, now!"

Pushing with the weight of his shoulder and one free hand, Cliff struggled to move the crate back over the threshold of Natural Selections. Dan placed both of his hands on the rough wooden edges of the box and pulled. The crate slid across the patterned carpet with relative ease, only pulling occasionally from splintered wood. Cliff's free hand was shaking; Dan was sweating heavily. Cliff pulled his other hand away from his face, finding it now thoroughly imprinted with blood.

"Alright, we . . . uh . . . need to make this quick." Cliff coughed out.

Dan nodded in response, removing his club from his belt. Cliff used his shaky free hand to lift one corner of the crate's lid, so Dan could slide his club in the crevice like a professional thief's crowbar. Huffing and puffing, both men pushed down on the club, slowly lifting the secure lid from its nailed edges. Sand began to spill over the edge of the crate. The men tossed the detached lid aside, finding the crate filled to the brim with the escaping sand. If the meteorite was packed in sand, reaching in to hoist it out from this angle would be impossible; their prize would have to be rolled out.

Cliff and Dan pulled down on the front panel with any adrenaline they had left, attempting to tip the crate forward. As they applied weight to the creaky wood, the rusty nails pulled free, sending the men toppling backward like bowling pins as the front panel peeled down to the floor. Sand cascaded out of the crate, enhancing the guards' forceful fall. Dust hung heavy in the air. Cliff flared his nostrils at the building pressure in his sinuses, then sneezed, launching a glob of blood and mucus toward the sand. It was too late to turn back now. Cliff's hand was still covered in blood, fortunately spared from granular sand, yet he wouldn't care for long. One of Earth's most valuable metals was here with them on the floor of Natural Selections. They just had to dig it out before saying "adios" to Sherwood Mall.

Dan used his club to poke through the sand that spilled forward from the crate. He coughed, then chuckled, "Where is it?"

Cliff's silence was deafening.

BOOM! The store shook with the vibration of a thunderous explosion. Dan and Cliff reached out to each other for cover. From the mall-facing windows, the red, white, and blue glow of fireworks illuminated the store. The relieved guards exchanged a glance, then slowly began to laugh for the first time since their heist began.

Cliff used his clean hand to dig through the sand, continuing between laughs, "That old lady . . . is full of . . . *caca.*"

Dan coughed as Cliff continued laughing hysterically. "There's no rock . . . it's a box of sand! Happy Fourth of July!"

Cliff lunged for the sand pile, definitively devoid of a meteorite, and sprawled out on his back to simulate making snow angels. The next thing Dan heard was the distinct sizzling of meat on a grill, immediately followed by Cliff's agonized screaming. Each grain of sand on Cliff's bloody hand burned with the sensation of sadistic acupuncture. Though Dan was struggling to stand beside him in the mess of sand, he managed to lift Cliff's shoulders upright. Blood from Cliff's nose and hand had caked on the sand; as the liquid melded with each granule, any trace of blood was absorbed . . . or, *swallowed* . . . deep into the mess of dust.

BOOM! Another explosion of fireworks overhead filled the store with an otherworldly glow. Cliff was whimpering in a fetal position, seizing from the unbearable pain. Dan pushed off the ground with his hands, ready to run, when a low rumble from the fireworks sent a tremor through the sand.

BOOM! The sand quivered with each explosion overhead. It felt as though the floor jumped an inch or two with each colorful blast. Dan watched in awe, mouth agape, as the dust started to twist and turn with the force of a vacuum. Slithering with snakelike fluidity across the carpet of Natural Selections, the sand formed a reverse funnel, sucking all the way back into the fossil pit. Continued flashes from the patriotic fireworks helped quicken the sand's sense of movement—and painted the squishy dinosaur model with a volcanic red hue. After each shell detonated in the spectacle outside, the store was again plunged into near-darkness.

BOOM! Back on the floor, Cliff's nose was now bleeding profusely, as he reached for the only fabric he could find nearby. His tender pink hand grasped a woven poncho hanging by the register, which he promptly used to cover his nose and mouth. Closing his hand into a fist around the poncho led to unbearable stinging, but it was the safest option, as the lingering dust began to burn his nose and esophagus. Cliff coughed blood into the poncho, adding a vibrant red to its already colorful appearance.

BOOM! Dan's feet dragged through the sand with great resistance, adding so much weight to each step that it became nearly impossible for the man to escape. The slithering sand pushed against Dan like an upstream current . . . eventually knocking him down with the force of a flash flood, dragging him into the fossil pit with the stream of sand. Dan attempted to scream as he tumbled backward, but the sound was suppressed by the sand, which quickly filled his mouth.

BOOM! Crawling on his elbows, Cliff felt the tingling in his palm deepening. Hesitantly lowering the poncho to wipe his hand clean, the motion of scraping off sand and dried blood also took chunks of skin with it. Groaning through gritted teeth, Cliff watched his skin flake away, then turn to dust before his eyes. Fireworks booming overhead drowned out his guttural screams of pain. Watching his hand disintegrate, his vision went blurry as he blinked dust out of his eyelids. His head throbbed with pressure, as though the supernatural vacuum were sucking his eyeballs out of his skull. His eyes became so dry they burned, then bubbled, then popped under the immense pressure. In a mess of blood and sand, everything that was once wet in Cliff's body was suddenly made dry.

BOOM! Dan's body hung over the edge of the fossil pit, too large to be consumed by the funnel. As he buoyantly rocked face down with the tide of sand, on the brink of consciousness, he felt a hand grasp his shoulder. Lifting his head slightly, expecting to greet Cliff, Dan instead saw rigid bones digging into his meaty arm. Through half-open eyes, Dan made out the outline of triceratops skull fragments, with piercing horns mere inches from his face. Spooning Dan in the fossil pit was a horrid amalgamation of mismatched dinosaur bones, an abomination held together with thick, bloody sand. Dan felt the overbearing hug of a bony ribcage closing in around his sides, like a fossilized anaconda suffocating him slowly. Dan barely held on to breath as he felt his insides burning, the bones pressurizing his abdomen and chest cavity. With tremendous force, the bone creature smothered Dan, juicing him like a plump blueberry, as sand gushed out of every orifice.

As the room fell dark, the crowd outside cheered. The nighttime spectacular was over. The spotless white tile floor just beyond the glass doors contrasted with the sandy, dust-covered floor within Natural Selections, experiencing the serene stillness of extinction.

~

The most explosive night of the holiday may have passed, but the big sale was just beginning. Mother Nature had work to do before the crowds returned in a few short hours. Thousands of sticky-fingered kids and horny teens would swarm Sherwood Mall over the course of the weekend; and now, there would be enough dust for each and every one of them. Mother Nature shook out the overfilled dustpan so its sediment load would cover Dan and Cliff's bones in the fossil pit, anticipating the visiting children who would excitedly dig them up. The leftovers had been sent into the sands of oblivion, like the dinosaurs before them, to be coughed upon in a brutal display of natural selection. The ancient shopkeeper chuckled to herself, before speaking in perfect English sarcasm . . .

"At least shopping malls will be around forever."

3
BIG BREAK
Austin Hinderliter

TIFFANY RUIZ DIDN'T JUST WALK down the mall. She didn't meander from storefront to storefront, looking at faceless mannequins modeling the latest fashions from The Gap, all their looks paling in comparison to hers. Instead, she strutted like the hot shit that she was—right down the center of the aisle, not moving aside for foot traffic heading for the exit. Shoppers gawked at her boldness, her arrogance. Tiffany knew the men were staring at her low-cut blouse, and the women were all jealous of her attributes and apparel that was out of their pay grade.

"The mall is now closed. Please complete your purchases and head for the nearest exit. Thank you for shopping at Sherwood Mall." The loudspeaker announcement rudely interrupted Kim Wilde.

Dragging neon pink manicured nails through her naturally blonde hair, Tiffany ignored the bulletin and moved farther into the mall. Although the traffic had subsided, an overweight woman in a much too-small tank top nearly collided with her.

Watch out, lady, Tiffany thought. *How rude! That woman better not have scuffed my glam party heels with the purple bows.*

All around her hung signs advertising explosive Fourth of July savings and patriotic flair. *How tacky! Just like that lady's outfit.*

Tiffany watched as a security guard chased after a boy with pockmark scars. She shook her head disapprovingly, which also shook her 24-karat gold hoops. Tiffany never missed a chance to show off her goods, both from God and Gimbels.

"Get back here, son!" the guard yelled. But by that point, the skateboarder was halfway to the exit. Tiffany was just glad they were on the opposite side of the concourse. She could not risk being taken out by such a goon.

She had to be flawless. Being knocked down could cause a chipped nail or, even worse, a bruise. That would not do. Even more unfathomable, a trip could break her crown. If that were to happen, the guard would have to restrain her because she would have murder pulsing through her veins. She looked over her shoulder just in time to see the guard round the corner as the skateboard wheels faded to the last lyrics of *Kids in America*.

Tiffany glanced at the purple kraft paper bag swinging back and forth by her side. Her crown and the odds and ends needed to make her even more fabulous were safe and sound.

It was two months ago that she had been crowned prom queen. She was a near shoo-in from the start. The only competition, if you could call it that, came in the form of Jenny Hall. But Jenny wasn't quite as tall as Tiffany, her hair not as blonde, and her God-given attributes not as generous. Thankfully, her classmates noticed these shortcomings. Jenny was the definition of Miss Congeniality.

Poor Jenny, Tiffany thought. She really missed out.

Tiffany had made the most of her achievement in the past sixty-one days. She had professional headshots taken. She had mastered the art of hair crimping. She had lost those pesky two pounds at aerobics. Daddy had even driven her to LA for a script reading for one of those daytime soap operas that every girl her age watched. She needed to land a role with an A-list hunk that made girls swoon. His eyes would be only for her, at least on the TV.

Driven by their jealousy, her career would land her among the stars—the who's who of Hollywood royalty. *Perhaps William Fichtner would do,* Tiffany thought. *I need one break, and I'm gonna get it no matter what.*

Pink neon pulsed through the West Coast script letters. The word *"Soundtracks"* was centered below in white. It wasn't the most glamorous option, but it was free, and every cent went toward her move to LA.

The letters' glow shined off the jet-black hair of Jesse Alexander, who was leaning against the wall with his left foot resting on the tile. He drummed his fingers on his left thigh—a compulsive habit Tiffany was accustomed to. His hand fell still as he saw her approach.

"What are you doing here, Jesse?" She would have ignored him entirely, but the gate to West Coast Soundtracks was down. Where was Heather?

"I need to talk to you."

Tiffany rolled her perfectly blue eyes. "I told you we have nothing to talk about."

"We have a lot to talk about." Jesse stepped from the wall and stood between Tiffany and the store entrance. "I told you you're not going to ignore me like this."

Tiffany stepped towards the roll-up gate. She could see inside the store, but there was no sign of Heather. "You're not going to ignore me like this, Tiff," Jesse continued.

"Just watch me," Tiffany said as she stared through the metal gate slats. "Heather, I'm here!" she called. Just then, she felt Jesse's fingers curl around her right forearm. The bag crinkled against her side as she was yanked violently around.

"Let me go!" Tiffany screamed. But it was no use. Jesse's fingers curled tighter around her arm.

He's going to break my arm! Panic-stricken, Tiffany looked down the concourse. Where was the security guard?

"You think you're too good for me now, huh bitch?" spewed Jesse. "You go off to LA, and suddenly your shit don't stink?"

Jesse was so close Tiffany could taste the alcohol on his lips and see the bloodshot eyes beneath his dark hood. For the first time, she feared what he was capable of.

"Of . . ." She tried to talk, but her mouth was dry. "Of course not, baby," she cooed, placing her left hand on his bicep. "You know I'll always be your girl." She hoped he didn't notice the tremble she struggled to control with her touch.

"Bullshit, Tiff! I heard from Foy you were out there slutting around. Probably going down on some big shot producer for a bit part in a TV show!" His hold on her arm tightened, and nails dug into her skin. In the nine months they had been an item, Jesse had never raised a hand to her. There had been one or two minor arguments, but everything had been smooth sailing. Sure, she didn't like that he drank—she was told it was both not a problem and none of her business—so she had never brought it up again. But when she told him she was planning a move to LA, Jesse Alexander erupted like a firework.

"Tiffany!"

Over her shoulder, Tiffany saw Heather rushing across the store. She had never been so glad to see another person in her life—she just never expected that person to be Heather Sprocket.

Jesse's hold loosened when he heard Heather approach, but he still hadn't entirely let go of her arm. He leaned closer, his eyes shifting from Heather back to Tiffany. "You think this loser is going to stop me?"

"No, but this loser is two seconds away from calling the police," Heather said, her voice now directly behind Tiffany, who was still pressed against the gate. "Now, let her go and get back."

Reluctantly, Jesse let go of her arm. It was then that Tiffany saw a flash of something in Jesse's eyes that chilled her to the bone. His dark brown eyes seemed to be burning, and she wasn't sure if it was from the neon glow of the West Coast Soundtracks sign above them or from something else — hatred. Anger radiated off him like heat from a blast furnace. But would Jesse Alexander *hurt* her? The enflamed mark wrapped around her arm screamed *yes*.

"This is between me and my girl," Jesse growled, looking past Tiffany and through the metal-slatted gate at Heather.

"It's about to be between you and the cops. Which one is it going to be?" asked Heather. Tiffany was in awe of Heather's bravado. Where was that bluster at school when she walked down the halls, her head down so far her chin pressed against her chest? The girl who never spoke unless her hand was raised had fooled everyone.

Tiffany heard Heather unlock the gate and open it behind her. She was afraid to take her eyes off Jesse. A fire still burned in his eyes, and she was terrified of what would happen when his anger erupted. She only knew she did not want to stick around to find out. She ducked down beneath the partially rolled-up gate and entered the store.

"Now get lost, scumbag," Heather said while quickly closing the storefront.

Tiffany stood just inside the entrance. Beads of sweat gathered on her brow, and she only hoped they hadn't ruined her makeup. Time would not allow her to redo her face from the foundation up.

She stared through the metal slats at her ex-boyfriend and, for one terrifying moment, imagined what their future would have held. Inevitably, bars would be in Jesse's life. His drinking was getting out of control. Now add domestic battery to his attributes. *I sure can pick winners*, Tiffany thought. *What does that say about me?*

Jesse continued to glare at Tiffany through the grating. Even worse, he showed no signs of moving. His feet were anchored to the floor like one of the metal palm sculptures that lined the concourse in evenly spaced intervals. Aversion in his eyes was just as sharp as the aluminum fronds.

Tiffany felt a light touch on her shoulder, and although she was staring directly at Jesse and knew there was no way he could grab her through the gate, she jumped.

"Do you want me to call security?" Heather stared between Tiffany and Jesse.

"No!" Tiffany said defiantly, shrugging herself loose from Heather's hold. "I came here on a mission. I'm not going to let some creep ruin it for me."

"You'll be sorry, Tiff. I swear to God you'll be sorry." His lack of emotion scared her the most, but she would not give him the satisfaction.

"Bite me, asshole." With that, Tiffany Ruiz turned on her heel and left Jesse standing beyond the closed storefront of West Coast Soundtracks, looking like a wild animal locked in a crate—ready to attack when freed.

The pink neon from the sign continued into the store, snaking along the ceiling like a pink, pulsating viper. It disappeared around the corner, where Tiffany could only assume the recording booths were.

She let Heather and the rolling neon guide her to the counter.

So many familiar album covers faced her—*Kiss Me, Kiss Me, Kiss Me* by the Cure, *Whitney*, and *Permanent Vacation* by Aerosmith, one of her favorites. *Did Jesse want to send me on a permanent vacation?* Tiffany shivered at the thought, crinkling the bag in her arms.

The bag! Please let my crown be okay!

Tiffany sat the bag on the glass counter and carefully pulled out the alloy crown decorated with crystals, white rhinestones, and other embellishments.

"Oh! Your crown is so beautiful, Tiffany!" Heather leaned on the other side of the counter, her elbows resting on the glass and her chin in both hands. Reflected in her glasses, which Tiffany thought were so unflattering on Heather's too-round face, were sparkling white rhinestones that glinted pink in the light.

Tiffany knew that the crown's value was more symbolic than materialistic. Indeed, the crown was beautiful, but its power outshone its value. Jenny, Heather, Nicole, Baila, and every other girl in the senior class were not awarded a physical manifestation of their beauty and popularity and, to be frank, perfectness. They did not have something that said they were the best.

Tiffany did.

"I'm just glad that creep didn't break it," Tiffany fumed. She looked down at the store entrance. Jesse was gone.

"Tiffany, your arm . . ." Heather pointed to the angry handprint that wrapped around her forearm. Her bushy brows were etched with worry. "I can't believe he did that to you," she continued as Tiffany gingerly inspected Jesse's farewell mark. The red skin would soon turn to a black-and-blue bruise. For now, a little Bonnie Bell Makeup Skin Concealer would hide it.

"At least that piece of shit didn't break my crown."

"But you're hurt," Heather said, still looking at the darkening mark.

"I'll heal." Tiffany was getting bored. Why wouldn't Heather just drop it?

"You know, if you ever need someone to talk to, I can be a pretty good listener." Gone was the bravado. Mousy Heather was back. "Or maybe you could talk with Mrs. Jefferies. I've heard she—"

"Oh right, Heather. Like I'm really going to talk with a high school guidance counselor who keeps a bottle of Jack Daniel's hidden in her desk! Mrs. Jefferies is a lush. She's the one who needs help, not me." Tiffany was over it all: Jesse, the blazing California summer, and especially this conversation. "There's a little thing out there called concealer, but based on your complexion, I'm not sure you've ever heard of it."

Heather's head fell so that when she next spoke, she was conversing with her dingy-white Converse. "Sorry, I was just trying to help."

Tiffany threw her head back. "I'm the prom queen, Heather. I'm going to be a star. I don't need anybody's help." Whatever Heather said in response didn't matter. She was talking to her shoes again, and Tiffany had no time to waste, especially after her altercation with Jesse. She could see Heather's mouth still moving, although the mouse's unpainted lips were partially obscured by strands of hair that dangled lifelessly when Tiffany turned on her heel to walk away.

"So, which booth is mine?" Tiffany asked, snatching her bag from the counter.

Heather finally looked up. Were those tears forming in her eyes? *God, grow up*, thought Tiffany. *Did this girl actually think we were going to become friends just because she did me a favor? It's not my fault the store hours are terrible and don't fit into my schedule. I had to get my nails done, pick out my outfit, and do my hair!*

"Last curtain on the left," Heather said, her voice squeakier than ever. "I have everything set up for you. You'll just need to hit record. There are also some outfits and props in the dressing room around the corner."

"Yeah, like I'm really going to wear any of that gaudy shit." Tiffany was already halfway down the aisle before Heather could answer.

Teeth? No teeth? Pouty lips? Tiffany's pearly whites were straight and well-proportioned, not too big for her face like Jenny Hall's. She decided she should show them off. After unbuttoning another button on her blouse, Tiffany practiced her best smile in the mirror.

I look deranged, she thought. She smiled once more, not showing as much gum this time. That's better. Would casting directors notice her megawatt smile? Tiffany hoped so.

She knew she needed to show a little more chest, so she unbuttoned another button, and then another so that just the top of her bra showed. It was more skin than she felt comfortable showing, but she knew there were a thousand girls just like her out there, all vying for the same part. Those God-given attributes would be put to use if it meant landing a part, even a bit part, as Jesse had called the roles she wanted to audition for. She had tried to explain that she needed to get her feet wet before jumping in headfirst. No casting director in their right mind would consider her for the role of the inevitable *Friday the 13th Part VIII* with no prior acting experience.

Jesse liked those kinds of movies, but they only made Tiffany uncomfortable. She knew the gore was fake. The nudity, on the other hand, was real. The thought of being naked on the big screen made her feel slimy, like she needed to take a bath. She wanted to be appreciated for her talent, but if her body had to help get her there, so be it.

She turned and stared into the video camera lens. She took a step back, putting her glam party heels on the adhesive feet in the center of the booth, which had the words "stand" on the left sticker and "here" on the right. Both clings were scuffed, and the heel of the right foot was starting to peel up from the tile.

So gross.

Conditions in the rest of the recording booth were no better. The booth was roughly five by five feet, with a mirror to the left and a small shelf in the corner on which the purple bag was set. Behind Tiffany was a black privacy curtain that doubled as the backdrop. Opposite that was the camera, partially extending from another black curtain. Laminated instructions were taped to the wall next to the mirror on what buttons to press and where to stand as if the stickers on the floor were not obvious enough.

Picturing teenagers and overweight brides to be lip-syncing to Cyndi Lauper made Tiffany want to hurl. *Just remember LA, girl. You've got to suffer for your art,* she reminded herself.

"Tiffany?" Heather poked her head around the curtain.

"What is it now, Heather?" Tiffany scoffed, irritated at yet another annoyance. Didn't Heather know she was just about to start recording her audition for *The Young and the Restless*?

"I'm sorry to bother you, but, uhm . . ."

"Spit it out, Heather!" *God, this girl is really on my last nerve.*

"I forgot my brother needs a ride home from clarinet practice. Spencer Sprocket. You might remember him from school. It's just over on Sycamore, so it shouldn't take me longer than fifteen or twenty minutes. Do you think, well, do you think you'd be all right by yourself until I get back? If not, I could call to see if my mom would—"

"Just go, Heather! God, I'll be fine. I'm not a child, you know?" Tiffany didn't mean to snap quite so hard, but Heather was beyond on her last nerve.

Tiffany exhaled, blowing a strand of hair free from her face. "Tiffany! Tiffany!" she squealed. "I have to go pick up my loser brother because being a loser runs in my family. Can we be best friends?" she mocked. "Get real."

The curtain fluttered behind her. Had Heather been there the entire time, eavesdropping just out of sight beyond the black velvet?

"Heather?"

Rings scraped against the pole as Tiffany yanked the fabric back. She stepped out into the narrow aisle. There were no signs of Heather. She jerked the adjacent curtain back, looking into the recording booth across from hers. It, too, was empty. "Heather? Are you still here?"

There were eight other recording booths between Tiffany and the main storefront. Each curtain was closed. They swayed slightly as she swept down the aisle, storming into the main storefront with both hands on her hips.

"Heather? What are you deaf?" The mall was quiet. Even the overhead music had been cut off. Tiffany was unsettled by the silence. Where was Kim Wilde when you needed her? Sherwood Mall was usually bustling with activity and the noises that went along with it: screaming kids begging their parents to take them into the toy store, kiosk workers spraying you with a sample of the latest fragrance, girls and boys flirting up and down the concourse. But not tonight. Tonight, the mall was dead.

A shiver crept down Tiffany's spine. She rebuttoned her blouse as she looked around West Coast Soundtracks. There were rows of CDs, vinyl, and cassettes, making the aisles of the narrow store cramped. Barely two people could fit side by side down them, and that was if they were normal size. *Jenny Hall would certainly struggle to fit around in here*, Tiffany thought with a laugh. It wasn't that Jenny was fat, per se. It was just that she did not have Tiffany's hourglass figure. No girl in the senior class had her figure. That's why she had been crowned prom queen.

Tiffany looked behind the counter. There was no sign of Heather. Just as she was shaking off her alone-at-night jitters, her eyes fell on the roll-up gate.

Her breath hitched in her throat.

She had seen Heather lock it earlier. Why was it now only partially closed? Tiffany stepped forward, one tentative step after another. The gap between the tile and the gate seemed to grow with each step.

She yelled the word she was afraid to say: "Jesse?" Mercifully, there was no response. Still, Tiffany pictured her ex-boyfriend leaning against the wall just outside the entrance. She listened for the sound of his fingers rhythmically drumming on his thigh. Her forearm throbbed from the thought of his fingers curling around her. She imagined them grabbing her neck, choking the life out of her. "You're not going to leave me like this, Tiff," he'd scream as her larynx crushed like a can of Slice.

Stop it, girl! You're scaring yourself half to death!

Jesse was not waiting on the other side of the wall. The mall was deserted — everyone was partying at barbeques and fireworks celebrations.

In a hurry to leave, Heather must have forgotten to put the gate down. Jesse was long gone, at home looking for his ex at the bottom of a bottle of Jack Daniels.

Metal was cold beneath her hand as Tiffany grabbed the bottom of the roll-up gate and pulled it to the floor. There was a lock in the middle, recessed between the tile. But where was the key? Heather must have it on her. No big deal. Heather said she'd be back in fifteen or twenty minutes. That would give Tiffany ample time to record her audition, grab the tape, and hit the road. If she hurried, she could even make it to Lacie Winter's Fourth of July Bash.

Lacie always threw the best parties, and Tiffany was royally pissed off that she was missing it. Of course, Heather couldn't —or was the better word wouldn't— move her work schedule around to accommodate her. Mousy Heather had probably never been invited to a party in her life. She didn't know the pains of missing the social function of the summer, so of course, she didn't share Tiffany's plight. Otherwise, she would have just changed her damn work schedule to Tuesday night.

"Back to work, girl," Tiffany sighed as she walked between two rows of vinyl. She hummed the lyrics to *Material Girl*. She glanced over her shoulder before rounding the corner to make sure the coast was still clear. She shook her gold hoops, annoyed that she had allowed Jesse to reach her.

But this was the end of that. She would record her audition tape and go to Lacie's party. Tomorrow, she would mail her VHS off to Hollywood. Her fingers would be crossed until she heard back from a producer. Oh! Tiffany almost forgot she had rebuttoned her blouse. Lack of cleavage could have cost her the role.

"Close call," she laughed while stepping back into the recording booth. Before she could finish with her shirt, she froze. Papers from her script had been strung across the floor. The purple bag was crumpled in the corner. Rhinestones caught the horror in her eyes. On the black tile, they looked like thousands of twinkling stars in the night sky. Her crowning achievement lay in the middle of the room, broken into several large pieces. It looked as if someone had removed it from her bag, sat it on the floor, and smashed it with all of their might. But who? And why?

Tears streamed down Tiffany's face, tracking black mascara with them. Her knees felt wobbly. She grabbed the velvet curtain to steady herself. Who would do such a heinous, ugly thing?

She backed up into the hallway, unable to take her eyes off her shattered crown. While wiping tears from her face, she caught sight of something moving to her right—no, not something, but *someone.*

The broken crown was not the only thing glimmering in the light. So, too, was the blade of a double-bit hewing axe. The figure holding it stood between Tiffany and the rest of the store, filling the walkway between the recording booths. They stood motionless like a black-clad mannequin, gripping the handle with black-gloved hands, with Tiffany directly in their sights.

She staggered backward as an ear-splitting scream erupted from her lungs. There was something hard behind her. The wall. She was trapped.

"Please! Please, no!" Tiffany wailed.

The mannequin watched her cower at the end of the hall. The axe's bit glowed pink under the fluorescent ceiling serpent that rounded the corner and snaked between the recording booths. The tail blazed above Tiffany like the dying end of a neon-blooded viper.

"Jesse?" Tiffany wiped snot from her trembling lips. "Jesse, is that you?" She sobbed while waiting for a response, for Jesse to rip the ski mask from his head and tell her it was all a game—a joke. But the mannequin stood still, watching her every move without the indication that this was for kicks. Jesse would not play these sort of games. Would he? The handprint-shaped bruise forming on Tiffany's forearm reminded her of his anger.

The mannequin took a step forward. Then another. Life surged through the axe-wielding figure as they began jogging down the hall with the axe still leading their charge.

"Jesse, stop! Please!" screamed Tiffany. Her hands trembled as her defenseless arms stuck out in front of her like dead limbs about to break from a trunk. One swoosh of the axe and she'd be yelling, "Timber!" With nowhere else to go, Tiffany ran back into the recording booth. Shattered crystals and rhinestones crunched underfoot. She spun in a circle, searching desperately for an escape. But there were no air ducts to crawl through and no dividing walls to crawl under. She was trapped.

"Please, God! Somebody help me!" Tiffany's terror-filled screams reverberated through the small booth. There was not even anything to use as a weapon.

The axe parted the curtain like a metallic Noah. The figure pushed its way through the wall of black velvet. Their eyes glistened in the neon light, and even though Tiffany could not see their face, she would swear her pursuer was smiling at her.

"Get away from me, you psycho! Don't touch me!"

The figure raised the axe in a flash of metal and wood. It barely registered. Time had slowed to a crawl, and just before the blade connected with tender, exposed neck flesh, Tiffany dropped to the floor. Shards of the broken crown cut at her hands, but better than the axe that shattered the mirror above her. Glass shards rained on Tiffany, cutting at her back. Tiffany crawled through the curtain and out into the hall, scrambling to her feet. One of her shoes came off as she staggered down the aisle, grabbing onto the curtains for support.

Vinyl and the store spun as she nearly collided with a display advertising the new Heart release. Tiffany looked over her shoulder just in time to see the figure emerging from the curtain, the axe now free from the mirror and wall. Pieces of drywall fell from the bit onto the black tile.

"Somebody help me!" Tiffany screamed at the top of her lungs. Where was the security guard she saw earlier chasing the boy on the skateboard? How could he not hear her screams? Surely, he was still on shift. It was then that a terrifying thought hit her. What if the guards also left, either by scheduling or choice to go enjoy the Fourth of July festivities? Was it possible that she was the only person in the entire mall?

No, not the only person left. The figure with the axe stormed down the recording booth aisle, right on her trail. Explosions filled the sky above the mall, shaking its skylights and bathing the structure in flares of red, white, and blue. The fireworks also drowned out the screams.

Boom. Boom. Boom.

The patriotic thunderstorm roared overhead, showering the city with shells and stars. "Please, what have I done?" Tiffany stumbled backward, not taking her eyes off the gleaming axe. "Jesse, I'm sorry! I'm sorry! I didn't mean it. I swear I didn't mean it!"

The figure stepped forward as Tiffany ran for the gate. She could hear the footsteps behind her, could feel the axe cutting through the air. She skidded to a stop, nearly colliding with the roll-up gate. She pulled upward on the metal slats, but despite her efforts, the gate would not budge. It was locked.

"Oh God, no!" Tiffany pulled harder on the metal gate, but it was a futile attempt. She was locked in. She pressed her face between two of the bars and shouted for help, pleading for the echoes to carry her screams to the security guard. "I'm locked inside West Coast Soundtracks, and someone is trying to kill me! Please help me!"

Boom. Boom. Boom.

Fireworks painted the night sky like a Jasper John's painting. Explosions cast long shadows across the concourse from through the skylights.

"Please! What did I do to deserve this!" Tiffany sobbed while shaking the gate.

"You know what you did . . ."

Slowly, Tiffany turned toward the whisper that came from behind her. The black-clad, axe-wielding silhouette stood only a few feet away. Once again, they were as still as one of the department store mannequins.

"You know what you did, Prom Queen." The voice, only a whisper, was further muffled by the ski mask.

"Jesse?" Tiffany was pressed against the gate. She would do anything to get even further away, but the mannequin was blocking her path back into the rest of the store. If she reached out, the tips of her fingers would graze the axe.

"Tiffany?" The voice came from behind her.

Tiffany spun around, coming face to face with Heather, standing on the other side of the gate. She could see her mascara-streaked reflection in her glasses.

"Heather!" She had never been so excited to see another human being in her life—again, not expecting that person to be Heather Sprocket. Tiffany's pink nails were chipped from scratching at the gate. Her fingers curled around the metal slats, reaching out for help. "Please! Unlock the gate!" She looked over her shoulder. The figure was gone. "Hurry up! Please help me!"

"What's going on, Tiffany? Did Jesse come back?" Heather's brow arched in confusion. She looked past the gate and Tiffany and into the empty store.

"He's trying to kill me!" Tiffany shrieked, still hanging onto the gate. At any moment, she expected to be yanked backward and thrown across the floor, where the axe would cut her open again and again. She would be like her crown—in pieces.

"I don't see anybody . . ."

"Just unlock the fucking gate, Heather! *Now!*"

Boom. Boom. More fireworks exploded overhead as the rest of the country celebrated America's birthday while Tiffany was just fighting to survive the night. *Boom. Boom. Boom.*

"Please hurry!" Tiffany screamed. Her eyes scanned the seemingly deserted interior of West Coast Soundtracks. Where was the son of a bitch hiding?

"Okay, I've unlocked it. Stand back, I'll pull the gate up," Heather said. Tiffany could not believe Heather was acting so calm. Then again, she had not seen the axe and mess in the recording booth.

"Thank you!" Tiffany wailed, staggering out of the store. The tile was cold beneath her bare right foot. "You saved my life!" She leaned on Heather for support.

"And you ended mine."

"What did—"

Before Tiffany could finish her sentence, Heather's fist smashed her directly in the center of the face. Before everything went completely dark, she heard the distant rumble of dying fireworks shattering above them.

~

Blood filled her nose, making it nearly impossible to breathe. Her head throbbed, but her face felt numb. She tried to talk but found it impossible. Something was tied around her face and over her mouth. A gag. Someone had gagged her. But who? And why?

"There's our girl!" a voice shouted. Someone slapped her on the knee. "Wakey, wakey, bitch!"

Tiffany tried to raise her arms but found them tied behind her back. What was going on? Where was she? As the room slowly came into focus, she saw two people standing in front of a black curtain.

"I bet you're surprised to see me here. Heather, maybe not so much. But then again, you are such a vain, egotistical person that maybe you are surprised." Tiffany recognized the voice but couldn't place it. Clara? Kelly-Anne?

She closed her eyes once more. She desperately wanted something to alleviate the pain pounding against her skull. Tylenol. Motrin. Anything to make the pain go away.

"You really don't get it, do you?" the voice said. "How about now, Shitbreath. That ring any bells?"

"I don't think she remembers, Jen," said Heather.

Jen? As in Jenny Hall?

Tiffany forced her eyes to focus. Jenny Hall stood in front of the black curtain wearing a black turtleneck, black gloves, and black pants. Her shoulder-length blonde hair was pulled into a tight bun. She looked like a floating head against a black plane.

"Why . . . are you . . . doing this . . . to . . . me?" Tiffany struggled to talk through the gag.

"It's always about you, isn't it Tiff?" Jenny laughed. "You want a motive? I'll give you a motive. Hell, I'll give you two motives." Her normally cheery voice was filled with venom. "I could live being your shadow. High school doesn't last forever, after all. I knew my day in the sun would come. When you won prom queen, well,

I could live with that. But when Foy Cordova confessed that you blew him to rig the vote, well, let's just say I went a little loco."

Tiffany tugged on her restraints. The rope tying her hands together and to the spindle of a chair would not give. The bind around her ankles was more lax, but with Jenny and Heather standing directly in front there was no chance she could free her legs without them seeing.

"You're . . ." *God, did it hurt to talk.* "Doing . . . this . . . to . . . me . . . because . . . of . . . prom?"

"Oh no, Tiff. Prom is just the tip of the iceberg! What you did to Heather here is so much worse," Jenny added, slapping Heather on the back. The girl stood in the corner, her head down and arms at her side. "It was actually Heather who got this whole thing rolling." Jenny shook her head. "Well, no, that's not really fair to say. It wasn't Heather who bullied Spencer. It wasn't Heather who called Spencer Shitbreath. Who made fun of him day in and day out with her clique of bitches."

Spencer? What is Jenny talking about? Tiffany wondered.

"See, Heather. This bitch doesn't even remember your brother—the one she drove to suicide.

"Jenny, maybe we should stop," Heather squeaked.

"I don't . . . I don't understand," Tiffany mumbled. The pain felt as if it would never end.

"It's no surprise you don't understand, Tiff," Jenny growled. "You never understand. You are so fucking blissfully unaware of how many lives you've ruined. You're a bully. A liar. A cheat."

"Jenny . . . Undo this. Untie me. We . . . we . . . can . . . talk . . ."

Jenny laughed again at that. "I think we're a little past talking, Tiff. Besides, with the fireworks over, we can't risk you screaming."

"You'll . . . never get . . . away with . . . this."

"Oh, Tiffany, of course, we will! We have the perfect scapegoat. Jesse Alexander! Now, did I tip him off that you'd be here tonight? Maybe. But when he grabbed you like that! Totally unscripted!"

"Jenny, maybe we should stop," Heather said meekly. "It isn't too late."

"It's beyond too late, Heather."

Too late for what, Tiffany wondered.

"Think about it, Tiff. We have your keys. Your car. You literally have Jesse's handprint bruised on your body. It's perfect."

"Jenny . . ." Tiffany began.

"Of course, it will be weeks, maybe even months or years, before they find you." Tiffany's blood ran cold. She tugged at the rope binding her hands. *Please! Please! If I could just get my hands free.* "You wouldn't be the first big shot wannabe actress that LA swallowed whole. Nobody has to know you never made it." Jenny leaned in. "That'll be our little secret."

Jenny reached down and picked up a piece of the crown. Tiffany flinched as she sat a broken piece on top of her head. Her crowning glory—shattered.

"Go ahead and hit the record button, Heather. I want to remember this. Well, enough with the chit-chat, Tiff," laughed Jenny. She picked up the axe leaning in the corner of the booth.

"Jenny . . ." Tiffany moaned, pulling in vain on her restraints.

"This is for the prom queen."

The axe fell down.

Again.

And again.

And again.

4
JILLY'S
John Martin

AMERI-GANZA! TYLER READ THE FLYER again before stuffing the crumpled paper back into his pocket. The air was thick, and the parking lot shimmered. A mirage sprang up at the far end. The sun was, mercifully, disappearing behind Sherwood, but heat still bore down from the yellowing sky. Somewhere, a lone firework crackled.

He'd locked his bike to a pole behind the mall's dumpsters. It stank but was shaded and hidden from the street. They'd kicked his tire the last time he left it at the rack. Fortunately, Jilly's had a spare that day. No reason to push his luck a second time.

Tyler pulled his hood and hurried around the building to the side entrance, sweat staining his undershirt, and his stomach was beginning to twist. Nobody ever used that door. A single Chick Tract littered the steps, this one crying about how Satan uses Halloween to touch kids or something. Tyler picked it up and tossed it into an overflowing trash can.

Like the other doors, it had a *Sherwood Mall July 4th* banner out front, advertising various sales going on throughout the mall. Tyler was biased but personally liked Jilly's' name better. He opened it, air conditioning blasting him and waving the banner, and for a moment, the beads on his forehead were like ice. Freezing. Cold and shocking, like plunging into a Slurpee. Refreshing. Far better than anything outside.

~

He'd first discovered Jilly's months ago. It had been early February, too cold to stick around at the park for long. But, he'd needed somewhere to go after storming out.

Sherwood Mall it was.

Back then, it was engulfed in pink streamers and paper hearts, and the gumball machines were stuffed with those shitty Valentine's candies that tasted like chalk. A vigil for the Challenger sat in the corner of the food court, surrounded by a congregation silently praying.

But then he'd found it—Jilly's—nestled in the narrow hallway sprouting from the Maxy's front door. He doesn't remember what first drew him to it. Maybe he'd seen an old NES, barely used, in the window. Maybe the cluttered oddities and preserved insects caught his eye. Or the Jilly's' smell. Worn leather books and the faintest whiff of formaldehyde overshadowed by a smattering of scented candles. Whatever it was, Jilly's was there. Quiet and peaceful in the sea of neon and pink and prayer that was Sherwood Mall that February.

~

The door clicked shut. Up the short flight of stairs and past the Cineplex, then a right. Another banner, this one reading 1776-1986, under an arch of red, white, and blue balloons.

"Faggot."

The shout echoed through the hallway, from the atrium or food court. It could've been directed at him again, but maybe not. He ignored it, pulling his hood tighter and scurrying down the hallway to Maxy's. Left at the department store. Through the narrow hallway. To the far end. To nearly the last store on the left.

Home. Safe. Swathed in the leather and formaldehyde and candles.

Jilly's.

~

His eyes had dried, but his nose was still runny the first time he'd wandered in. The store was quiet. The counter empty, save for a small desk fan buzzing at its edge. Tyler crept to the back, pretending to peruse books and wiping his nose on his sleeve.

His mom had found his dice tucked away in the back of his closet. At the bottom of his second-to-last drawer, summer clothes piled on top. She'd called Eric's mom in a fit, then Jason's. They'd, in turn, called Sam and Patrick's parents. All before the boys got back from school.

Alex's car was in the driveway when Tyler rode home, and his heart sank. His stepdad only ever came home early when there was a crisis.

They threw his dice on the kitchen counter. A Nat 20. Funny.

They screamed at him about how D&D summons Satan and his minions. And they didn't raise him to be like that. And who lured him to this lifestyle.

"Probably that queer, Mr. Potter," Alex grumbled, despite the fact that the English teacher had a wife and two children. As if he was in Tyler's life enough to know that. Tyler screamed back and demanded to know why his mother was lurking in his room. She stammered about some bullshit about looking for clothes to donate, but Alex slammed on the table. The dice rattled. He shouted louder as if he had authority over Tyler for any reason other than having a fat wallet.

Then, the dice went to the trash but never made it. At the last moment, his mom turned, shoving them in the garbage disposal. Tyler stared, the wind out of his lungs. The disposal whined and stuttered. It coughed up blue plastic chips into the sink.

They demanded to know who the "ringleader" was. Tyler never gave up the Dungeon Master, because you do anything for friends.

But Patrick did. And Jason got shipped off to some *pray-away-the-devil* school a month later.

⁓

"Hey, Tyler," Ms. Bateman called from the desk, smiling. "So glad you're coming tonight! It's gonna be one to remember."

She was older but as spry as any teenager, and her salt-and-pepper hair was stained a new dye every month. This month was blue. She had an accent Tyler loved but couldn't place, holding onto her O's a note too long, speaking quicker than molasses but slower than water. Like fresh tree sap, maybe.

"Hey," he said, smiling back. "Yeah, I'm looking forward to it."

She stood, straightening the *Ameri-ganza* flyers on the counter. "The others'll be here soon. There's snacks in the cabinet if you want anything. Help yourself."

Tyler did, opening the nearest cabinet to reveal rows of Dr. Pepper, Doritos, and some kind of unlabeled chocolate pudding. His favorite, the perfect mix of salty and sweet. He went to pull out the food but noticed a smudge on the floor. One small, black drop, inky and thick. The ceiling must've been leaking again.

Tyler told Ms. Bateman about it when she walked by. She corrected him, told him to call her "Paula, or Polly," and wiped it up. She wasn't worried about it. "Happens all the time, the store's old."

⁓

When D&D collapsed, the friend group collapsed with it. Everything was Church on Sunday mornings, nights, and Wednesdays, and somehow, they all managed to get sent to ones on different corners of town. Tyler got grounded for a month. Eric for two, but then he moved across the country to his dad's house. Sam got pulled out of football. Only Patrick got off scot-free. Apparently, Satan couldn't dig his claws into the JV Quarterback.

They all blamed Tyler like it was his fault his mom was a bitch, and Alex was a nut. He wasn't the one that ratted about Jason. He didn't send anyone away or kick Sam out of football. But still. They all sided with the Golden Boy, Patrick.

Only Polly listened. Intently. Nodding along and sitting on a counter, one leg crossed over the other. Listening to the boy she found in the back of Jilly's, pretending to peruse the books.

The tears came again even though he tried to fight them. She opened an old dresser with worms preserved in jars on top and pulled out a box of tissues.

"That sounds terrible," she cooed. She told him he was always welcome at Jilly's. That it would always have what he needed.

He stayed late that first night, after the crowds went home and the ambient pop music died. Past when the stores had closed, and the neon went dark. Polly drove him home.

"Here you are," she said, parking and tugging his bike out of her back seat. He thanked her and turned to the door. She stopped him.

"Hey, wait," she said, taking his hand and pressing something small and glassy into it.

It was a vial of black nail polish.

Tyler recoiled. "The hell is this for?" he asked.

"For you. I found it in a cabinet and thought you may need it."

"I don't need this."

"Maybe not yet. But maybe you will," she said, smiling. "Our little secret. You don't have to use it if you don't want to." And she closed his hand around it. "But hold onto it."

~

Today, the polish was chipped. Tyler studied his fingernails, considering if he had enough time to strip the old coat and paint on a new one. Polly had said that the others would be there soon, and with them would come the chaos of tonight. Jillys' private *Ameri-ganza* celebration. Invite only, but based on the stacked flyers, *invite* was a loose definition. Tyler was curious how many people would show up.

A large hand landed on his head, tousling his hair. "Hey there, sport. Glad you came." It was Brian, smiling. After

Polly, Brian had been the second Jilly's regular he'd met. Tall and blond, and with a patchy John Lennon beard, he had the vibes of an old hippie that had cut his dreadlocks but never truly integrated with society. He worked odd jobs and lived in a trailer in the "bad part" of town, as Alex said it. But Tyler had been to his place twice, both times for dinner. Brian's barbecue kicked ass.

"Thanks! Happy to be here. Planning on any more barbecues?"

Brian chuckled and told him the next would be on Sunday.

"Is that Brian?" called Polly. "Fantastic. You two, get your asses back here and help me move this."

The two men obeyed, winding through the cluttered aisles. Past ancient dolls, every kind of preserved animal, and a few maps a century or more out of date until they reached the Employees Only door. Then, through the storeroom and in the back, they found Polly dragging an old wardrobe into the maintenance hallway. The three lifted it, squeezing between a pipe and the yellow tape circling the *other* door, avoiding stepping inside. The sign beside it said *Safety Hazard*, after all.

Tyler was winded, but the three managed to move the wardrobe to the front. Polly had a *Negotiable* sticker waiting. She cleaned out a spot in the far corner for it, taking an old wagon wheel and a statue of a Dalmatian — missing one ear — and moving them to the discount pile. Tyler thought about taking off his hoodie, but didn't.

The front door opened. The bell rang, and shitty pop music momentarily floated in.

"Anyone here?" Maria called.

"Well. Look who decided to show up," Brian hollered back, grinning. "Like a blister after the work's been done." Maria found them, hugging Brian and Polly, then threw her arms around Tyler. She was a couple of years younger than him, maybe 12 or 13, and bounced between the other two's couches. Tyler never asked why she'd run away from home.

But Polly had brought her in a year before him and made damn sure that she enrolled in school that August. She'd gotten an A-minus on her last math exam.

The four worked. Moving boxes and ordering the mess. Getting the store situated for the night, and for the sales that would be ongoing during the long weekend. Laughing. Chatting.

Then Maria asked Tyler about Patrick.

"Have you talked to him?"

"Yeah," replied Tyler, tight-lipped. And Polly nudged her, giving her a single head shake.

~

He'd changed. It started the next Monday after the dice. Avoiding Tyler's gaze in the halls. Dodging him in the few classes they had together. Sitting with the football team at lunch instead of with the dwindling friend group. Overnight, he was too cool for Tyler and the others. A jock. An All-star. A *Golden Boy* that couldn't be caught dead with those losers. Outcasts. Fags.

Even though it had been Patrick that planted a kiss on Tyler's lips at Sam's 12th birthday. Now, Tyler hated him for it, and he'd hated himself since the party for kissing him back.

But that was all in the past. Patrick always had a rotation of girls swooning over him, even when he had been with his former friends. Now, his little crowd of disciples grew into a mass of cheerleaders and jocks and assholes. Tyler never told anyone about that night, not even the others. Because you do anything for friends.

Tyler yelped as a wooden pole fell off the rack, cracking against his knuckles. It shouldn't have hurt, but they were still bruised from a week ago.

"You okay?" Brian asked, concerned.

"Yeah. Still a little sore." And to prove he was fine, he lunged back into the work, sweat staining through the hoodie's armpits. But then, he crammed an old basketball too tight on a rack, and a can of Speed Stick fell, splattering on the other side.

"Shit. I'm sorry. I'll—"

"Tyler," said Polly, placing her hands on his shoulders. "Look at me. Deep breath." And she mirrored him, inhaling through her nose, holding it for five seconds, and blowing out for eight. "You're fine. Don't apologize, it happens. We'll always have more."

Tyler's knees felt weak, and his bruised fists clenched and released.

"Tonight's a big night. You're just nervous," she said, calmly. "If you need to take a walk, go ahead. We've got it held down here."

But Tyler didn't want to walk. He didn't want to leave the store because what was out there for him? Cracked tile floors? Jilly's had that. White brick walls and pink, blue, and purple neon lights zig-zagging across the ceiling? He hated it. It was like looking at the sound of a fork scratching a plate. Towering, canyon-like hallways leading to an atrium that would crisply bounce slurs at him from every direction, with the grand prize of a shitty fifty-cent hotdog from the food court? Pass.

So Tyler didn't go on a walk. He sighed and trudged to the back, through the storeroom, into the hallway, found an old desk, and sat, crisscrossing his legs. Staring at the door circled in yellow tape.

It was old, and had it not been anchored to the wall, he'd have assumed it was another oddity. Brian had once said it was pine, but it was so stained and worn and chipped that the wood could've been anything, really. The brass hinges had long since tarnished, and the knob discolored from countless hands. Its frame had symbols carved along it, as weathered as everything else. Tyler had never seen them before, but he assumed they were runes, or from some ancient people long gone.

There were other carvings, too. Dicks, mostly, but a smattering of other graffiti. The cleanest read, "L+P 4 Evr," scratched inside a heart. Another, someone had painstakingly carved a poem in the softwood, full of "thees" and "thous." Tyler liked that one the most. There were a few spray painted on. Others, too, were written with Sharpies.

Knock, knock, knock, knock.

Four quick, sharp raps against the other side. From fatless knuckles, or what Tyler imagined a cane rapping on a door to sound like. Or maybe bone.

Knock, knock, knock, knock.

Again. Leisurely. Soft. Like an old friend stopping by for a chat or when the missionaries showed up at his house. His mom always let them in, and Tyler always disappeared into his room.

He'd been sneaking out to Jilly's for a month when he first saw the door and heard the four taps. Polly was with him, and when he'd asked why it was there, she shrugged, saying, "It's always been here." Then she'd whisked him away to help move products, the tapping ceasing. His hands were moist. His eyes kept searching for the door, curious where it led. But he'd never opened it. The tape and sign were warning enough, but the carefulness of the others, too, warned him off wordlessly. And so, the door faded into the background. The knocking, drowned out by pop music and humming AC units. Just another quirk of a very old store.

～

The next day was the first time. He shuffled into school, pushing through the throngs of students. Talking, shouting, throwing water bottles and crumpled paper over him at each other. Smoking. Kissing. Whispering. Giggling.

QUEER

He read his locker. Then again. The hallway went silent, the mass of bodies pressing into him. His breath caught, his hands trembled, and he turned, peering through the crowd at who had written it.

Patrick. Leering at him, snickering. Along with the other jocks.

～

"How was school today?" Alex said, walking past him to the bedroom.

"Fine." As if Alex was still close enough to hear. He thought about telling what happened. To a teacher or even to Alex and his mom.

But he didn't. It would be his word against the quarterback's. And because you do anything for friends.

~

The next day, he walked into school with his head held high. Wet, black nail polish smearing his fingernails.

That night, he called home, leaving a voicemail that he was spending the night with his friends. Polly invited him to her apartment — so it really wasn't a lie — and stripped the polish. Then, she showed him how to use the base coat, then paint, let dry, then another coat, and drying, before applying the top coat.

"It's tough the first few times," she said, grinning. Maria smiled, too, from her bed on the couch. "You have to be careful not to pick your nose while it sets."

They laughed and ate McDonald's while his fingernails hardened.

Alex slapped him when he saw. He screamed at him, spewing all the names that the kids at school wrote on his locker. Demanded he take it off, who would've done such a thing, poisoning his mind like that?

Tyler refused. They didn't go to Wednesday night bible study. They took away his NES, then his Walkman. Through the paper-thin walls that night, he could hear his mom and Alex mumbling. Alex was crying. He'd never heard that before. "No!" Alex raised his voice, then fell to a mumble. "Our son isn't a queer."

That next afternoon, Tyler didn't go home. Jilly's had a brand new NES on sale.

~

When he walked back into the store, the Ameri-ganza fliers had been put away, and the center was cleared for space. Polly had lit another candle, this one called *sniff-my-nuts*, and smelled of hazelnut and almonds. His polish was still chipped. Damn, he should've taken the break to fix it.

Outside, a crowd floated by and Tyler's heart caught in his throat. The football team. The jocks. The guys that were so much cooler than you who could ruin your life with a single joke, and with their cheerleaders following.

Orbiting the herd. Decked out in their jerseys, two tossed a football back and forth over the group, and the rest passed a lighter around, smoking.

Patrick wasn't with them.

"You okay, sport?" asked Brian, setting his hand on Tyler's shoulder. The team wandered past, oblivious.

"Yeah. Just a bit nervous, is all."

The older man smiled. "Hey, that's okay. Ameri-ganza can get hectic. It means you're normal. Human."

Tyler unclenched his jaw. He didn't realize it had been so tight. Then he sighed. "I don't know if it's gonna happen." Tears welled up, but he opened his eyes wide the way Maria had shown him, and they dried before they could fall. "I-I-I want him to come. I really do. But I don't know if he feels like that."

Brian's eyes met his, and he cocked a half-smile. "About you? It's hard, you know. At your age. All your hormones and such." Tyler winced, grinning.

"Ew, gross," he laughed.

Brian chuckled too. "But seriously, if he does, great! If not, it's no big deal, there will be others. Time will go on. Sure, it'll hurt, but one day you'll meet someone new." He finished, tousling Tyler's hair and turning, his old boots clicking on the linoleum.

～

It was over a month ago when it happened. May 12th or 13th, less than a week before school ended.

Tyler strolled in, shoulders pulled back and jaw tight. Ready to take the words on his chin.

But that day, they never came.

He found out what had happened from the whispering at the back of the class and just-too-loud conversations at lunch. Patrick's dad found the loose board under the bed. He'd pried it open. There was a single vial of black nail polish, unopened. But that wasn't it. It was stuffed with men's swimsuit magazines, their pages stuck together and stinking. A dozen of them, but the way the girls in the back chittered about it made the number jump to hundreds. By the afternoon, love letters to men across the country had dug their way into the rumors, too.

Patrick hadn't shown up to school that day. Nor the next. On Friday, he came, sporting a black eye that was no longer swelling. Nothing new was scrawled on Tyler's locker. Nobody flicked his ear in the hallway or spat gum at him in History. And at lunch, Patrick sat at an empty table on the other side of the cafeteria.

That Monday, Tyler overheard that there was an opening for QB.

~

Then, there was this morning, July 4th. He'd been out, riding his bike with a new wheel that didn't quite match the older one. The knuckles on his right hand were bruised, and the scrapes almost healed. It was cool, but humid, and his hoodie stuck to him. It'd be a hot day when the sun rose higher.

He saw Patrick sitting on a swing in the empty park. Alone. Elbows on knees, and head hung. He almost didn't stop, he knew nothing, *nothing*, good would come of it. But then he slowed and turned, cursing himself on each pedal back. He fell in the swing beside Patrick's. "Hey."

Patrick was quiet. "Hey."

They didn't say anything for a long time, listening to birdsong and feeling the first sweat bead on their foreheads. Patrick winced every time a car sped past. Finally, Tyler sighed and said, "I'm sorry this happened."

Patrick didn't look up. "I am, too."

They stayed like that, the swings bobbing back and forth until the first rays cleared the shadows and fell on them.

"Are you doing anything tonight?" Tyler asked, looking at him. Patrick never answered. Then, Tyler reached into his pocket and pulled one of the two crumpled flyers from it.

"Would you want to?"

Patrick looked at him, then the paper, then slowly reached out and took it. "Ameri-ganza?" he asked.

"It's not put on by Sherwood. It's our own, private thing. Low key. Won't be many people there." The next words caught in his throat, but he pushed them out. "I'd like to see you there."

Patrick grimaced, the paper crinkling in his hand.

"I'll think about it."

~

Now, it was July 4, 7:43 PM. The crowds were seeping in, and even though Jilly's wasn't near the main entrance, they still found a way to crowd the hallway like sardines. Meandering forward, wrapped in a sea of red, white, and blue. Many wore those cheap plastic Uncle Sam hats. A few babies wailed. High schoolers, some that Tyler recognized, shuffled along with their families, aching to be somewhere cooler than Sherwood Mall's *July 4th Sale-o-rama*. The fireworks would start at dusk in the field across from the big parking lot.

And when they started, and everyone was distracted, Patrick would, hopefully, come. He'd lock his bike to the pole behind the dumpsters that stank but were hidden. He'd slink through the side door, far away from the crowds. He'd creep his way to Maxy's but take a left into the hallway. He'd find Jilly's. He'd be home.

With Tyler.

He watched the crowd while Polly set up a plastic disco ball and Maria pulled food from the cabinets. They were, mercifully, thinning and soon would congregate in the atrium, leaving this half of the store empty.

A cold sweat broke out on Tyler's forehead. What if they didn't? What if there were stragglers, or kids who snuck away to smoke or couples for a quickie?

What if Patrick saw them? Got cold feet?

Left?

He tried to shake the thought away. He told himself that Patrick wasn't a pussy, that he'd come. When the lights went out, and the fireworks started, and the mall was quiet, he'd be there, tapping on the front door. But still, his hands shook. He looked down at them, studying the pattern of bruises.

~

"Tha-fuck have you been?" Alex demanded. It was 3:15 am. Five days ago. He'd tried to sneak back in through his window.

It was bolted. Shit.

So, with his head held high, Tyler walked through the front door.

They were both waiting for him, and Tyler could smell the liquor on Alex's breath. His mother was curled in a chair, her nose buried in the newest Chick Tract. Missionaries must've come by.

"Hey!" he snapped again. "Look at me when I'm talking. Where. Have. You. Been?" He pushed into the little hallway from the front door to the living room, puffed his chest out, and lifted his arms as much as he could without feeling like he looked like a jackass.

It didn't work. And Tyler's dry, red eyes bore into the jackass.

"Move."

Alex's mouth twitched. His face got redder, like a tomato. He barreled closer, his stinking breath rolling over Tyler's face, filling his nose and sticking in his eyes.

"I said," he seethed. "Where. Have. You. Been."

~

Knock. Knock. Knock. Knock.

It was late. The mall was closed. The last of the July 4th decorations had been put up.

Knock. Knock. Knock. Knock.

Sharper this time. Faster. It caught his attention, like when the mall's background music cut out after he'd gone deaf to it.

It was different.

Knock. Knock. Knock. Knock. Again. Heavier. Louder. *Desperate.* Like a starving man begging for food.

"It happens all the time," Polly said, holding the other side of the globe. "Come on."

But her face was tight. Her lips were thin. She didn't meet his gaze. And she didn't look at the door.

"Wait," said Tyler, lowering his side of the globe. Its wooden feet, shaped like paws, balanced, and he let go, turning to the knocking. "I want to know what —"

"TYLER!"

Polly had never yelled. He shrank, and he saw something he'd never seen before. An adult apologized to him.

She sighed. "I'm sorry. That wasn't fair of me."

Knock. Knock. Knock. Knock. Knock. Knock.

Her eyes met his, then bounced to the wall. Then to the ceiling. Then to the door. She sucked her lower lip in, then released, and blew air from her nose.

"Okay. Help me move this. And let me call the others. But, Tyler?"

He picked up his end again. "Yeah?"

"Please. Just, please. Try and have an open mind about it."

And then it was dark. Brian and Maria walked in with weak smiles. Not looking at him.

"Hey, sport." Brian fiddled with something inside a dresser. Maria twitched, bouncing on her feet.

Then, the man closed it and handed Polly a length of thick rope.

"Come with us," she said and nodded at Brian. Tyler and Maria followed her to the back, through the Employee door, and stopped outside of the yellow ring of tape.

THUCK. THUCK. THUCK. THUCK. THUCK.

Banging. The door shaking, the frame cracking. Flecks of paint chipping and showering off. The room echoed with it. The building shook with the blows.

THUCK. THUCK. THUCK. THUCK. THUCK.

Tyler's heart pounded in his ears. His knees locked and breath caught, and every nerve in his body screamed "RUN," but he couldn't, his legs wouldn't obey.

THUCK. THUCK. THUCK.

"Oh, for fuck's sake —" Polly threw the rope at Maria. Then stomped over the tape, balled her fist, and banged against the door just as loud. The other side went quiet.

Tyler stared, wide-eyed, at the trespass they all were so careful to avoid.

Then, tightness around his waist. His eyes darted. Maria with the rope. Pulling it securely, knotting. The other end was already tied to a pipe running up the wall.

"What's —" but he was cut off by a crash near the front of the store. Then, the entry door shutting. Locking, a thick bolt sliding into place.

"Maria, go stand over there," Polly said, pointing to the far wall. Maria obeyed. Tyler yanked the rope half-heartedly.

"Guys, what's going on?" His voice shook. No one answered. The noises began again. But this time, it was long, dragging noises against the old door. Like fingernails. Or claws.

"I-I don't want to do this anymore!" He yanked harder on the rope.

"It's okay." Brian. Carrying two long rods, each with cloth balled at the end like a boxing glove. One had a hook below the ball. "You'll be fine." He handed the one with the hook to Polly, then braced his against the door.

"Please!" Tyler begged, trembling. "Please don't do this." He no longer cared about the knocking. He just wanted to go back to the way things were.

Polly turned to him. "Sweetie," she said, drawing in air. "Tyler. The rope is for your own safety, I promise. We're showing you this because we love you. We *trust* you."

"Do you think he's ready?" Brian asked, concerned.

Polly didn't answer and turned to the door. She guided the hook onto the doorknob. "This," she leveraged the rod. The doorknob twisted. "Is Jilly."

The door exploded open, held back by only the rods. Growling. Scratching. The frame shaking and splintering, the wood bowing as the mass of flesh surged. Tendrils curling, writhing, wet slapping against the walls and floor. It opened more. The flesh-wall grew and pushed the door. Polly and Brian struggled. Holding it back.

They slid.

The door's other side, plastered in sinew and pulsing veins. Coiling. Stretching. Tyler yanked like an animal tied to a slaughtering pole. The rope pulled tighter. Black ooze dripped from the thing's pores. It fell down bits of hair and fingernails and teeth that sprouted haphazardly across the mass.

Then the eye opened. Like some great squid's eye, the size of a dinner plate. But it was human, with an iris a deep, thoughtful blue.

And it saw Tyler. Twitching. *Blinking.* Focusing, finding his body tied to the wall. It recoiled like a tiger. Hungry.

And then, Jilly's mouth opened. Long. Vertical, stretching from below the eye down the mass. It split, tearing skin and fat apart. Red, hot blood sprayed from the gash and mixed with the pooling black grease. It spasmed. Ruptured. Splayed open further. It lunged, the maw prolapsing, rolling out and pulsing into the room with such force that Brian stumbled. Fell. Dropped the rod, and Polly couldn't brace the door on her own. The shock threw the door fully open. Thundering against the wall. Tyler's ears ringing. His legs failing. He collapsed, pressing his body into the corner. As far away as he could manage from this mass.

The skin boiled. Bone fragments pushed and broke the skin; teeth sprouted from the mouth. Bleeding. Clicking, scratching against each other. Chaotic. They twisted in waves, reaching out at Tyler and pulling back. Clicking. Scratching. Guiding its prey into the black hole at the center like a lamprey.

Then, Jilly's dripping tongue lurched from the hole. Long. Thin. Muscular. Ribbed with chipped bones like a goose's tongue and covered in human fingers. They curled at Tyler like they were beckoning a child.

As if to say, "Come here. Just a little closer." It whipped and thrashed and drew itself long. The fingers found the floor and scrambled. Gripped. Pulled the organ as far as it could go, then further. Crawling at Tyler. Crawling to the edge of the yellow tape.

Polly's rod struck the tongue. It screamed with a thousand voices. It recoiled. It yanked. Teeth and blood and fingers ripping from the muscle in the retreat. The tongue disappearing in the mouth. Brian slammed the door with his rod. Jilly hissed. Thrashed. Pushed. Polly joined him. Pushed back. Battling the thing. Attrition. Struggling.

Tyler's fingers found the knot. Yanked. Fingernails digging into the hemp. Polish chipping. Blood pooling under his fingers. He tore. Screaming. The knot fraying. Coming loose. One more pull. Looping his fingers in the hole. Ripping. Rope loosening. Kicking. Squirming. Polly shouting. Brian lunging. The door closing another inch. Rope coming free. Tyler jumping, kicking it off. The world blurring. Charging forward, shoving Maria. Through the door. Into the main room. The building rattling. Black grease dripping from the ceiling. The front door. Almost there. Free. Free. Safe.

But the grate was locked, and the door was bolted and his sore fingers couldn't grip it. He couldn't see the key anywhere. He yanked anyway. No use. Behind him, the monster's cries were dying. The old door slammed shut.

Then, heavy footsteps growing louder. Running. He turned, and the three were there closing the distance.

And Polly was in front. Hands outstretched, palms open. Cooing.

~

"Well? I'm waiting!"

Tyler stared down at the jackass with the red tomato face and his forehead vein bulging. This thing. This little imp. A parasite that couldn't comprehend the world past the artery it suckled from. A cuckoo bird that planted itself into his nest, his home, and screamed day and night, begging for more food. More attention.

More authority.

"And what's wrong with your hands?" Alex finally noticed something about Tyler. "Why are they so fucked up? Is this some ritual? Did some fagg—"

Tyler didn't remember throwing the first punch.

Alex's red face snapped back, blood spewing from his nose and across the hallway. He stumbled, tripping on a shoe. Falling back, head thudding against the wall. His mom's scream.

His body lunged. His left hand curled into a fist, broken nails digging into his palm. A wild left hook cracking into Alex's jaw. It felt so weak.

But Alex's head struck the wall again. Louder. Solid. Tyler's body slamming into his. Ribs popping. Cracking. Falling onto the stepdad, his chest caving under his weight.

Then, screaming. His mom's. His. Alex's gurgling, all mixing in the house while his fists windmilled. Slamming, finding meat. Cracking in his hands or Alex's face, it didn't matter. Wet splattering. Teeth breaking, flying.

And then it was over. His heart pounded in his ears, his nervous system was on fire. His mom was sobbing. Grabbing him, pulling him off of Alex.

And he slapped her. He told himself it was just recoil. It was adrenaline. Just the moment, and that he didn't mean it.

And he knew he was lying.

He didn't sleep that night. He lay in bed, numb from the day. They'd left for the hospital. The next morning, only one new message on the answering machine. It was Mom calling from a payphone. Breathless. Tired.

"Alex wants you to know he's sorry that he's been a bad father. And he isn't going to press charges, in case you're worried. He loves you. I love you." *Click*.

Tyler sighed, falling onto the couch, the house silent. Blood drying in the entryway. And fell into a deep, deathlike sleep.

And that was five days ago.

～

"We weren't going to hurt you, Tyler."

Polly had cooed, calming him. Now, she sat across from him in the circle of chairs, silently eating a cupcake. The plastic disco ball spinning.

"Do y'all like the cake?" she asked, looking up at him. Tyler's was untouched.

"I do." Maria had already finished hers and was eyeing Tyler's.

"Maria, there's enough to go around," Brian said, motioning to the cabinet. When it was opened next, Tyler knew the tray of cupcakes would be full, as if they hadn't been touched. Jilly would see to it.

Outside of the store, the hallway was dark. The first firework popped.

"She, Jilly, provides for us. She stocks this place with what someone needs," Polly had said, sitting on a conveniently placed chair. *"Tyler, she loves us. Like you love us, and we love you."* Brian stood behind Maria, hands on her shoulders. She had dry tears on her cheeks and Tyler's stomach knotted. He'd hurt someone he cared for in his mad escape.

"Was the rope too tight?" Maria whispered. "I-I'm really sorry if it hurt. I just didn't really know that I was gonna have to tie it, you know?"

"No, no, you didn't do anything," said Tyler, tears welling up in his own eyes. Tears for the people that had just tied him to a pole and showed him a monster. People he loved.

His friends.

"It's just," Brian started, glancing at Polly. She nodded, and he continued. "Well, you saw Jilly. She's old. Hungry, and she loses control sometimes, that's all. The rope was to *protect* you, Tyler. What if she somehow reached further? Grabbed you? The rope was for your safety, sport." And he smiled.

Tyler felt the raw skin around his stomach. Still bruised but healing. He wondered if Jilly's had other things. Painkillers, maybe? Something better than the Aspirin she usually provided. He opened a drawer, but instead of painkillers, he found a hoodie. Crisp and laundered, the exact same as his current one, down to the size. He sniffed the sweat stain under his armpit. Yep, ripe, and changed into the new one. It smelled of lavender.

Patrick loved lavender.

Knock. Knock. Knock. Knock.

Four quick, light raps at the front door. Timid, like a mouse hiding from a tomcat. More fireworks. The show was starting.

"Patrick, hey," he opened the door. The hall was empty except for the boy. He didn't answer but smirked and looked down at his hands. They had wet, black nail polish smearing the fingernails.

"Hey, Tyler." Almost a whisper. Tyler stepped back, and Patrick crept in, shutting the door behind himself.

"You must be Patrick!" Polly beamed, opening her arms as if to give him a hug from the end of the aisle. "Tyler talks about you all the time."

Patrick blushed.

Tyler grimaced.

Polly strode through the aisle beside them, rummaging through shelves.

"Tyler, I'm," his voice caught. He choked. The first tear rolled down his cheek. "I'm sorry for what I did. Thank you for inviting me tonight." He looked up at Tyler. Tyler stared at Patrick's wet nails.

"Where'd you park your bike?" he asked.

"The dumpsters, beside yours. Where you said people wouldn't see it."

Polly closed a drawer, pressing something into the back of her leg, and came around the corner, behind Patrick.

"Well, well, well. Look at *these* two lovebirds," Brian strolled up behind Tyler, his voice almost normal. But Tyler could hear the flatness underneath. The force he was using. Again, Patrick blushed and looked at Tyler. Their eyes met.

Polly swung. The hammer fell.

~

Jilly needed meat. Live, twitching meat. But it didn't have to be conscious. Polly was merciful, at least. Practiced with the mallet. Patrick crumbled, wheezing and twitching as Tyler broke, sobbing. Polly and Brian dragged the body to the back.

"It's gonna be bad," Maria hugged him and whispered in his ear. "It always is, watching for the first time. But you'll get used to it. I promise."

Jilly always demanded they watch her feast. They obeyed, Tyler numb as the door opened. Patrick's body jerked, lying inside the yellow tape.

He cried. Bawled, and the others bawled with him, both for the savagery of the feast and for the pain Tyler felt. Watching his childhood friend and the boy who kissed him be ripped apart by the mouth. The eye, twitching in euphoria, in orgasm. The remains of Patrick's arm, splattered and chewed, resembling ground beef, sliding into the hole at the center of the teeth.

Bones chipped. Broke. Crushed, the sound drowned out by the fireworks above. And still, he watched. Even through the pain and the revulsion, he never took his eyes off of the meal. Not as Patrick's leg tore off. Not as his head squeezed in the mouth, popping like a grape. Not as Jilly finally, mercifully, wrapped her tongue around the last leg, curled around the shoe, and sucked in like it was pasta. Because that's what they needed him to do. And you do anything for friends.

All that was left of Patrick in the world was a bike, chained where no one would've seen him stop, and crimson blood and carrion seeping over a circle of yellow tape. Then, Jilly's tongue sopped up the latter. And Patrick was no more.

~

On Sunday night, Patrick was reported missing. On Monday, the cops came to Tyler's still-empty house and questioned him. Someone had driven by and seen the two boys at the park. But they wrote their notes and left, with the older of the pair mumbling something about "not wanting to get involved with their kind of activity."

On Wednesday, Alex and his mom came back. His mom stayed. Alex left for a motel. The news said that Mr. Potter was called in for investigation for everything from Patrick's disappearance to pedophilia to occultism.

No charges were filed, but he wouldn't be the English teacher the next year.

And then, Friday. Exactly one week after Ameri-ganza. Tyler, now, had a job at Jilly's and spent his day ringing up the few customers that trickled in and sweeping up dust that always seemed to pile in the quiet store. The cash register was never empty. A new bike, with *SALE — Gently Used*, balanced beside the counter.

He heard a knock from a dresser and turned, laying his broom down. Another knock, the second drawer from the bottom. Four light taps. He bent and opened it.

In the dresser sat seven blue, plastic dice. A Nat 20.

5
SKIN DEEP
Reece G. Donnell

A S SHE CLOSED AND LOCKED THE salon door, Betty Gamble sighed contentedly. Turning the sign over, she glimpsed *"Sorry, Betty's is closed,"* and felt that familiar pang of excitement. Even after ten years of owning her own place, it still tickled her seeing her own name on the sign.

"Y'know," she began, "we always do so well during . . ."

Her words were cut off by a shattering of glass, causing Betty to spin on her heel. Standing before one of the salon's booths was her assistant, Lacie Blake, and on the floor, tiny pieces of the vanity mirror lay. Lacie looked at Betty sheepishly and shrugged.

"Sorry, Bet," she said. "I was cleaning behind it and, I guess it got away from me."

Betty only smiled, as Lacie quickly grabbed a dustpan and broom.

"That's okay," Betty assured, walking toward the mess. "You know, in the whole year you've worked here, I think that's the only mistake you've made? Pretty impressive, if you ask me."

"Well, I've had a lot of practice," Lacie said, putting the dustpan down and taking the broom. "Not as much as you, of course." She swept up the shards, careful not to get them under the cabinet.

"35 years!" Betty exclaimed. "Ten years on my own. Man, how time flies. But, I've only been here, at Sherwood, for the last three."

"Just curious," Lacie said, sweeping. "Why did you move here to the mall?"

Betty shrugged, letting her weight fall onto her good leg.

"It seemed economical," she said, shifting. "There's far more foot traffic here than on Main. Besides, Sherwood didn't have a salon. Well, they didn't *still* have a salon—not after Ginger's purple hair factory went out of business. I tell you, she had those old ladies looking like cotton balls!"

Betty laughed to herself, giving herself a lookover in the mirror. No, her hair . . . was perfect—Well as perfect as it was going to get. Ginger had nothing on her.

"Somebody missed a rare opportunity," Lacie smiled, dumping the shards into a small trashcan that typically held little more than hair and discarded gum wrappers.

"I suppose," Betty said wistfully. "But I don't suppose I'll be here much longer. At my age, I might wanna think about hanging up my apron."

"Nonsense," Lacie replied with a subtle chuckle. It was outlandish, she knew. Betty still had many years ahead of her. "Fifty-five is still young—besides, you love this place."

"I do," Betty responded with a smile, exposing her large front teeth, the left slightly overlapping the right.

Lacie sat the pan back down and returned to get the rest. With one last sweep, the remains of the shattered glass rested in the dustpan. She leaned on the broom and sighed.

"So, what were you saying? I mean before I . . . interrupted," Lacey asked.

"Oh," Betty began with a dismissive wave of her hand. "Just that we always do so well around holidays. You know people 'round here love to spend their hard-earned paychecks in support of Uncle Sam."

Betty leaned on the counter by the cash register before glancing at her watch. It was later than she expected. Time really does fly . . .

"Naturally," Lacie agreed. "Especially during the Fourth of July, there's so much going on, what with barbecues, fireworks right outside, and the parade downtown. And of course, ladies want to look good. Did you know that more babies are conceived in the US on July Fourth than any other day?" Lacie punctuated her statement with an assured nod, giving weight to its factualness. Betty looked down at her wrist once again.

"Incidentally," she began anew, "why do you keep looking at your watch?"

Betty blushed, caught.

"Well, since we have to close up here, Joel and I are going to miss all the festivities outside," she began, getting progressively more flushed. "So, he's fixing a . . . private dinner in his backyard. With fireworks, apparently."

"Oh . . ." Lacie said with a nod. "Aren't they illegal?"

"Illegal?" Betty asked.

"The fireworks?" Lacie clarified, placing the broom back in the small, floor-to-ceiling cabinet beside the booths. Lacie knew that it didn't stop the most determined of them, but she didn't take Betty for a lawbreaker.

Betty covered her mouth and shooed her employee away.

"I just have so much to do!" Betty exclaimed. "Closing here, then going home and getting ready."

Then, it came to her. A sudden thought. Lacie's eyes brightened with the idea.

"I know!" She cried in excitement. "How about I close here? But first, I'll give you a little touch-up."

Betty immediately began to shake her head. She knew she was already perfect — as perfect as one could expect a middle-aged, hard-working woman to be.

"No, I couldn't ask you to —"

"I'm offering!" Lacie cut in. "I'll trim your split ends, give you a manicure, then do you up like you're Joan Collins herself. You're just as elegant as she is, a *real* lady. These girls today, with their mullets and bubble perms . . . Makes me ill having to do those . . . It'll be a real treat for me, Bet, and it couldn't hurt."

Before Betty could commit, Lacie was already ushering her to one of the booths.

"Well . . . okay," Betty relented, sitting down as Lacie gave the back of the leather chair a slap. "That last coloring did dry my hair out a lot."

"Peroxide *will* do that," Lacie said, knowing full-well that Betty already knew. It was hard to turn-off the know-it-all attitude as a fresh apprentice. She threw a cape around Betty and fastened her in.

Betty frowned.

"You're not using one of the booths with a mirror?" she asked.

Lacie picked up a pair of scissors from a nearby cart and playfully snipped the air.

"What's the matter?" Lacie asked. "Don't you trust me, Bet?"

Snip . . . Snip . . .

"So," Lacie began, as hair started to glide from Bet's frame, falling into her typical song-and-dance routine she gave all the customers. "Big date, huh?"

It was small-talk; not something everyone was fond of, but Lacie enjoyed it. She loved getting to know someone for an hour or two and then —*poof!*— they were gone. If she were lucky, she'd see them again in six to eight weeks. If she wasn't, they'd just be a memory, like a dream she often wondered was real or not.

Snip . . . Snip . . .

The conversations meant very little to most. However, she knew there were a fair amount of her customers who enjoyed them. It was their reprieve from their day-life, where they could feel encouraged to say anything, unfiltered.

"Mm," Betty muttered. "To be honest, I'm not sure how long it will last with Joel. Hey, do you think I could pull off the Madonna cut? I've been thinking about it."

Snip...

"Oh?" Lacie responded. "Hasn't it only been a few months with Joel? Madonna? On you? Didn't you *hear* what I just said about today's egregious style?" Lacie gave her a smile, although Betty couldn't see. It was a habit she did when customers were sitting in front of the mirror.

"Yeah," Betty sighed. "This place takes up a lot of my time. Especially if I want to stay at the top. Y'know, there's talk of another unit here becoming a salon? I'm not sure how to feel about that."

Snip... SNIP...

"You really love what you do here, huh, Bet?" Lacie asked, taking a few strands and pulling them up to straighten them before cutting away the deadends.

SNIP...

"Of course," Betty replied emphatically. "What we do is so important. We make people look their best, and that way they feel better. It makes you feel good at the end of the day."

Snip... Snip...

"Ah, you mean that's what *you* do," Lacie corrected. "I've got far less experience than you."

"You've been here a year. It'll be ten before you know it, and I've never had anyone better. I don't think you've ever even made a single mistake."

"Thanks," came Lacie's flat reply. She didn't know if she should be flattered or if Bet was just talking her up.

SNIP... SNIP... SNIP...

"What about you?" Lacie asked after a beat.

"What about me?" Betty responded.

Snip...

"Well," Lacie began with an unmistakable glee, "you have, what? Thirty-five years of experience? That's a lot of happy people. Unless... they weren't all triumphs. Surely you must've had some disasters?"

Snip... Snip...

"Ah, beauty fails!" Betty laughed. "I've had a few, not many, but a few."

"Such as?" Lacie asked, keeping the conversation flowing. "I need the *details*, Bet. Share all the juicy gossip."

Betty chuckled and sighed. It wasn't something she thought about all that often.

"Okay, lovely," she said. "But this stays between us, okay?"

"You got it, I won't tell a soul, Bet."

. . . Snip . . .

"Well, it was 1951," Betty said with a chuckle. *How the years have gone by so fast.* "I'd only been on the job a few months — still training, really. And we had this client, Mrs. Franklin, she was ancient, but loved a purple rinse . . ."

. . . Snip . . .

"I don't know what I did," Betty said, then laughed. "But I turned it *green*!"

Snip . . . Snip . . . Snip . . .

"But I suppose it doesn't really count as a failure," Betty continued. "Because she *loved* it!"

Betty roared with laughter as her head began to jerk around in the chair, but Lacie's hands never wavered. She paid attention to what Betty was saying but never missed a strand out of place.

"Is that all?" Lacie asked once Betty had quieted down.

"That's all," Betty repeated.

Snip . . . Snip . . .

"Nothing else you can think of?" Lacie asked. "Nothing that . . . made someone cry? Or required fixing? Or maybe even a refund?!"

Snip . . . Snip . . . Snip . . .

Betty suddenly straightened in her chair; Lacie's rapidly intensifying tone alarmed her.

"No," Betty said. "No, that's all . . . So, anyway, about that Madonna haircut . . ."

Snip . . . Snip . . .

"You're telling me," Lacie began anew. "That Betty, the Queen of the Salon, has never had a disaster? Because, you know, Bet . . . Sometimes, when it all goes wrong, it can ruin someone's life."

Betty felt Lacie's fingers run through her hair, pulling up strands and snipping them. She winced just a little as Lacie pulled a little too hard. She felt the loose pieces fall around her, landing on her shoulders, the back of the chair, and floor.

Snip . . .

"What?" Betty managed, pulling forward just a bit

Snip . . . Snip . . . Snip-Snip . . .

Lacie's speed increased. *Snip-Snip-Snip-Snip-Snip-SNIP . . .*

Betty tried to turn in the chair, but Lacie immediately planted a hand on her shoulder, taking a final snip at the base of Betty's neck.

"Lacie, I think that about does it, now," Betty said, trying to hurriedly exit the chair. After getting her feet underneath her, she stood.

Lacie laughed. "How do you know, Bet? You can't see a thing."

Instinctually, Betty's hands reached for her long blonde hair but found it was gone. Her eyes widened in horror as she felt the uneven mess of cropped hair left atop her head. Shoving Lacie out of her way, Betty ran for one of the booths with a mirror. Her hair had been clipped completely on one side, and at the back. The left side still retained some length, but only a few sad wisps. Her hair had been savagely hacked, in some places right down to the scalp.

"What have you *done* to me?!" Betty screamed.

"Take a look," Lacie said, pointing to the checkered floor. "Take a look at your best feature, Bet."

Behind the chair, a mound of bleached hair lay. Taking it in, Betty sobbed, before turning back to the mirror and staring in disbelief.

"*WHY*?!" She demanded. "You . . . you bitch! You're *fired!*"

Suddenly, hands seized Betty's head, yanking it backwards. She felt Lacie's breath on her face as she spoke softly.

"You'll find out, Bet."

Suddenly Betty was propelled forward by Lacie's hand, and her head hit the mirror with a sickening *crack*. Briefly, stunned, she shuffled backward before collapsing. Then everything went black for Betty Gamble.

In the blackness, Betty felt the phantom snips as the strands of hair continued to fall around her. It was pain that first brought her back to consciousness. Distantly she could hear music, then as she slowly began to open her eyes, she found herself staring at the salon ceiling, squinting at the fluorescent lights shining back at her. After a moment, she realised she was reclined in one of the salon's basin chairs

"Don't you sometimes think it's real, but it's only false emotions that you feel?"

The words and music didn't match anything Betty was hearing. She'd heard Kim Wilde at least three times today alone whilst she worked. No, this music was much older—from Betty's youth.

"What . . . ?" Betty slurred.

Trying to pull herself up, Betty found herself unable. She was bound to the basin's rim by something tied tightly across her neck. Looking down as far as her restraint would allow, she also saw she was again cloaked in a salon cape. Suddenly, Lacie Blake's face appeared over hers.

"Ah!" She cried with mock surprise. "Welcome back, Bet. Did you have a good nap?"

Betty's head throbbed, and the music wasn't helping, although vaguely, she recognized the song.

"Don't you just *love* Johnnie Ray?" Lacie asked with a smile. "I did, but now it only makes me remember what you did."

Betty frowned, fighting to get words out through her grogginess.

"What . . . I did?" She managed. "I don't—"

"No!" Lacie screamed, pushing her face against Betty's. She grabbed Betty's cheeks, cupping her hand over Betty's mouth and giving it a shake. "Of course, you don't remember, Betty."

"I've only known you a year, Lacie . . ." Betty whimpered.

"That's not true!" Lacie snapped. "And that's *not* my name."

Something felt oddly waxy about Lacie's skin, as Betty felt her employee's nose press against her cheek. Lacie pulled back and offered a sickly smile.

"Well, let me give you a hand remembering, Bet. Your facial is ready, and we need to get this show on the road before Joel gets here. You want to look your best, right?"

Lacie straightened and took in a deep breath, before slowly blowing it out. Betty watched as her assistant closed her eyes, clearly building her nerve. Lacie raised both fingers to her eyeballs and removed two small lenses. To Betty's surprise, one of the eyes was milky white beneath.

"Lacie?" Betty whispered.

Not entirely sure what she was seeing, Betty watched as Lacie threw her hair back, and began to pull at both ears. Slowly, her face began to peel away, the ears, then the forehead, the cheeks, the nose. Finally, Betty stared up at a visage she didn't recognize, as Lacie held what had once been her face aloft and lifeless. Before she could stop herself, Betty shrieked.

"That's right," Lacie said. "Disgusting, isn't it?"

Betty's face was seized in Lacie's beautifully manicured hands, and she pressed her disfigured face against Betty's nose once more.

"Take a look," she whispered. "You did this."

What stared back at Betty barely looked human. The skin was raised, calloused and pink. The beautifully made-up lips no longer existed, just one fine line represented her mouth. A mass of withered, wrinkled tissue amounted to cheeks, and deep, raised scars covered the entire grim image. There were no eyebrows, eyelashes, or any features that would identify Lacie as a human being. Mercifully, Lacie pulled back before cocking her head down at Betty.

"Starting to ring any bells?" She asked.

"Who are you?" Betty choked.

Lacie threw her hands up in the air with an exasperated laugh.

"I can't *believe* you!" She screamed. "The worst thing that's ever happened in my life, and it's not even a blip on your radar! You're such a *bitch*. Completely self-centred, only caring about getting to the top."

"Lacie, I . . ." Betty began.

"*THAT'S NOT MY NAME*!" She bellowed. "Do you have *any* idea how much I wanted to vomit when you called me that every day for the past year?"

Hesitantly, Betty shook her head as much as the restraint allowed. The woman that wasn't Lacie cackled again, before moving out of Betty's view.

"Well, I'll give you a hand, shall I?" She began, bordering on hysteria. "Think back, Bet. It's 1952, you're young and green, and all the girls are oblivious to the fact that Johnnie Ray is as gay as Christmas."

The woman Betty didn't recognize stared down at her once more, her eyes burning with hatred.

"There's a dance coming up," she said, her tone suddenly calm. "And you're working at Charlotte's Salon."

The name struck Betty like a knife through the heart, she hadn't thought about Charlotte's Salon in years. Closing her eyes, it suddenly all came rushing back, the dinky little salon, her chain-smoking boss, and the accident . . .

"Alice . . . ?" Betty whispered.

Suddenly, Betty remembered it all, as though a chest buried in her subconscious had been unearthed. Lacie had given her the key, and everything burst out and began to play before her eyes. It was a movie she didn't want to watch, but she couldn't look away from.

It wasn't particularly busy that day, it was around three in the afternoon when Betty and her boss Charlotte Brennan had been in the back room. They mixed their respective bowls, Betty's, a nourishing face mask for a pretty teen, and Charlotte's, a mixture of 30% peroxide for Mrs. Tibbits.

"So, he said that they're just *friends*," Charlotte said, blowing out cigarette smoke. "I wasn't born yesterday; this isn't my first time at the rodeo. There's something going on between him and that waitress."

Betty's mouth fell open at her boss' nonchalance.

"Well, I mean," Betty began carefully. "If there *is*, won't you be upset . . . I mean if it ends?"

"*No*," Charlotte snorted. "I was done with him a long time ago. He got me this place, that's all I wanted."

Betty laughed uncomfortably as she continued to mix her bowl.

"Besides, there are plenty of better options," Charlotte said after a moment.

Betty cocked a hand on her hip.

"Oh?" She said with mock surprise. "Such as?"

Charlotte Brennan came in close, eyeing the two clients sitting beyond the curtains before speaking.

"You know Johnny Collins?" Charlotte whispered.

"Yeah?" Betty agreed. "He works over at the drive-in?"

Her boss stepped back and nodded assuredly.

"That's who I want," Charlotte said.

Betty let the mixing brush fall from her hand.

"*Charlotte*!" She exclaimed quietly. "Isn't he still wet behind the ears?"

Charlotte waved her away with a chuckle.

"Not a chance," she affirmed. "In fact, I've already had some."

As her boss came in close to whisper her final words, Betty was about to let out a delighted shriek. However, the conversation was abruptly halted by a loud *smash*.

"Oh, Jesus!" A voice cried from the salon floor. "What the hell have you done now, kid?"

Rushing through the curtains, Betty and Charlotte froze, seeing the mess that greeted them. Mrs. Tibbets stood over her young son ready to strike, and the salon floor was covered in glass.

"Stop!" Betty screamed.

"What happened?" Charlotte immediately followed.

Mrs. Stanley Tibbets lowered her hand and turned to the shocked workers.

"I can't ever control him," she explained. "He was running around, and he tore one of your mirrors off the wall before I could stop him."

Now that the shock had passed, Betty and Charlotte saw the mirror frame, lying empty on the floor.

"Well, don't hit him!" Betty exclaimed.

"It wasn't a good idea to bring my kid here, was it?" Mrs. Tibbets asked with a confused frown.

"Not really," Charlotte muttered.

"There are plenty of other things for him to do," Betty said. "He's probably just bored."

Carefully avoiding the broken glass on the floor, Betty approached the cowering child.

"Hey, Mister," Betty began, crouching. "This is kinda dull, huh?"

The child nodded timidly.

"Well, I've got an idea," Betty continued. "How about, I give you fifty cents and you can go across the street and see that Marilyn Monroe double feature, huh?"

The terrified child immediately lit up, as Betty dug in her apron pocket.

"Get yourself a popcorn and soda too," she smiled, pressing the money into the child's hand. "We'll send mom over when she's done."

With that, the child skipped over the broken glass and out the salon door. Betty watched to make sure he disappeared inside the movie theater across the street.

"Well," Charlotte stated loudly. "Let's get movin'."

Betty turned to her client, a girl under one of the dryers, and smiled apologetically.

"I'll be right with you," she said. "I'm so sorry for the delay."

"Chop, chop!" Charlotte ordered from the curtained doorway. "We've lost enough time as it is!"

"Right . . . " Betty replied, awkwardly stepping over glass shards. "What about the . . . mess?"

"We'll clear it up once we get these treatments going," Charlotte instructed. "If we waste any more time, these ladies will be here until after closing. Now, get going!"

Feeling fear seizing her insides, Betty ducked behind the curtains and quickly retrieved a bowl from the counter. Gingerly, she made her way to her client beneath the dryer.

"Sorry about that," Betty said, lifting the dryer from the young woman's head.

"Oh, don't worry," her client began. "I'm real glad you could fit me in. The other places were jam packed 'cause of the dance."

Betty inspected the hair set in rollers and nodded approvingly.

"Well, your hair's set," she confirmed. "Now, for the beauty treatments!"

"Ooh, goody!" the client exclaimed. "I just have to look great."

Betty gave her bowl one final mix.

"So . . . um," she stuttered, bending to meet her client's eyes.

"Alice," her client offered.

"Alice," Betty repeated. "You're going to the high school homecoming dance, huh?"

Alice's cheeks immediately filled with color and she giggled.

"Yes," she said. "I'm so excited, it'll be the first time my fella and I have been out officially."

"Oh?" Betty asked, "Who's your fella?"

Betty began to apply the mixture in her bowl to Alice's face.

"Johnny Collins," Alice replied with a smile. "You might know him; he works over at the drive-in on weekends."

Betty felt herself flush, but she said nothing. She continued to apply her mixture to Alice's face, remaining silent, hoping her awkwardness hadn't been clocked.

"I just want to look good for the dance," Alice said eventually. "I've seen what some of the other girls are wearing. I can't afford a new dress, so I thought, maybe some beauty treatments."

Betty chuckled, glad the silence had passed.

"Don't you worry, honey," she smiled. "This face mask will turn you into a whole new woman."

Betty stepped away after covering the last of Alice's exposed flesh and sighed.

"Okay," she began. "Now, we just let that sit for fifteen minutes . . . Twenty if you want to look *really* good."

Alice's face began to contort with discomfort, and she touched Betty's hand before she could move away.

"Excuse me," she frowned. "Is it supposed to itch like this?"

Betty waved the teen away with a smile.

"Oh, don't you worry, honey," she assured. "That just means it's working, getting all the mess out of your pores."

Once again, Betty stepped over the broken mirror pieces and disappeared behind the curtain. She intended to sweep up the glass after she'd washed out her bowl, so set to work in the sink. After a few minutes, Charlotte appeared in the kitchen doorway, rolling her eyes before slamming a coffee cup on the counter.

"What're you doing back here?" Betty asked. "I thought you were *so* eager to get these ladies finished up?"

"That damn Tibbits woman," Charlotte whispered. "Asked me if I could 'Irish up' her coffee. I swear, have we got two weirdos out there?"

Betty put her clean bowl on the side and reached for the nearby broom.

"What?" She asked with a bemused smile. "There's nothing wrong with mine."

Charlotte Brennan blew out a theatrical sigh and snorted with laughter.

"Oh, *really?*" She chortled. "Well, she's out there on that seat fidgetin' like a cat in a room full of rocking chairs"

"Sorry," said a voice from the doorway.

Betty and Charlotte turned to see Mrs. Tibbits there, her upper face caked with a runny greenish goo.

"I don't mean to be a pest, dears," she continued. "I just think there's something wrong here."

Charlotte took a step forward, puffing her ample chest out in anticipation of an argument.

"I beg your pardon, Mrs. Tibbits?" She pressed.

Betty cocked her head at the mixture running down the client's face, it was quite the sight.

"Oh, I don't want any trouble, ladies," Mrs. Tibbits quickly responded. "It's just . . . well, something's not right here, see?"

To illustrate her point, the mother rubbed some of the greenish substance onto her finger.

"The bleach," she began. "It's never run like this before, and it doesn't even itch. Is it some kind of new formula or—"

Frowning, Charlotte stepped forward and began to investigate her client's head. Distantly, Betty felt panic seize her insides, but she remained silent. Charlotte sniffed at Mrs. Tibbits' matted hair, her frown deepening.

"This isn't . . . " she began.

"GOOOOOOOOOOOOOOOOOOD!"

The piercing scream cut off Charlotte's words, and sent all three women hurtling back out onto the salon floor.

"Oh, Jesus," Betty whispered as she took in what greeted them.

Alice twirled frantically in circles around the salon, shrieking and crying as she flailed her hands before her face.

"Get it off, get it *off!*" She cried.

Charlotte quickly rushed forward, attempting to grab one of the teen's arms and hold her still.

"It's burning!" Alice screamed. "*God*, it's *burning!*"

"Help me!" Charlotte roared.

Betty, her trance broken by her boss' demand, began to move forward. Before she could, Alice broke free from Charlotte's grip, flailing anew. One of her arms connected with Charlotte's face and knocked the salon owner flying backward and onto the floor. Alice continued to scream, no longer able to form words, alternately clutching at her face and reaching out for anything that might help.

"HELP MEEEEEEEEEEEEEE!"

She stepped on a stray shard of the glass on the floor. It slid out from under her foot as she fell backwards in a pinwheeling frenzy.

"No!" Betty heard herself cry, realizing what was about to happen, but powerless to stop it.

With a catastrophic crash, Alice burst backward through the salon's plate glass storefront and collapsed onto the street.

"Jesus Christ!" Mrs. Tibbits shrieked.

Alice's wailing continued as she lay face-up on the street. Charlotte hurtled forward from the floor and threw the salon door wide, bursting into the street. Betty and Mrs. Tibbits quickly followed, and all three stared down at the stricken teen in horror.

"Oh god," Charlotte whispered. "Oh, good god."

Betty felt her stomach churn at the sight before her. Her client's face was an angry red mess beneath the caked-on mask. Blood ran from several large slash wounds across her forehead, cheeks, and neck, and a sizable shard of glass jutted from one eye. The teen girl scarcely looked human anymore.

"Help me," she whispered weakly. "It burns . . ."

People began to crowd around the scene as an ashen-faced Mrs. Tibbits turned to Betty Gamble.

"What have you done?" She whispered.

"That's right!"

The scream brought Betty back to the present, in her own salon, bound by the neck to a hair washing basin. The grotesque, inhuman face stared down at her, the remaining eye seething with hate.

"Now you remember," Alice said coldly.

"Oh, my god," Betty managed.

One side of Alice's withered mouth curled into a sickening smirk.

"That's right," she said. "Not pretty, is it?"

Then her face disappeared, and the rustling of tools sent an icy fear through Betty's body. She began to struggle with her restraints.

"Alice," she began frantically. "Alice, I'm *sorry*! It was an accident!"

"Sorry?" Alice repeated bitterly as she slammed bottles down, pouring from one, then another. "You're not sorry, bitch. Christ, this is probably the first time you've thought about me in *years*. Too busy clawing your way to the top."

"I *am* sorry!" Betty cried. "It was a terrible mistake, but it was an accident."

"Doesn't matter," Alice said coldly, frantically mixing a bowl. "We're not even, you took *everything* from me, and now . . . I'm going to do the same to you. It's time for *your* facial."

Alice threw her head back and cackled to the sky.

"Oh, how I've waited for this day!" She cried. "You don't know what it's been like, the taunts, the surgeries, the *masks*. And every day, I dreamed about getting back at you! Here we are! All that time learning goddamn beauty treatments, working in dead-end salons, all to get to *you* . . . It'll all be worth it, because I'm going to *win*. I'm *finally* going to get you back."

"I don't think so."

The voice was calm and determined, and most alarmingly, it came from right over Alice's shoulder. Before she could turn her head, a blinding pain struck her. Alice screeched, and her knees began to buckle. Leaning on the counter for support, she turned slowly and saw Betty standing behind her, completely free, fixing her with a stare. A large pair of hair cutting scissors jutted from Alice's shoulder, missing her neck by mere centimetres.

Before she could say a word, Betty lurched forward, taking Alice by the scruff, and pulling her close.

"Let me give you some advice," Betty growled.

Swirling Alice around, Betty let go, and watched as her employee hurried toward one of the basins. The porcelain connected with Alice's ribs with a crack, again making her cry out in agony.

"When you want to take someone hostage," Betty began coldly. "Maybe tie up their goddamn hands first. Maybe . . . don't do a half-assed job where there are *plenty* of sharp things around."

Betty approached confidently, seizing Alice by the back of her neck.

"No!" Alice muttered.

Wrenching the scissors from her shoulder, Alice spun and began slashing out wildly. Betty dodged the first attempt with a swift jump backward. Alice's second swing clipped her left cheek, leaving a long, bloody gash. Betty brought a hand to her face as blood trickled onto the tiles below.

"You bitch," she said with that same steely determination. "I'm going to kill you."

"Not if I kill you first," Alice screamed as she sprang forward once again.

Betty seized the arm holding the flailing scissors before they came anywhere near her this time. Alice struggled against the seasoned beautician's calloused grip, but got nowhere. Grabbing her free arm, Betty again pulled Alice close, before driving a knee into her crotch, and delivering a brutal headbutt to Alice's deformed nose. Falling backward and landing with a thud, the scissors flew from Alice's grasp. As her boss stood over her, Alice Kaleb was completely at her mercy.

"You idiot," Betty said coldly. "How the hell do you think I got here?"

"Lying on your back?" Alice wheezed.

Betty responded with a swift kick to Alice's ribs. She spasmed in pain, before rolling over onto her side in defeat.

"All your years of planning," Betty began. "They didn't amount to much, did they? I would've thought such rage should make you a criminal mastermind. But I suppose it can only go so far if you're *stupid*, huh?"

Alice made no attempt to reply, she was curled up on the floor, breathing heavily.

"Did you *really* think you could best me, bitch?" Betty began anew. "I've been doing this for 35 years; I've clawed my way to the top. I did what I had to do to get to where I am."

Betty advanced on the stricken Alice.

"That means I've put a lot of people in the ground," she continued. "You're just one more to add to the count. Look around, *Alice*, this is *Betty's*, I've worked my entire life to get here, and no one's going to stop me now. Not you, not Charlotte Brennan, no rich ex-husband too tight with the purse strings! I've beat them all, and I'll keep winning. And I'll look incredible doing it, because *I'm Betty Gamb—*"

Betty's words turned into a guttural groan and pain exploded inside her stomach. Looking down, she saw Alice, her hand clutching something that was deep inside Betty's abdomen. Blood began to gush out of the wound as Alice pulled a shard of mirror glass free, letting it clatter back to the dustpan on the floor. As Alice rose, Betty fell to her knees, trying to desperately hold her hands over her stomach. She could taste the blood in her throat as she rapidly tried to catch her breath. Alice was behind her now, leaning down and gently putting her hands on Betty's shoulders.

"You always need to have a back-up plan, Bet. I thought some broken glass might come in handy," she whispered in her ear. "Shame you didn't slip on it, though, eh?"

The world began to swim before her, as Betty collapsed onto the floor. Far off, she heard Alice's voice fill with merriment.

"Now, it's time for your facial, Betty, dear."

Betty Gamble swayed in and out of consciousness, catching only snatches of what was going on around her. She was aware of bandages being wrapped tightly around her midsection, her hands being bound behind her back, and something being applied to her face. It was the tingling sensation that finally brought the world flooding back. When everything came into focus, Betty found herself in a salon chair, her face feeling heavy, as though it was caked in mud.

"Wha . . . ?" was all she managed.

Alice knelt before her; her disfigured face horrifically close to Betty's.

"Don't worry, Bet," Alice smiled. "I was sure to tie your hands this time."

The tingling Betty felt became a constant itch.

"You're going to be so beautiful," Alice said. "Just as beautiful as I am. But will Joel *love* your new look?"

Betty's face began to burn, she could hear her skin beginning to quietly sizzle beneath the caked-on mask. She couldn't help herself, and quietly began to moan.

"Hurts, doesn't it?" Alice asked. "Don't worry, hon, that just means it's working."

Alice let out a merry giggle as she spun Betty around in the salon chair.

"Please," Betty said through gritted teeth. "Please don't *do this*. After everything I've worked for . . . Don't take away my brand!"

Sighing in disgust, Alice grabbed what remained of Betty's hair, yanking her head backwards.

"You're still not sorry, are you?" She asked. "All you care about is your precious salon, and those second-rate looks of yours."

Alice bent in close, staring at her disfigured visage over Betty's shoulder. Her employer shivered from the constant pain, but managed to hold her tears at bay.

"Well, guess what, Bet?" Alice whispered. "Vanity is a sin . . . and karma is a bitch."

~

"Betty?"

Unusually, the salon door was open when Joel West tried it, and that worried him. What worried him more was the state Betty's salon was in. A dustpan full of broken glass was on the floor, and to Joel's horror, one piece was covered in blood.

"Oh my god," he whispered. "What the hell happened here?"

A trail of blood led away from the dustpan, and gingerly, Joel followed it. Along the way, a large pair of scissors were also cast aside and dripping with blood. Beneath one of the salon's chairs the blood trail stopped. In the chair, facing away from Joel, someone with short blonde hair sat hunched over and sobbing.

"Betty?" Joel repeated. "Betty, what's going *on*?"

The figure lifted their head slowly and took in several shuddering breaths.

"Joel . . . ?"

It was unmistakably Betty's voice.

"Betty, what on earth happened to your hair?" Joel asked.

"We can still love each other, can't we?" Betty answered.

Joel frowned, reaching out towards the chair, Betty visibly stiffened as he did so.

"Tell me you still love me," Betty sobbed as the chair slowly spun. "Tell me I'm still *beautiful!*"

Upon seeing his lover's face, Joel West stumbled backward. A lump rose in his throat and he thought he might vomit.

"We can get married!" Betty screamed.

Her once impeccably made-up face was red raw, still glistening with the dew of freshly exposed skin. Her nose had melted entirely away, leaving only two uneven holes in the center of Betty's face. One eyelid had dropped off completely, whilst the other hung by a thread and bounced sickeningly with each movement Betty made.

"*Jesus Christ!*" Joel exclaimed. "What *are* you!?"

What was left of Betty's lips cracked and bled into a deranged smile as bloody spit ran down her red-raw chin.

"I'm *BEAUTIFUL!*" She shrieked.

Throwing her head back, Betty Gamble bellowed a demented laughter, finally realizing that her beauty was only skin deep.

6
TANGERINE BLUE
Billie Karras

1. An Egg Lain

THERE WAS A FLY in the car.

Burt was driving (had been now for what seemed like forever), but since Heather was only along for the ride, she was able just to sit, body pressed snug against the passenger door, and watch the little insect as it perched. It was above her head, where the faintly rattling window met a tattered red headliner, and wasn't black nor hairy but painted with a smooth emerald iridescence that was really quite stunning. Under the yellow glare of passing streetlights, colors danced upon its alien body with a kind of kaleidoscopic brilliance; the fly had the metallic gleam of a piece of carnival glass, or the swimming face of a soap bubble, or the sheeny scrim on the surface of a lakeshore oilslick, and Heather, for her part, was utterly transfixed. The most hypnotic thing of all, however, was not its prismatic anatomy. It was its utter *stillness*. Flies were busy, twitchy creatures—constantly rubbing, constantly preening. They never just *sat*. Could it be that it was asleep? Could it be that it had died? Or was it possible (and at this she felt a fevered, sweaty chill) that *it* was watching *her*, too?

Heather licked her lips. They were very dry.

This shit, she thought, *might just be a little too good.*

Presently, Burt hit the turn signal. The old Pinto was filled with its mechanical *click-click-click*, and Heather's head lurched as the car dove leftward into a narrow suicide lane. Momentarily dazed (well, *more* dazed), she forgot the fly long enough to have a look out the windshield. On the other side of the road, cars blew past them in a steady stream of too-bright headlights. Then, like a rack shot in a movie, the Sherwood Mall came into focus at last, technicolor-hot and bright.

Heather had to marvel at the buzzy glow of its signage. It stood like a neon monolith, flinging fans of green up into the low clouds above, splashing shades of blue onto the palm trees around. Its tall brick walls seemed to tower over all else, and sprawled so widely she couldn't even see both ends. There was nothing like it at all in Canyon Springs. It looked like a dream made real, constructed not of unconscious secrets but of concrete, of marble, of glass. Heather couldn't believe she'd never been here before. She'd have to make Burt bring her back during daylight. Perhaps next weekend . . .

She looked at him now. A handsome man with a solid Roman profile, with thick dark hair and a distinguished manner of posture and dress. She couldn't believe she'd met him in their dusty little town, where modernity was a dirty word and reading was for women, children, and faggots. Burt was a real intellectual, dark and moody and full of poetry—and yet he never talked down to her, never made her feel less than. Heather knew she was dumb, knew she was inexperienced, but if Burt knew it too, he didn't show it. It was for this, above all else, that she thought she loved him.

Cheeks burning, suddenly overtaken with affection, she reached out for his thigh and rubbed it. He let a hand slip from the steering wheel and met her own, squeezing gently. *What a catch*, she thought. She stretched her legs, flexed her toes. *What a catch*. And then a rhyme: *Here at last.* And how funny that seemed just now. *Here at last. Here at last. Heeeere at lasssssss —*

Then she remembered her fly.

"Lose something?" Burt asked, amused at the sudden lapse in bubbling laughter to his right. Now she was craning her neck, peering up to look at the headliner, leaning back to inspect the rear window.

"No," she sighed, settling back into her seat. "Well, yes. There was the *prettiest* fly, right —" and she pointed at the tattered headliner's edge, "*here.* And it was just *sitting* there, you know? Sitting there and staring at me. I was beginning to think we were friends."

"But of course," he chuckled. "Who wouldn't want to be friends with you?"

"Oh, lots of people." She stared at the line of traffic coming up the opposite lane. It seemed to go on forever. "Say, listen, are we gonna make it, Burt?"

"I certainly hope so," he said.

"You mean we're late?"

"Late for what?" There was the faint edge of a grin in his voice, and she slapped his arm.

"The *movie,* you dildo!"

"Hey now," he said sharply, but he was still grinning. "Sure, sure. We'll make *that.* I was just saying, if you really wanna *make it —*"

"Oh, you pervert. Do you talk to your wife that way?"

"As a matter of fact," said Burt, "I do not."

They were turning in now; the mall's cinema stood just ahead. The marquee, lined with flashing white bulbs and lettered huge and red, read **TANGERINE BLUE — ALL NITE!** Burt parked, and Heather said, *"All* night? Burt, how long *is* this thing?"

"I dunno, babe." He killed the engine, stuffed the keys into his brown tweed jacket, and pulled out a crinkly bunch of cellophane. "You know the French. They just go on and on."

Heather didn't, actually. She liked action, romance; the slow stuff, often subtitled and always self-serious, bored her. Still, she nodded. She knew he wouldn't be able to keep them from finding a motel for longer than a couple hours. The weekend could only afford them so much time.

Presently, Burt was busy rolling another joint. Heather debated begging off—she was still pretty stoned from the drive—but then it was lit and between her lips, and before she knew it, her head was filled once more with warm lavender haze. It drifted heavily from between her plump lips, hung for a moment in the air like a ghost, and then vanished, frightened by discovery, by light, by her sudden rush of breath. She took another drag, then handed it back to Burt. And the ritual continued.

"This," Burt said, coughing, "is very good grass."

"You old hippie," Heather laughed. "No one calls it *grass* anymore."

"Ah, of course, of course," he said. "Very good *pot.*"

Heather took a last puff, snuffed it out, and kissed him through his beard. "Come on," she said. "We're gonna miss the oranges."

They opened their doors then, but just as Heather was about to step out, she saw a familiar face just inches from her own.

"Oh, *hey*, little lady." The fly was right where it had been, just between the open door and the Pinto's raggy headliner. And, as before, it was utterly still.

Burt's door clunked shut, and, muffled, he said, "You find your friend?"

She squinted at it. With the car off and the way the shadows were, the colors its body had shone with earlier were now absent entirely. She raised a hand to it (she couldn't bear the thought of it trapped in the car, buzzing impotently against the glass until either it beat its own head in or starved to death), intending to shoo it out once and for all. But her reflexes were slow and her reaction was all but nonexistent, and she didn't realize it hadn't flown away—hadn't even tried to *crawl*—until her hand was actually touching it. And when the insect's gossamer wings began to beat, when its legs snapped, when its bubble-face body finally burst, it was with the kind of sickening little *crunch* that Heather, in her horror, could hear only in the tender nerves of her teeth.

Burt was in front of her now. He stood just beside the open passenger door. His Oxford shoes were scuffed; the crotch of his slacks was dusty with ash and fuzzed with the detritus of his amateur joint-rolling. Heather looked at it, his crotch, and then her gaze drifted down to the wet smear of fly on her hand. The wings were crumpled. Its eyes had ruptured, and their liquid redness, mixed in among the white of its guts and the black of its broken carapace, made it look quite like the fly had actually bled. Inside, Heather's own guts did a roiling somersault. Outside —

"Hey, honey," Burt said, oblivious. "You coming or what?"

~

They had to go in through the mall itself, as the theater had no outside entrance. The time was something like nine, perhaps even ten (Heather wore no watch, and the Pinto's dashboard clock was busted), and the place was eerie in its huge, bright emptiness. Its ceiling zig-zagged with more neon — here blue, there pink, and everywhere accented with a deep violet that was as hard to look at as it was beautiful — and these were reflected brilliantly off the sterile white of the walls and floor tiles. Heather snuck a guilty look behind, checking for smudges of dirt tracked in by way of her scuzzy old Chuck Taylors. She hadn't even scuffed the wax.

They rode an escalator up. Heather stayed close to Burt's side, pressing herself into the safety of his large frame, wishing she could crawl inside it. The fly incident had really upset her, and although it was probably nothing more than the pot and the drive, her jangled nerves and her girlish empathy, she really did feel like there had been something *intentional* in the pretty little thing's ultimate inaction. She couldn't shake the feeling that it had *wanted* to stick her with its murder. The notion was oddly violating. Suddenly, she wanted to be home, and quite badly. She didn't give a shit about the movie. She only wanted a bed, and a drink, and perhaps—

But they were already at the cinema's mouth. Before them stood a single besuited old woman, very tall and very gaunt behind the glass of her dim, smoky box office. And as they approached, she nodded them a very slow and very weary greeting. "Two for *Tangerine Blue,* I presume?" came her voice from the little amplifier. It was full of gravel and static, and carried with it a refined trace of Transatlantic. Heather kept her eyes fixed firmly to the speaker's grating; she did not want to allow any of what was happening inside her, any of this strange and stoned turmoil, telepathic passage through the woman's glass and into her wispy, liver-spotted head. She feared, however, that it was already too late. For when she risked a single peripheral glance at the woman's large, drooping ears, they suddenly turned inward, toward *her,* like a pair of fleshy satellite dishes just honed in on a cosmic transmission.

Heather looked away at once, cheeks inflamed. Beside her, Burt was retrieving his wallet. "Here you are," he said, and slid over a five.

The old woman took it with fingers that were impossibly long, impossibly thin. "You're just in time," she said, tearing their tickets. "Well. Here you are. Theater 7 will be to your left, just up that way. And may I offer you any . . . *refreshments?*"

The way she said it, Heather knew that the question had been directed at *her.* At once, the urge to blurt something foolish was so strong that it actually almost came out. *I'm his niece,* she wanted to say, or, more innocuously, *my father and I, et cetera . . .* but, blessedly, her tongue was much too dry to say anything at all. Burt murmured something in the affirmative, and she followed the two of them (the old woman had emerged from her cage to serve them further, sighing all the while) to the concessions stand. As the popcorn bags were loaded and the soda cups were filled, Heather recalled a conversation they'd had—her and Burt—that had played, more or less, through her mind for weeks. Now again, repeating itself once more within the folded recesses of her brain as Burt paid the old woman a second time, as he gathered their things and led her down the lighted corridor toward the theater, toward their seats, toward the mystery-meat amalgamation of light and sound and screen and celluloid so confoundingly titled *Tangerine Blue* —

Now again the scene played.

I'm going to tell you something you already know, he'd told her, *but it needs to be said all the same.* This was after the first time (in fact, some of it had still been drying into the rayon of her rumpled dress even as they spoke), and the hour had been late; the Pinto was lit only by the streetlights and a cluster of candles set precariously atop the dash. They were in the back seat together, bare feet socked into a cluttered pool of books so deep Heather couldn't even see her toes: there were your Fitzgeralds and Hemingways here, your Poes and Popes there, and even (Heather was intrigued to note this despite the fact she'd never read a word of her) a few ragged copies of Erica Jong.

What we're doing here, he'd gone on, *is dangerous, not only for me but also for you. So we'll need to be careful. For starters, we can never be seen together in town this way. Naturally. And what we just did, lovely though it was, can never happen again — not* here. *Right?*

She, of course, agreed. The car was parked only a few houses down from her own.

Second: we must never draw attention to ourselves. No furtive looks. No guilty faces. Christ knows there's nothing to feel guilty about anyway. It isn't illegal for a woman to be out with a man, is it?

She'd laughed, shaking her head, absurdly flattered at the implication.

Of course it isn't. But that's what it's all about, right? The name of the game, babe — be cool. People see what they want to see. And oftentimes, what they want to see more than anything else in the whole world is this: nothing at all. So can you dig it, babe? Can you be cool?

Heather considered this honestly. She thought of her mother, just up the road and sleeping; she thought of Burt's wife. How might she feel if she knew about this? But that was a foolish question, a *dumb* question. Heather knew how Burt's wife would feel. It was exactly how *she* would feel.

Can you dig it, babe? he'd asked. *Can you dig it?*

Heather decided that she could.

And then, in spite of all Burt had said, they *had* done it again, right then and there. At some point during, while her ass was up and her left cheek was smooshed down against the upholstery, she'd found her eyes wandering over the books again. Their covers were splashed in shadow, a dead-pulp sea of authors and titles the likes of which she could only faintly make out. But her eyes adjusted, and among the books, she now saw, was a scattered pile of graded papers. At the top was one of her own. It had been hastily composed the night before, typewritten and full of slash-throughs, and across the top of it, staring up at her like the sly wink of a bleeding eye, was a big fat *C*.

Heather might've been offended—hell, she *should* have been offended. But when he turned her about to take her some more, this time from the front, she had wrapped her legs around his pale, skinny shanks all the tighter. It was only high school, after all, only one *C*, and besides—

Given the essay, he'd been rather generous.

~

They took their seats midway up the rearmost row, Burt to Heather's left and Heather to Burt's right. The cushions were a rough, splotched velvet, sticky with spilled Cokes and hardened with a thick crust of congealed popcorn grease. Heather tried hard not to think of this filth as she shifted her weight, tried hard not to imagine what unholy thing was scratching the insides of her knees, tried hard not to associate the smell of the buttery bucket in Burt's lap with whatever nameless nightmare lay festering just beneath her ass . . . blessedly, she couldn't see much. The theater was dimly lit; below,

Heather could just make out the crooked shapes of the other filmgoers. The rows were packed. Beyond them was the screen. It was a dead man's face, moonish, gray, utterly devoid. For a moment, Heather moved to speak, wondering if something might be wrong. Then she settled back. It was only as the funny old ticket-woman had said, of course. They were just in time.

"Guess we won't be doing much making, then," Burt whispered.

"What did you say?" She truly hadn't heard him.

"Nothing, babe."

He patted her thigh, then offered her the popcorn. As she took it, she also took his meaning. The thought of lovemaking in these awful seats made her want to hit him even as her fingers rummaged through corned grease. *Does he think I'd do that?* she wondered. But beneath her incredulity, the thought *did* excite her—at least a little.

"Do you think I'd do that?" she asked. She'd meant it to sound sexy, demurely playful. It came out low and full of teeth.

"Aw, I was only kidding around," he said, and took back the popcorn.

Heather ate her handful, wanting to apologize but not knowing how. She soon forgot; the popcorn was wonderful, hot and crisp and absolutely soaked in butter. Each bite seemed to make her tongue engorge with blood, each swallow sent shivers up her stomach that seemed somehow to come out through her toes, and it was very strange, and also very good. She took a sip of soda, Cherry Coke. It soon turned to gulps.

Suddenly, a voice: *"Hey, let's get this going, buddy, will ya?"* It came from one of the rows up front. Large, male, and furious. In response, the mouse beside it squeaked, "Bucky, please . . ." Heather scanned the backs of heads. Her eyes had adjusted somewhat to the lack of light, but still she couldn't tell who had yelled. They all looked the same. They were all without faces.

Then, as if the yeller had reminded some sleeping projectionist just what it was that they were all here for, the lights died completely. For one pregnant, sore-necked moment, the theater was blacker than blind night, and Heather waited with bated breath. The darkness held; in it, the rustle of bags, the crackle of wrappers, the liquid rattle of iced drinks in cardboard cups. Somewhere, she thought she heard a fly buzz. And then the screen exploded into white.

She felt a big hand on her thigh then — Burt's. She must have jumped. He stroked her a moment, tracing large, manish fingers across her thin flesh, tickling the tiny hairs that grew upon her so faintly it was as if they hadn't been there at all until he'd touched them. She put her hand on his. Her fingers were strange to touch with, not quite pins-and-needles but in the ballpark; they felt crumbly, like beach sand. She flexed them. They did not disintegrate.

On the screen, there was still only white, the sort of mad absence that could drive a man to murder, and over the speakers, a discordant cacophony of instruments she couldn't begin to identify began to drill her ears like shards of ice. Somehow, that made things better, though. At least there was *something*.

Am I here? she wondered now. *Am I really?*

But before she could reflect any further, the nothing-white onscreen began to soften, morphing first to the easy color of clouds, then warming to a thick cream, and finally cooling to a deep, sapphiric blue: big and full and beautiful. The blare turned to music, flutes and cymbals and bass and keys all working in tandem, and together they created a sound of such sweet, easy normality that Heather's spine tingled at the sound of it. It was only muzak, the kind of mindless pleasantry that played over every Shop Smart, every Stay-Mart, every goddamned department store in the country. But there was something else in there too, some dissonant, complicating factor. Perhaps it was a theremin. Perhaps it was only the fuzz inside her head.

Eyes to the screen, Heather groped for more popcorn. It had grown cold.

2. The Worm Emerged

Although she had a feeling, Camille Laurent did not for sure *know* that she was being watched. She was, in fact, completely unaware that, until a few moments ago, she hadn't even really existed at all. And why should she? When the opening white-to-blue reels of *Tangerine Blue* had finally given way to picture, she was in the back room of the grocery store in which she worked, just as she had a dozen times before, sitting on a banana crate and peeling an orange. Within her was all the evidence of a life long-lived. She remembered how her father had died (young, drunk, and drowned in a puddle of rain on his way back to his barracks from a blurry night spent in an English pub); she remembered her eighth birthday, during which her mother had been too busy at the *bordel* to be home and Camille had tried, through grim, determined tears, to bake her own yogurt cake. She'd fudged the ratios somewhere along the line, had ended up with nothing to stick her candles into but a flat and sticky mess. She was only nineteen, after all — she remembered most everything about her own life. It did not matter that none of it had happened, because to her, it *had*. She was a person; she dreamed when she slept; she bruised when hurt; yes, Camille shat and pissed and ate and smoked —

And here, now, as the emptied citrus skin fell to the dirty floor beneath her swinging feet and that unseen (but suspected, yes, *suspected*) eye lingered upon it, she indeed lit a cigarette. She smoked it serenely, unwatched but only for the moment, for then the eye was on her and her thin, pale, sullen face, and watched Camille alternate between fruit slices, Turkish Royal drags, and tired, dreamy sighs. She was real enough, sure: her tonsils were gone. So, too, was her appendix. And yet all these things were only nothing, a pile of money tricks, smoke and mirrors, an actress and a set and an Arriflex 35 BL3. But how could it matter if she didn't *know?*

"Ah-hem," a gruff voice interjected from behind her. "Smoking on the bananas again, are we, my sweet?" It was M. Durand, the boss. He spoke, of course, entirely in French. But hey, babe, as we say in good, clean American: what are subtitles for?

"My feet are killing me," she said, not meeting his eyes.

"So let them." Durand neatly plucked the cigarette from her lips. He held it for a moment, only half-gone, before putting it to his own. He breathed deep and, when he removed it to exhale, there was the faintest smear of lipstick left on his lower lip. He grinned, licked it away, and let the cigarette fall. "We don't need you *alive* at the register, dear. Only to work there."

She stared at the floor, mouth quivering, then dropped the remainder of her orange, stomping off, her short heels clicking madly all the way. Durand watched her go, as the eye watched *him*. He lingered for a moment, looking now at the pile of peel and the fruit splattered and the cigarette still smoldering just beside them. He stooped to pick it all up . . . and on the way down turned his head toward the space on the banana crate where she'd sat. He hovered there for a moment, temples shiny with sweat, a man looking for something lost. Then he sniffed, long and deep.

Only missing that one small beat, Durand resumed gathering the trash. He put the smoke out, straightened, gave a glance about that was not quite guilty, and stuffed the dripping handful deep down into the front pocket of his red grocer's apron.

Unheard to him and everyone else in his world, a single drum beat, and then a steel-stringed guitar began to play. The piece was arpeggiated, minor-keyed, hot.

Presently, as the eye flashed on Camille at the register, she was making change for an old man in a bowler hat. He frowned behind his large mustache, fidgeting, irritated. She came up short, had to crack a new roll of francs, and outside, Camille smiled at her fingers. She meant it for him, but the old man either didn't see or didn't care. And inside, where the eye couldn't hear her at all, she wondered: *Am I really here?*

And as with the last sparrow left before winter came, a clear, mournful whistling rose up over the guitar. It soared high and yet utterly lost, alone and bone-cold. It danced in pitch a beat or two, higher, higher, higher, turning from a mere few bars into a phrase. And then, with that, the scene changed anew.

~

Burt had to pee—normal enough for a man who'd drunk what had seemed far too much Cherry Coke to have ever fit in that little cardboard cup, and it still more than half-full—but a funny thing had happened at some point between the time he'd first sat down and now.

He couldn't get up.

It was only the opening credits. The funny, western-sounding piece of music hit a lull as *Un Film de Andre Auclair* was declared over black, and then the song picked up again, and the film went on. It was a montage: shots of shelved soupcans, of adding machines, of the largest citrus display ever committed to film. The pretty broad in the picture was hanging up her apron in the break room and gathering her things to go; the day was over, and so the lecherous old boss—Burt thought the actor looked a little like one of the killers he'd seen the other night in an old rerun of *Columbo*—was locking up the store. Then he was getting into his car, the last left in the lot, starting it, checking the rearview mirror for—

And all at once, her blue eyes filled the frame.

Burt forgot about the pain in his bladder for a moment as the girl—Camille—leapt forward, slipping a mean-looking cord around the boss's bulging throat in the process. She pulled and, as they struggled, the music reached a fevered, haunting pitch as the words *MANDERINE BLEUE* screamed down at the theater like a billboard set right upon the centerline of an interstate highway. Then the title disappeared, and the shot cut to outside the car (it was a Buick, Burt now saw). The engine tried to catch, missed, then sputtered to life, just lurching forward as the scene cut again to black.

Well, Burt thought hazily, *it's certainly not Godard.*

The film soon picked up again: centered in the frame was a squalid country house, paint-chipped and ugly. The car was outside, and the girl, downy dress wrinkled and torn slightly at the armpit, was dragging her boss up the stoop and in through the door. An older woman (the mother? the sister?) was in a stupor on the couch; she stirred in her pile of blankets and fashion magazines. An overfilled ashtray, set precariously atop her ample bosom, toppled off and onto the floor.

"Camille?" she slurred, although that could've just been the language. "A boyfriend?" Her subtitles were just out of sync.

"Go to sleep, Mother."

Then the girl was in a bedroom, which was much more intentionally furnished than the rest of the house. Still, it was in even more disarray. The vanity mirror was shattered, the lampshade cracked. The shot cut to the closet: it appeared to have had a bomb go off somewhere in between the girl's hanging dresses and the plastic laundry hamper. Camille was on the floor, fingers poring over a collection of tweezers, needles, thread, and knives, and the boss lay inert on a heap of newspaper. Burt thought he looked smaller than before.

The girl paused, licked her lips. She seemed to be contemplating and stopped to light another cigarette. Then she clamped it between her teeth, screwed up her face, and reached into the pile. When her fingers came up, they held a tiny, glittering blade.

Burt couldn't believe how realistic it all looked. She cut him neatly—there was hardly any blood—and the skin which parted from muscle and tendon looked not at all like rubber latex. Sticky strings of scarlet trailed up as she parted face from skull, and it all looked too warm, too thick; the naked eyes from which he blindly stared seemed too moist, too fresh. They looked, to him, like they'd really *seen* things like the morning paper, like the legs on the first girl he'd ever slept with, like that last horrified glimpse of windshield and sun-visor and her awful, beautiful blue eyes.

The camera pushed in, and Burt saw now that the man's whites were splotched with red, but it wasn't splatter: Camille obviously worked clean. It was his capillaries, burst from shock and asphyxiation. Burt could have vomited. Instead, he only drank more Coke.

He gave a sidelong glance at Heather. She had gotten the popcorn bucket out of his lap at some point, was really going to town. Suddenly, a thought came to him, a recollection of a dream he'd had once in college that had been occurring to him more often than not lately. In it, he had fucked a baby.

Oh, Jesus, he thought, *not with this again. Stop.*

But of course he couldn't. It was the goddamn grass, he knew, what else? The dope, the reefer, the pot.

It hadn't been a *good* dream, alright? Jesus, no. He'd awoken confused, horrified, crushed with a guilt so heavy he couldn't breathe. And these were feelings which had carried over from the dream itself—they weren't in reaction. In it, Burt hadn't known *why* he'd done what he'd done; *it* hadn't even happened *onscreen,* so to speak. He only *had,* at some point, and the entirety of the dream had consisted only of the aftermath. He'd stared down at the infant (*unhurt,* he reminded himself again, *babbling and whole and unhurt*), and it was with the feeling one might have after running someone down after a night at the bar: the helpless sinking of one's own life caused in an instant by the sort of crash he wasn't even awake enough at impact to have felt anything more than the tiniest of bumps in the road. *It's over,* he remembered thinking upon waking, when the dream had still seemed real. *And everyone will know.*

The through-line was not lost on him. There were only two reasons for this memory to resurface now, and the main one was sitting right next to him. *She's seventeen,* he thought as he had many times over the last few weeks, *not seven* months. *She's practically a woman, for Christ's sake.*

And that was true. But *still*, man. Heather thought of him as a kind of sage, a world-wise, artsy thinker, and she thought of him that way because he'd wanted her to. But it was a lie. The truth was, Burt had never read *Fear of Flying* either. He only owned it because he'd read a review in *Playboy* and thought it sounded like something he should.

He tried to push these thoughts away, tried to focus on the film. Camille was still cutting up her boss, and how this scene made it past the censors, Burt couldn't guess. He struggled to remember where he'd heard of it—radio, newspaper, errant talk in the teacher's lounge—and couldn't. It hadn't really been about the movie anyway, of course. It had been about what came after; this showing at Sherwood Mall was only something to do in the interim, something to give the sex and his image some semblance of legitimacy. Burt was no philistine. Burt was an *aesthete* with a capital B.

He sighed, shifted—God, but these seats were uncomfortable—only again he didn't move. The urge to urinate was quite bad now, and he tried to stand a third time, this time more forcefully. He gripped the armrests tightly, pushed with his arms and legs until they began to shake with the strain, and still . . . nothing.

He began to feel a tightening in his throat. All this reflection, all this guilt, not to mention the odd, pseudo-Freudian paralysis—could it really just be the drugs? He'd smoked his fair share of tea in the Sixties, had even experimented with certain psychedelics during his time in a Santa Clarita folk band. Never had he experienced anything like this. It was heavy, and sweaty, and it was as if his ass were literally glued to the seat. *If Hollywood ever gets ahold of this stuff,* he thought, *they'll be putting it in the Mike and Ikes by next summer. Steven Spielberg, eat your heart out.*

"Heather," he whispered now, unable to keep the rising claustrophobia out of his breath. "Heather, I think we'd better g—"

That was when he saw her, and how he'd missed her thus far, Burt would never know. He could have screamed, *should* have screamed, at the very sight of her, but somehow he didn't. He'd never know how he managed that one, either.

The girl was different; she was not the Heather he'd driven to a movie fifty miles out of the sticks so she could feel like they were on a real date without risk of being recognized; she was not the girl he sometimes found himself wishing were dead — not in any hateful, murderous way, but in a car-wreck way, an overdose way, Christ, even a nasty-slip-in-the-shower way would do, because she was a mistake, a *sweet* mistake, yes, but a mistake all the same because she could *ruin* him, as easy as pie or a child's flattened skull beneath the left-front tire of your red old Pinto, and then it really *would* be just like the dream after all, baby or no baby, guilt or no guilt, seven*teen* be damned —

But it *was* her. There was no mistaking that.

This is how it was:

She was fat, *really* fat, and that really *was* the first thing he'd noticed. Her breasts, small and pert just twenty minutes ago, were now huge, mountainous things; her nipples, having burst free of a lace brassiere God knew how long before, poked through from beneath her dress like the thick ends of burnt sausages. Her left arm, bulging, rippling, and lined with pink stretch marks, was curled around the popcorn bucket like it was a life ring. Her face, jowled, triple-chinned, and huge, was smeared with grease, flecked with white crumbs. It was looking at him now, utterly puzzled.

But that wasn't it — if it were, he certainly *would* have screamed, for in his heart, Burt was truly no feminist. It was her *skin* that had held him together: white in that low, spectral glow of the projector — not caucasian, but a godless, whale-flesh *white* — and it held within it just that same quality as the slick, slimy sheen of dead fishbelly. *That* was what held him together. Because —

But she was still looking at him, was actually leaning *toward* him, and as he smelled her at last (hot butter mixed with sour, rotten onions), his bladder let go. It warmed his thighs, pooling inside the crack of his ass and dripping down his legs and onto the floor. He looked down to see where it went, and yes, *glory* be to *God* —

There were flies in his seat, millions of them broken, dappled, oozing, and they had congealed into a kind of soupy glue. But that was ridiculous, of course — how could he have missed them? For God's sake, he *remembered* brushing the crumby leavings of the last person to have occupied this seat before he had ever sat down. No, there had been *no* flies, none at all except for the one in his car. And that one was dead.

He reached down toward his hallucination and touched it. His fingers dipped at least half an inch into a layer of cold slime. Burt retrieved his hand, inspected the digits in the blue movie-light. There were legs under his nails, and he could have laughed, because it was really quite simple, friends and neighbors, really quite simple indeed: the marijuana had driven him insane. And say —

Wasn't there a movie about that?

Heather was speaking now, something-muffled-something-something. A furious *"Shhhh!"* came from somewhere in the rows below, choked, garbled, as if spoken through a mouthful of television static instead of the usual mouthful of not a goddamn thing. He gave her an eyebrow that rose for miles: *what?*

"Are you alright?"

He looked down at the popcorn bucket, unable to answer. It was still full. Her fingers were . . . *worming* around inside it, quite bonelessly, curling this way, writhing that. Burt closed his eyes, opened them again. Heather remained as she was. A slick, oversized, bipedal worm.

What do you think Freud would've made of this? he wondered. Dimly, his stomach rumbled. He looked down at the popcorn. It was still full.

Heather patted his thigh with her sickly soft, sickly animated maggot-fingers: *You okay, darling?* He could feel their little mouths through his slacks, not biting, only probing. His piss was cold now. The fishy stink of it stung his nostrils almost to the point of pain.

Just ride it out, he thought. *You're not insane, man, you're just bugging* out. *It's like we used to say in the old days, right? Turn on, tune out, drop in.*

"Yeah," he croaked at last. "I'm okay."

"Shhhhh!"

Heather, conspiratorial, grinned. Her teeth were gone. Burt reached for the popcorn, smiling back, and took a great big handful. It was still full. He chased the corn with Cherry Coke. That was full, too. So he tried to forget about it: *turn on, tune out, drop in.*

He tried.

He *tried.*

~

In the film, Camille Laurent was seated in front of the broken vanity mirror, hair in a bun, face scrubbed of all lipstick and rouge. She was naked, and Burt, in spite of his ongoing descent, thought she looked pretty good. But it didn't last. Like the gathered pieces of a brand new outfit, meticulously and with a tight, concentrated frown, she began to put on Durand's skin.

Soon enough, she *was* him. The film cut abruptly to Durand, only a few inches shorter than he'd been before, walking out the door and back to the car. He got in, started it up. Back on the couch, Camille's mother slept on. The dream she was having was plain on her face — it was in the serene curve of her drooling lip, the gentle ease with which her eyes waltzed behind their closed lids. It was a dream unmistakably sweet, yet pickled all the same.

Burt forgot himself for a while, and what a blessing it was. At around the three-hour mark, the picture became pretty good. He munched the whole time and, despite each sloppy, overdrawn handful, the bucket indeed remained full. Eventually, his clothes began to tighten;

his neck began to bulge; his chest grew into tits. At some point, he moved to undo his pants, a feeble attempt at some extra room for his new-spilling belly. But when he touched the buckle, he found he couldn't quite grasp it. His fingers had lost their bones.

3. An Incubational Interlude

Camille Laurent was no longer M. Durand—Heather had lost track of the names somewhere between the porno-mag model and the member of French Parliament. Presently, she was only a housewife, occupying a pleasant colonial plantation house somewhere in the western part of Georgia. Heather was grateful for the continental shift. It made things easier to follow.

Not that that was saying much. *Tangerine Blue* had puzzled her greatly. The surface was easy enough to make out—the lead character was lost, not of home, nor of place, but of herself. She (he?) wanted to be someone else, anyone else, and so had gone through myriad identities the way Heather herself sometimes went through outfits. But what, Heather wondered, was the *point?* Was it really so simple as . . . what? A public service announcement? Love the body God gave you; look within not without; just be your fucking *self?* For *eight hours?*

Heather was aware of her own metamorphosis. Oddly, it did not frighten her. She was still stoned and, at this point, pleasantly so. Her head hummed with warmth, her body likewise, and she felt like the very Earth itself had embraced her into a snug, motherly hug, the way you felt in the depths of a good bath—soothed and fetal, completely relaxed. This was due, in large part, to the literal cocoon that had formed around her. Her wormskin, once slimy-smooth, had now thickened to a brown, brittle shell that was as cozy as it was strange. She couldn't move, of course, but that was all right. She hadn't the urge. There was the movie to keep her occupied, now in its seventh confounding act, and Heather, well . . . Heather wanted to see how it all came out. Maybe, she thought, Camille would go back to her mother. That would be nice. She missed her own terribly.

Burt, on the left hand, was not doing near so well. *Tangerine Blue* had lost him completely, and his own cocoon was more prison than home. It was hard to breathe inside, and his toes and fingers itched terribly. He was no longer sure of mere hallucination. Really, Burt reflected, he was no longer sure of anything. It was the high that would not quit, and Christ, what a nightmare.

He wished he could turn his head, wished he could look at Heather. He thought of her as she'd been in class: a pleasant student, pretty and sweet if not terribly bright. Her compositions were half-assed, dubiously argued; her penmanship borderline retarded in its blocky, oversized scrawl—not to mention the myriad misspellings which Burt suspected even an invalid wouldn't make. What was it that attracted him to her in the first place? Could it really have only been her legs, her ass, her tits?

No, he thought, *it couldn't. She was sweet. She is sweet. And she makes me sweet, too.*

But at what cost? He wondered this as a dull throbbing began in his encased arms, his legs, his back, his face. The pain, low and deep, reminded him of nights spent tossing through his early teenage years: low light streaming in from the window, belly sticky with furtive semen (he would let it dry there, for he did not want his mother to discover stained sheets), and a discomfort in him that was more than simple guilt, more than simple barely-adolescent disquiet in the dark. It was physical, and it seemed to emanate from within his very bones. Growing pains, he'd supposed, but he had never guessed they'd have been that literal. And now, as he experienced these again, he realized that what he wanted more than anything, not just *now* but for the past decade, was to return to that bedroom once more, to drift off to sleep at last and awaken, hours later, back within the uncomfortable, uncertain and yet totally *sweet* years of his youth. His mother, still living, making eggs in her plaid house-

dress and her starched apron. His father, straight from
the dreamy canvas of a Norman Rockwell, smoking his
pipe and reading the paper and greeting him, *heyyy, look
who's finally up* . . .

He recalled the morning on which school had most
recently returned. He'd had a dream the night before,
in which he had already grown old and died, and on
the other side of life was not heaven nor hell but only a
room: four walls and a roof, a single bed, a bedtable, a
lamp with a carnival glass shade. There were no clouds,
no loved ones. Only him, and still old. Eternity passed,
and no angels came to visit, no demons came to torture.
He only went on aging in that little bed. His already-
wasted muscles withered to thin jelly; his skin sagged for
a thousand years until finally beginning to actually drip
off his bones, like candlewax, hanging there as the bark
of a dead tree and drying to cracked, flaky leather. But
still he lived. And the last thing he remembered upon
waking was his life as a pile of dust, still in that bed and
still lucid, thinking of his mother and his father and his
childhood and adolescence and early adulthood, all of
them gone, out of reach, locked up behind that great steel
trapdoor of time itself, time itself, time itself.

He had met Heather for the first time that day, fourth
period. The dream was still with him. She'd worn a short
dress and, along the shadowed insides of her cream-col-
ored thighs, Burt could actually *see* the youthful vitality
of her. It was in the glow of the skin, and he remembered
thinking (with only the mildest of self-remonstrations),
if only I were her age. But as it turned out, he didn't need
to be. And now, in the theater, he realized something
else. She really was wonderful. What of her spelling, her
inexperience, her habit of open-mouthed chewing? She
was fun and good and easy to get along with, and she
was *sweet*, and when this was all over, whatever *it* was,
he thought he might soon ask her to marry him. And
what of his wife? *Yes*, he thought, vicious, triumphant.
What of her?

Beneath the cocoon, from between the place where his shoulder blades used to be, Burt's wings began to sprout.

Beside him, so, too, did Heather's.

~

Camille Laurent knew that things were close to the end. *How* she knew this was still a mystery, greater than all others. She was no longer sure why she had stolen any of the skins, was no longer sure of what it was she was searching for. Once, she'd thought that when she found it—the perfect *her*—she would know. The fact that she hadn't, the fact that she *didn't*, was so frustrating it made her want to scream, to scream and scream and scream until her throat was shredded and bleeding and the thing watching her (for now she *knew* it was, only she didn't know how nor whom nor why) would have no choice but to scream too. But she couldn't. Screams were useless. Some of the people she'd stolen had screamed plenty— boy, *had* they—and it hadn't made a bit of difference. Screams were useless. Besides—

She'd only just put the baby to sleep.

So Camille sat on the sofa, smoking, ruminating. The body she wore was a slack, pudgy thing, from her inactivity and its recently-concluded pregnancy. Why, she wondered madly, had she picked a housewife? A stewbum would have been near as degrading, and then she wouldn't have needed to endure the husband night after night. He was a boring man, a crude man, smelly and just as insufferable as all the rest of them. Once, she had thought that to *be* a man would be the answer to all her ills, but she had tried that time and again. Men were lumbering, oafish creatures, ugly and rough, and all the patriarchal power in the world was not worth its utter *weight*. She had been businessmen, heads of companies, heads of state. She had been lumbermen, and tillermen, and barkeeps. None of them were good, none of them were right. A man was expected to be consequential, to shake things, to build—a man was expected to *stand*. But Camille, for her part, didn't want to stand at all. Camille only wanted to *be*.

She snuffed her cigarette out against her thigh. The skin there sizzled, puckering. She thought of the baby, pink and new in its crib, with a father and a home and a whole life ahead of it. She wondered if it knew she was not its mother. It was not easy to soothe.

She sighed, hating it, wishing to *be* it. But that was hopeless. It was tiny. She could not possibly hope to fit inside its skin. Only . . .

Perhaps she could.

Camille sat up. It was like she'd heard a voice, not within, nor without, but *above*. Could it be that *this* was what she'd been looking for all along? Not an established life, not a mere costume, but an entirely new one? That could be her. The infant had a father—a boor, yes, but a kind one, attentive, nurturing. She could not love him as a wife, no, but as a daughter? Yes. Camille thought she could.

She leapt to her feet. Then she padded into the kitchen, selected a paring knife, and headed for the nursery. She had nothing to lose, of course. And besides, she wasn't even there. Not really.

～

Burt and Heather watched the proceedings with bated breath. Surely this could not be the end. Burt could relate—he wanted, he'd come tonight to realize, something similar. A fresh start, a new leaf, and how newer could one get than actual infancy? Ah, who but the French? Of course, his life was a real one, and Heather was the best he could do, but still, he got it. And from inside his cocoon, not moving, Burt saluted Camille Laurent.

Rob that cradle, babe. Rob it good.

Heather did not at all share these sentiments. True, she had been dreading an ending wherein the message was sanguine, *Tangerine Blue* being such a long film that was at turns painfully boring and breathlessly shocking. But now that it seemed the end would come with the live skinning of a baby, she felt . . . well, *cheated* was the word that came to mind. *That* can't *be it*, she thought. She tried to shake her head, realizing just after she did that she hadn't been able to move at all for hours—and was surprised to hear a sharp *crack* come up from somewhere below her ears.

She didn't have time to worry about it, though, for Camille was in the baby's room now. The camera hovered above its crib like a ghost; it cooed down at the theater like a dove.

As she watched, a new thing began to happen beneath her cocoon. Heather noticed it like she noticed all the rest—hardly at all. She was too absorbed. But now she had no choice, for it was making the film hard to see. Her head, or something inside it, was bulging out and upwards, pushing itself against the hard interior of the cocoon, cracking it further, pushing it away from her face and so making her view from behind it distorted and blurry.

To her right, she could hear a similar sound. It was happening to Burt, too.

He nibbled a hole, she thought madly, for in the deep parts of her, she *did* know what was happening. *Yes—he nibbled a hole, and pushed his way out, and—*

Her new head burst through at last. She turned to look at Burt; he looked right back.

They had not emerged as butterflies.

～

The husband, tired and dirty from his work at the local quarry, burst through the door just as the knife had begun its plunge. His shout was shocked, strangled. He started forward—

But only too late.

The eye drank of the infant's blood as greedily as the floral sheets beneath it, lingering there in grotesque close-up even as the husband wrenched Camille away, even as he threw her to the floor, even as he beat her. The sound of his screams was broken only by those of his blows, flat, meaty, crunching. Still, she did not scream. The baby had died easily, and now its blood no longer gurgled from the short slit in its throat but only trickled slowly, from the slit itself and from between its tiny velvet lips. Its eyes were open, glassy, horribly real. The eye did not leave them for several minutes.

Then it did. The husband had Camille by the throat, straddling her, and was still raining down upon her face with his free fist like a boxer who wanted not only to win, but to kill. But the boxer was exhausted, grew weaker with each throw. He was sobbing now, wheezing. Beneath him, Camille lay perfectly conscious. Her front teeth were shattered. Her nose was broken. And courtesy of his wedding band, her cheek was sliced down past the politician, past the whore and the artist and the lawman, all the way down to the stubbly jowls of M. Durand's. She was laughing. The eye shifted sideward then, and the reason was made clear. Evidently reaching for it throughout her long beating—

She had finally reached her knife.

She punched it through the husband's temple; it went in with the sound of a wet, snapping branch. He slumped over, blood drooling from beneath his hairline, and Camille got shakily to her feet. She was no longer laughing. The husband was dead, and the baby, now fatherless, was utterly useless.

She touched her face, felt the shredded folds of ruined skin, and roared, impotent. Years without mistakes, years of close calls proved just that, and now this. She had blown it. *She had blown it.*

Furious, confused, and vaguely violated by the bodiless voice she'd earlier heard—wanting only to rip and tear and shred and *hurt*—she hooked her broken nails into her ruined cheek and pulled.

The housewife's face tore open, a living mask made of many others, to reveal that of the fourth-act-montage's Russian oligarch. Camille used the knife to dig deeper, twisting for purchase, down past the politician, the photographer, the waitress, the porno-mag model. Flesh and blood flew this way and that, over her shoulders like limp, dripping Christmas paper, and as the layers peeled away, the skins became progressively darker, more soft, more putrid. She'd worn them a long time, and what, after all, does old meat do but rot?

She could feel the eye on her, could feel it as bodily as she'd felt it all her life. The eye, the *eye*, invisible but as there as the air and the atoms within it. She wondered what it looked like, that eye. She wondered how it would feel between her teeth.

And then she was Camille Laurent again, unsheathed at last. She stood there a long time atop her pile of gore and empty skin; she was a redwood, a mountain, a reborn monolith. But her own skin, so long buried in dead, festering flesh, had become necrotic. Her fingers were black. Her nose had melted away. In its place were only twin channels, red at the borders and crusted dark along the edges inside. They were not empty—they ran with mucus and pus and hordes of short, white maggots. Exposed to the open air, they fell stunned, bouncing off her wasted breasts and down to the floor below. She stood there a moment, feeling them writhe between her toes, and stared straight ahead—right into the eye itself. But did she know it was there? Did she really?

Yes, and how she'd always *hated* its constant surveillance. But she would close it. Yes, she would close it. And then—

Camille raised the knife and sprang. She knew not why she did it, just as she did not know the reasons for a great many of her actions—the murders, the skinnings, the thefts—but this one was different. All the rest had come from the fat fingers of a Frenchman named Andre Auclair, pounded into an old Olivetti over a period of weeks as he drank and ate and whored and congratulated himself through it all. But this action, this *act*, had nothing to do with him at all. And as she sliced into empty air, as she began to stumble forward, as the world around her went black entirely—

The knife caught on something stiff in that vacuum of darkness, something flat. It tore through with a hollow sound of ripping canvas.

Camille fell in after it.

4. And So, a Fly

The film was over. The lights came on, and Burt and Heather got slowly to their feet. Their legs were stiff, all twelve of them; they stretched, yawning, fluttering their wings. The blood that ran through them was cold as the saline given during a transfusion, and with it, they shivered, silent for the moment, unsure of what to say, unsure of what to do.

Camille had had no idea at all of what she'd been doing to the people watching her, no more than the sun is aware of all the bastard life it's seeded upon the Earth. It simply *exists*, there, and there, and there. And while the power of cinema is a psychic one, so too is it physical. For through its flickering, the wants and needs of its characters become the wants and needs of its audience, at least until that flickering stops; so, *too*, does their pain. Who has not wept at Scarlett O'Hara's trials, her self-imposed heartbreaks? Who did not cry when E.T. finally went home? Camille had wanted to transform all her life, and so, as *Tangerine Blue* finally ended, as she'd emerged from between that sliced sheet of silver screen, as her eyes had adjusted to the projector's glare of rolling credits and the hazy darkness beyond it, Camille, an impossibility herself, had seen *her* audience at last. And they were just as she'd made them.

From their place at the back of the theater, Burt and Heather watched as the buzzing swarm of flies writhed atop her. They had sprung forward at once, unthinking, and Camille, out of her film and into the world of the living, had screamed in mad terror. The couple stayed where they were—they felt neither hungry nor particularly vicious. The popcorn sat heavily in their new burbling stomachs, churning there, burning. So they only watched, watched as a small, skeletal hand burst from between two giant carapaces, watched as it groped for purchase, watched as it found none. For a moment, they thought they could make out Camille's head, still noseless but now slicked with bright blood. Then it disappeared under a slopping glut of acidic vomit, and the crowd, ever the tough one, slurped up what remained.

"Do you, uh," Burt began. "Should we go down there?"

"No," Heather said. She had seen enough. "Let's just go."

They flew out the theater, down the hall and into the lobby. "Enjoy the show?" the old ticket lady asked in her dry, still-human voice. Burt and Heather only buzzed on, out and into the Sherwood Mall at large. The neon was dead, the fluorescents out. They landed, scuttling the rest of the way toward the glass double-doors of the side entrance. Through them, they could hear birds chirping, could see the infant dawn's blue glow as it rose far off in the east. *All nite,* Heather thought with glum irony. *They weren't kidding.* She sighed, reached for the handle with one fuzzy, insectile leg —

But Burt stopped her.

"Hey, listen. Should we . . . do you still wanna make it? I mean —" He coughed through his moist proboscis, twiddled his spindly legs. "I saw a motel on the way in, just a ways away. Do you . . . still wanna go? With me?"

Heather thought about that a long time. Did she? She thought of her mother, due back soon from her holiday trip; she thought of Burt himself, how he made her feel, how she was sure she made *him* feel. He was a married man, an *old* married man, and she was only seventeen. What would his wife think? And what might *she* think, in ten years, or fifteen, twenty? Could she be happy with him? Or would she only be disappointed in Burt and in herself?

At last, she thought of *Tangerine Blue:* its matryoshka madness, its (quite literally) three-dimensional finale, its trite, cloying ultimate theme. *Just be yourself,* she thought emptily. *So is that it? Is this? Is it really?* Burt was still looking at her. His huge eyes glittered hopefully; the colors beneath his shimmering wings danced. *He really is pretty,* she reflected, and at this, she had to smile. *The prettiest fly, the prettiest fly, just-oh-just the prettiest fly. But . . . but . . . but . . .*

"No," she said at last, still smiling. It had turned sad. She gave his head a slow stroke, kissed his eye. And again she whispered, "No. I don't think I do, dear."

Burt sagged, crestfallen, and Heather opened the door to go. But before she could fly away, she had to stop once more, for the dim morning light was gone, as were the cars, the lot, and everything else. In their place was only stark emptiness, a space not just whitely blank but actually *devoid*, made not of earth and air nor celluloid and light but this, only of this: flat, unprinted pulp, dry and dead.

Heather, not knowing what else to do, looked back toward Burt.

He was gone, too.

7

THE GREAT COMMUNICATOR
Adrian DeLeon

A FTER HE HEARD ABOUT THE SCARS, a man who went by Stan Carnell called Eddie for a job. Eddie, tired and delirious from a long day in the sun, sat twisted up in his landline, confused as to how Stan even got his number. He didn't know it was because of how he looked yet.

The meeting was a few days later at Sherwood Mall. Eddie didn't think much of it until he got there, remembering that it was the Fourth of July. The mall was pulsing with music, streaming American flags, and big blow-out sale posters in shop windows for new sneakers and VCRs. Most of all, it was swelling with people. Smiling parents, horny teenagers, and pimpled employees crowding in currents over the tile flooring.

People had always stared at the twisted markings on Eddie's face, so he avoided big crowds or town gatherings. Independence Day and other holidays ingrained into Americana were always filled with families. Kids watched Eddie's face with interest fairly often, and he didn't mind. It was their parents who yanked them away and avoided looking at what remained of his face.

Eddie reached up to pull down his *Reagan '84* hat, further obscuring their view.

Two years before, Eddie had been to a rally, back when his scars were still waxy-looking from a distance with a bright red shine.

A guest speaker at the podium had pointed him out of the crowd, shouting, "See folks! Even the most vulnerable and disfigured Americans in our society love President Reagan. Isn't that true, son?"

The crowd jeered, and Eddie nodded in response, mostly because he didn't know how else to answer. The man had called Eddie up to the podium. Eddie listened with anxious hesitation. There were some cheers but also gasps once they got a look at his face in the sunlight. One teenager in the front seemed as if he would vomit.

"Don't you have a great love for our president, son?" The man on the podium had asked.

Eddie started, but he was still getting used to having less lip than before, the words coming out slurred or muffled. His chin would become damp from saliva that flowed unrestricted when he spoke.

"Well, I certainly—" Was all Eddie got out before the man laughed and shouted, "That's right! That's right! Thank you so much, you beautiful soul. Somebody get this gentleman a free hat for his trouble."

Eddie knew most of the audience didn't understand what he said either, but for at least an hour, people looked at him without feeling afraid, so it wasn't so bad.

Eddie took to wearing the hat every day after that, and it helped with not being the center of attention. Its blue color was fading, and the fabric was worn thin at the edge of the bill, but the hat made him feel safe.

Stan Carnell was sitting on a bench by a big fern growing in the center of the walkway. The first thing Eddie noticed was the guy seemed short, had a symmetrical face that was easy to look at, and was drinking a can of Coke out of a blue straw. He wore a bright-colored shirt, like many of the younger kids wore, though he definitely seemed to be in his 30s.

Over the phone, Stan told Eddie to meet him in front of Jack's Toy Box. People flowed in and out at a steady pace, but the store was always full of kids running around and mothers scolding. A Jack-in-the-Box's head hung over customers from the store's sign. Its slow animatronics hummed as it slowly turned its head, side to side, and forward and back, as if springing.

Eddie sat down next to Stan and asked, "This seat taken?" barely slurring as he said it.

"Not at all," Stan said as he stood up to shake Eddie's hand. "You must be Eddie Crumney."

"What gave it away?"

"Oh, well. I think you know. Come on then, sit down."

Eddie felt a pit in his stomach about his looks preceding him, but Stan's friendliness helped Eddie into a slight ease. Being in a crowded shopping mall like that was always easier when someone was with him.

"Coke?"

"Nah, I'm okay. What's the work you need?"

"Right to business, huh? I like it, I like it. Me, I have a clinically diagnosed aversion to work myself, so I usually put it off if I can. Have a Coke."

Eddie disliked making a fuss, so he took the unopened can, popped it, and then set it on his knee. He stared at Stan until the man straightened up from his slouched posture and got to why he called.

"Well, fine. On to business. You see that chick in there with the striped shirt? In those pastel colors and a white collar."

"I don't see her," Eddie responded, uneasy.

"Next to the board games."

She looked around the store listlessly and seemed to be following a much more enthusiastic eight-year-old. Her face had a lovely glow to it under the lights inside the store, dark hair falling over one shoulder as her hands played with it, aimlessly. She seemed young for someone with an eight-year-old, but still close to Eddie's age.

"Go talk to her."

Eddie looked at him in disbelief.

"Yeah, go talk to her. One conversation. One hundred bucks."

Eddie stood up and looked around to see if anyone was watching their conversation. "You just making fun of me? We just setting up the ugly guy for some practical joke? Well, I'm not falling for a trap where I get run out of a toy store and have someone's heels thrown at the side of my head."

"Slow down, bud. When you talk fast, I can't understand you at all, and you're spitting everywhere. Sit down, sit down. I'm not pulling your leg, though. I told you it would be easy, simple work. Just go in there and chat her up. Ya know, just don't make her too uncomfortable. A nice little conversation. Distract her for a few minutes, and I'll pay you the easiest hundred dollars you've ever made."

"What do you get out of it? Swoop in after she gets freaked out by the guy with a fucked up face?" Eddie wished he hadn't used so many Fs, the sounds coming out in hot puffs of breath instead of any well-formed words.

Stan gave a mild shrug and smiled a menacing, toothy smile. "Something like that," he said.

Eddie turned away.

"Okay, hold on. Hold on. Two hundred, huh? How about two hundred?"

When Eddie looked back, Stan had his wallet out and pulled out four 50s. It *would* be easy money. Eddie thought to himself that he would never want this to be a regular thing, but he had already driven out here and put himself through the stress of being exposed in a crowd like this. Walking away with a couple hundred bucks wasn't so bad for him. At least it would be worth the trouble. Eddie's hand reached out for the money, but Stan pulled his hand back and retrieved a single fifty for him.

"Here. You can have the other three after."

Eddie pocketed the cash, pulled the bill of his hat down lower, and then faced toward the toy store. The crowd swelled to a larger size more suddenly than wind changing direction. Eddie would have rather made the money digging holes at the construction site. A burning sensation flooded his cheeks, and his chest tightened.

The only thing that benefited Eddie was that everyone in the crowd was enamored with the sale. Board game BOGO, blowout sale on Barbie clothes, a crowd of boys surrounding a rack of fake rifles that whirred and clicked when you pulled the trigger, screams and shouts. It was busy and wild enough that Eddie was just another invisible shopper. In a crowd like this, he could be no one, which was all he's ever wanted to be for a long time.

The woman he was supposed to talk to was looking at a fully stocked wall of stuffed bears, her lips pulled into a pout. Eddie came up to the same wall and picked up one of the stuffed bears by the cardboard display it sat in. He flipped over the bear in his hand, pretending to read the back. He was sweating now and felt his perspiration rubbing off on the cardboard. Moving on from the stuffed bear, he looked for anything else to stare at while he thought of something to say to her, but the bear kept staring at him with an angry expression in its plastic eyes.

Then, it started singing *Row, Row, Row Your Boat*. It kept eye contact with Eddie, and he felt it looking at him.

"Pretty expensive, huh?"

Eddie was slow to realize she had spoken the words to *him*. He gave a slight nod and caught her with his peripheral vision. She was on the side of his face that looked a little better, though still recognizably damaged. She was looking right at him, though, he could tell that much.

Pretty expensive?

Eddie looked at the price of the bear he had just picked up.

Seventy goddamn dollars?

Eddie choked out, "Yeah, I wasn't ready to start a new credit card today, so I guess I'll have to wait for a clearance sale."

She laughed. It was soft and quiet, but you could hear the smile in it. Eddie felt the warmth of it on his cheek, like being woken by sunlight in the morning.

"Yeah, I thought it might be a good gift for my niece, but I think I'll have to save up and get her one before

Christmas. She wanted a stuffed animal that could read her stories. They're expensive, but they're the same price as a Teddy Ruxpin, and on top of that, they don't just lip sync to the sound of whatever cassette you put in there. I don't know how it works, but they all have their own voice."

"Yeah, well, it's something. That's for sure."

Eddie turned his head to get a look at her, but she was looking right at him. He nearly gave himself whiplash as he turned away.

She let out a small chuckle.

"Looking for a good gift?"

"Yeah, something like that."

"Family?"

"No, I'm in the store for a . . . colleague. I don't really have . . . any o' that out here."

"I see."

The kid she had been following around the store ran up to show her one of the toy rifles and asked her if he could get one.

"You'll have to ask your mother," She said.

Three other boys his age ran over, one of them holding the same toy rifle and the other two holding plastic tomahawks. One of them had the same bright platinum haircut as the guy from A Flock of Seagulls. Eddie chuckled to himself, wondering if that made him more or less aerodynamic. They sprinted past screaming and weren't the only kids running full speed as if they were at the city park.

"So, not yours?" Eddie asked.

"No, that's my nephew. My sister's at Jeweler's Palace on the other side of the Cineplex looking at some necklaces, and he was getting antsy, so I offered to bring him here with me while I shopped for his sister. I figured it would just distract him for a while, but it looks like it'll get his energy out too."

Eddie watched the kid run by one more time. He made the mistake of letting his guard down, and he was turned with his bad side facing her.

"Do they hurt?"

Eddie blushed a little and pulled at his hat. It felt silly how low he pulled it at first, re-adjusting it to the position it was in when he got to Sherwood Mall.

"Yeah, sometimes. It's like an ache. Just in my jaw."

The side he had tried to keep closest to her only had one patch of leathery, sagging skin. About an inch long stretch by his chin. The other side was twisted canyons from his forehead stretching down to just below the corner of his mouth. It was the place where his eyebrow used to droop slightly over his eye; to most onlookers, the skin seemed old and sagging. He felt if it weren't for the right side of his face, he might've looked like a normal guy with a fairly attractive scar on his left side.

"You a vet?"

It wasn't an unusual question, some thought he might have been in Vietnam and that he was scarred terribly from napalm or was the result of some Viet Cong torture. He was too young to have been in Vietnam, but the scars made him look older.

"No, it was just an accident."

"Sorry," she rubbed her hands nervously on her pants, "That was rude of me."

"No, no. It's okay."

Eddie turned to look at her head-on, and she didn't flinch or look away. Her eyes didn't trace the lines of scar tissue; she just looked right at him.

"Eddie," he said. He stuck out his good hand for a shake, the one with normal skin. He tried to seem less damaged, but knew when he said his own name, he made a face that looked like he was chewing.

She grabbed, shook it once, and then just held it, keeping her amber eyes fixed on him. Then she said, "Lee Tomlinson," in that same voice you could hear the smile in, even if it was too subtle to see on her face.

Then, one of the bears on the wall behind them started singing a song from a children's cartoon. Either the wiring was bad or the batteries were dying, because the song slowed down and changed to a darker key.

They both laughed nervously at each other.

"A lot of money for something so creepy," Lee said.

When she looked back at him, Eddie felt she wanted to ask about how it happened. So, Eddie just kind of blurted out, "It was a car accident."

"Oh, I'm so sorry. You know you don't have to explain anything to—"

"Drunk driver."

"I'm sorry. I hope he got what was coming to him."

"Uh, she didn't, since it was Idaho three years ago. It was still legal to drink and drive. Her kid was with her, they're okay though. And cops didn't see any reason to charge her."

Eddie remembered them saying, "Why ruin another life when this guy's life is already ruined?" They were talking about not ruining her kid's life, Eddie assumed, but he always felt a layer of hypocrisy or maybe even laziness in it.

She stood motionless, listening. People used to ask, back in Boise, where they knew him: *What happened?* The questions and the worries, and old friends not hanging out, because when the beer dribbled out of his poorly shaped mouth, it made them too depressed. Eddie noticed people asked less if they didn't know what he looked like beforehand, so he moved to California to get away from it.

Lee posed as if she had another question she wanted to ask, but she scanned the room once with slight worry in those attentive eyes.

"It was lovely talking to you. You can phone me if you like. I'm in the yellow pages."

Eddie nodded.

"You'll call me, right?"

Eddie nodded again, harder, and then laughed, watching her disappear into the crowd. It was difficult not to feel as if he scared her away, but asking him to call seemed so genuine.

She walked away toward the display wall, which featured plastic swords and cheap slingshots.

Eddie left without buying anything.

When he walked out, Stan began clapping. "Well done, Frankenstein. That was perfect."

"Yeah, yeah. Give me the cash. We're done. I don't wanna do this again."

Eddie felt sick thinking about this weasel going in there and flirting with Lee.

Without getting up, Stan pulled out $150 and held it out to Eddie, who gripped it hard and shoved it in his pocket while he looked around. Anxiety set in that they looked like some urban drug deal he'd seen in those *Just Say No* ads, but no one was looking at them. Kids were waving tiny American flags, and shoppers kept coming in droves for discount Chucks and new Nintendos. The neon lights reflected shades of purple from the floor. For the first time since he watched two headlights collide with his driver's side door, Eddie felt okay being here. He felt hidden enough that he could be happy.

His thoughts were interrupted by panicked shouting. They grew into frantic pleas begging, "Jay! Jay! Where is he? Where is Jay?!"

Eddie saw Lee jogging back and forth, in and out of the store, calling out for her nephew. Scanning the entire stretch of Sherwood Mall. She eventually screamed and went back into Jack's Toy Box to ask the cashier if he had seen a boy with a Joe Montana jersey who had been running around earlier with a plastic rifle. She asked every person who would listen if they had seen him. Someone called mall security, but nobody had a clue where the boy went.

Lee had fallen on the ground outside the store, tears and snot were running down her face. Her cheeks were red, and her voice was scratchy. It came out in croaks to answer questions the security guard had for her. Eventually, they put some kind of announcement on the intercom asking for Jason Garrick to return to the front of Jack's Toy Box, repeating two or three times before ending the transmission with an aggressive click.

Eddie turned toward Stan, his nails digging hard into the palm of his hand, while Stan sat there smiling and holding his coke can gently between his index finger and his thumb, the straw sitting absently on his bottom lip.

"What the fuck did you do?" triplets of spit came down on Stan's face when Eddie pronounced the F again.

"I dunno what you're talking about," he was almost laughing.

"This ain't funny, where's the kid?"

"I wouldn't know."

"So this is what you do? You send fucked up looking guys to go distract baby sitters and moms while you sit back and hire some other goon to kidnap him."

"Bud, I can't understand what you're even saying." Stan was whispering this now, only loud enough for Eddie to hear. "I don't know where the kids go and I don't care what happens to them, but if you do, I can tell you they promised me they don't kill him unless they feel they have to. Or an accident. Accidents do happen, you know."

Eddie let his hand fly, and his palm knocked Stan's Coke can onto the ground in a clatter not loud enough to draw attention. His other hand wrapped its fingers around Stan's throat.

"No one will believe you. I've been sitting here the whole time; there's a camera right above us that will prove it. I'm just some guy, enjoying a day at the mall, and if you knew what was good for ya, you'd do the same. Move on. There isn't anything you can do about it."

Toward the end Stan began gasping his words out and choking, until eventually Eddie let him go.

When Eddie looked around, he saw Lee, still sitting on her ankles, talking to security, but now she was watching him with this confused and hurt expression. He didn't think she'd be able to tell what he and Stan were talking about but was sure that from afar his behavior gave way to suspicion.

Eddie scanned the walkway and noticed three kids whispering around the trash can in front of the nearby department store. One of them had that god awful platinum hair Eddie recognized. He walked towards them, trying to keep his body more relaxed than it had been during his conversation with Stan.

When Eddie approached, the kids were whispering, but they all went quiet upon seeing the sagging skin on his face. In the shadowed lighting away from the purple neon lights above, it was easier to tell what was scarred and what was healthy; the scarred skin taking on a more ashen color. The blood drained from the children's faces, and Eddie didn't know if it was him or something else, maybe a combination of both.

"Hey, you kids, see what happened to that other kid? Jay?"

They all shook their heads. The platinum blond child at the front shook his head slower and with less conviction, as if in a trance. One of the children Eddie had seen with a plastic tomahawk asked, "What happened to your face, mister?"

Eddie hesitated before saying, "I lied."

They all gasped and looked at each other.

"This is what happens to liars, you know. Now I'm gonna look like this forever."

This time, Eddie really let the spit fly when he said *forever*.

Two of them began to silently cry.

Then Eddie added on for good measure, "And it hurts."

~

Getting back into the store made Eddie anxious. There were fewer people inside, but plenty of people outside whispering and talking about it. The crowd only dwindled because shoppers would walk by and talk about the boy who had gone missing. Parents avoided bringing their kids in as if the store was to blame.

One security guard hung around the entrance, but paid no attention to Eddie.

They must be looking for the kid more than they're looking for a kidnapper, Eddie thought.

He hadn't seen Lee and assumed she had gone to look or perhaps meet up with the kid's mom. Eddie felt a cold sweat at imagining Jay's mother hearing the message on the intercom. Did she scream? Did she cry? Did she keep a silent demeanor while sprinting to the other side of the mall until the panic set in and she began calling her son's name? Did any of it feel real?

Eddie remembered his own mother visiting the hospital in Boise. He remembered her weeping and saying it felt like a bad dream. He was covered up in bandages, and his mom asked the doctor three times, "Are you sure that's my boy? Are you sure that's my Eddie?"

Eddie had a good impression that no one hauled Jay out of the store, and the kids he had been playing with confirmed it. As they turned a corner, they saw a hand wrap around Jay's mouth, pulling him behind a shelf. When they caught up, the only thing around the corner was a wall.

Kids don't just disappear. *Except for when they do,* Eddie thought morbidly. Still, no one had seen anything, so he's probably still inside. Hopefully Stan lied, and the kid is just lost in the storage room. Eddie could scoop him up and bring him to security.

The kids told Eddie they last saw Jay just after they chased him past the wall of talking teddy bears. When Eddie walked by the wall, one of the bears was singing *Rock-a-Bye Baby*, but something went wrong with the electronics again, and it began repeating the final verse. It short-circuited and never fully finished the word *Breaks* before starting again.

After that, the kids chased him and passed along the "kiddie toys." It seemed they were talking about an aisle of big, soft stuffed animals. Just on the other side of that aisle was where they saw Jay get taken, between the shelf of action figures and what the platinum kid called "girl stuff." Platinum-haired-kid had a good memory. He told Eddie it was because he saw the He-Man toys right next to where he had never seen Jay again. He was hoping his mom would buy him some.

There was an oddly spaced gap right between the action figures from the dolls. It was the first time Eddie noticed the paint job on the other side of all the displays and racks of toys. It was a golden tan color that matched the uniform the employees wore. Paired with some khakis, you might blend right in with the paint.

In the center of the wall was another small *Patriots Sale* poster in big block lettering and a red, white, and blue color scheme. Eddie checked that no one was watching him, then put his ear to the poster. He knocked softly. It gave a thin, hollow sound that rang longer than he thought was right. Other than the gap between shelves being strange, there wasn't anything else off-looking about the wall. Eddie assumed there would be a seam to pull with his fingernails or that pushing it would naturally spin the wall open. It felt too solid.

Eddie was going to move on and look for a way into the back room of Jack's Toy Box, but then he noticed a slight chip in the floor trim. There was only a few millimeters' gap between two chunks of molding. Eddie knew if he wasn't looking for something specifically, he would've never noticed.

He got low and tried to pry at it with his fingers, but he didn't have enough leverage. The wall was sturdy in its spot. Maybe even locked from the other side, though Eddie hoped not.

He knocked again and whispered, "Jay? Jay, are you in there?" He looked around while he waited for an answer, but all was still and silent.

One couple had noticed him do that, so he backed away from the wall and feigned interest in the He-Man toys. He sauntered casually around the store, looking for something to give him leverage to open the wall with. Light reflected off a thin plastic sword that Eddie figured would do well enough.

When he returned to the wall, Eddie then jammed the sword hard into the small gap. The plastic was thin enough that it didn't make much noise, but it didn't move the gap very much. Eddie tried again with more force, and this time felt the sword go deeper into the floor molding. He got lower to the ground and pried open the wall until it popped. It wouldn't crack open very much, not enough to swing into the aisle at least. It only opened a foot and a half, so from the aisle, shoppers would never see it past the shelving unless you were right in front of it, watching.

The tip of the sword was bent, hanging at a funny angle like a broken bone. Eddie didn't want to leave evidence right in front of the hidden door, so he squeezed through the opening with it, despite how silly it felt.

Eddie expected something like a storage room. He worked as a shelf stocker at a grocery store back in Idaho before the accident, so he expected something with tall ceilings and pallets of toys from deliveries. But instead, it was a five-foot-tall crawl space that Eddie had to bend down low to walk through.

Once he got close to the end of the corridor, he started to hear faint singing. Childlike voices. The air was cold. A chemical smell held a grip over the air, and Eddie couldn't place it, but he felt it smelled like the finishing oil he'd use to preserve wood at a job site. The feeling of it was thick in the air, and getting stronger. Once he made it to the opening at the end of the crawlspace, Eddie was coughing and holding the collar of his jean jacket over his mouth.

The room was poorly lit, but he saw a workbench on the closest wall. Streaks of a brownish red color were across it, and the table had scalpels and knives sitting along with the wiring tools he'd normally see electricians carrying around. Pliers. Wire cutters. Copper wiring.

The voice was coming from the teddy bear, its mouth at moments perfectly in sync with the song and sometimes completely off. The voice sounded like a child, very obviously not a toddler but not a preteen.

A bright light hung above a table in the center of the room. A mostly clean wooden table that looked as if it was designed for woodworking. Clean except for the dark stains on the far side of the table.

It wasn't a lot, just little droplets of red. Eddie always imagined things that were stained with blood would be covered in it, like his steering wheel the night of his accident. The way the blood poured down his leg from the gash above his knee. Before the fires got to him, he couldn't even see the color of his jeans anymore. But this was nothing, just a few little sprinkles. It could've been anything from an oil stain to paint.

His hands shook, and his chest felt heavy. Because if it was there, if it was blood, that meant there was no point cleaning it. Because there's no point in cleaning something that will just get stained again. Eddie felt himself separated from the situation. As if he didn't know why he was doing this anymore, but he remembered Lee sobbing on her knees. He thought of how scared Jay's mother must be. How he had his own role in this. He took the money. He might as well have pulled the trigger.

And he stood there, supposedly the hero. With a broken plastic sword and a face that makes old women faint. The ridiculousness of the horror itself made Eddie chuckle and calmed him down.

In the corner, away from the light, he saw a small figure move. Low to the ground and shaking like an animal. Its back was to him, breathing heavily. Eddie reached up over the work table and turned the hanging light towards the corner, where he saw a child locked in a cage.

"Jay?" He called out

There was no recognition of Eddie in his face, but he looked relieved at first and started shaking the cage. When he saw Eddie's face, he recoiled. He never spoke, opening his mouth to shout, but no sound came.

"Jay? Is that you?"

The kid nodded desperately.

Eddie dropped the sword with a clatter on the concrete floor. He approached quickly and yanked on the gate, but it didn't budge. A large metal lock wrapped its claw around the handle. Jay silently wept as he watched Eddie. Extending one finger up at him, asking for a moment, Eddie ran over to the first workspace by the entrance

He grabbed some wire cutters first, then a hammer just in case it didn't work.

His plan was to try to cut the thin metal around the lock and remove it, and if that didn't work, he'd hammer it off. Though he wasn't sure how much time he had or how loud he could be before whatever creep did this to Jay would show up.

Eddie got to work, but Jay turned wide-eyed and started shaking the cage. His hands gripped hard and wild.

"Quit that," Eddie said, "Too much noise. I need to keep this still."

But the shaking became more violent, and Eddie saw a screaming terror in Jay's eyes that couldn't make it past his throat.

That was the last thing that happened before the needle went into Eddie's neck.

~

When Eddie woke, he was tied by his wrists and his ankles. A bright light was blinding him, and he couldn't turn his head to look away from it. Leather straps wrapped around his forehead and kept his head still.

Two figures looked over him. One was an older man. He had short, clean-cut silver hair. He was thin, his collarbones visible through the surgeon's gown he wore. The other was the same acne-ridden teenager from the cash register.

What's going on, Eddie said.

"Ah, ah, ah. You shouldn't push yourself," the man said. He poured a little water into Eddie's mouth.

The teenager looked at the man as if waiting for instructions.

"Send them out."

"Are you sure?"

The man chuckled and started stroking Eddie's hair.

"Who will they tell?" He asked. His laughter was growing. "Send both of them out, but zip tie the boy."

The teenager followed as instructed. He pulled Jay out of the cage and zip-tied his hands behind his back, they unstrapped Eddie. The older man pushed Eddie off the table, and he fell hard onto the pavement.

I think you sprained my wrist, asshole, Eddie tried to say. The attempt gave him a pain in his throat, and he coughed violently.

"Ah, I said 'don't push yourself'. It won't heal right if you keep trying to talk."

Eddie looked at the man, confusion and anger filling his eyes.

The man paid no mind and walked slow, with a sense of drama. He got to the other workbench, the one next to the entrance in the cold concrete room. There was a teddy bear, same as the others. It held an American flag and had that same hat Uncle Sam wears.

The man squished the soft, fluffy paw, and it began singing *America the Beautiful*. This voice was different from the other bears, it sounded older and more familiar to Eddie. His head was pounding, and he tried to beg, *Can you please turn that off?* He broke into another coughing fit.

He grabbed his throat, and thin scratchy lines touched the palm of his hand.

His hands shook as he reached for the broken plastic sword, which sat delicately next to it. The shiny plastic was enough to get a warped reflection out of it.

The first thing he saw was his face, just like everyone else saw in him. A reflection that for the last three years always made him think, *that's not me.* The one that made his own mother say, *Are you sure that's my Eddie?*

The second thing he saw was the thick black stitches on his throat just below his Adam's apple. The bear continued singing, and the arm holding the American Flag began to wave it back and forth.

Please shut it off, Eddie tried again.

"It's incredible what can be done in a free market," the older man said. His smile was twisted by the way the light hit him right above his head. In the deep darkness of the shadows on his face, a dark void that went on forever. Such deep blackness on his pale skin. "It's also such a shame you could never use it properly. You used to have such a beautiful voice."

Once again, his voice was stripped from him. A voice he lost and had to work hard for years to win back, just to have it ripped from his flesh all over again. Metal shards and engine fires, scalpel in the dark, it was all the same.

Eddie's throat started to burn hot, like steam was coming out from deep within him and blistering his insides. He stopped trying to talk and turned away, tripping on the ground on his way out. When Jay realized they were free to go, he began running down the narrow crawl space and out the secret door into Jack's Toy Box.

Eddie followed, his head fuzzy from whatever drugs they used to keep him asleep for the procedure. The echo of the voice that had been taken from him, not now but years before, called out to him.

Thine alabaster cities gleam undimmed by human tears.
America, America. God shed His grace on thee.

The lights behind them shut off, and in the dark, he wept.

By the time he got outside the crawlspace, the sun had set.

He fell down at the entrance of the store, which seemed closed or closing soon. There were still a few groups of shoppers, but no one noticed them appear from the opening in the wall, which shut smoothly behind them. Faint pops and fizzles came from outside, which Eddie realized was most likely why the store was so empty.

Through the haze of blurry vision, Eddie could see Jay running into Lee's arms and Jay's mother running not far behind.

Eddie could hear Lee saying that she was so glad they stayed close to the store, that they knew he'd come back.

That was before they noticed the stitches on Jay's neck and his hands tied behind his back. They screamed. Eddie barely held himself up through the drug haze that the man put him under.

When Lee's eyes found him, her mouth twisted at the sight of Eddie, and she shouted that she had met him in the store, that he must be a sex creep or something because he wasn't in there with a kid, he just looked around and left without buying anything.

Before he could try to say anything, he was tackled to the ground by security. He felt a rumble in his chest from how hard he had hit the floor.

Eddie wanted to tell them about the secret door, the crawlspace, how the man behind the wall would keep stealing their voices until someone stopped him, but nothing happened, and a screeching burn in his throat came back. The taste of blood filled his mouth.

The security guard got low to the ground and said, "You'll be going away for a long time for what you did to that kid, you fucking sicko."

Eddie was faintly aware that they must not be able to see his stitches. They must be obscured by the blood dripping down his chin in a steady stream.

Stan was still drinking from a Coke can, sitting at the bench in front of Jack's Toy Box. Eddie's Reagan hat sat comfortably on the man's head.

He gave a salute and walked away.

8

BALLIF'S BOO-DOIR
Liam Ray III

IT WAS HALLOWEEN. Neon lights of orange, purple, and ghoulish green crept in classic strands throughout the store whilst the bewitching smell of pumpkins billowed as if every present jack-o-lantern sighed with seasonal content. Through crackling speakers, the stereo conjured a sonically sinister elixir of toccatas, fugues, and dances macabre. Among cobwebs that were, for the most part, authentic, layers of shelves were adorned with commodities ranging from cute to cursed and back again: carving kits, costumes, masks, makeup, wind-up spiders, poseable skeletons, rubber limbs, kooky comics and magazines, bottles of fake blood, Trick-Or-Treat buckets, and a monstrous amount of gimcrack nicknacks. These horizons of horrors eventually lead one to the front desk, atop which sat a bottomless bowl of candy for every palette — and there was never a limit to how many pieces one could take. Most popular was the *haunted house*, which resided at the back of the shop, full of gimmicks and gotchas where patrons were guaranteed that one good scare to which they were all entitled. It was *always* Halloween . . . at least as far as Ballif's Boo-doir was concerned.

Outside of the store, however, the 4th of July, as the distant treble of rogue fireworks implied. That particular Friday had folks out in droves to the Sherwood Mall, patriotically participating in the celebrations. This is not to say the Boo-doir was left out of the day's proceedings; prominently displayed were red, white, and blue makeups at a discount, sparklers in the shapes of ghosts, witches, and skeletons, and American flags featuring carved pumpkin faces in place of the standard fifty stars. Even the coffin in the center floor was repainted red, white, and blue. Still, the odd outlet was a world unto itself, Samhain forever in full swing, missing only the crunching of crisp autumnal leaves. A sound substitute approached in the form of one Morna Ballif, the owner of the Boo-doir and someone who, by her own account, had been "old a long time, but stubborn a lot longer," teetering gracefully behind a half-walker, half-scooter decked out in orange and black streamers. The handles boasted the embossed words: "Trick" and "Treat." She, herself, was in full regalia as a not-so-creepy clown and, in place of where a big red nose might traditionally be, was a faux firecracker complete with fuse.

Manning the front desk was Teddy Kratky, a horror-themed-Hawaiian-shirt-and-torn-punk-jeans-wearing-geek-of-theatre-junior-in-college who, observed Morna and noticed with discomfort that her transportation had accrued a particularly crunchy piece of popcorn on its left wheel, manifesting the misophonic nightmare of a crackle, squeak, and squelch with each revolution. Teddy squinted in the likeness of Clint Eastwood, eyeing the little yellow butter stains left on the white tile floor in her wake. The pain came to a halt as Morna entered the store, parked near the front desk, then offered a smile to Teddy that he wasn't sure was bigger than normal or just the clown makeup working overtime.

"Happy Lost Sock Remembrance Day, Morna!" Teddy hailed.

"Happy Lost Sock Remembrance Day, Teddy. How has the afternoon business been?" Morna asked before checking her face paint in a nearby mirror.

"Slower than last year," Teddy reported, "But the sparklers are a sleeper hit, and I got a guy to buy one of the Halloween flags without realizing what it was, so that's something. How was your coffee with Jim?"

"How do you know I had coffee with Jim?"

"Your smile was just, I don't know, *more* today."

"It's just the coffee. Gives me gas."

Teddy leaned forward and peered over his glasses, "When I said things were slow, I meant legally pronounced dead. Please give me something interesting here. How was Jim?"

"Jim was . . . a gentleman. He already had my usual ordered by the time I got there, and I found out he's a music lover."

"Knew it. Hey, you oughta make him a mix tape. " Teddy said, handing her a bottle of spirit gum.

"A mix tape?" Morna looked away from Teddy and back to the mirror, applying the solution to her nose where part of the firework was peeling.

"Yeah, it's a romantic gesture kind of thing. Make a mix of songs you both like, he'll listen and love it while thinking about you. Total magic charm."

"Witchcraft, huh? I like the way you think. I never really had much luck with anything past a Victrola, though, and I'm still trying to figure out compact discs. I am curious to listen to these Talking Heads I've heard so much about."

"Of course you are," Teddy snickered, "And it's cool, I can help you with the tape. I just hope Jim has a tape player."

"I suppose, if he doesn't, I could just invite him to my house."

"You have a tape deck at your house?"

"No, but if I've already got him there, I don't really need the tape, do I?" Morna side-eyed Teddy with a subtle grin.

"Morna Ballif! You scandal!"

With all due theatricality, she retrieved a fake dismembered hand and gently bonked Teddy on the head with it, "Oh, get your mind out of the gutter, boy. I meant we would likely take in a spooky movie on the television and popcorn."

Teddy rolled his eyes, "Speaking of, I think you tracked some popcorn from the food court on your wheel. Want me to get it?"

"That's okay, you've been *so* overworked today, and I need the exercise."

Teddy smirked and shook his head as Morna carefully lowered herself to the floor. From a pouch hanging on the front of her transport, she pulled out a napkin and used it to peel the straggler off. The strands of sinewy butter and oil clinging to the rubber reminded her of that funny little nightmare man movie she'd seen recently. And speaking of nightmare men, two obnoxiously posh and polished white Oxfords appeared on the floor before her, followed by the clearing of a throat that needed no clearing.

"Morna Ballif. Let's chat," said an annoying voice attached to the aforementioned obnoxious Oxfords.

Morna knew those shoes, that annoying voice, and the ugly individual to which they both belonged; a cold, corporate monster of a lesser Frankenstein, "Ryan Glade. Let's not."

Teddy sighed a very audible, unwelcoming sigh, then quickly moved to help Morna back to her feet, but she managed and kindly motioned for him to stand by. At the same time, a man and his two kids entered the store and perused, keeping Teddy preoccupied. Once upright, Morna looked Glade in the eye and gave him an insincere smile, which likely didn't land effectively due to the clown makeup. Glade, out of character, smiled back and went to say something, but Morna, fighting stiffness in her legs, moved behind the counter and shuffled some items around. Glade followed with pest-like determination.

"Happy Independence Day, Morna," Glade said through a grin that could almost certainly eat shit.

"And may the Fourth be with you," Morna muttered.

"No, no. I said *Independence*. I know your ears aren't what they used to be."

"Did you just come here for semantics or can I interest you in some spooky sparklers?"

"Nothing semantic about it. Today is Independence Day for both of us, because sometime tonight, a paper will be signed that means I'm finally free of you."

Teddy, who had just pulled a mask down for one of the kids, perked up at this comment and peered over at Glade as Morna finally locked eyes with the man, furrowing her brow, which cracked her face paint in the process.

"Is this some sort of a joke, Ryan?"

"I'm not the one dressed like a clown," Glade said, trying unsuccessfully to shake a piece of popcorn off his shoe.

"I beg to differ."

"Cute, Morna. But it's nearly over, and not even your little quips can bring me down today." Glade then leaned on the counter, making sure to tower over her. Teddy noticed this total eclipse of a doofus but could not step away from the two boys, who both wanted to try what seemed like every mask the Boo-doir had to offer. Still, he listened as Glade continued with malicious merriment, "I've put up with you for six and a half years. Before that, Gina's father put up with you for twice that long somehow. I don't know how he did it. I don't know why he liked you. Three weeks in and I was already so sick of your year-round spookshow bullshit, partly because you haven't turned a substantial profit here since 1974. If you'd just start charging an entrance fee for that attraction—"

"I'll never charge for the haunted house. If you would take a chance and go through it, you might finally see some charm in being one of us Autumn People," Morna asserted.

"Or you could shit your pants, which would be my personal preference," Teddy added.

Glade shook the comments off and resumed, "*And* because I couldn't stand the thought of another Halloween with you in your element, let alone several more years, and because I'm almost sure you'll somehow outlive me and I don't want another generation putting up with you, I worked out a deal to shut . . . you . . . down."

"You can't. This space is still in Gina's name."

"Not after tonight. You see, I've spent the last year having a big ol' change of heart, and I've convinced my wife that I finally see what her father saw in you and this place and that I'd love to be a part of it. Best part is it really worked and even better than I could have prayed for. I thought she'd just offer me a partnership, but she's signing the whole space over to me."

Teddy could hold back no longer. Pointing at Glade with a zombie mask in hand, he shouted, "You piece-of-shit-wastoid!"

The once pending patrons dispersed, sent off with a smug little wave *goodbye* from Glade. Teddy stormed over to the desk beside Morna, fuming, but she placed a hand on his shoulder.

"Teddy, mind your language when there are people in the store. And Ryan Glade, you should be ashamed of yourself."

Glade raised his eyebrows in feigned confusion, "Oh? For what?"

"For being a malformed, conniving, self-centered, soul-curdled son-of-a-bitch."

Just for a moment, Glade and Teddy both looked at Morna in such silence that their blinking was the loudest sound in the room.

"Right, well," Glade smarmed, "like I said, you can't bring me down today."

"Maybe not. But Gina can," Morna said with a smirk, pointing beyond Glade. The victorious gesture was accentuated by her frilly sleeve.

He spun on his heels, his Oxfords squealing on the tile below like a record scratching before taking in the sight of Gina Glade, his wife and, by all means, his antithetical partner. She donned a bright blue sports jacket and matching red, white, and blue plaid sweater and skirt, complete with a satin white bow which fluttered as she approached with what seemed to be a matter of some urgency.

"Hi, honey!" she called, still closing the distance.

Glade turned his head in profile, eyes alternating between Morna and Teddy, "Say anything to my wife about our business here, and believe me, I'll have the legal means to make things even harder on you."

Morna wasn't outwardly fazed, but she did glance at Teddy with a look that indicated they might not want to push their luck. Gina approached, hugged Glade, and offered a sincere smile over his shoulder.

"Hello, Miss Ballif! I feel like I haven't seen you in ages."

"Morna's pretty busy today with the sale, unfortunately," Glade ushered Gina—with slight reluctance from her—further from the front counter, "Not that I'm not happy to see you, but why the surprise visit?"

"You're the one who surprised me. I told you last night I'd be here to visit my friend Robin, but she mentioned you were around. Is everything okay?"

"Peachy, yeah, just fine. I just . . . can't stay away from the—" Glade practically vomited the word "Boo-doir."

Gina's eyes lit up, "I can't begin to tell you how happy that makes me. Papa would be glad to know you've got such big plans to keep it going."

"Absolutely." Glade scooted Gina a little further away, "So, how are you?"

"I'm okay, but I heard some really sad news that a young man was just killed . . ."

"Oh?" Glade feigned interest but peered back at Morna, who appeared invested in the news.

"Mhm, these darn fireworks! I know folks love them, but they're so dangerous. I guess someone set off a big one, and it flew right into this poor boy's chest. The impact stopped his heart before it blew up."

"Wow. Well, it's great we ran into each other, but I probably should g—"

"Let me show Miss Gina here my costume you were complimenting earlier," Morna said, having snuck up behind the couple.

Gina clapped her hands excitedly, "Oh my gosh, yes!"

"Please, no," Glade said, possibly pleading to a higher power.

The higher power made no comment, so Morna positioned herself uncomfortably close to Glade and handed a giant gag lighter to Gina, who looked on like a curious child at Christmas, unlike Teddy, who now awaited the coming chaos like a gremlin.

"Gina, will you be so kind as to light my nose?"

"Oh, I don't know . . . I was just telling Ryan—"

"It's harmless, I promise."

"Okay then, " Gina grimaced.

Glade had no way of knowing what would happen but braced himself anyway as Gina ignited the long fuse. The incendiary string sizzled its way into Morna's cylindrical schnozz, yet nothing happened. Gina looked puzzled while Glade unclenched. Then, "AH-BOO!" Morna had sneezed a marvelously theatrical sneeze, accompanied by a bountiful blast of green confetti, which now resided almost completely on Glade, giving him the appearance of an angry, ugly cookie.

Gina burst into laughter, teasingly brushing some of the confetti off, "I love it! Isn't that so cute, honey?"

"Yep. Cute." Glade took over removal duty.

Morna offered a modest bow, "Thank you, thank you. It was so nice to see you again, Gina. Please stop by any time and soon."

"Count on it. I'm so sorry it's been so long. It just seems like Ryan always has something come up that keeps us from visiting. I've missed you and this place so much."

"I've missed you, too," Morna said as she and Gina hugged, "But don't worry. I'm not going anywhere."

Glade snapped a glare at Morna, who continued, "In the meantime, why don't you take a couple of sparklers and some candy for the road?" She handed them to Gina, who graciously accepted. "By the way, do you happen to know the name of that young man who was killed?"

"Oh, Dominick, I think? I can't remember the last name. Why?"

"Just curious, thank you. I hope you have a good Fourth of July."

Practically sweeping Gina away, Glade gave his best bad acting, "Hope you have a good one, too, Morna! Can't wait to talk with you tonight about all our plans!"

The unlikely couple departed as Morna scooted back into the store, rejoining Teddy behind the counter. The two sat in contemplation for a while, affording Morna an opportunity to affix a new fuse to her nose, until Teddy finally broke the tension.

"My bad. I shouldn't have said today was slow."

"That's okay. I'll just take it out of your wages for the week."

"Fair enough. So, what are we going to do about Glade? I mean, he can't actually shut the place down, right?"

"He can't. This place is too important. As for what we're going to do, you just leave that to me. I've got a lot to do between now and tonight, but it will work out."

"I hope so."

"I know so." Morna frowned at him, the clown paint exaggerating her expression, before she put her fingers to the corners of her mouth to form the frown into a smile. "Not every horror story has a bad ending."

Morna squeezed Teddy's shoulder in assurance, then tottered her way into the haunted house. During the hours of operation, Teddy was usually the one to look after it, setting up props, fixing the animatronics, and occasionally acting as a guide that would make William Castle proud. Despite Morna's devotion to the Boo-doir proper, she only entered the haunt on rare occasions and never mentioned why. Teddy had worked there for three years, but it wasn't until this day that he finally recognized a pattern: death. He was almost certain that Morna would go in shortly after she'd learned of someone dying. A little over a month ago, it was after Dr. West had succumbed to old age. In April, it was that new high school art teacher, Mrs. Chenus, who was killed in a head-on collision. Before that, a construction worker, the head of the local paper, and more. Teddy thought he might as well ask Morna about it, especially if the Boo-doir was getting shut down. Or maybe he could follow her in there this time and see what she does. Or maybe—

"Theodore!" The friendly voice was that of one Shannon Walker who had just entered the store with her best friend, Lily Young.

"Happy Haunted Fridge Night. How are you two?" Teddy asked.

"Stressed, broke, tired, constantly feel like I'm gonna ralph, but I graduated at least. You?

"Hoping I can say the same next year. Well, mostly the graduation part."

"For sure, but in the meantime, we should celebrate."

"Celebrate?"

Lily stepped back to the counter, now wearing a werewolf mask, "We're moving to Los Angeles in a couple weeks."

Shannon clarified, choosing a piece of chocolate from the bowl, "Going to try to make movies."

"We'll probably be someone's coffee slaves first." Lily rolled her eyes.

"I'll miss seeing you two around. Send me something cool or edible or both and send me Elvira or Stephen McHattie."

"We'll try our best. So, for tonight, we were thinking . . . you've got keys to this place, right?"

Lily removed the mask, her glasses fogged over, "Shan wants us to spend the night in the Boo-doir. Specifically the haunted house."

Shannon shot Lily a look, "Nice tact and your do's dented."

Teddy sighed, "Bogus timing. Major Dickweed might shut down the store this same night."

"Oh shit." Shannon said soberly, "Morna's going to do something about it, right?"

"It kinda hinges on some meeting tonight, so I don't know."

"Can *we* do something about it?"

"I wish," Teddy lamented. "I don't know what I'd do without this place."

"Me either."

"Me too." Lily unmussed her hair then mused, "Is there any harm in us trying this since it might shut down anyway? Go out with a spooky bang?"

"Yeah, how about it, Teddy?" Shan asked, hopeful eyebrows raised.

Teddy thought of Morna. She'd kept composed, but he knew she was worried and her vague 'plan' wasn't terribly reassuring.

"Meet me back here a few minutes before closing," Teddy relented, "but first, you've got to wait and see Morna's nose."

As the festivities outside of the mall grew to a muted cacophony, Sherwood itself had begun to draw its blinds for the night as a gentle darkness swaddled each neon light leading back to the final bewitching beacon that was Ballif's Boo-doir. Morna, who had returned and indeed obliged Shannon and Lily with an explosive sneeze, appeared to be in better spirits, yet indicated nothing further of her ideas to foil the Glade's villainy. The remaining hours had gone by without much fuss and without much more in the way of business. Teddy swept up bits of green confetti, stray popcorn, and the general dirt of the day, and all the while devising a plan to stow himself and his friends inside the haunt for their sendoff spooktacular. His plan was bold, risky, with no holds barred: He would ask Morna for permission.

As she finished with the register, Teddy saw a window to inquire, but was immediately distracted by the ringing of the store's phone. Morna answered, but her once improved spirits turned to sickly poltergeists. Whoever was on the line affected her entire posture and the clown again donned a frown. Teddy observed the one-sided conversation until Morna gave the final word.

"Have it your way, Ryan. I'll see you on the other side." Morna wasn't one to slam a phone down, but she did let gravity have its way with the receiver as it thrashed back into the cradle. "Teddy, I have a very big favour to ask of you."

"Yes I'll help you hide Glade's body."

This gave her a much-needed chuckle, "In time. For now, this might sound a little odd, but would you mind awfully staying here after closing?"

Teddy's eyes widened, "Yeah, sure. Totally."

"Oh, good, I was afraid you might have plans. I've been left with no choice but to go and discuss the potential shutting down of the Boo-doir. Summoned by the dork lord, himself."

Teddy smirked, emitting amused air through his nose, "Good one, Morna. I have two questions: One, why exactly do you need me to stay?"

"I don't trust Ryan not to try something drastic tonight and if I can't be here to watch over things, I need someone I *can* trust. What's your second question?"

"Can I invite my friends? Lily and Shannon?"

"I think that would be all right. Just no hard drugs, no testing the spirit board, and most importantly, no going into the haunted house. There was an issue with it earlier, and I need to call someone to look at it. It's not safe right now, understand?"

"Understood."

"Good, and thank you . . . I'll let security know you'll be here. I'll need to come back at some point be . . . well, at some point. But the sooner I go, the sooner these matters can be settled. Wish me luck."

"You got it. Happy Birthday."

Morna smiled, this time only with her eyes. Teddy noticed she was not bothered enough to remove her makeup for her forthcoming meeting. Instead, she simply added a black and white sweater to her ensemble and via her trusty Trick-Or-Treat mobile, vanished from the store. Lily and Shannon, who had been waiting just outside, peered in cartoonishly from either side of the door. Teddy gave them an all-clear thumbs-up and, though he looked forward to the night to come, he also knew he wouldn't be able to keep his friends out of the haunted house.

~

The entrance to the haunt was a decrepit oak door which once belonged to the Morningside funeral home, adorned with a slightly paraphrased notice: *Abandon all courage, ye who enter here*. The door creaked open heavily, and Teddy led the way, followed closely and curiously by Shannon and Lily. At first, the three merged with the deepening shadows until the door closed eerily behind them, cutting out all light.

"Not to kill the vibe, but thanks for letting us come in here," Shannon whispered.

"Don't mention it," Teddy whispered back. "Especially not to Morna."

A pre-recorded scream shattered the silence and brought with it the full-tilt activation of the attraction: Theatrical lights flooded the hallway with a deep blue and plum concoction alongside flickering faux candles on the walls. Meanwhile, sounds like chains rattling, wind howling, and other monstrous moaning supplemented the score from *The Fog*, which rumbled through the floor. A pneumatic wolfman pounced toward the three and, though secured behind a pane of glass, he still earned an excited yelp from both Shannon and Lily as well as a salute from Teddy.

Further along, was a plethora of paintings on the walls with eyes that seemed to follow them. Once they arrived at the last painting on the left, it dropped, revealing a zombified dummy quivering and cackling behind it.

"Hey, Lily? Remind you of anyone? Your ex, maybe?" Shannon teased.

"Nah, this guy at least knew when to drop dead."

The trio took a left at the end of the hall, where they then squeezed through body bags hanging from the ceiling, one of which called for help. Past this was a small corridor of clowns, then another small hall with mirrors for walls, leading to glow-in-the-dark writing stating *DEAD END* above an upright casket. As they approached, Lily scowled into the nearest mirror where her face now odd and misshapen, "So Teddy, have you seen what Morna was so worried about yet?"

"No, I've been looking out, but everything seems normal. It's just weird."

"Totally weird, too, that she didn't tell you what the problem was. Not like you haven't helped fix broken things in here before, right?" Shannon asked.

"Well, to be honest, I don't think the problem is that something is broken."

The three moved closer to the casket and Lily inquired further, "What, like, something to do with that Glade dude trying to shut the place down?"

"He's definitely an issue with a lot of issues, but no."

Teddy reached for the handle to the upright casket. The lid flew open, disturbingly divulging the maligned visage of a woman in her mid-30s, clothes tattered, glasses cracked, and auburn hair tangled. Lodged in her pale face were shards of glass among bruises, abrasions, and blood.

Shannon and Lily screamed.

The woman screamed.

They all screamed.

The casket door slammed shut, leaving the trio to stare blankly ahead for a moment, before conferring through wide-eyed contact what they had just witnessed.

"Was that . . . a new addition?"

"Nope . . ."

Teddy motioned for his friends to stay back and although neither of them did, he cautiously reached for the handle to the door once more. No surprise this time as he revealed the centerpiece of the haunted house: the dining room. It was decked out with enough gothic furnishings, bones, and cobwebs that The Addams Family would feel welcome there. In the middle was a round, ornate table affixed to a turntable, slowly spinning as a strobe light chandelier shone down onto it. Seated there were six skeletons in comical attire, articulating with each rotation of the table. Hiding among them was the mysterious, ghastly woman from before. Teddy entered the room with mustered confidence, backed up by Shannon and Lily who were both nervously amused.

Teddy called out, "Hey, who are you?"

The woman poked her head up slightly, though partially obscured by the revolving skeletons, "Who are *you*? And where's Morna?"

"I'm Teddy. I work for Morna and Morna is out on business right now. Happy National Name Yourself Day."

"Name Yourself Day? I don't think that's real."

"It might be some day. So what *is* your name?"

"Oh, I'm Stella. Stella Chenus."

"Stella Chenus? As in, that art teacher?" asked Lily.

"Who was killed in the car crash?" added Shannon.

Teddy stepped closer to the table. "Right, no offense, but isn't Stella Chenus dead?"

The table's rotation brought the woman back around to the trio. Upon realizing her hiding spot was compromised, she stepped off, "It is a little harsh when you say it that way, but yes. As a matter of fact, I am, um . . . dead. I thought maybe Morna would have mentioned me before."

"I love Morna, but apparently she doesn't tell me shit." Stella grimaced. "I'm sorry."

Shannon, who for some time now had been staring at Stella's wounds, had to ask, "Does that hurt?"

Stella covered her face ineffectively. "No, but I suppose I look a fright, don't I?"

"Yeah, but it's cool. You look cool," Lily assured.

"Oh." Stella lowered her hands and smiled for the first time. "Cool!"

"So, not that you don't perfectly fit in with the place," Teddy inquired, "But really, why are you here?"

"Oh boy . . . loaded question," Stella sat down at the table only to remember that it moves, then awkwardly got back to her feet, and cleared her throat, "Well, um, you see, this place is like . . . a toll bridge to, I suppose you could say, the other side of the veil? Most like us have to wait until Halloween to cross, but since Morna has made it Halloween forever here, that bridge is always open. We can come and go as we need to see our loved ones, finish unfinished business, check on our cats, et cetera."

"Bitchin'," Shannon declared.

"Dude," Lily smacked Teddy's arm, "Why didn't you tell us you worked at a portal to the spirit realm?"

"I mean, retail *is* Hell," Teddy said half-seriously, "So, Stella? Or do I call you Mrs. Chenus?"

"Oh, you can call me . . . gosh darn it! Now I have that Blondie song in my head. Anyway, sorry . . . Stella is fine. I don't think you were one of my students, so no reason for the formality."

"Well, Gosh Darn It Now I Have That Blondie Song In My Head, it's been nice to meet you and now I actually wish I could have taken one of your classes. That said, this place is in some pretty big trouble, so do you have any idea of what else is bothering Morna, specifically about the haunted house or this supernatural toll bridge thing?"

Stella's grimace returned. "Yes, which is why I'm worried she isn't back yet. We have a new one crossing over tonight and she asked me to meet them when they arrive, but I don't know how to handle the rest."

"Handle the rest of what? Who's arriving?"

"Oh, um . . . him."

Stella pointed just behind the trio, causing them to turn and see the newest spectre to Sherwood Mall: a young man who had, embedded in his chest and leather jacket, a large, unexploded firework.

"Dominick?" Teddy asked with eyebrows raised.

"Yup." Dominick gave a little wave. "Thanks for not screaming at me and stuff."

At that, the attraction where boisterous noises and lavish light had once been, was now absorbed into an abyss.

"Wow, nice timing, Teddy." Shannon said, her voice echoing slightly in the void.

"Agreed, but I didn't do that."

"Are we in the ghost portal thing now?" Lily asked.

"Um, no. This isn't how it works." Stella said.

"I think the power just went out, is all." Teddy said as he tried to move closer to the casket door. "Everyone be quiet a sec. I think I hear something."

He gently pried the door open and listened closely. Though distant and muffled, there came an uncannily familiar sound. It was an unset rhythm of soft crackling. It was a faint pattern of crunchy squeaking. It was—

"Popcorn," Teddy whispered.

"Is it Morna?" Stella asked.

"No, it's not her wheels, but someone totally stepped in popcorn and they're totally right out there."

Dominick whispered, "I thought being dead was weird, but here we are listening to ominous popcorn noises."

"Shit, we can't risk more trouble for the Boo-doir. If anyone sees these . . . undead people. " Teddy called out with a louder whisper in the direction he hoped Stella was in, "What was it Morna needed to help you handle for Dominick?"

"Morna's created a sort of canvas of conduits here. Certain props and decorations in this haunted house are sort of possessed by those of us who have passed on. They give us a place to anchor our energy for crossing and a lot of other sciencey things I don't entirely understand, but that's what Morna needed to bring here tonight: another conduit so that Dominick could possess it. Oh! Which he has to do by midnight."

A dull crash made itself known a short way from the group, reverting them to silence until Stella finally whispered again, "I'm sorry, Morna really is so much better at explaining it."

Teddy managed his way toward the table where Stella was. "No, thanks, I think I get it. I just have no idea when Morna will be back."

Shannon whispered blindly, "And I'm guessing we can't just grab something off the shelf for Dom to possess?"

"No, Morna's always made it clear that our conduits have to be something personal to us."

Dominick chimed, "You guys could go snag my dad's GTO. That would be pretty rad."

"I don't think we have time for a joy ride," Lily advised.

"Well, I think I've had enough of being left in the dark for one day. It's probably a stupid move for a horror fan, but I'm going out there," Teddy said, adjusting his baseball cap for maximum bravery.

"It's totally stupid," Shannon began.

"Which is why we're coming with you," Lily finished.

Teddy spoke dryly, "Your funerals."

The trio traced their way back through the haunt, the increasing commotion in the main store thankfully drowning out most of their stumbling. As they approached the entrance, a foul smell singed their nostrils. Teddy took a deep breath, braced himself, and flung the old oak door open, which generously creaked in the process, revealing none other than the creature himself, Ryan Glade, tampering in the store's breaker box which sparked slightly as he spun on his heels in surprise.

"Jesus!" Glade shrieked, "What the hell are you doing here? Don't you mall maggots have anything better to do?"

"Just working the night shift, which reminds me, I didn't see your name on the schedule, so what the hell are *you* doing here?" Teddy asked, nodding to Glade's various tools, gloved hands, and generally sketchy appearance.

Glade appeared to flip through his mental Rolodex for an appropriate excuse but sighed, "No use beating around the bush . . . Turns out the place can't be mine if Morna doesn't sign, and guess who didn't want to sign? I'm moving onto Plan B."

"Can't believe I'm saying this, but sabotage seems low, even for you."

"Sabotage? No, no, no. I'm just doing my due diligence by pointing out all the problems this place has." Glade took a couple steps forward as the popcorn stuck in his obnoxious Oxford continued to disgrace the floor with its unbuttered friction. Teddy and company watched as Glade pointed out said problems around the store, "Broken fire extinguisher, untraceable odor—likely mold, exposed wiring, and that death-trap of a spookhouse. So many safety violations."

"*You're* a safety violation," Shannon sneered.

"You won't get away with this," Teddy said.

"What do you plan to do about it, exactly? It's just your word against mine. And last time I checked, I was an outstanding member of this town. You're just some shit-kicking Satanic punks."

Just then, Stella appeared between the trio and Glade, the latter tilting his head in confusion as he was stared down by the artistic apparition.

"Firstly, these are good kids and you should set a better example. Secondly, punk is cool and you clearly don't understand Satanism. Thirdly . . ." She smirked, "You wanna see some *real* punk-ass Satanic shit?"

On cue, a cold wind blustered through the store, rattling everything from the ceiling to the floor, enough to wake the dead. Both doors to the haunted house flew open and from them came dozens upon dozens whose post-mortal coils had brought them to defend the Boodoir. The spirits, including Dominick, supported Teddy and his friends whilst they surrounded Glade on three sides. Stella gave Teddy a wink, who shared looks of awe with Shannon and Lily.

Glade breathed heavier, eyes squinted, "You . . . You're all dead."

"Is that a threat or an observation?" Lily asked.

"What's the matter, Glade? Wanna add an exceeded occupancy violation to your list of problems?" Teddy teased.

Glade's nerves betrayed him. His feet moved him slowly away from the semi-circle of spirits, but he willed his arms in a passive gesture, "Teddy Kratky . . . let's talk."

"Ryan Glade . . . let's not."

Glade shrugged, then rabidly lunged toward Teddy, only to be intercepted by Dominick. Glade strangely came to a halt and stranger still, Dominick had disappeared. The store fell silent for a moment until Stella spoke.

"Oh, boy . . . "

Glade turned away from the wall and faced the others, but two things were now different about him. First, he now had a familiar firework lodged in his chest. Second, he spoke with a similarly familiar voice, "Uh, dudes?"

Stella stepped forward, "Dominick, you need to get out of there! A living person can't be your conduit. I don't give hall passes for possession!"

In a blur, Dominick's spirit evacuated the vessel. As he looked to the crowd of his cohorts, he noticed them looking back with more concern than before. Teddy saw Dominick's confusion and pointed to Glade. The firework had not reverted back but, instead, remained in Glade's chest.

Dominick winced and stepped away, "Sorry, dude, I guess that's yours now."

Glade, with blood starting to seep from his mouth and new combustible ligament, stumbled back against the wall, landing precisely against the exposed breaker box and received more shocking news. He managed to pull himself away, but by then, the volts had taken their toll, igniting the firework's fuse like so much insult to injury. With quick thinking, Teddy ran to the coffin at the center of the store and kicked open the lid, motioning to it thereafter. Shannon and Lily nodded to Teddy, then to each other, then grabbed Glade by his arms and launched him, with the aid of the other spirits, into the coffin. Teddy kicked the lid shut and obtained distance with the others. All in the store observed as the coffin transitioned from apropos set-piece to its original intended purpose where a percussive *POP!* agitated the container after which only came bellows of faint smoke and deathly silence.

Teddy approached the coffin and with relief, muttered, "Ah-boo."

A frail but friendly hand landed on his shoulder.

"Happy Halloween," Morna said.

"Happy Halloween," Teddy repeated, "You kinda missed all the excitement, but I'm glad you're here."

"I'm glad I'm here, too. Looks like you had quite the happening."

Teddy nodded, "Is everything going to be okay?"

"I don't see why not. The lawyers sided with me and, even if they didn't, Glade's got more problems now than a lawyer can handle. We can make repairs easy enough and handle whatever else wicked this way comes. For now," Morna tossed Stella a pair of fuzzy dice from Dominick's father's GTO, "That boy only has a few more minutes. See that he hops into this conduit. We'll find a place for it later. The rest of you can go back now and thank you all for your help."

And so, all the spirits, including Stella and Dominick, returned to the haunted house, leaving only Shannon, Lily, Teddy, Morna, and Glade's barbequed bits in the main store.

Morna continued, "And thank *you* three, specifically. I didn't intend to put you in this situation tonight, but I'm beyond grateful that you were here. Lily and Shannon, if you need anything at all, consider it done. And Teddy, I expect you to go and live a life of your own, but as long as Sherwood Mall stands, so does the Boo-doir, and I'm sure it would go to good hands if you ever want it."

"What about Gina?" Teddy asked.

"She unfortunately saw the true side of her husband tonight at the meeting with the lawyer, but after Ryan stormed out, she and I had a long talk. I guess what Ryan had said earlier that day did make me realize I'm not going to *actually* be around forever, despite what he may have thought, so in the event that something should happen to me, Gina and I agreed with the lawyers present that you're my official successor."

"That's the nicest thing anyone's ever done for me, but nothing is going to happen to you. Sherwood will always be here, which means the Boo-doir will always be here, which means it will always be Halloween, and there's no Halloween without you."

Lily rolled her eyes and Shannon pretended to gag.

Morna lost control of only a single happy tear, then shook her head, "You've never been a brown-noser before, Teddy. Don't start now. If you want another raise, you know you can just ask."

"Cool. Can I have a raise?"

~

With the remaining 4th of July weekend, Teddy did, indeed, receive his raise. The store closed that Saturday for clean-up and repairs, and Ryan Glade's remains were cremated; a modest funeral held as a part of a same-day service holiday sale. They would later be brought by in a jack-o'-lantern stylized urn by Gina, an act of bittersweet spite, stating that he would have loved his final resting place to be the store. There would, however, be several instances of visitors claiming they could hear screams of 'Nooo!' coming from the funerary receptacle. By that Sunday morning, the store was open again, and the news of Glade's demise brought waves of new patrons. Shannon and Lily were not among the regulars, however, as they were busy packing their bags and looking at their two fresh tickets to Los Angeles—courtesy of Morna—where they planned to make their own debut horror film, *Ballif's Boo-doir*. Morna, alongside several more coffee dates, movie nights, and mix tapes with Jim, delighted in the festivities, foot traffic, and freedom she'd not experienced in years and, though her exploding firework clown nose might have been considered in some amount of poor taste, she nevertheless continued to entertain, sneeze confetti on customers, and wish all a Happy Halloween.

9

BLEED FOR ME
G.D. Bowlin

"THE MALL IS GONNA LIKE, um, close in . . . fifteen minutes? Yeah, fifteen. Happy Fourth of July or whatever."

The crackling voice blared over the speakers in Send-A-Smile, and Cassie rolled her eyes behind the register. She dropped her elbows onto the counter, resting her chin on her upturned palms, and snapped the pink gum between her teeth.

"Oh, and uh, the Fireworks Extrava—whu?—Extravaganza will kick off in Corbett Field, just behind the mall, at dusk."

"Inspiring," she said to the silent store.

She didn't find much to celebrate on July Fourth, and she certainly didn't care about the fireworks display in town that many seemed to be closing up shop early to observe. Of course, with her mom working a double shift, she had nothing to come home to but creepy, drunken "stepdad" Randy.

As much as she hated working at Send-A-Smile, it was better than being at the trailer, so she was happy to volunteer to stay after on a holiday to stock shelves and take inventory. She could use the extra money as well since she didn't even get to keep all her cash. Her mom took half and called it rent while she spent it on boxed wine.

Cassie had to remind herself things would get better. At the rate she was saving, she'd have enough to move out by the time she graduated high school. Every bit of overtime she could get would help with that, too.

She looked out the glass wall behind the cash register and watched as the last of the shoppers shuffled lazily out to the parking lot. Workers closed the metal shutters and locked up their stores, their movements automatic and jerky. *Automatons*. She never dreamed she'd be like them, but there she was, shilling greeting cards and Hummel figurines.

Her boyfriend Ty would have called them all "Corporate wage slaves."

He had tons of little terms like that, a vocabulary picked up from punk records and anti-establishment zines. His big talk made her laugh, but, more importantly, it inspired her. Empowered her. She'd never known anyone like him. She'd met him out in the parking lot after work one night, sitting on the curb and smoking a cigarette. He'd been handing out anti-Reagan leaflets outside the mall and just sat down next to her, like she'd invited him.

"Do you want to change the world?" That was the first thing he ever said to her.

Who says things like that? she'd thought. She'd said yes, traded him a Marlboro Red for a leaflet, and they'd been inseparable ever since. He didn't go to her school, so he hadn't heard the rumors about her, most of which weren't even true. Illicit tales about what she'd done with other boys. When she finally confessed to him some of the true ones, he said he didn't care. He didn't believe in shame. He loved her the way she was.

She was thinking about Ty's blue eyes, totally spacing out, when she suddenly felt she was being watched. She scanned the mall through the glass. Nothing but white tile flooring, white brick walls. A big, empty void.

Then she saw him. A man standing in front of Tandemonium. He definitely hadn't been using the tanning beds there. He was pale white, balding and thin. Tall, well over six feet, and wearing a navy blue suit. He was impeccably dressed, absolutely still, and staring directly at her with deep eyes set into a gaunt face. They looked impossibly dark. Black, even.

Cassie wracked her brain, trying to ID the creep. He wasn't a regular customer of the store. She didn't recognize him as one of the mall's daily hangers-on, certainly not one of the teenage mall rats or elderly folks who speed-walked around in their neon tracksuits.

The man didn't move. Didn't blink. He just . . . watched.

Those deep, dark eyes made a strange, sick feeling rise up in Cassie. A tightening in her chest, like she felt when she found Randy looking at her whenever she bent over around the trailer. She shuddered and turned away.

Then the lights in the mall shut off, the massive overhead panels going black one by one until only the pink and blue hues of the mall's garish neon accent lights remained, bathing everything in an eerie purple glow. She peered through the glass, but the man was now gone. Vanished into the shadows.

Suddenly, a hand gripped her shoulder tightly and pulled. She staggered backward and whirled around, heart pounding, half-expecting to find the man somehow standing behind her, his horrible stare penetrating her.

It was only Kathleen. As always, a giant, toothy grin was plastered on her face. The owner had to look perfect. She had teeth sculpted by orthodontia, proof that her New Age, hippy affectations—her braided hair and crystal necklaces—were all adopted. Subtle crow's feet and laugh lines betrayed the fact that she'd been born in the post-war suburbs, just in time to really, like, *be* there for the Summer of Love, man. Cassie forced herself to not gag at the thought. Hippies creeped her out.

"Are you sure you're okay with working tonight? I bet your family's gonna be grilling out for America and watching those fireworks, just missing the heck out of you," Kathleen chirped.

Not likely. "No, they have, uh, other plans. They had to go out of town. It's just me and the VCR tonight," Cassie lied. There was no reason to let anyone know anything more about her home life than they needed to.

"Aw! All alone on the Fourth of July? That's so sad, Cass,"

Kathleen reached out and stroked Cassie's arm. Long nails ran along her goose-pimpled flesh, and Cassie inadvertently pulled away.

"Well, *Kath*, a girl needs her alone time too, right?"

There was something unsettling about Kathleen. Nothing as outwardly menacing as the creep who had just been watching her, although he wasn't so different from a million other guys throughout Cassie's life, just more obvious about it. No, the issue with Kathleen, Cassie had decided after months of working for her, was that she seemed . . . empty. So cloyingly positive that she couldn't be real.

Cassie chose to ignore it until she could find a better job. Preferably something that didn't involve selling bergamot-scented candles.

"You can always come home with me," Kathleen said. "My chosen family would be more than happy to have you over for a tofu burger and a Tab. We can push this inventory work to next week."

An image of a bunch of dreadlocked white people sitting at a massive dinner table flashed in Cassie's mind. Slowly, they all turned toward her, Kathleen's rictus grin plastered on their faces. Incense and sage smoke filled the air. Crystals stood about on blood-stained altars. They would sacrifice her to the God of Hemp.

"No, it's okay, I really want to get that overtime money for next week's check. I don't mind being alone, anyway."

"You are such a free spirit. I love it. Well, my home phone number is taped there by the phone. You call me if you want, and I'll come pick you up and bring you home with me if you change your mind. We'd love to have you in our family for any holiday."

"Cool . . . thanks."

Kathleen placed her palms together, gave a small bow, and walked out of the store, woven sandals flapping on the tile floor of the mall beyond.

Cassie took a deep breath and closed her eyes, trying to shake off the unsettling feeling that Kathleen was trying way, *way* too hard to get her to meet her family. It wasn't the first time she'd extended an invitation like that. Cassie doubted there were actually bloody altars, but who knew what was going on behind the doors of whatever weird commune the aging hippie lady lived in? Some sick New Age cult, probably. People in tie-dyed shorts flagellating themselves in front of a big screen TV playing old Woodstock footage.

Cassie reached into her purse and rummaged through the pile of wrappers and keys and cheap lipsticks she'd shoplifted from Judy's. She came up with two items, both of them from Ty: One, a necklace made of a strand of ball chain. Two items hung from it. The first was a guitar pick that Ty claimed he had caught in the crowd of a Dead Kennedy's show when East Bay Ray had thrown it from the stage. The other was a double-sided razor blade. The steel edges shown in the yellow overhead light of the store. Careful not to cut herself with it, she turned it over in her hand and read the words Ty had written in red sharpie: "Bleed for Me." He had blunted the blade, for her safety he'd said, but it was still capable of leaving a cut. She liked it that way. Kathleen wouldn't allow her to wear it in the store, and it felt liberating as Cassie clasped the chain around her neck. The cool metal of the razor pressed flat against her chest.

The other item was a mixtape he'd created just for her. A list of bands that he had introduced Cassie to. Most of them were politically charged, like the Dead Kennedys. They brought to frantic, urgent life a sea of new ideas that Cassie had never been exposed to. The tape meant a lot to her. The fact that Ty had made it just for her was, of course, a big deal, but so were all of the bands, young men and women who had been able to articulate ideas that she had felt for so long but hadn't been able to identify in herself.

She slapped the cassette into the small boombox she kept under the counter for late-night work sessions. "Degenerated" by Reagan Youth blasted from the tinny speakers.

The music followed her as she danced through the store, bopping past the shelves full of clown dolls and greeting cards and fake flowers, her long, black, shaggy hair whipping around her head until she reached the back office. The rhythm left her as soon as she entered the room. There was something unsettling about the space. It was so sanitized. As empty of personality as she suspected Kathleen to be. Piles of accounting books, a filing cabinet that Kathleen kept locked at all times, and an odd painting in a gilded frame. A mandala pattern with a third eye in the center of it. Crudely painted, as if done by a child. Gazing into the third eye, a chill ran up Cassie's spine. *If there's a hell,* Cassie thought, *it's eternity locked in a room just like this one.*

She suddenly got the feeling that she was being watched again, and not by the third eye. The same sensation that had plagued her earlier when she'd caught the tall, bald man watching her. Cassie looked behind her into the dimly lit store. No one. Nothing.

She shook off the eerie feeling and grabbed a boxcutter from the desk drawer and a couple cartons of fresh stock. The word "FRAMES" was stamped on the side of each one. She carried them down to aisle three, one of only six aisles in the small store. Careful of the contents, she delicately set the boxes down, pulled the boxcutter from her back pocket, and slashed along the taped edges.

The frames inside were all the same. Green and gold, in a marble pattern, surrounding a stock image of a happy, blonde family all smiling with their arms around each other. It didn't look anything like her family. She wondered if she and Ty would ever have a family photo like this one. The idea left her hot and flushed, blushing.

If they did, it sure wouldn't be in a totally cheesy frame like this one, she thought.

The phone rang and she jumped, startled. The frame fell from her hands and shattered on the floor, the thin, patterned carpet not enough to save it.

"Dammit! What kinda dweeb calls the mall after closing?"

She hurried down the aisle toward the register and, for a moment, wondered if Kathleen knew she had broken the frame and was calling to scold her; that she had been somehow watching her this whole time.

Hands shaking a bit, Cassie picked up the phone. Before she could speak, she heard Ty's voice.

"How's my girl?"

God, she loved when he called her that. No hint of ownership in it, only dedication. She was his, and he was hers.

"Just got started. I'm listening to your tape, actually. Makes work not suck so bad."

"Those songs changed my life, Cass, I swear. Is Crazy Kathleen giving you a buncha bullshit?"

"Ugh, she's the worst. But no, she left me alone to put all this stuff up. Just a bunch of useless crap," Cassie said, twisting the phone cord around her finger.

"American capitalism at work," he said, his low, husky voice making her feel like he was lying there beside her in bed, whispering in her ear. "We live in a disgusting, throwaway culture, Cassie."

"So gross. I'd invite you over, but the mall closed early. Everybody went to see the fireworks or grill out or whatever. Ugh, gag me. Wanna . . ." she hesitated. As much as she wanted to see him, she didn't want to sound desperate, clingy. She'd seen that in her mother's approach to men. She hated it. "I dunno, wanna hang out later or whatever?"

"Down. See you soon," he said, then added, "Stay safe," and hung up.

A man of few words. She gently placed the phone down into its cradle. She cracked her knuckles and decided to take the night on with renewed vigor. The sooner she got Kathleen's crap done, the sooner she could be with Ty, driving around and smoking cloves and making fun of all the middle-class posers.

She got to work back in the frame aisle, bobbing her head along to the music. The boombox was now loudly playing "Hellnation" by the Dead Kennedys.

Until it wasn't.

The song cut out mid-chorus, and the little shop was filled with a sudden, uneasy silence. Cassie waited for the tape to click, telling her the side had been filled and it was time to turn it over. The click never came. She was filled with a sick feeling in the pit of her stomach, and she didn't know why. Tapes broke all the time. Maybe Ty had cut the song short by accident. She wrapped her arms around herself. Held herself tight.

Forcing herself to take one step, then another, she tentatively walked back to the checkout counter. Her boombox sat on top. The cassette deck was open. The tape was gone.

"Not cool, man . . ." Cassie murmured in the eerie quiet of the store.

Tap. Tap. Tap.

Footsteps. They were coming from the back aisle, deep into the store.

"Who's there?" Cassie called out.

The footsteps stopped. No answer came.

Her chest tightened. Her adrenaline raged. She took off running toward the office, sprinting as fast as she could. The footsteps picked up again, faster and faster. She didn't look back. She couldn't. The steps got closer, feet clomping against the cheap store carpet.

She reached the office, slammed the door shut behind her, and flicked the flimsy lock in the center of the knob. It would hold her attacker off, but not for long. Her eyes darted about the room, desperately searching for an escape route in the windowless little hellhole. There was a ceiling vent above the desk. Her only hope.

She leapt up onto the desk and examined the vent more closely. Too tight for her to squeeze into.

Bam, bam, bam! Violent banging filled the room. A flurry of kicks and punches against the thin wooden door.

Among the sparse supplies on the desktop, she spotted it: the telephone. Cassie jumped down, grabbed it, and brought it to her ear. No dial tone. With shaking hands, she pulled on the phone cord, pulled and pulled, until she found the end. It was cut. Frayed wires poked out from the end, mocking her.

The knob rattled as whoever was on the other side jerked on it.

She silently prayed that Ty would show up. Visions of him kicking down the door and sweeping her to safety in his pale yet muscular arms flashed in her mind, but she knew they were only fantasy. Deep down, she knew the truth. She was all alone. Same as she ever was. Against the bullies at school who called her a whore, against the pig of a stepfather who tried to make her into one, against the mother who was too far gone to care what she was.

She'd fought all of them. She would fight whoever this was, too.

She needed a weapon. Her eyes settled on a dusty old snow globe on top of the filing cabinet, featuring Snoopy wearing a Santa hat. Cassie grabbed it and felt its satisfying weight in her hands. Not exactly intimidating, but it would have to do.

"Sorry, Snoopy," she said. "You're out of season."

Squaring her shoulders, she turned toward the door, shaking fearfully in its frame, barely holding up against the blows of her attacker.

"Listen up, scumbag! I don't know who you are, and I don't give a shit. If you come through this door, I will pulverize you! I am armed, and I am pissed, and you will not fuck with me!"

The pounding stopped just as suddenly as it began.

"Oh great, more creepy silence. Thanks a lot."

She crept closer to the door and listened. She thought she heard footsteps . . . Were they receding? It was tough to tell. She listened for a long moment. Nothing. For all she knew, her attacker was still standing by the door.

"Ugh, God, get it together," she said to herself, then rummaged through Kathleen's desk drawers, coming up with a roll of scotch tape.

Clambering under the desk, she rooted around until she found the other end of the phone cord. It was still plugged into the wall. Probably a long shot, she figured, but if she taped the cord back up just so, maybe it would reconnect. She carefully laid the two ends of the cord against each other on the carpet. Her hands weren't shaking any longer. She was steady as a rock.

As she worked with the tape, she tried to figure out who could be attacking her. It couldn't be a practical joke from Ty, he would never want to frighten her. Besides, he didn't have much of a sense of humor, even a cruel one like so many other boys she knew. The pervy watcher from before seemed the most obvious choice, but security always did a sweep to get any loiterers out at the end of the night. Could they have clocked out early on account of the holiday? Then there was Kathleen. Perhaps she had come to kidnap her and feed her to the hippie cult.

She wrapped the last bit of tape around the phone cord. Cassie put the phone to her ear and listened to the dial tone. *Fuck. Yes.* She began to feverishly punch in the numbers. Nine . . . One . . .

A key slid into the door.

Ice ran through Cassie's veins. Before she could punch in the final number, the door swung open, revealing Kathleen. The woman stood there with the same grin spread across her face, but her eyes were searching and strange.

"I knew I shouldn't have left you alone in here," she said.

"Stay back, Kathleen, I'm warning you!"

"Cassie, I hate to say it, but uh, whatever you're doing right now is not up to Send-A-Smile's standards of behavior."

Cassie raised the snow globe high, ready to strike should her boss attempt to get any closer.

"Sweetie, you are clearly unwell. Why don't you let me take you home with me?"

"Why, so your weirdo cult can sacrifice me to a moon goddess? Get real!"

"For Gaia's sake," Kathleen sighed. "If you don't want to come over, you don't have to. I just forgot my wallet, I'm not here to kidn—"

Before she could finish her sentence, a claw hammer slammed down on her head. The claws bit into the flesh of her scalp and shattered through her skull. Kathleen's eyes rolled back in her head as rivulets of blood poured down her face. Still, Kathleen stayed on her feet. Her arms braced themselves against the door frame. Her mouth flapped open and closed like a carp out of water. Then, the gloved hand holding the hammer yanked it down, pulling away the left side of Kathleen's skull, exposing her brain, leaving long strips of flesh hanging limp, and she fell to the floor, dead.

Then the watcher was standing in the doorway, looming, staring at her with his sinister, darkly probing eyes. His face was a flat, expressionless mask. The hammer, gripped tightly in his black-gloved hand, dripped Kathleen's blood onto the dirty carpet.

Without hesitation, Cassie flung the snow globe at him. He tried to duck, but she'd anticipated him and aimed a little low. The globe shattered against his shiny bald dome. Shards of thick glass jutted from his flesh. Water, blood, and glittery snowflakes poured down his face.

He clasped his head in pain but did not utter a sound. Cassie rushed him, pushing him into a rack of "Get Well Soon" cards. She sprinted away down the aisle, heading for the entrance. She was nearly to the checkout counter when she stopped dead in her tracks.

The rolling gate had been brought down over the entrance. Its heavy metal framework secured by two padlocks at the bottom. Cassie was trapped.

Then a sharp kick hit the back of her right knee, and her leg fell out from under her, and she was on the ground, gasping in pain. A gloved hand roughly grabbed her hair and pulled her up until she was seated with her legs curled awkwardly under her. A witch awaiting her beheading.

She looked up to find the bald man's inscrutable, wet face staring down at her.

"Cat got your tongue douchebag?" Cassie asked.

Predictably, he did not respond.

A figure stepped slowly out of the aisles beyond them. Ty. He *had* come. Her love was there to save the day. She wasn't alone in this fight after all. Cassie's heart leapt in her chest.

Then it sank. As he emerged from the shadows, she saw that he wasn't rushing to help her. He was sauntering forward with a smile. And his clothes, his hair . . . he was neatly groomed and wearing a blue suit with a red power tie and an American flag tie tack.

He walked up to her. So close that the tips of his polished dress shoes almost touched her rug-burnt knees. He gazed down at her.

"I told Charles here that you'd be a fighter, but you really outdid yourself. Very nicely done. I'm proud of you, Cassie. Really, I am."

"What . . . What is this? Who is this freak?"

"He's one of our enforcers. A good one. Dedicated. Say hello, Charles."

"Hello, Charles," Charles said, his voice a low monotone.

"Why are you doing this?" she asked, wincing against the hold Charles had on her.

"Well, as you can probably gather, I am not the *punk rock* ne'er-do-well you believed me to be," he said, using air quotes around *punk rock*. He began to pace back and forth in front of her, gesticulating with what he imagined to be a politician's firm, commanding presence. To Cassie, he sounded like a PTA board member practicing a lame speech in his bathroom mirror.

"Charles and I belong to a group. A secret group. We call ourselves the Founding Fathers. We are dedicated to upholding American values. Life, liberty, and the pursuit of happiness for all white American men and, of course, our loyal, pure, dignified white women."

"Aside from being pretty white it doesn't sound like I'm included in that category," Cassie said bitterly.

"No, I wouldn't say so. You are, however, very useful to us. You see, each year on the Fourth of July, we make a sacrifice in the names of our prophets: George Washington, Benjamin Franklin, Thomas Jefferson."

"What about Kathleen? Did she work for you?"

"Crazy Kathleen? No, she's what we would call collateral damage."

"*You're* crazy, Ty. *This* is crazy. You get that, right? You have to get that."

Ty grinned at her. "Blood waters the tree of liberty and all that. Say what you will, but we've been killing young ladies for more than a century and a half, ensuring American supremacy across the globe. Could be a coincidence I suppose, but why stop now?"

Cassie spit on Ty's perfectly shined shoes. "Well if you want a virgin sacrifice, you're shit outta luck, dude."

"Oh, don't I know it." Ty winked at her. "No, you're actually perfect. Only the blood of an um, *experienced*, girl will do. Why snuff out the light of a pure female vessel? That would be a waste. No, we only take the lives of promiscuous women such as yourself. The punishment for your transgressions makes the sacrifice to our Founders much more powerful.

"That's why I adopted my little punk persona. The rakish male feminist. I was looking to entrap a free-spirited girl just like you."

"I trusted you. Ty, I-I loved you," was all Cassie could say.

"I know. I am sorry for that. I went a little overboard, I think, but . . . well, I don't know, maybe I did like you as well. This is very sad for me too, you know," he ran a hand through his perfectly coiffed hair. "Charles, restrain her, and let's get her out of here. The barbecue will be starting shortly."

Charles pulled Cassie to her feet. He began to bind her hands with a length of roughhewn rope. As she struggled against his large, clumsy paws, she remembered the dull blade hanging around her neck. *Bleed for me.*

It wasn't great, but it was all she had. It would have to be enough. She would not die at the hands of these men.

Cassie fought like mad, flailing her arms back and forth, and managed to get an arm free from Charles' grip.

Ty scoffed. "Oh, Cassie, come on now. There's no use fighting. You were born for this."

Ignoring him, she threw an elbow back into Charles' groin, hitting him square in the balls. He doubled over in pain.

"My little Ronnies!" Charles groaned.

Cassie shook the rope off and let it fall to the floor. She turned on Ty and locked eyes with him, fire blazing in her gaze. Ty backed away, trying to control his nerves.

He stammered, "Ca-Cassie, don't make this escalate."

Cassie snapped the ball chain from around her neck.

"You were right about one thing, Ty. I was born for this. Now bleed for me."

With the razor gripped between her thumb and forefinger, she rushed at Ty, baring her teeth in a vicious grin, and, with all her strength, slashed for Ty's throat.

10

BENEATH STILL WATER
Jason Harlow

S AMANTHA FELT A BULLET OF sweat on her forehead as
she gripped the steering wheel in frustration, having
already circled the hectic parking lot in her dad's Celica
Supra. From the passenger seat, her best friend Tiffany
cranked the A/C up once more, an effort to alleviate the
oppressive heat. She wore a custom black camera strap
around her neck that carried her Polaroid OneStep.
They scanned their eyes in every direction, puzzled
and irritated by the lack of unoccupied parking spaces.

"This place is absolutely packed," Tiffany remarked.
"It's like a *madhouse*." She felt no need to make mention
of the salient red, white and blue signage that covered
the majority of the premises. "I guess the Fourth of July
weekend really brought a crowd."

"Yeah, no kidding," Samantha responded, glaring out
the window to her left as the blinker clicked. "I get that
there's some really sweet deals going on," she began, "but
I didn't expect the entire freakin' *city* to be here today."

Noon was still a quarter-hour away, but the Sherwood Mall had drawn an almost unprecedentedly large
crowd—which both girls quickly recognized a silver
lining in. Samantha wanted to surprise her mom with
the new nectar lavender haze candle that had just been

released; her mother's birthday was Monday. Likewise, Tiffany's main goal was to snap photos for the local newspaper's *Stars, Stripes, and Snaps* photography contest; after all, the fifty-dollar cash prize was more than she made at her bowling alley summer gig in three days.

While neither of them was insincere in expressing their purpose for going during what they knew to be the busiest time, they were mostly excited about the possibility of witnessing cute boys in their sleeveless shirts and short summer shorts. Surely, that would make the hassle of navigating through the mob of impassioned mall-goers much more bearable, they figured. Although they knew they'd be seeing plenty of cute guys at Jade Brookside's party later that evening, they were both feeling profusely confident in their brand-new blouses and mini skirts, and they knew that seeing more people could only shift the odds closer to their favor.

"Do we need to snag some fireworks while we're here?"

"Jade said it wouldn't hurt to get some if we could."

"Key phrases right there — *wouldn't hurt. If we could.*"

"Remember who ate the last piece of her birthday cake last year?"

Tiffany shrugged, smirking. "Touché," she declared, prompting a brief chuckle from her best friend. "Well, you know, I could get out and hold our place in line at the fireworks stand while you keep cruising around looking for an empty spot."

"Works for me. I'll pull up right by the water fountain, and you can jump out real quick."

Tiffany exited the car, making sure to dispose of the Taco Bell bag she had acquired from the drive-thru half an hour prior. Sherwood didn't have the best food options anyway. And certainly no Beefers. She squinted her eyes as she used her left hand to shield them from the sun.

Several other children, the oldest of which looked a few years younger than Tiffany, threw coins into the rippling swirls in the center of the water fountain. They were all dressed in some combination of red, white and blue. Some of the younger kids donned face paint of color-correlated superheroes, such as Captain America and Spider-Man; one particularly rambunctious kid sported a pair of star-spangled sunglasses that matched his red and white Chuck Taylors.

Loud footsteps caught the attention of Tiffany as she made her way into the line. She turned her head in the direction of the noise and noticed, through the abundant crowd, a sickly pale, emaciated child running as if in danger. The kid wore a dirty white t-shirt and ragged blue jeans, and his face told the story of someone who had seen far better days. Despite his disheveled appearance, his movements were swift, and as far as Tiffany could see, he had essentially vanished in the tumultuous parking lot.

Some of the people in line noticed the boy and looked concerned; others simply were too occupied in their own doings to notice. After a few seconds had passed, everyone standing in line was no longer looking in his direction.

When Samantha finally caught up to Tiffany, she had made her way through the bulk of the line, with only a few groups of people still waiting in front of them. "This is the most far-out fireworks stand I've ever seen!"

"You could say that again. This thing's huge! And would you look at the *line*? It's gotten even bigger than it was when I first walked up!"

"No kidding! If it went back any further, it'd be all the way to Times Square!" The two best friends shared a laugh.

"Hopefully, we can run in here and find a gift real quick. I just need to grab that candle."

"Okay, yeah, don't worry about me holding us up either. If I don't see anything exciting, I'm not snapping any pictures."

They exited the fireworks stand after stuffing their purses with enough Roman candles, firecrackers, and bottle rockets to light up the forthcoming evening's obsidian sky. They couldn't help but notice the Sherwood Mall sign that shined brighter than ever before, the patriotic fringe garland that wrapped around it serving as an immediate indicator of the Independence Day extravaganza.

Upon entering, they gazed in amazement at the spirited decorations: red, white, and blue balloons bounced around, being slapped by kids and adults like a volleyball in a high school gym. "This is *amazing*! They really went all out for Independence Day," Tiffany observed.

"No kidding! This looks even better than the *Winter Wonderland* theme they did for Christmas!"

After gazing up and noticing the crowdedness of the upper level, the entrance seemed to be the least packed area in the entire mall, composed mostly of smaller parties or individuals sitting on the benches waiting to meet up with others. This allowed the tandem of teen girls to scope the scene a bit and get a feel for the unusually large crowd.

"Does Branson Blanchard still work at Thread Count?"

"Wouldn't know. Haven't been in a couple months. It's not like I need new bedding every week," she teased.

"Well, I really wouldn't mind if we *happen* to run into him. Ya'know what I mean?" Tiffany smirked.

"Yeah, yeah, and I wouldn't mind if we *happen* to run into *Rob Lowe* either, but let's try not to get trapped here all day."

"Oh come on, if we make a few pit stops it's not the end of the world. We still have about five hours until the party."

"I know, I know. I just don't wanna have to wait around on you to seek out your perfect Prince Charming out of all the people here."

Tiffany lifted her head and twitched her nose, sniffling. "Golly! The food court smells better than ever today. Not only did they go all-out with the visuals, it even smells amazing today too!"

"Give me a break, you had that Beefer less than an hour ago!" Once Tiffany mentioned it, however, she couldn't help but notice the comforting fragrance of fresh bread clashing with the robust, smokey hot dog scent.

Tiffany laughed. "Don't judge me, but I'm gonna try one—oh, look! Even Dog House Delights is running specials!" she exclaimed, pointing ahead. Samantha spotted it in an instant—a man dressed as Uncle Sam held a white sign, its vibrant blue text visible from the distance—

"4TH OF JULY
SPECIAL!
JUMBO HOT DOGS
99 CENTS!"

"There's no way I'm gonna pass that up!"

"Gee, if you were any hungrier, you'd be a *tapeworm*," Samantha ribbed, gently punching her best friend's arm.

"I have an idea. You go snag the candle you wanted to get for your mom. I'll head over to the food court and then go to the lower level and snap a couple pictures of the arcade. Meet me outside of Frill Seeker in about fifteen."

Though nervous about a potential logistical pickle in such a buzzing environment, Samantha agreed. "Sounds good to me. See ya then!"

"Catch you later!"

Being alone in the Sherwood Mall seemed a bit overwhelming for Samantha. She realized the mall likely hadn't been this busy all year as she listened to the unrelenting and echoing sounds of voices, footsteps at every pace, the pinging noises made by the elevators, and cash registers opening and shutting. What Samantha didn't realize, however, was that just as she entered The Cozy Corner, from a distance—someone was staring at her—*watching* her every move.

Someone was *waiting for her.*

Waiting for a chance to strike.

⁓

Samantha returned to the bench and sat down with Tiffany, who sat alone with a rectangular red and white-checkered paper basket with few remains of a once-jumbo hot dog.

Tiffany glanced over to Samantha with a shameless grin. "These loaded fries sure are out of this world!"

"I think, if anything, your *appetite* is what's *out of this world*."

"Yeah, yeah . . . Did you find the candle you were looking for?"

"Well, I actually didn't end up going. The line was super long. Did you get any cool pictures of the arcade?"

Tiffany shrugged. "I didn't go. Got a bit distracted. I ended up walking over to Thread Count. Branson wasn't working. But guess who got a new weekend job?"

Samantha furrowed her brow. "Get outta here."

"I start next week. They were so busy the hiring manager said she wished I could've put my uniform on right then!"

"Well, uhh, congrats." Samantha tried to hide her annoyance but could hear her tone struggle. "Oh. So, I guess we need to head to the Cineplex now? I mean, *if* you're still wanting to take some pictures."

"Yeah, let's go. Don't worry, we won't take too long."

Tiffany could read Samantha's displeasure in the situation, so offered up a new conversation piece in an attempt to repair the mood as they walked in the direction of the theater. "Say, anyway, are you excited for tonight or *what*?"

"Yep, and I'll be wearing the cutest Independence Day outfit this town has ever seen! It's gonna be a blast!"

"Ha! You could say that again! When Jade's older brother gets a hold of these fireworks, it will be a real *blast* indeed."

The two girls made their way up the escalator, strolling past the purple neon lights from the food court as they made their way to the theater. Tiffany couldn't help but notice from a distance the sign for *Skate-O-Rama* had been taken down, its aluminum roll-up gate touching the floor to prevent access to the once-vibrant entryway.

"I'm still so disappointed about the bowling alley," Tiffany mentioned.

"Did we ever find out what's supposed to be going in there?"

"Mom says the development company who owns the mall is keeping it a secret. They say there's been a ton of construction going on after hours, though."

"Well, Tiff, what do *you* think it's gonna be?"

"I think it'll become a new 3-D movie theater. At least that's what happened when the one in Allendale went out of business."

"That would be wicked! Remember that Starchaser movie that released in 3-D last fall? That was the bomb!"

"Well, maybe if my guess is correct, we can catch some more wicked 3-D films."

"That would be awesome," Samantha stated while coming to a stop. "Let's just keep going."

"Come *on* . . . Let's just snoop around a bit. As busy as this place is, we'll blend right in!"

Samantha groaned inwardly at Tiffany's eagerness. They continued pressing on until they noticed, taped to the large double doors to what used to be *Skate-o-Rama*, a sign that read:

DO NOT ENTER

"Dang. I guess we'll just have to find out when everyone else does."

"You sure about that?"

Samantha's heart sank. "Wh-what do you mean?"

"They, uhh . . . they didn't close the doors all the way."

"You're *kidding*."

"See for yourself."

Tiffany gently pressed her foot against the center of the double doors, where a small gap had been inadvertently created.

"I wouldn't."

"Do you have to be such a chicken?!"

"It's got nothing to do with being a chicken. I just don't see the point."

"Are you kidding me? We could just sneak in real quick!"

"Get real, Tiffany. That's the dumbest idea I've ever heard."

"More like the *best* idea you've ever heard! How do you know there's not something totally rad behind these doors?"

"Give it a rest. We don't want to risk getting in trouble!"

"Seems low-risk, high-reward to me. What better way to win the photography contest?"

Samantha couldn't think of an objection fast enough. "Come on, this is gonna be so rad! When I win, I'll give you half the money! Let's go!"

Moments later, they walked slowly through a dark entryway, the only light being a neon blue trim along a wall. They trekked less than ten feet forward, enjoying a strident saltwater fragrance.

Teal blue water filled their entire line of sight on each side. A school of blue tangs slowly glided through the water to their left side. A giant pink jellyfish sat idly on their right side.

"An *aquarium*," Samantha whispered.

"This is so cool."

Their feet inched forward at a slow, steady pace as if to mitigate a potential echo from the considerably hollow building.

"Is anyone else here?"

"It sure doesn't sound like it."

"Let's get out of here. We're probably on closed circuit, anyway. Security's probably gonna come get us any minute now."

"Come *on*, Sam, let's check out what's around this corner. I wanna make sure I get the best picture ever!"

Samantha offered no response as the two continued through the quiet halls of the aquarium. On one side, they witnessed large bullfrog tadpoles that resembled snakes—on the other, tiny pink seahorses and mandarinfish that resembled a psychedelic optical illusion or a pack of Skittles.

"*Look*, Tiffany, let's—"

"*Ssshhh!*" Tiffany interrupted, placing her hand near Samantha's face. At the end of the hallway, a door was open. They couldn't get a concise look, but the part of the room they could see resembled an animal care room or a research facility.

They watched as a man in a black suit stood across from two old, strangely sophisticated, overweight men who looked nearly identical. They wore matching outfits: lifted black shoes, black pants with suspenders under a white button-down shirt, and a black top hat. Their facial hair was one of their biggest differentiators, and that was only because the slightly taller one had a shorter goatee.

Samantha and Tiffany watched as the two near-identical men exchanged handshakes with the man in black. Even in their hushed state, they could barely hear what the men were saying from the distance.

"He tried to run away earlier, but we got him now."

"S'long as he won't give us any issues."

"Oh no, oh no. That's taken care of."

"Good deal. How much longer?"

"We're letting him feed now, so he'll be fine for a while. How long did you say it was until your next stop?"

"About four hours," answered the brother with the longer goatee.

"Oh yeah, oh yeah. He'll be fine."

"We'll get him out of there in just a minute and have him on his way with you guys."

"Okay, we'll go ahead and move the crate over here," said the brother with the shorter goatee. As if on cue, the two brothers turned around and walked several yards backward to a dark corner that was unable to be seen from Samantha and Tiffany's perspective. Seconds later, they wheeled a large device covered in a black sheet back to where they had previously stood. They repositioned it slightly, moving it to a forty-five-degree angle that revealed to Samantha and Tiffany an embroidered logo on the linen that read:

"TRUMANN BROS. CIRCUS
EST. 1981."

"I'll go ahead and check on him now, actually," the man said to the two brothers.

Samantha looked over to Tiffany with a serious tone. She barely moved her mouth when she spoke. "Let's go back." With that, the two friends turned around.

As they made their way to the exit, Samantha noticed something out of the ordinary —*something* she had never seen before.

"Whaaa-wh-*what* . . . *is* . . . *that*?"

From inside the tank, a large creature sat idly, its tired and weak molten yellow eyes the least puzzling thing about it. Whatever it was, was considerably eerie and abnormal. It was too human to be reptilian but too *reptilian to be human*.

The creature swayed back and forth, causing the turquoise water to move at the same pace. Moments later, the creature placed its sharp, alligator-like teeth through the pair of mandarinfish.

Samantha looked over to Tiffany, who stared in shock and horror. She felt her heart pounding through her tight blouse like the bass drum in some of her dad's favorite rock songs.

Back and forth, back and forth, the water stirred.

The two girls surely weren't expecting to encounter anything of this nature, and Tiffany couldn't let the opportunity go to waste. She pulled her Polaroid One-Step up to her eyes.

Click!

From the distance, a voice —the voice of an enraged, threatening man —could be heard.

"Whoever's in here is a goner! Show yourself, you meddling idiot!"

Samantha and Tiffany simultaneously felt their hearts sink and their body temperature rise higher than that of the pizza in the food court. Neither of them had ever felt such an intense rush of astonishment and fear at the same time; they knew they were risking some consequences by entering, but they never had a plan for getting caught.

Their instinct said run. So they bolted toward the entrance, retracing their previous footsteps, only backward and at a much faster pace than before.

Footsteps followed as they neared the entrance. They grew louder as the deranged man nearly caught up to them, his feet tattering in rhythm on the ground. Samantha and Tiffany reached the heavy steel door and successfully exited, slamming it behind them to create a larger distance and a hopeful exit.

They swiftly navigated through a crowd of people, occasionally brushing against, bumping into, or otherwise aggravating unsuspecting mall visitors. Moments later, they made a knee-jerk decision to burst into the candy store.

"How awesome is *that?!*" Tiffany asked rhetorically. "I *knew* it'd be worth it!"

Samantha hated that she couldn't offer a rebuttal, and also hated that the events that had transpired would likely only enable more compulsive behavior and bad decision-making from her best friend. "I'm still in shock over what we saw. Wh-what *was* that thing?"

"No idea! But don't worry, if I win, I mean, *when* I win this contest, I'm still gonna give you half the money."

"That was so crazy," Samantha exclaimed, her hands resting on her knees as she tried to catch her breath.

"Do you think those guys are gonna keep chasing us?"

"I say we exit through the department store, but let's play it safe. Let's look as nonchalant as possible, and get to—"

Samantha's eyes widened as she interrupted herself. She stared intently into the distance, away from Tiffany. "Sir! Excuse me, sir!" She exited the candy store, racing through dozens of concerned passersby.

"Where are you going?!"

Tiffany spotted Samantha in the distance. She had successfully snagged the attention of a tall black man, who held a fountain drink in one hand and was dressed entirely in black. She was standing in the middle of the aisle, conspicuously expressing concern to the man—while causing concern to the surrounding mall-goers.

Tiffany watched on, occasionally catching glimpses of the man's facial expression and body language. She noticed he was wearing a security uniform—and that he was clearly disinterested. Samantha raced back toward Tiffany through the droves of people. Her face told a story of disappointment, which she vocalized as soon as she returned to the outside of the candy store.

"That security guard was going on break and couldn't have given any less of a shit."

"Well, let's just get outta here!"

As Tiffany turned around, the man who they had seen strike a deal with the circus owners appeared, grabbing her shoulders forcefully. He lunged his face closer to hers. "Hand that picture over to me! Now!"

"I'm sorry, sir, we didn't mean any harm!"

"I said NOW!"

She tossed the camera over to Samantha. Samantha dropped the bag with her parents' CD to the floor and caught it, her face hollow from shock and panic. The man's eyes remained fixated on Tiffany; his face took on a crimson hue.

"Give me the camera right this very moment!"

Tiffany swallowed the lump in her throat. "I-I can't give you that, sir," her voice trembling as if shards of glass were committing an act of trespassing in her throat. "I didn't even get a good shot of the tank, I promise!"

The man paused, his face still. His black sunglasses kept her from seeing his eyes, but she knew he was staring directly into *her* eyes.

He instantaneously and unexpectedly shifted focus, charging toward Samantha. Just as she began running backward, the man clamped his palm across her mouth, silencing her while subsequently dragging her with him through the crowd of people.

"Hey! Somebody help, somebody help! He took her! He *took* my friend!"

Tiffany chased after Samantha and her kidnapper, but shortly after realizing they were out of sight, Tiffany's mind raced. Did she need to race to the security office or use a store's phone to call for help, she wondered, with each passing second becoming more crucial.

She turned around and was immediately startled by two men swarming her on each side — two men dressed identically to the man who had just kidnapped Samantha.

~

Samantha woke up to a bright white light shining in her face, with nothing but cold, gray concrete walls surrounding her.

Suddenly, *a noise*.

The table on which she lay made a repetitive squeak as she descended downward. She knew she wasn't in the room alone.

Sedated and unresponsive, her body lay still as her eyes went wide. Two people stood above her, both of whom were wearing protective goggles, surgical hats, and operating masks. Samantha couldn't hone her vision into their eyes or make out any of their facial features.

"This is it, Doc. The last thing we need," called Dr. Langston, her eyes following her forearm as she lifted the syringe.

"This singular dose will be strong enough," Dr. Coffman informed, pulling his protective goggles down. The white light cast from the screens surrounding them caused a glare in his goggles that was almost blinding for Samantha, who was given none. She hoped the two mad scientists were unaware that she was awake, but had no time to ponder their lack of compassion as the doctor leaned closer, hovering intently.

Dr. Coffman's gloves gave Samantha's left arm a light squeeze; a clear fluid was promptly provided by Dr. Langston, who patted her down with a damp white cloth. Samantha wished to scream, but even if it were possible, it would surely prove to make no difference as Dr. Coffman injected the syringe into her arm.

"That takes care of that one."

"And now . . . the other."

~

The two scientists stared into the tank, cringing as they slowly looked over to the other. Dr. Coffman, known for his incredibly impressive success-to-botch ratio, had no explanation as he struggled to look directly into the disappointed eyes of the black-suited agents.

The words struggled to come out as he remained in disbelief. "It seems there's *been a*—a mistake, a miscalculation, a—*contretemps*."

From outside the glass, the two doctors and the mysterious man dressed in black stared intently at the creature in the tank. Its skin was scaly, its hands were webbed, its eyes were yellow. Samantha's evolution was complete.

But Samantha wasn't the only creature they watched. From where they were standing, another creature rested idly in the tank behind her. The other creature had an insatiable appetite and had grown much larger.

The larger creature no longer sat idly, commandingly zooming through the tank. As Tiffany sized up her prey, the water rocked again, *back and forth, back and forth*.

Before Samantha could muster up the ability to move, Tiffany's serrated teeth ripped through Samantha's scaly reptilian abdomen with ease, further darkening a fraction of the once shiny turquoise water with a bloody crimson spout. Dumbfounded, their eyes widened in amazement and in horror.

With a vice grip caused by the newly-acquired piercing teeth she sunk into Samantha's scaly neck, the menacing, indestructible Tiffany vigorously bounced her head up and down, attempting to squeeze every ounce of life that belonged to her once best friend. Samantha's heart came closer to failing with each passing second as rippling bubbles of dark blood overtook the no-longer vibrant tank. Tiffany flexed her unwavering strength as she slammed Samantha's face into the tempered glass repeatedly.

The ten-million-gallon tank now belonged to their inadvertent infernal reptilian humanoid creation, and there would be no stopping her. All signs of life became absent for the creature that once was Samantha; her ribs shattered, her midsection punctured by the suffocating pressure. The now-gargantuan Tiffany slowly descended until the only movement in the red water was the few bubbly ripples caused by the gluttonous devouring of her lifeless ex-best friend.

The slimy, crackling sounds made by the shattering bones and chewing of cartilage sent chills down the spines of the deranged spectators. The three of them exchanged nervous glances before their eyes returned to the water.

Tiffany stared back at them, her eyes more menacing than ever as her stare pierced their souls. They couldn't help but notice that, once again, she had grown.

"We have to stop this one. Before it's too late."

They knew that soon enough, their creation would become hungry again. Soon enough, their creation would prove to be too big for the tank. And soon enough, their creation would become *too big for them to control*.

But Tiffany would have to spend her time in the glass confines. And the most radical Fourth of July weekend party would have two fewer visitors. Jade likely wouldn't be too thrilled about not having as many fireworks at the party as planned, but at least *she* wouldn't have to worry about running out of food . . .

11
TANDEMONIUM
AudraKate Gonzalez

THE BIKINI IN THE REFLECTION of the store window mocks me. I wrap my arms around myself to hide how absurd I look in my uniform before entering the salon. A T-shirt with the image of a tan body, bursting cartoon cleavage, wearing a polka dot bikini, covers my torso. The wardrobe was chosen by the manager of Tandemonium, my new job.

It's the latest tanning salon located on the ground level of Sherwood Mall. The manager, Stella, claims it's the hottest spot for those looking to get some color this summer. Stella jokes that the only place better for a tan would be directly on the sun. She's even hired extra staff for the summer months to stay on top of things. And with the busy Fourth of July weekend, it's a good thing she did.

An electronic bell rings as I step over the threshold.

"Welcome to Tandemonium, how can I—Oh, Amy!" Stella looks up from the front counter. "Ready to start your first shift?"

I nod. "Totally." Not really. I'm more nervous than ever. Mostly just afraid that someone I know is going to see me in this ridiculous outfit. I look at Stella and notice that she isn't sporting the uniform. Humiliation must be reserved for her employees. *Cool.*

"All right, let's go through everything you learned from the orientation walk-through and then I'll leave you to your shift. I have some last-minute things to prepare for Independence Day, so I won't be around, but it's pretty simple." She checks her neon green manicured fingers. A terrible color choice for someone like me: pale skin and red frizzy hair, but it's a great contrast to her dark skin and permed blonde curls.

I go through my mental checklist of things from the orientation aloud. "Tanning beds are down this hall. There are six total. Only one person per room. Timer is by the front desk and each bed works on a dial. Customers can do no more than twenty minutes but no less than ten. Lotions are required and can be purchased at the desk. Customers are not permitted to bring their own lotions. Tanning beds must be sanitized after each use. At lock up, all tanning rooms are to be individually locked, lights shut off, and gate pulled down and locked."

Stella smiles. "Excellent. You'll be great! If you have any questions, jot them down, and I'll get to them tomorrow."

"You got it," I say through a forced grin.

"Oh! I do have to remind you of one thing from orientation that you might have missed."

I missed something?

"It's probably the *most* important thing."

Oh, that . . .

"Don't disturb any of the customers during their tanning experience. If I hear of any complaints, it could result in your termination."

"Right, got it. But just one thing . . . what if there's an emergency? Like a fire or robber or—"

"*Do not disturb the customers during their tanning experience.*" Stella's eyes glow with annoyance.

I nod my head in submission and keep my lips in a tight line to avoid saying anything else that she might not like to hear.

She blows out a nervous puff of air. "I'll see you later." And then she flits away, her heels clicking across the white tile, and out of the store. I take my place behind the front counter, which is shaped like a giant surfboard, and begin my workday by organizing the tanning lotions. All the names are really cheesy. Solar Glow, which promises a shimmering effect; Cosmic Bronze, which says it bronzes instantly; and, Nebula Nectar, which claims to darken as the day goes on.

Seeing the lotion options, I'm thankful for my freckled, ghostly skin that turns into a tomato in the sun. Although, I would be lying if I said I wasn't a little envious of the girls who do tan. It hides so many flaws and ends up making them all look like golden goddesses.

The electronic ding echoes across the store.

"Welcome to Tandemonium, how can I help you?" I ask the woman who has entered the salon. Her skin is incredibly dark. Like a leather couch or a piece of jerky. I keep my face blank, though, reminding myself that my job is to get people in the tanning beds and not tell them that their skin is damaged beyond repair.

"Twenty minutes, please." She begins to scan the many lotions. "Which lotion do you recommend?"

I look at my pale skin in disbelief. She can't think I've ever tried one of these in my entire life, right?

"I'm not sure. It's my first day. But I can let you smell the samples to help you choose."

I set the samples in front of her, and she proceeds to open the lids and smell them. When she opens the lid to Solar Glow, some of the liquid squirts out onto the counter. A green sludge plops down and emits a strong odor. A sweet metallic scent, like a flower I've never smelled before, with an undertone of decay tickles my nose.

I grab a paper towel to wipe up the mess, but when I turn back around, the sludge has inched from its original spot.

"I—did you—" My words aren't coming out right because I'm so confused. But the woman stares at me as if I'm an invalid, so I ignore the urge to ask her if she saw the green goop move, and I clean it.

"I'll take this one." She hands me the bottle of Solar Glow.

I ring her up and lead her to room number three.

"Just holler if you need anything," I tell her as she shuts and locks the door behind her. I get back to the front counter and turn the dial for room number three to twenty minutes. Turning up the knob on the radio, I finish organizing the lotions while listening to a song belted by Whitney Houston as the time passes.

A loud *thump* from down the hall makes me jump.

I tell myself that the woman must have dropped something, but when a muffled noise resounds over the radio, I can't help but react. I check the dial on the wall. She still has five minutes left on the clock.

Indecision gnaws at me.

It's against the rules of the job to interrupt a customer's tanning experience, but what if she slipped and fell? She could be hurt. Or passed out. I think it's a terrible policy not to check on a person if something could potentially be wrong. So, hoping the excuse of it being my first day will cover my ass, I ignore the job rules and jog to room three.

My tentative hand forms a fist as I reach up and knock on the door. "Ma'am, is everything alright in there?" No response. I knock again, a little more frantic. Still nothing. The bright blue light from the bulbs of the bed glows from beneath the door.

I steel myself, squatting down, and press my right eye against the keyhole. There's a hazy, gray cloud that unfurls from the tanning bed. Thinking that the tanning bed could be burning our customer alive, I race to the front of the store to grab the keys to the room. Running back with the keys in hand, I bump into the woman exiting the room.

Her skin is covered in a glowing sheen. It makes her look serpentine, almost the color of pea soup under the lights, but I'd never tell her that.

She huffs, sticking her nose in the air. "Did you need something?"

"I'm sorry. I thought—" What did I think? I can't exactly tell her that I thought she was being barbecued. No, that would sound ridiculous.

"Isn't it your policy *not* to disturb the customer?"

"Yes, but . . . Wait . . . How do you know that?" It's not like we advertise the employee rules to the customers.

The woman fumbles over her words, tongue-tied, before she comes up with something. "That's common in every tanning salon I've ever been to."

Giving her leather skin a once over, I realize there's no point in me arguing with an expert on the subject of tanning salons.

"I'm really sorry about that. It won't happen again."

"I'll be expecting a discount the next time I return. *If* I return." She storms out of the store, and I'm left wondering if I'll have a job at the end of the day.

I look into room number three. Nothing appears out of the ordinary with the room itself, but the tanning bed holds my attention. It's basic. Normal. An enclosed shell of acrylic covering UV light bulbs. No burn smell. No scorch marks. Nothing that would have created the smoke from earlier. Had I simply hallucinated it under the stress of it being my first day? It could be possible . . .

Grabbing the bottle of disinfectant, I begin to spray the bed down. When we went through orientation, they emphasized the importance of cleaning the beds after each use to prevent customers from getting funguses or any sort of cross-contamination from person to person. Thinking about the whole thing really makes me wish I had some gloves on right now.

I'm putting a lot of elbow grease into scrubbing the bed clean when my hand comes across something sticky. A gag creeps its way up my throat. It's remnants of Solar Glow. The goo no longer smells like flowers at a funeral, but instead just smells like burnt flesh. My hand begins to tingle from where I touched the goo, and I can feel it turning numb. I shake my hand out, trying to get rid of the feeling, but it only intensifies. Either I'm allergic to the stuff, or this is something to do with the ingredients it's made of, and the UV lights activate it.

With a trigger-happy finger, I spray the remnants of Solar Glow. It sizzles and, to my disbelief, inches away from me and my bottle.

What the hell—

Before, when I thought the lotion had moved, I had easily written it off as my mind playing tricks on me. But now? There was no denying it now. This smelly slime was alive. Or at least reactive to cleaning chemicals.

I hit the green goo with the disinfectant one more time to watch it wither and shift beneath the droplets. My eyes are hypnotized by the foreign material, wondering what exactly this stuff could be made out of and if I should tell Stella that she may want to consider recalling all of the bottles.

"Hello?"

There's a knock on the open door that startles me. I bash my head on the lid of the tanning bed and let out a loud curse.

Well, that's not professional at all.

"Oh, I'm so sorry. Are you all right?" A new customer rushes over to check on me. I was so engrossed by the goo that I didn't even hear the *ding* of someone entering the salon.

I rub the spot on my head that's surely going to be bruised, but I brush it off. That and the weird goop in the bed. It's time to get back to work. I make the executive decision to quarantine room three, and not market Solar Glow to anyone else for now. Not until I can talk to Stella about everything. I may not know much about the world of tan skin, but I do know that lotion is not supposed to be able to move.

Shutting the door behind me, I usher the customer to the front counter and continue my shift. In the back of my mind, I can't help but wonder what the lasting effects of Solar Glow will be for the woman who used it.

~

The rest of the day goes by without incident. Not because I think nothing is going on behind my back. No, I'm still highly skeptical about these foul-smelling lotions and what's going on in the tanning beds. But the salon is a revolving door of bronze gods and goddesses. It's been a never ending hustle of getting people a bed, starting the timer, wiping down beds, yada, yada, yada. They walk in in a rush and then leave with blank, content faces, completely ignoring me on their way out, which would seem rude to me if it wasn't for the fact that I've been running around like crazy.

I was supposed to be relieved of my shift hours ago, but the girl that was meant to take over decided not to even show up for her first day. I called Stella on her clunky Motorola DynaTAC, which had terrible reception, to let her know we were crazy busy and the other employee didn't show up. Instead of getting any kind of sympathy or help from her, I got a gleeful cheer and a "I knew we'd be swamped! Sounds like you've got everything handled," and then the *click* of her hanging up. Superb boss, truly.

It isn't until close to closing time that things *finally* begin to slow down, and I can take a break to eat my, now cold, dinner from the food court. Mall pizza. Not very nutritious, but definitely greasy and delicious. The perfect food to reward myself with after a crazy day.

I almost spit out my diet soda from excitement when I see a familiar face come bobbing through the entrance of the salon. My best friend from college, Maggie, has a giddy smile on her face when I run around the counter to swallow her in a hug. We jump around like children. It's like no time has passed between us, even though it's been two years since we last saw each other. She looks the same. Tall, brunette, model good looks, and natural olive skin tone.

Maggie steps back to take me in from head to toe. "Who in the world would hire Casper the ghost to work the front counter of a tanning salon?" She snorts in a cute, piggy way. And she hasn't lost her sense of humor that always knows how to roast me in a way that puts me in a good mood.

"I assume they wouldn't want to hire someone who'd be tempted to spend all day in the beds. So, I guess I'm the right ghost for the job."

"Do you like it?" she asks.

I pause for a moment. Do I like it? The job itself isn't bad, but the weird stuff that happened earlier . . .

"It's gonna pay the bills. Not exactly where I saw myself, but that's something you have to accept when you drop out of college early." I sigh. I don't regret my decision to drop out of school, but I do regret not fully thinking through the consequences of it. "But what about you? When did you make it back to town?"

"A couple of days ago! Sorry, I didn't reach out sooner. Had to do all the family meetups first before I could make time for friends. I stopped by your house earlier today and that's when your dad told me you'd gotten a job here." She drags a hand over the bottles of lotion at the counter. "Figure I could use a fresh base tan before the Fourth of July festivities this weekend. Maybe we can go get drinks after you're finished here?"

I nod enthusiastically. "Definitely."

"Awesome." She motions toward the lotions. "Any of these that you recommend?"

I scoot the bottle of Solar Glow far away from her. "Any but this one."

Maggie picks a different lotion, and then I set her up in room five for twenty minutes. The last twenty minutes of the day before I shut everything down.

While Maggie's tanning session starts, I clean and lock things up. When I shut off the radio, that's when I hear the noise again. The same sounds as earlier. Some bumps and then muffled grunts. And it's all coming from room number five. I must have ignored them when things got busy, but now the noises are practically slapping my eardrums.

Knowing that Maggie is one of my friends, I don't think she'll have any problem with me checking in on her.

I unlock the door and step inside. All of Maggie's things are lying in the corner along with the lotion she picked. The tanning bed is still running, but the lid is sealed almost completely. I don't think the beds are supposed to shut like this. "Mags? You okay?" I push on the lid. Tug at it. Try to pry it open, but the stupid thing won't budge, and Maggie isn't responding.

Smoke begins to unfurl from the bed, filling the room with a terrible-smelling fog. "Maggie, if you don't answer me, I'm going to call 911." I'm trying to calm myself down by making it a half-hearted joke, but my frantically beating heart is very serious about calling for help.

"Maggie!" I scream as I wedge my fingers in between the bed and the lid and force it open. All those years of working my butt off in the gym, bodybuilding with the boys, pay off. And my mom wanted me to join her aerobics class. *Pfft.*

The lid flings open, knocking me off balance. I quickly regain my footing and scramble to the bed, but there's no Maggie inside.

Instead, I'm greeted by a trap door where Mags was once lying. The base of the bed has opened like a giant mouth, revealing a chute that goes to God knows where.

"Mags?" I yell down the chute. My voice echoes back to me. There's a faint whimper in the dark distance, and it's all I need to send myself down to the depths of hell.

The slide spits me out into a dank, shadowed tunnel system. I look up to where I once was. I can see the faint glow of the tanning bed way above me. There are rungs on the wall next to me that lead up to where I used to be. It makes me feel a little better knowing that I'll be able to get back up there. But I still have to find Maggie first.

The air is thick with moisture. My nostrils fill with the smell of mold and earth. The cylindrical walls that surround me are made of thick concrete. Water drips from them, and moss grows in spotty patches. I must be somewhere underneath the mall.

The only light comes from a room ahead of me. I take a deep breath and move forward toward whatever awaits me.

My short walk takes me to the end of the tunnel and it opens up into a cold chamber. A shiver runs through me as I scan my surroundings. Here, the moss has changed from something earthly to some sort of bioluminescent plant that casts a familiar green glow. It pulsates with an eerie rhythm, as though the plant is alive and breathing. In the center of the room are multiple pods that look unlike anything I've ever seen before. Each pod is connected by cords and pipes. The pods to my left appear to be stained with . . .

Is that blood?

Bile rises in my throat as I approach the pods. I push it back down, hoping that what I'm seeing is actually not blood but rust. But when the sour metallic smell invades my nose, I know it can't be anything other than that.

There's a large machine in the center of the chamber that clicks and groans. The central console of the machine displays a translucent screen covered in various symbols that I don't recognize. Nothing looks like it's from our world. It all looks futuristic. Alien.

My foot steps on something squishy, and when I look down, there's a puddle of blood. I scream and stumble backward, falling into a pit and landing on a pile of something that smells like decay. Whatever is beneath me is soft. I slowly open my eyes and cry out when I see that I'm lying on a mound of hundreds of skinless, decomposing bodies. Their exposed muscles, tissue, and bones glisten in the soft glow of the green light.

Some of the bodies still have their eyes, and they stare at me as if I can do something to save them now.

A pair of eyes that I recognize blinks at me. A whimper escapes the body, and I hear the slight whisper of my name. A croak of "A-Amy." The sound is pitiful. Barely audible. But it still cuts through the macabre silence like a knife.

I swim through the bodies; the sensation of their clammy corpses against mine almost stops me, but I push on. My voice cracks as I shout, "Maggie!" The desperation that's building inside of me is almost palpable.

A tear drips down her skinless cheek, mingling with the gore that covers her. The sight of her suffering makes my legs want to buckle.

When I reach her, I pull her slippery body into my arms, and she screams in pain. Her cries pierce the air, reverberating through the chamber. The weight of her fragile form, what's left of her, tells me that she doesn't have much time left. There's no way she survives this.

"They—they're . . ." She tries to choke out words, but it's difficult to do so with the blood filling her throat. Her bright red face tries to plead with me to understand.

"What, Mags?" I ask, my own tears now falling. I'm hardly hanging on to my composure.

"They're . . . taking . . . " she wheezes, "*skins*."

The pounding of my heart over the softness of her voice makes me question what I just heard.

"What? Who?" My voice shakes. I wait for Maggie to answer my questions, but I'm greeted with silence as her eyes roll back and her head lolls to the side. Her gummy body goes slack as the last breath leaves her lungs.

The sound of heels clicks from somewhere above the pit I'm in. I glance up, Maggie's lifeless form still in my arms, to see my boss, Stella, standing in the glow of the light.

"Didn't I tell you not to disturb the tanning experience?" She turns on her heels and shouts, "Bring her here."

Someone approaches me from behind, but before I can do anything to defend myself, everything goes black. The sensation of slithery hands grabbing me is the last thing I feel before I'm knocked into unconsciousness.

When I wake up, panic sets in. I'm strapped down with metal bars inside one of the pods I saw earlier. Across from me, inside the other pod, a translucent gray creature writhes and shifts from inside like a nightmarish blob of silly putty. It doesn't have eyes, but I can't shake the feeling that it's watching me intently.

I wrestle against the unforgiving restraints but to no avail. The metal bars dig into me as I try my hardest to break free.

Stella's grating heels get closer until she's standing in front of me. "I thought you were going to make an excellent employee." She clicks her tongue in disappointment. "Oh well."

"What are you *doing?*" I manage to demand even in my terrified state.

"What I have to do so that me and my children can survive."

"Your children?"

Stella motions to the blob across from me.

Maggie's words echo back to me.

They're taking skins.

The blob begins to take shape, creating the outline of a human form, attempting to match my height and weight as it prepares itself for my flesh.

The revelation of their assimilation to become human rocks me to my core. All those bodies in the pit. People that came to the mall just wanting a simple tan for the summer, only to have their skin stripped from their bodies and then be discarded like trash. These creatures now walking among us. Humans none the wiser.

"You're monsters!" The rawness in my voice matches the raw terror in my wildly beating heart.

She laughs at my reaction. "No, but nice guess." Stella moves closer to me and begins to slather me with lotion. I gag. Solar Glow.

The lotion spreads, wiggling like a living blanket. Tingling numbness washes over me. Once the goo has coated my entire body, Stella smiles. "It was nice chatting with you, but it's time to go."

"Why the lotion?" I choke as the door closes.

Her muffled voice comes through the glass window. "It prepares the skin for extraction. Oh, and it prevents you from feeling *too* much of the process. I do *so* hate to hear the screams of you pathetic humans. It's like nails on a chalkboard."

I thrash against the restraints. The cold metal bites into my wrists and ankles. "Let me go!" I screech as the machine gets louder and louder, a deafening hum that begins to drown me out.

Stella's face makes one last appearance as she steps in front of the tiny circular window, her expression gleaming with sadistic pleasure. "Sorry, but rules are rules. No disturbing the customer during their tanning experience." She cackles as she walks away, listening to the sound of my blood-curdling screams as my body is stripped of my skin.

12

A SIMPLE ACT OF KINDNESS
Vincent St. Claire

MARLENE POUTED AS A SPECIAL news report interrupted her Saturday morning cartoons. Harold Greely was last seen leaving his job at the plastic factory on Monday, June 30th, and had not contacted his wife, friends, coworkers, or extended family. Being eight years old, Marlene couldn't fathom why they would stop *The Smurfs* to show her this.

Her brother Tony stumbled down the stairs with a plodding, zombie-like lack of elegance. He meandered toward the television set and cranked the volume dial back four notches.

"Hey!" shouted Marlene, staring up at him with a frown.

"You'll wake up the neighborhood," he scoffed. Marlene stuck out her tongue at him before returning her gaze to the cartoons.

Tony was a youth of small stature—technically an adult, as he had celebrated his eighteenth birthday a week earlier. This was his last summer before heading to the University of Southern California, and he had spent it working day and night at Lorenzo's Pizzeria. Mercifully, they gave him the weekend off after his grueling Fourth of July Friday shift. He couldn't complain too much. The time-and-a-half pay had resulted in a nice chunk of money, and he didn't intend to put it all in his college fund.

Tony made his way to the kitchen and rummaged through the pantry. Even after he turned it down, the TV could be heard loud and clear from the kitchen — Marlene would be lucky to make it to High School without hearing aids. With a sigh, he opened the lower cupboard door and pulled out the box of chocolatey cereal stashed behind his mother's healthier options. Maybe she had been right when she said that it had stunted his growth and didn't do his complexion any favors, but it was his weekend off, and he was going to enjoy himself. Tony grabbed the milk from the refrigerator. An entire side of the carton showed a black-and-white photo of a boy around Marlene's age. Thick letters above it read, "HAVE YOU SEEN THIS CHILD?"

After he poured himself a bowl of what loosely passed for cereal, Tony sat at the dinner table and shoveled the soggy morsels into his mouth. Tony had loved the stuff since he was a kid and probably still looked like one eating it. While he had watched his classmates grow to six feet and have their skin clear by the end of high school, he was still five-foot-one with a patina of cystic acne across his body. He was ridiculed by many of the popular students and was eager to reinvent himself at USC.

Tony gulped another spoonful of cereal and heard his mother Helen's footsteps descending the stairs. He tried to wolf down the rest before she could see the trash he was eating — more sugar than cereal, she would call it.

"My God, Marlene, don't sit so close to the TV. I ain't got vision insurance!" His mother spoke at her usual volume: louder than most people screamed.

"OK, Mommy," said Marlene dully without moving an inch.

Helen was a beefy woman in her late forties. Her hair was tied up in curlers, and she wore a bathrobe dulled from years of constant use. She was originally from New

York and spoke with an accent thick enough to turn heads in this part of the country.

As she stepped into the kitchen, she grimaced at the cereal box. "Jesus, Tony, you're gonna stunt your growth."

"A little late for that, ma," he replied.

She pulled out a box of bran flakes for herself and nestled into the seat adjacent to her son. She was about to pour herself a bowl when her eyes shifted to the picture of the little boy on the milk carton.

"You're shitting me. This's Jimmy Carmichael from Marlene's class!"

"You know that kid?"

"Yeah, I talked to his mother at parent-teacher conferences. Oh, I bet they're worried sick!"

"Another guy just went missing," said Tony between mouthfuls of cereal. "It was on the TV right before you came down."

Helen shook her head and set the milk carton back on the table. "Sometimes I feel like there's no kindness left in this world."

The two silently finished breakfast as the TV blared from the other room. Since her husband George left the family four years ago, Helen had become very protective and, to a degree, smothering toward her children. Though she was excited for Tony to begin his new adventure at college, she dreaded seeing him leave.

"What's on your agenda for today?" she asked, finally breaking the silence.

"Well, I was thinking of going down to the mall to check out the Fourth of July sales. I made some extra dough yesterday and want to get some new clothes for school."

"Don't blow all your money," she said, pointing a finger into his face. "Your scholarship ain't gonna cover everything, and I can barely pay my *own* bills."

"Relax, ma. I'm just getting some clothes."

"And be home at a decent hour."

"I will."

"And not in the back of a police car."

"Jesus," he laughed.

Helen got up to stand next to him, towering over her son even though she wasn't a tall woman. She put a hand on his shoulder and gave him a motherly smile.

"I know I ain't gotta worry about you getting in trouble, but watch after yourself."

"Is this about the milk carton kid?"

"No." Tony looked at her, not believing her at all. "Well, maybe a little."

"Ah, relax, Ma," said Tony with a scoff. "It was a grown man and a little kid. I doubt their disappearances are related."

"Don't you make light of this."

"I'm not. I'll be careful. Really."

Helen kissed her son on the forehead and grabbed both of his shoulders. "I know, I gotta cut the umbilical cord. I just don't have many more chances to be a mom before you move away."

"It's okay, Ma."

"Have a nice day off. You deserve one."

While his mother and sister resumed their morning routines, Tony prepared for the day. He finished combing his shower-wetted hair and looked into the bathroom mirror with lingering disappointment.

Throughout high school, Tony's style had been generic and unobtrusive. He didn't fit into any of the jock, nerd, goth kid, or headbanger stereotypes and felt phony dressing like them. If he wanted to make a statement once he landed at college, he would need to look around for inspiration—something that represented him, but with a little flash. He couldn't allow himself to be dismissed as the short, pizza-faced kid for another 4 years.

"It's time for a new look," he said to his reflection, "but what should it be?"

~

The wind was perfumed with palm trees and sea salt that hot summer day—the perfect atmosphere for his five-block trek to the bus stop. His stretch of the neighborhood was not particularly illustrious. Small houses with chipping paint and unwatered lawns were the rule rather than the exception. Still, it had never been known as dangerous or crime-ridden, which made the recent disappearances all the more unsettling.

When he arrived at the stop, there was a spattering of odd characters: a bearded man in a dirty coat far out of season, a middle-aged black woman in glasses with a stern look on her face, and a man in a white collared shirt handing out little comic books about how everything enjoyable in this world was the path straight to hell. Tony pulled out the headphones of the Walkman he had stashed away in his pocket and put them on, not listening to the tape but hoping that it would prevent any of the crowd from talking to him.

As he waited for the bus, ignoring eye contact with the strangers, another man joined the queue. He was a little taller than the boy, perhaps 5'6", and a decade or so older. The man styled his hair, which crept back at the temples, in a messy pompadour. Though he seemed hip and confident, what really grabbed Tony's attention was the man's jacket. It was a style that Tony was beginning to see more of now that *Top Gun* was dominating the box office—a dark brown leather bomber jacket with a rust-red wool collar.

Tony imagined the man must have been boiling in the heat with it on, but that jacket could be just the look he needed for college.

The man noticed Tony eyeing him and gave a sarcastic smirk.

"Take a picture, kid. It'll last longer."

"Sorry," said Tony, diverting his reddening face from the man. "I just thought your jacket was cool."

"Ya do, eh? Christ. Sounds like old man Huwell was right."

Tony looked back at him, confused, but the man in the jacket held up a finger and fished around in his jacket pocket. He pulled out a business card and handed it to Tony. It read: *Huwell's Fine Leather Goods at Sherwood Mall.*

"That kook pays me to wear this thing around town and hand out cards. It's nice in the cooler months, but Je-*sus* does it bite the big one on days like this."

"How much would something like that set me back?"

The man shrugged. "Beats me, kid. This is a floor model. But I'm sure he'd work something out for you."

Screeching brakes bowled over every conversation as the bus pulled into the stop. The homeless man, the grumpy woman, and the Jesus freak all got into the vehicle, but the man in the jacket started to walk away.

"Aren't you getting on?" asked Tony.

"Nah, man. I'm workin'. This was just one of my stops." He popped the wool collar and strutted down the street. "See ya 'round, kid."

"Hey, you riding or not?" shouted the bus driver, leering at Tony impatiently.

"Yeah, sorry."

Tony got on and found a seat in the back. He pulled his headphones back on and hit the play button. Though he loved this mixtape, he couldn't focus on the lyrics or the music. His mind wandered to that marvelous jacket.

~

Tony studied the mall directory sign and found Huwell's Fine Leather Goods by the mall's C wing entrance. It was an oddly shaped section, like a rectangle grafted onto a baseball home plate. The store seemed large for being so niche, but Tony figured they must stock quite the inventory.

It was a predictably busy day at the Sherwood Mall. Nearly every window was plastered with signs advertising Fourth of July sales. Smells of cinnamon buns, soft pretzels, and Orange Juliuses wafted through the air when they weren't overtaken by the ghastly combination of perfumes emanating from department stores. People filled every inch of the halls, pushing against each other like herded animals as they marched toward savings with single-minded determination.

When Tony reached the leather store's facade, he was stricken by how out of place it looked. The mall was a sterile white with neon buzzing everywhere, but Huwell's looked straight out of a TV western. Cedar paneling covered the walls and floors, and the signage was written in an Old West typeface. A rack of leather jackets was against the back wall, and there were displays for shoes, purses, and gloves. The odor of fresh-cut leather was powerful. Almost too powerful—like an aerosol leather was sprayed to amplify the natural smell. Still, a strange metallic funk lingered beneath.

Tony felt a hand touch his shoulder and jerked around to see a jovial man in his sixties. He was as anachronistic as the rest of the store, wearing a suede vest, suspenders, and hand-cobbled leather shoes.

"Welcome to Huwell's Fine Leather Goods. I, of course, am Mr. Huwell, the Genius of Leather. How can I help you today, sir? New shoes? How about a fine pair of gloves for your mother?"

"Oh, uh, I was looking for a jacket."

The man put his hands on his hips and narrowed his eyes. "Let me guess, one of those bomber jackets like Tom Cruise wears."

"Yeah," said Tony, laughing nervously. The man seemed larger than life, and the boy didn't think he had much chance of steering the conversation.

"Jerry must be doing his job! He thinks I'm nuts having him walk around town in our jackets, but I tell you, boy, my sales have skyrocketed ever since. A little advertising goes a long way. Come. I'll show you where they're kept."

Tony needed no help finding the single rack that hung leather jackets, but the man ushered him toward it. It dawned on Tony that this storefront was tiny—much smaller than it appeared on the directory kiosk. It wouldn't be unusual for some of the space to be allocated for inventory, but this store's backroom must have been three times the size of the sales floor.

"Well, here we are," said the man as he flipped through the jackets on the rack with dextrous fingers "They've had quite the surge in popularity as of late. We've hardly been able to keep them on the shelves. I'm sure we'll have something that will fit you. Never fear. What is your size, son?"

"Small," said Tony, scratching at his shoulder. "Maybe Extra-Small if you've got it."

"No shame in that, my boy. We weren't all born to be linebackers. Here we go. I'm afraid Small is the best we can do. What do you think about this one?"

The man held out a jacket, identical to the one on the man with the pompadour, though noticeably smaller. Tony grabbed it and began to look over the garment. He noticed the tag had no brand, just the logo printed on the store's sign.

"Do you guys have your own clothing label?"

"Of course. In fact, we do quite a bit of tanning, cutting, and stitching at this very location—locally sourced hides, only the finest."

"Interesting," said Tony weakly.

"I challenge you to find a mass-produced sweatshop jacket from the name brands of higher quality. Quality used to *mean* something. Nowadays, a pair of shoes won't last more than a few months. Junk, I say."

"I'm sure it's great. How much is that?"

"That piece in your hands can be yours for $150." Tony gulped—that was more than he made in a week. The salesman must have noticed his expression and put his hand on the boy's shoulder.

"Little steep for you? You must understand that these are all handcrafted pieces and will be a little spendier. No matter, I'm sure we can work out a sort of financing plan for you. Not to worry at all."

"You really mean it?"

"Yes sir, I do. Here, why don't you try it on? We have a little changing room in the back with a mirror. Come this way."

Once again, the man was on the move, darting across the sales floor without waiting for Tony's response. Before he could catch up, the man stood by a door next to the check-out counter. A small black sign reading "Employ-ees Only" hung on a tiny hook.

"Don't let that sign deter you, my boy, just go through this doorway, down the hall, first door on your left. I'll be right here writing out a financing plan should you decide this jacket is indeed for you. Go ahead, take your time."

The man stood by the door with crossed arms, tap-ping his foot.

"I can just try it on out here."

"Do you see a mirror around here, boy?" Huwell brought his arm around Tony's shoulders and began to walk him toward the entrance. "Don't be silly. You'll want to see how you look."

Tony hesitated to go to the changing room, but didn't think the salesman would get off his back until he saw himself in the mirror. He gave Mr. Huwell a weak smile and passed through the door to a small hallway with the same white floors and walls as the rest of the mall. A set of fluorescent bulbs flickered like strobe lights at a dance club. The funky smell that cut through the leather was stronger here, and he felt his stomach begin to churn.

Tony opened the first door on the left as instructed and walked into the small room. It contained a coat rack, a folding chair, and a long mirror on the opposite wall. It was strange for a store that didn't sell clothing outside of jackets, gloves, and shoes to have a designated changing room. A mirror on the sales floor would have been less of a hassle.

His body began to shiver, and Tony was suddenly grateful for the jacket in his hands. This room felt five to ten degrees cooler than the rest of the hallway, though he couldn't figure out where the draft came from. When he looked into the mirror with the jacket on, his heart sank.

It was *huge*. Tony had enough room for another person. His reflection was painful—a reminder that his body would always betray him. With a frown, Tony put the jacket back on its hanger. He told himself it was a stupid idea, anyway—Top Gun would probably be old hat by the time he started school. Tony would have to find another style somewhere else in the mall, but at least now he could save some money.

He grabbed the doorknob and was puzzled when it wouldn't open. Strange—he didn't remember a lock on the door. He didn't even remember closing the door behind him. Tony tried again to no avail, the knob turned around in his hands without catching.

"Hello?" he said in a loud voice. "I think I locked myself in." He was met by silence. Odd, Mr. Huwell couldn't have been more than twenty feet away.

"Mr. Huwell? Can you hear me? I'm locked in here." Still no response. Could the man really be that engrossed with the paperwork? A shuffling sound from the adjoining wall crept into the changing room. Tony wondered if another worker was back there sorting inventory. He faced that direction, toward the mirror. It was worth a shot.

"Hello? Can you hear me? I think I locked myself in."

Suddenly, the shuffling stopped. The hairs on the back of Tony's neck shot up. What could be going on? He tried the door again, pushing his shoulder against it and jerking the knob with more force.

"Mr. Huwell," he said, shouting now. "Please, I can't get out. Can I get some help?

If he could have heard his surroundings over the bark of his voice, Tony would have noticed the movement continuing behind the wall—footsteps in the connecting room traipsing to the mirror. If he had just turned around, he would have seen the mirror on the wall begin to shake.

"Hello? Anybody? Help me, please! I'm trapped in here."

A stillness overcame him. In that instant, he could sense someone on the other side of the door. They were waiting for him. Perhaps they had been the whole time.

"Goddamn it, will you just get it over with?" said the voice behind the door. Tony recognized it immediately as Mr. Huwell's, but it was different now—cold, joyless, and for the first time, real.

Something crashed behind him. He turned to see that the mirror had swung open on a hinge, slamming against the wall and revealing a hole cut in the drywall behind it. A set of eyes glinted through the blackness. They moved closer, and the light from the dressing room outlined the face around them. It came into the light, and Tony shuddered with recognition. The pompadoured man peered in through the hole, staring at Tony with a sickening smile.

"What? What's going on?"

The man, now adorned in a stained leather apron, stuck one foot in through the hole. It was only about two feet by four feet, and the man struggled to crawl through, fighting for balance as he held something in his hand. Tony continued to pound against the door, but felt a weight on the other side. Huwell must have been on the other side holding it shut.

"Hey, this isn't funny. Let me out!"

The man in the apron was inside the dressing room now, carrying a sturdy mallet. Tony looked for some escape, some path to salvation, but the hole in the wall was his only exit.

"Just keep still, and this'll be over in a second."

The man started toward Tony, tapping the mallet against his palm as he approached. The stench of tanning fluids and rotting meat emanated from him, growing stronger with each step closer. He licked his lips with anticipation, taking things slowly as if he took pleasure from the boy's growing terror.

"Help! Security! Anybody"

Annoyance flooded the man's face as he bolted toward Tony. He grabbed the boy's face with a muscular hand and covered his mouth. Tony tried desperately to struggle free, but the man pulled him toward his body.

"You really think they don't know what's going on here? That the mall isn't in on it?"

He was done playing around. With a violent motion, the man swung the mallet above his head. In another second, he would slam it down into Tony's skull. Seeing his life about to end, Tony did the only thing he could think of. The coppery taste of blood flooded into his mouth as he bit down into the man's palm.

"Oh, you son of a —"

The wound forced the man to loosen his grip. Tony squirmed out of his arms and thudded onto the floor. Holding his bleeding hand to his chest, the man swung the hammer over his head and lurched after the boy. Tony, still crawling on the floor, launched his foot upwards. A crunch rang out as his foot connected with his pursuer's groin. The man doubled over on the floor with eyes wide open, clutching between his legs. Tony needed to get out of there, and fast. With nowhere else to go, he dove through the hole in the wall.

A relentless stench overcame Tony as he climbed into the production area. Industrial fans the size of full-grown men blew frigid air onto piles of hides. Meathooks lined the walls of the expansive room, dangling carcasses high above his head to bleed out. Tony figured there must be a back exit somewhere in this room, and kept running, ignoring his burning lungs.

He kept his pace, seeing the light of day cutting the outline of an overhead door at the end of the room. The smell made him nauseous, and the fans made his skin break out in gooseflesh, but he continued his sprint. More of the hanging bodies passed by, and Tony felt like something was off. He turned his head toward them, and realization squeezed hard against his gut. The sides of meat swayed with the blowing of the fans, but they were not cows, goats, or even livestock at all.

The macabre sight brought his escape to a halt. He gazed up with a slack jaw at the body hanging to his right — sliced open from groin to throat and dripping blood into the drain beneath it. Tony recognized the face, even though it was bloated and drained of color. He didn't want to believe it, *could* not believe it, but there was no doubt. Dangling on the hook was Jimmy Carmichael, the milk carton kid.

He thought he was going to be sick. If he looked, Tony was sure he would find the man from the news report as well, but there was no time for that. His life was on the line. Tony bolted toward the door, getting closer — more light crept through it now. He finally reached it, feeling renewed hope as it wobbled against his weight.

Tony slipped his fingers underneath the door and tried to pull it open. He grunted and strained with all his might to lift the shutter, but it was locked closed. What now, what now? He had to stay calm. There must be a button to lift the door, and he had to find it with the meager glow spilling from its edges.

The only thing illuminated was a dumpster in front of the door. It was still too dim to make out the details of its contents, but there was enough light to paint the general picture, and the smell filled in the rest. Rotting, skinned corpses were piled atop each other. This must be a loading dock where the dumpster would be trucked away. The realization made Tony sick, and he bent over to vomit.

Before he could, he felt a hand grab the collar of his shirt.

"Stubborn little shit, ain't ya?"

~

Helen spent the next two weeks frantically searching for her missing son. She became a frequent sight at the Sherwood Mall, handing out flyers and talking to every employee of every store. The desperate mother made multiple television appearances, looking more ragged each time, pleading for anyone with information to come forward. The police came up with no leads, and though suggestions of connections to other recent missing persons were offered, no pattern could be deciphered.

After a busy morning hitting every store in the mall's A and B wings, Helen took a brief respite at the food court. She popped a stream of pretzel bites into her mouth that she barely tasted and slurped down an Orange Julius fast enough to give her a serious brain freeze. It didn't matter to her. Nothing mattered now except finding Tony.

Small crowds of teenagers whispered to each other and pointed their eyes toward her. "There she is, the mother of the missing boy," they would be saying. "How sad. She doesn't look like she's slept in weeks."

She crumpled up her baggy, empty now except for a teaspoon of coarse salt, and threw it along with the half-finished smoothie into the trash. She would repeat the process in the C wing—going from door to door, employee to employee, showing Tony's picture, and asking if they'd seen him around. If this wing were anything like the last two, it would result in scores of eye-rolling teenagers telling her they still hadn't seen anything and one or two requests from management to leave the store.

After another half hour of fruitless inquiry, she stood in front of the last place she could imagine Tony visiting: a kitschy leather goods store. She sighed as she entered, ready to get it over with and take her search to somewhere more promising.

Helen nearly choked on the smell of leather. There didn't appear to be an employee available, so she wandered around the store, eyeing the wares. Everything seemed to be of exceptional quality—the handbags were cushy with a bright sheen, the shoes looked stylish and durable, and the jackets would have looked good on anyone. She continued her dallying, stepping over to a tiny display featuring a variety of hand-sewn gloves.

As she was about to pick up a pair, she could sense someone standing behind her. Hellen turned around to see a man of late middle age smiling at her.

"How do you do, ma'am? Welcome to Huwell's Fine Leather Goods. I, of course, am Mr. Huwell, the Genius of Leather. I guarantee you will not find finer leather goods anywhere in the region. What can I help you with today? Would you like to try on some of those gloves?"

"Oh," said Helen, who dug into her pocket to produce a wallet-sized print of Tony's senior photo, "My name is Helen Grady. This is my son, Tony. He, uh—he went missing a couple of weeks ago. The Fourth of July weekend. The last I heard, he was headed to the mall, and I was wondering if you'd seen him."

The salesman grabbed the photograph and studied it carefully. After a few seconds, he frowned and shook his head.

"I'm terribly sorry, ma'am. I'm afraid I don't recognize him. I was working that weekend as well."

Helen took the photo back from him. "Well, I didn't think this would be the kind of place he'd gravitate toward anyway."

The man looked hurt by the comment. "Yes, well, you might be surprised where boys his age might want to go."

"Yeah, I suppose."

Helen began to turn away, but the salesman grabbed her shoulder as she took her first step toward the exit.

"Er, I hope it isn't rude of me to ask, but how is the search for Tony going? Are there any—oh, what do they call them, leads?"

Helen tried to keep it together but burst into tears almost immediately. The salesman tried to console her by patting her back with an awkward hand.

"No. I know that he was headed to the mall, but it was the Fourth of July, and this place was busy as all get out. We don't even know if he made it here for sure."

The man was caught off guard as Helen buried her face into his shoulder. She had been on the verge of tears this whole time, and his shoulder had been suitable enough to cry on. He continued to pat her back, now with a little more confidence. The salesman could not contain his smile, but forced a placid face before she brought her head up.

"What's just awful is that the police aren't putting as many resources into it as they could because he's eighteen years old. An adult, but just barely. He'd only been one for a week when he went missing. The cops say lots of men his age leave home, but that's not him. That's not *my* Tony."

"Eighteen? That boy was eighteen?"

"I know, he looked younger. But that doesn't matter to those —those *pigs.*"

He gave Helen a sympathetic smile and nodded his head. As his mouth curled into a frown, he crossed his arms and examined the woman.

"I do wish that there was something I could do to help you."

"No, it's all right. You've been as much help as anyone else in this mall."

The man took a step closer to the display of gloves.

"I'll tell you what, ma'am, I know this is no consolation for your missing boy, but why don't you let me give you something?" He bent over to snatch a particular pair of gloves and handed them to Helen. "This is a freshly sewn pair of gloves. Hell, it's a freshly *tanned* pair of gloves. The hide it came from was mostly unusable. Very small, most of it covered in blemishes —the whole works. But a very small patch was truly exquisite. I saw you eyeing them earlier. Go ahead. On the house."

Helen stared at the gift in disbelief.

"Oh no. I couldn't."

"Please. I won't take no for an answer. It's the least I could do."

She examined the gloves carefully. They were a truly impressive work, soft and pliable. Unable to contain her curiosity, she slipped one on her hand.

"My God, it fits."

"Like a glove?" asked the salesman. They both laughed mildly.

"What is this leather? Kidskin?"

"Yes, you could say that."

"I just —I can't believe your generosity."

"My dear, it is but a pair of gloves. I have an entire display full and more in the back room. I could tell from the moment you walked in that this pair belonged to you."

"Well, thank you."

"Any time."

Helen waved to the salesman and started to exit the store. She couldn't explain it exactly, but she felt much better than when she entered a few minutes earlier.

"Best of luck on the search, ma'am. I hope your boy gets home safely and soon."

"Yes, thank you very much."

She stepped out into the open mall with a renewed sense of purpose. There were still a handful of stores left in this area, and four sections of the mall to go. She had the funny feeling that if she kept at it, she would find Tony, and everything would be all right. It was crazy what a simple act of kindness could do for a person.

13
LITTLE KING
William MacFarland

JAMES DIED AGAIN. He wanted to throw the controller at the television. Instead, he watched, again, as pixelated insects swarmed his pixelated body. How long had he tried to beat this dumb level on this dumb game?

"Man, this level is bullshit."

"Yeah," Chris said. "My brother told me that there was a cheat code to get infinite lives."

"Sure." James got up and turned the television off. He turned back to Chris, who was squaring up to throw another dart at the target.

"What were you saying about the mall?"

"I said that my brother told me," Chris paused to squint at the bullseye, "there's a guy who works there with black eyes."

"Black eyes?" James crossed the basement to sit on the large couch. "Like punched-in-the-face black eyes?" He balled both his fists and mimed punching himself in the face.

"No." Chris laughed and threw the dart. Missing the target completely, it stuck into the wood paneling. "Like all black, no whites." He swirled his fingers near the whites of his own eyes.

James considered this, his brow furrowed. "Ya right." He had grown more comfortable calling out his friend's wild claims, especially when those claims came via Chris' older brother.

"No, for real. My brother said that some kid in his class said that the guy's eyes are completely black." Chris threw another dart, missing the board completely. He paused, considered. "And the walls are full of meat."

"What are you talking about?"

"Yeah," Chris nodded, as if agreeing with his own story. "There's a store at Sherwood where the walls are full of meat, and the dude working there has black eyes."

"That's bullshit. A wall is full of meat? What the hell does that even mean?"

"Not a wall, the walls. Like all of them." He crossed the room and sat on the floor across from James.

"Oh yeah?" James knew this story was garbage, but he was curious about where it was going. Chris' older brother was known to tell all sorts of stories about all sorts of made-up crap. Once, he had convinced the two of them that the local Catholic Church was actually home to a secret coven of witches, that the neighborhood was built on a cursed Indian burial ground, and Bloody Mary haunted the nearby woods. What made Chris' brother so believable was that he acted like he believed what he was saying. The more James hung around Chris, and by proxy, Chris' brother, the more he realized that they were two weird kids who told weird stories. But they weren't all that bad, he guessed. Weird friends were better than none at all.

"Yeah," Chris said, picking at the orange fibers of the carpet.

"Sure," said James.

"No, for real," Chris said. "My brother said that he was talking to a kid in study hall, and that kid's dad worked at the mall as a janitor or something."

"Whatever. If that was true, everyone would know about it. It'd be on the news or something."

"It is true." Chris got up and sat next to James, his eyes wide. "My brother said that the kid told him that his dad saw some really gross stuff leaking out of a wall in one of the hallways behind the stores. The kid said his dad was checking it out 'cause he thought there was a busted pipe or something."

"For real?"

"That's what he said the kid said."

James looked at the basement walls, letting his mind wander. "What about the guy with the eyes?"

"Oh, that was the weirdest part. My brother said that the kid's dad said that — "

"James!" Both boys jumped. Chris ripped the cover of the comic he had been holding.

"James! Are you down there?" He got up and ran the short distance to the bottom of the steps, stumbling over his feet.

"Yeah! I'm . . ." He looked over at Chris, who was already packing up to leave. "We're down here." His mother stood silhouetted in the rectangle of the door frame, hands on her hips.

"Tell your friend to go home. We need to go out." She walked away before he could respond.

James turned to deliver the news, but Chris was already standing, backpack in hand. The two boys exchanged an apologetic look. *Sorry, you have to go. Sorry, you have to stay.*

"I'll tell you the rest later," Chris said.

"Yeah, sure."

"Later."

"Yeah, later." James sighed as he watched his friend ascend the steps, a familiar heat flushing his cheeks.

~

When his mother told him that they were going to the mall, James felt excited. Excitement that was immediately extinguished when he saw the folded newspaper advertisement near her purse.

Little King Clothing's 4th of July Spectacular!
Let SALES and Freedom RING!
All suits and vest sets are twenty-five percent off!
All ties and slacks: ten percent off!
Free tie pin with each purchase!
This sale is a BLAST!

Illustrated boys in suits and ties waved American flags, and to James, they all looked miserable. Not a parade of fine young men dressed to impress, but anguished prisoners in a forced march.

"You need a new suit." Her tone was matter-of-fact, but not unkind. Not yet, at least. James wiped his hands on his pants and cleared his throat.

"Mom, I—"

"Your old suit is too small," she interrupted. "You need a new one."

The thought of clothes shopping with his mother was an unhappy one, all past experiences having ended in arguing or embarrassment, or both.

"Mom, I really don't—"

"Your grandparents' anniversary party is next week."

James imagined himself being paraded around the store, having to try on one suit after another. He would have the illusion of choice, but in the end, *she* would choose for him.

"Mom, I really don't want to go."

She cleared her throat and looked at him. "I don't know why you're being so difficult."

"I'm not trying to be—"

She cut him off again. "The family will be there." She paused, considering her words. "We need to make a good showing." Her voice was tight, tears welling in her eyes.

James knew that the conversation, such as it was, was over. If anything mattered to his mother, it was putting on a *good show*. Especially if that show was in front of her parents and the rest of the family. His face flushed, and he clenched at his jeans.

"Ok."

"What was that?"

"Ok," he said, staring at his feet, hating all of this. He hated this, and he hated himself for not standing up to her. If he had the guts, he would have really argued. He would have told her to fuck off with her good showing and that she should try to make a good showing of herself for once. But James didn't have the guts—those had been taken away years ago. His stomach churned with what was unsaid, his emotions an unrecognizable landscape. A feeling he was all too accustomed to.

"Good." She was smiling. The tears were gone. "Now go get in the car."

Walking out, James caught a glimpse of Chris. He was pedaling his bike in lazy circles around the cul-de-sac. James thought about Chris' story of meat-filled walls and the black-eyed man.

~

Little King Clothing, like the rest of the mall, was decorated in full for the Fourth of July holiday. Bunting hung from the ceiling in great swooping splashes of red, white, and blue. Classical piano renditions of patriotic music played discreetly through hidden speakers. Poster-sized copies of the advertisement hung at intervals around the store. It was well-lit, well-furnished, and just as awful as James had expected.

He followed in his mother's wake as she walked among the racks and displays. Having gotten what she wanted, she was happy. Not only that, but she had put on her public persona. A version he liked and wished he could experience more often.

"Look at this," she said, stopping in front of a display. Faceless mannequins, each with an American flag in hand. "You would look so handsome in this," she said, pointing to the middle mannequin.

James eyed the mannequin. The three-piece set was one of the ugliest shades of blue he had ever seen and was identical to one of the outfits in the advertisement. It looked even worse in person, and it made James' eyes hurt.

"Mom, I don't really like tha—"

She turned on him and hissed, "Don't start."

James squinted, a sharp pain hitting him in both temples. Headache?

"That is quite stunning." James and his mother jumped at the unexpected voice. "A summer sky." The voice was soft, gentle, and it made James' skin crawl. Both he and his mother turned in unison to face the smiling sales clerk. "Blemishless."

James and Chris loved to watch horror movies, creature features, and slashers alike. He and Chris would laugh and talk about how, if they were ever in that situation, they would either run or try to fight. Being boys of their age, and wanting to outdo one another, they always chose to fight. They would never run away, and they would make fun of the victims for freezing up like idiots.

Staring into the black eyes of the clerk, James understood why those characters froze and never ran or fought.

Staring into those black eyes, he felt trapped in his own body, wanting to scream, to run, unable to do either. Frozen. Fight or flight concepts without meaning. The shock of what he was seeing disconnected everything. *I'm in a dream,* James thought. *This is a nightmare.* And following that, *Chris was right.* And with that, the edges of his vision darkened, his breath caught in his chest, his knees buckled. He felt himself going away somewhere deep.

"Goodness," the clerk said, smiling. Thick ebony clots clogged the sockets where its eyes should have been. "It looks like our little gentleman is unwell."

"James?" His mother's voice was full of concern. "Honey, what's wrong?" Soothing concern, no hint of the previous hiss. An act.

"Here," the clerk said. "Let's get our Little King off his feet."

James couldn't think. It was as if the static of a monstrous radio was slowly being increased, scattering his thoughts. He blinked his eyes, trying to clear them and his mind. He felt himself being led, a hand on each arm. Everything was a faraway sensation, distant, removed.

And then he was sitting in an overstuffed armchair across from the dressing rooms.

"There," the clerk said. James felt his head lift to look at The Clerk. The black clots, if they had been there in the first place, were gone. In their place were the most dazzling blue eyes he had ever seen. Eyes the same color as the suit his mother had pointed out. The head static cleared as quickly as it arrived.

"Now, isn't that better?"

"Thank you so much, I don't know what came over him," his mother said. "James, thank the kind gentleman." She gave his shoulder a hard squeeze.

"Than—" James swallowed and tried again. His breathing had steadied. "Thank—" His voice was weak, making him sound years younger than he was. "Thank you."

"Not at all. Now," the clerk said, turning toward James' mother. "Is there anything I can help you with today?" He gestured towards the racks of clothes. "All suits and vest sets are twenty-five percent off." He smiled. "All ties and slacks, ten percent off." The clerk turned toward James. "And you receive a free Little King tie pin." He gestured to his own tie pin. The small gold crown glinted in the showroom lights, causing James to squint.

James stared at the blue eyes, trying to make sense of what he had seen. What he had thought he had seen.

"Thank you." His mother was smiling. She looked happy. *Hadn't she seen?* "I would like to see that suit," she said, pointing to the mannequin. "In a slim fit, please."

"A woman of taste," the clerk said. And then his mother did something that surprised and disturbed James.

She giggled.

Laugh, yes, but never a giggle. She sounded like one of the girls at his school, and was smiling like when they had a dumb crush on someone.

"Right this way." The clerk took his mother's arm and led her back to the display.

James watched them. The clerk's hand had moved to the small of his mother's back—strange. James turned away, rubbing his temples and trying to make sense of it all. He had seen the black eyes; he knew it. His body knew it, felt it. None of it made any sense. Did he really think that his mother, of all people, would giggle at someone that looked like that? Would let someone — *something* — like that touch her?

No.

He knew that.

She would have been the first one to scream for help. Black eyes were far from a good showing.

But what had he seen then? Chris' story must have gotten to him more than he thought. He came in here looking for something, and when it wasn't there, his mind made it all up. That had to be it.

But he had seen something.

Hadn't he?

James picked at the upholstery of the armchair. A nervous gesture, a distraction. Small brown strings came loose that James balled between his fingers and dropped to the floor. He took a deep breath — *smell the roses* — and exhaled — *blow out the candles*. It was a phrase his teacher used and one that he and Chris made fun of, but it helped. It was helping now. *Deep in, slow out.* He could feel his heart slowing, his insides uncoiling. James flicked the other string ball to the floor.

He looked around. A few shoppers, not many, walked through the store. His mother stood enthralled by whatever the clerk was saying. She stood facing him, mouth agape, eyes wide, nodding to whatever he was saying.

James picked at another loose thread and breathed in deeply. *Deep in, slow out. Deep in, slow —*

Someone coughed, breaking his concentration.

James looked towards the dressing rooms. The middle curtain was drawn shut, and James felt sympathy for the poor kid who was in there. They sounded sick. Really sick. James winced as another barrage of wet coughs erupted from behind the curtain. Gross. James wrinkled his nose at the noise while a sly grin spread across his face. How would the clerk react if someone barfed up their food court nachos on his well-cared-for carpet? From the sound of it, James wouldn't have to wait long.

He waited, but there was no rerun of food court nachos.

The kid had fallen silent except for a series of short, wheezing gasps. Deciding that he really didn't want to see—or hear—what happened next, James got up to walk around. His mother would find him soon enough after she decided it was his turn to try something on.

James made his way through the store, remembering the times he would hide in between the racks, pretending that he was in a top-secret fort or a hidden cave. He felt safe in those tight spaces. He felt the urge to do that now, but never would. He was too old for that stuff, and he felt sad that he was too old for that stuff.

James stuffed his hands in his pockets and kept wandering. He walked the perimeter of the store twice. Zigzagged between all the racks twice. Counted the sales posters and buntings.

Twenty each.

Forty total.

How long did it take to pick out a suit? James was ready to walk the perimeter again when he stopped near the front entrance.

You should leave.

The thought surprised him. Butterflies filled his stomach as he looked out into the concourse. James felt a tidal pull from the crowd and took one step forward, out of Little King. It would be exciting to slip away and experience a moment of simultaneous freedom and rebellion. James smiled at the thought of it. Who knew? Perhaps he could slip away for a bit without her knowing. His heart thudding and his mind decided, James took another step out of Little King. He took one last look, checking if he was clear to escape.

She was nowhere to be seen, and neither was the clerk.

The store was empty except for whoever was gagging in the dressing room.

James tried to remember if he had passed his mother and the clerk amongst the racks. He couldn't. As far as he knew, they hadn't moved from the display with the trio of mannequins. His brow furrowed, and he returned the step he had taken. Where was she?

She left.

She left you.

He shivered. There's a huge difference between leaving and being left. The thought made no sense—she would never let him out of her sight, especially when the mall was this crowded.

What if she left because you were arguing too much?

What if she got tired of your whining and decided to leave you?

A slow, creeping sensation of cold dread flooded him, as if his heart had started pumping ice rather than blood. James was starting to worry but refused to lose control. He was not going to freak out. He would keep his cool, but he wasn't sure for how long.

The walls are full of meat.

Chris' words bobbed to the surface of his mind, pale and terrifying. Pinpricks dotted James' back, setting the short hairs on his neck on end. It was as if an invisible finger, icy and dead, ran down the length of his spine. James stood on tiptoe and craned his neck. Little King was, in fact, empty. His heart began to race. If she had left, why hadn't she told him? Did she leave him because he had upset her in the car? He stepped from the concourse tile to the showroom carpet.

A fresh wave of phlegmy gags erupted from the dressing room.

He clenched at his pant legs, his knuckles turning white with the strain. *Deep in, slow out. Smell the roses, blow out the candles.* He felt his chest tighten and his knees grow weaker.

He wanted to run.

"Mom?" The question pleaded for a response.

Nothing.

Somewhere in the mall, a woman—not his mother—laughed. It was a bright, happy sound that was quickly overtaken by the monotone drone of the crowd. It all sounded far away. Dreamy, thick. The gasping from the dressing room stopped abruptly. Silence hung over the emptiness of Little King Clothing like a fog.

He wanted to run.

His mind told him to run.

But where? Out into the mall, screaming her name? Did he really want to be another crying kid who had lost his mommy? No, but whatever embarrassment he'd feel would be preferable to how he felt in this moment. James stood rooted to the spot, waves of indecision crashing over him, robbing him of his ability to act.

Stay? Leave? Wait? Look?

What was the right thing to do?

Deep in, slow out. Smell the roses, blow out the candles. His eyes started to brim with tears, and he wiped them away.

Deep in, slow —

The mental static and nausea from before returned, cutting the thought short.

"You look unwell."

The words hit James like ice water. The hand that came to rest on his shoulder felt heavy. Dead. There was no mistaking who was standing behind him, and yet it made no sense. Seconds before, the store was empty, the entrance clear. James swayed on the spot and closed his eyes, wishing to wake up, knowing full well that it was a stupid wish. A wasted wish.

Another cold hand came to rest on the other shoulder and squeezed. It was gentle, which made it much worse and more unwelcome. "Your friend —" Warm and fetid breath, like the gasp of a corpse, puffed into his ear and assailed his nostrils. " —wasn't wrong."

Like a puppet, mindless and without autonomy, James was turned to face The Clerk. The clear parts of his mind pleaded for him to regain control, to run, or at the very least scream for help. But those parts were being drowned out by the howling in his mind —the static was now a roar.

There were no flowers to smell or candles to extinguish.

James stood face to face with a demon, a thing that masqueraded as a man. A creature of outer darkness with teeth that were far too small and far too many. James felt himself slipping the way one slips in a dream — an abrupt, slow sensation of zero control. *You did see it!* His mind screamed. *He tricked you both, you did see it!*

The fiendish grin expanded across its plaid face as The Clerk smiled even wider. "That's right." Its tone was that of an impressed teacher. Globules of black pus leaked from its eyes in thick, tarry rivulets. "You did see," it chuckled, licking at the corner of its mouth, smearing the black slime that ran there. The sound turned James' stomach. It sounded more like whatever was behind the dressing room curtain than a laugh. "You are an observant young man. I must confess," it lowered its voice to a whisper, a tone of *just between you and me*, "you took me by surprise." It tittered, and James thought he would go insane at the sound of it. That he was going insane.

There was a wet, tearing sound from the dressing room, and The Clerk looked up. The pressure in James' mind lessened. The Clerk gestured towards the dressing room with a gnarled talon.

"How about you and I go see what all the fuss is about."

"My mom." His voice was weak, barely a whisper.

"What about her?"

"I —" Again, indecision flooded James. He wanted to know where she was. He wanted to know if she was okay. He wanted to see if she was coming back. He wanted to know why this was happening. He wanted to know if he was, or had gone, insane. James opened his mouth, but his words failed him.

Again, he found himself being ushered to the chair near the dressing room. As he sat, James caught sight of The Clerk's tie pin. All rational thought evaporated as water on a hot skillet. The small gold crown was gone, replaced by something far worse than oozing, black eyes. All rational thought evaporated as water on a hot skillet. His young mind split along unseen seams, never to regain its former structure. The sane world of a few minutes before was gone, flipped inside out, and torn.

What James saw pinned to The Clerk's tie answered the questions that had raced through his mind.

She was not all right.

She was not coming back.

He had not gone insane, but would be going shortly.

"Beautiful, isn't it?" The glee in The Clerk's voice was evident. "One of many, I assure you, but this one is special."

James closed his eyes, trying to escape into the blackness behind his eyelids. The Clerk's face floated there in that blackness, its smile awful and predatory. "You are observant, and we can't afford to lose such a fine young gentleman such as yourself. "Look."

James' eyes snapped open. The Clerk stood in front of the dressing rooms, *its* hand gripping the closed curtain. A late-night host from hell, introducing its next guest.

"Please." The whispered word was all that James could manage. He didn't want to see what was behind that curtain.

"It jitters and crawls back there." The Clerk's voice was reverent, full of awe. The fissure in James' mind widened. The fabric curtain was swept aside with a flourish.

The room was empty.

A poster hung on the back wall. Nothing more.

Images of mangled children marched across the faded poster in a nightmare parade. Each one more anguished than the next, their suits stained with the slime that poured from their eyes.

"The hunger is back there."

Blooms of moisture began to soak through the paper, reducing the images to abstract blurs and smears.

"It roams back there."

That's what it looks like when you melt, the fading part of James' mind thought. *That's what it looks like when you melt.*

"It fills back there."

There was a thick gurgling sound of a clogged drain releasing its foul contents. The Clerk stepped into the small cubicle and ran one long finger down the middle of the poster. Yellow liquid poured from the opening.

"It births."

A mass of mottled gray flesh, pulsating with unnatural life, pushed through the wall. The stench was immediate and oppressive. The scent of spoiled meat and long-festering trash.

Smell the rot, breathe out the filth.

James gagged, and the mass of corrupted flesh retched in response, the same wet sound he had heard before. Kind calling to kind.

"Isn't it wonderful?" The Clerk said.

James sat mute and motionless as a veined tendril slapped loose off the opening and fell to the dressing room floor. The boneless appendage unwound itself in large, lazy loops, like a sedated python.

James' mind raced and tripped along a twisted nightmare corridor, but he could not look away. Within the texture of that slithering thing, he saw small pearlescent inclusions. They bulged, splitting the veined skin and spilling onto the floor.

Teeth.

James' tongue instinctively ran along his own at the sight of them.

"Oh." The Clerk looked up towards the front of the store, its smile widening to Cheshire proportions.

"Wait here," said The Clerk as it strode to the front. James' muscles relaxed, the mind static lessened, but not by much. He turned to follow The Clerk's progress.

A woman had entered the store. James' heart fluttered. *She would see, she would help. She would see, and she would get help.* James cleared his throat. He would scream for help. He would scream for help and run to her.

Nothing.

He pushed against the arms of the chair to stand, but his arms and legs betrayed him. He tried to call out for help, but *his* voice failed him. The thing in the wall squelched and writhed. James willed his desperation at her.

Help me. Look. Get out! Get help! RUN!

The Clerk greeted her with the same charm and class that it showed his mother. The woman smiled in return, blind to the grinning horror in front of her.

She can't see.

The woman gestured to the newspaper in her hand. No doubt that it was the same advertisement promising that the *Little King's sale would be a BLAST!* The Clerk led her to a rack of dress pants, her expression cheery and impassive. The face of someone running a quick errand, in and out, and on to the next thing.

The appendage slithered along the carpet, sounding like heavy boots in thick mud.

"Help." James' voice was small, weak, nothing more than a wisp of a thought. The expanding mass throbbed and spluttered in response. The softened drywall buckled under the weight of the thing. Fluids oozed and dripped, befouling the well-cared-for carpet.

She would see, and she would get help. He would scream for help. He would scream for help and run to her. All he had to do was scream, and the nightmare would end.

The woman looked up in James' direction, offering him a polite smile.

"Help." He whispered, wanting to scream the word. He was unsure if his lips were moving, and the whisper wasn't imagined. Her brow furrowed, and her smile wavered. *She can't see, but she's starting to feel it,* he thought.

He was living a nightmare, and this lady was buying dress pants.

The woman accepted her free tie pin and left the store. James watched her go, tears streaming down his cheeks. He pushed himself to a standing position, feeling that he might be able to move, to run away.

"Very few see." The Clerk said, moving from behind the counter. Invisible fingers picked at the fissure in James' mind. The static returned. His legs weakened from under him, and he fell back into the chair. The Clerk's proximity robbed him of his mental clarity and physical strength. "Some *feel*, but they don't *see.*"

The jittering flesh in the changing room had split in several places, revealing a tangle of bone and muscle. Pale, unblinking eyes emerged from one of the larger growths. The quivering mass pushed further, releasing a tangle of what looked like fingers. They fell writhing onto the pus-soaked carpet, squirming as a nest of snakes.

"Look at her." The Clerk gestured towards the woman who was retreating into the crowd. James followed the gesture as if an invisible string connected his head and The Clerk's wrist. "Look at them." A long pause hung between them. The crowds bustled past, unaware. James watched them with eyes that were beginning to blur. "Oblivious to the wonders around them." Its voice dripped with contempt, with hatred. "That dumb bitch doesn't even feel it." The Clerk looked at James, eyes twin abysses of unknown space. "But you do." The Clerk smiled. "You see and feel and that," The Clerk paused to consider its words, "is exceptional."

"Yes."

James felt something tug at his foot.

James looked down to see a cluster of fingers engulfing his right sneaker. The sight of this would have horrified him moments ago, but he watched it with a detached blankness.

His mind, stretched past breaking, was no longer his.

"Yes."

"The most wonderful thing." The Clerk said.

"Yes."

"It makes a good showing, doesn't it?"

"Yes." The phrase triggered some thin memory, but James couldn't hold it. A glimmer of something faded and then was gone. "A good showing."

James patted the warm flesh that had enveloped his leg. His hand stuck and would not pull away. The warm sensation that spread over the place was pleasant. Distant. This was happening to someone else. Someone far away.

"A good showing."

The laugh that followed layered and folded in on itself like a monstrous reverb on an old amplifier. It rolled and echoed inside James' head and through his small frame. Pressure built behind his eyes. A howling wind blew through the open spaces in his mind.

"Wonderful." The Clerk grinned.

"Yes." James mouthed the word.

"Wonderful."

"Wonderful." Tears rolled down James' cheeks, but there was no sadness or fear. The areas of his young mind that were once filled with emotion were at the bottom of the sea floor. Dark, vast, and empty.

Tendrils swayed in front of his face in slow, rhythmic arcs. Pulpy masses prodded and plucked at his arms, his cheeks. The sightless eyes studied him. The thing from the wall jittered and roamed.

"Wonderful," James repeated.

"Truly." The man said.

James could hear the murmur of the shoppers and faint rhythm of the mall's music. The thing in the wall heaved itself further out of the opening, and James smiled. With his free hand, he wiped the tears away from his face.

It came away black

He smiled.

He cried.

14
PARRISH PHOTOS
Vanessa Leonardo

THE SHUTTER SNAPPED CLOSED and then mechanically opened again, like a giant blinking eye. Lyle adjusted the aperture slightly by turning the wheel two then three millimeters using his thumb and forefinger. The subject was centered now but kept moving. It didn't know that it needed to stay still for the picture to be crisp and perfect, but Lyle pressed the shutter release anyway.

Click.

The film winder adjusted to the next negative. But not quickly enough.

The subject was moving away from him now, surrounded by others, but he was less interested in them today. Sometimes he took pictures of them all, but today he was focused on his favorite one. She was dressed head to toe in red, white, and blue—fitting for the holiday weekend. Her long brown hair grazed the top of her shorts. Her bangs seemed to tickle her small nose until she brushed them away. He had seen her at school, but they'd never spoken. Lyle didn't speak to his subjects. It ruined the magic.

But he could watch her.

She and her group of friends were loitering outside Timberline Outfitters across the way from Parrish

Photos, but as they finished their ice cream cones—hers was chocolate with chocolate sprinkles and whipped cream—they began edging out of sight. Where to? Lyle wished he knew. He wished he could follow his subject—but then it would see him. And once the subject saw the photographer, the magic was gone.

The one-way privacy window film that he had installed after the store officially closed kept him hidden. No one had reason to look into the now-empty store. And if they were to try, they would only see their reflection.

They wouldn't see the small setup that Lyle had created for himself. The few cameras he pilfered from the last day of the *Going Out of Business!* sale, the tripods and stands set up at every window, the collection of film reels stacked in precise piles, organized by company name, width, and amount, just as Mr. Parrish had taught him. And most importantly: his gallery. Seven photos were pinned against the wall in a neat row, each depicting his favorite subject as of late.

She was the perfect subject, beautiful yet mysterious. Sometimes, when she'd keep still long enough for him to get a decent shot, he thought maybe she knew he was taking her picture. Like she was being a better model. Making him a better photographer. Each photo on the wall was of her on a different day: one with her boyfriend (Lyle assumed it was her boyfriend since his arm was around her), another of her laughing with her best friend (some girl with big earrings and even bigger hair), another of her pensively thumbing through *The Collector,* one with her little sister, another of her eating ice cream—this time vanilla with rainbow sprinkles and cherries on top—one of her at a payphone. And Lyle's favorite. One of her looking straight in his direction.

Almost directly at him.

As if she could see him.

But he knew that was impossible.

Lyle checked his watch. There were only ten minutes left before the mall closed. It was 4th of July weekend, and "normal kids," as his mother liked to call them, would be out watching fireworks, at a bonfire, on the beach, drinking in the dunes, or whatever else they did.

Instead, Lyle was going to retire to the darkroom to set up the chemicals and lay out the bins that he had used and cleaned yesterday in order to develop today's film.

He took his time. There was no rush. He had nowhere to go, plus he couldn't leave until security was gone for the night, and that wasn't until all the stores were closed and the workers had gone. The fireworks would act as a distraction, too. He'd practically be invisible. The last thing he needed was someone catching him leaving from the back exit of the closed store, though Lyle dreamed up a few excuses just in case: "Mr. Parrish asked me to grab a box of receipts he forgot," or "I'm still cleaning out inventory as a courtesy!"

Parrish Photos had shut down over a month ago. Mr. Parrish, the namesake and owner, had tried to keep up with a competing store in the other wing of the mall, but even with Lyle's help, he couldn't. The brand new 1-hour photo turnaround time they were advertising was just too quick for him. "It's just not the way we used to do things," Mr. Parrish explained when he realized his business had failed. "It was okay that things took time, but now, everyone wants things *now now now*. They have no patience! Good things take time . . ." He pressed a handkerchief to his nose and waved Lyle away, as if Lyle hadn't already seen him cry several times that last day. But at least Mr. Parrish had retirement to look forward to. Long days resting and relaxing. No stress. No responsibilities.

With the store closed, Lyle had nothing. He couldn't go home. His stepfather already loathed the few hours Lyle was in the house just to eat dinner and sleep. "Something about him just creeps me out," his stepfather had said to Lyle's mother, who in return, responded, "That's just because he looks like his father."

"But you don't think he's like . . ."

"Nah, he's harmless."

"I don't know . . ."

"Remember, he was the one who got him sent away. Lyle has a conscience."

Lyle did look exactly like his father, which didn't help his social life. Since his father's arrest, his face was plastered on every news channel, newspaper, and magazine cover. The same dark brown eyes, squared jaw, long face, and thin lips followed Lyle everywhere in some form or another—like a funhouse mirror: an older, meaner version of himself that reminded him to hide.

A baseball cap, sunglasses, and a hoodie were the only things that kept people on the street from yelling slurs at him, as if he were the one who had committed the crimes.

So Lyle preferred to hide in the store. He hadn't told his parents that the store closed. They didn't ask him about work anyway. They just wanted him out of the house as much as possible. Since no one came to clean the store out or set up a new one, Lyle just kept showing up and resumed his work. Though that had changed from helping customers pick out cameras and developing film to harnessing his own craft, watching his subjects, and composing his gallery. He knew it couldn't last forever. Eventually, someone would want the space for another pretzel stand or a tchotchke store. But until then . . .

After sliding his hands into plastic gloves and putting on his safety goggles, Lyle poured the developer into the first processing tray. The pungent smell caused his nose to wrinkle up. As much as he loved developing film, he still hadn't gotten used to the strong smells. They instantly brought him back to his father's dark room, the one place where his father was calm, maybe even happy. Lyle was allowed to help, but only sometimes and never alone. These few memories are the ones he tries to hold onto when he hears about what his father did, *allegedly*. The few moments when Lyle felt wanted and connected. Like he had a real family. Lyle took his time pouring the stop bath and the fixer, making sure to take all safety precautions. Mr. Parrish had been adamant about that.

"Make sure you don't spill the chemicals on your skin or clothes!" Mr. Parrish had repeatedly warned. "If you get them on your skin, it can change your skin color and give you a nasty rash. If you get it in your eyes, it might blind you! So be careful."

Once the basins were filled and in order, Lyle placed a pair of tongs next to each one. He thought this was what a coroner must feel like before dissecting a body, on the precipice of unearthing something never before seen by the world, discovering hidden secrets, bringing to light what's been kept in the dark. In a sense, producing magic. It made his fingers tremble and his teeth chatter with anticipation.

"*Sh!*" a voice whispered harshly.

Clumsy, heavy footsteps echoed from the other side of the locked door. Lyle held the tongs up like a weapon.

Another voice stifled a giggle.

"I told you they wouldn't find us!" a male voice said.

Were they in the store?!

"So what's the big plan exactly?" a female voice answered, a bit accusatory.

"We stay in here until the security guards leave. Then we find our way up to the roof and set off these M80s my uncle got me!" The male voice laughed along with a second male voice. Lyle counted at least three of them, but guessed there were more based on how many footsteps he heard.

"So you just want us to sit in the dark for an hour? You can't be serious, Billy," the same female voice as before said. "Why couldn't we hide out at Betty's Salon or Beyond Basics?"

A second female voice chimed in: "O.M.G. Becky, you are such a buzzkill. Obviously, it's because the workers are still there. I'm sure we could light a match or something and get a light in here." This one's voice was much snarkier, and it sounded like she was chewing on something. "Hey Trent, light my cigarette, will you?"

"Sure," the second male voice said.

Lyle heard the flame spark, the end of the cigarette crinkle, and then a deep inhale followed by a breathy exhale.

OK, Lyle thought. *I can wait an hour. Keep the door locked, don't make any noise, and pretend not to be here.* Lyle was used to this. These were skills he had mastered when his parents came back from the bar angry, drunk, and looking to beat someone up besides each other. Ones he had honed when his father was still around, and brought another young girl home who liked to scream while he took her picture. As long as he stayed hidden and quiet, no one knew he was there. As long as no one knew he was there, he was safe. "I thought this place was empty," Becky said. Her delicate footsteps pitter-pattered slowly around the room as if she were surveying everything. Lyle imagined her greasy hands moving the tripods, putzing with the film boxes, and ... *Uh oh.*

His gallery.

Lyle swallowed the vomit that shot up into his throat. The acid burned his tongue, leaving a bitter, rancid taste in the back of his mouth. He pressed his lips closed with the tongs.

Just stay hidden, he reminded himself. *Just be quiet. Don't get caught.*

"Oh yeah," Billy said. "Looks like someone left a bunch of stuff behind after it closed down. Do you think it's worth much?"

"You're not going to steal it, are you?" Becky asked.

"Why not? It's not technically stealing. The stuff's been abandoned. It's not like anyone is going to use it ..." Trent said. The film compartment clicked open and then shut. "Smile ..." The filmless camera shuttered.

"Woah, what the hell is this?" Billy asked.

Oh no ... Lyle balled himself up in the corner of the dark room, tongs on his lips, tears streaming down his face. He had gotten too comfortable and hadn't been careful enough. He knew he should have taken everything down when he left, but he got too cocky. He got too smart for himself. Just like his father.

"I'm a bit too clever for my own good," his father, Rodney, had said after the arrest. Though he said it with a smirk as if he were still being a bit too clever for his own good. Clever wasn't the word his mother used. Nor the word the media used when talking about him. They preferred sicko and monster and evil.

"Becky, come and see this," the second female said.

All the footsteps shuffled to one side of the store, followed by gasps.

"What the fuck is this?" Billy said.

Lyle kept his lips clamped shut even tighter. A stream of piss made its way down his right leg. It was hard to breathe. His nose was clogged from crying, and he needed to open his mouth, but he was afraid they'd hear him cry out.

Just don't see . . . He prayed they wouldn't find his gallery. That they would just leave now, leave him in peace, to make his art, to be left alone. It was dark in there after all. How much could they possibly see? *It would be okay,* Lyle told himself. *It would be —*

"Is that a picture of you?" Billy said.

"Um," Becky answered. "That's you, isn't it?"

"And me," Trent said. "And you, Carla."

"But we're in the background," Carla added. "The photos are all of you, Becky."

"Give me another match," Billy demanded, his tone stern and serious now.

Lyle couldn't take it any longer. He tried to breathe through his nose, but the snot had bubbled and clogged both nostrils. His eyes felt like they were ready to burst from their sockets. The tongs had dug deeply enough into his skin that he could feel the prickly sensation of broken, rushing blood. He unclasped the tongs and took in a deep breath. It was as though he had been underwater for minutes, suffocating. His lungs inhaled. His throat throbbed. His lips trembled.

And then he coughed.

"Did you hear that?" Billy asked.

No no no, Lyle thought.

"Is someone there? Hello?" Trent followed suit.

Quick, tempered footsteps made their way outside the dark room door. The handle jiggled. "It's locked. I think someone is in there!" Billy said.

"Let's get out of here," Becky said.

Carla agreed.

"No, I want to talk to this guy. Hey!" Billy started pounding his fist against the door. "Stand back. I'm going to bash it in with my shoulder."

"I'll help," Trent added.

Lyle rushed to the other side of the room, made himself as small as he could for his tall frame and wide build, and tried to tuck himself into the corner beneath the shelves. It took them three coordinated hits to bust open the darkroom door. It took everything in Lyle's power not to yelp out loud. He kept both hands over his mouth and clamped his eyes shut tightly, hoping that if he couldn't see them, they couldn't see him.

"Ugh, it's rank in here," one of them said.

Lyle covered his ears. Their voices were now muffled in the distance. Yet, still too close. He needed to make himself smaller. But how small could a five-foot-ten-inch boy really get?

"What is this place?"

"It's a dark room to like make photographs or something."

"The yearbook uses one at school. It's where that weird kid, Herb, is all the time."

"Where is he?"

"There's no one here."

"The door was locked from the inside. He's gotta be in here."

"Look at all this shit. It looks like someone has been here recently."

"Take a look at this."

Lyle braced himself.

"More photographs . . . Becky, this one is of us today."

"This just keeps getting creepier and creepier . . ."

"Hey!"

Lyle felt a hand on his ankle and a powerful yank.
His back slammed onto the floor, but he still kept quiet
and kept his eyes shut. "Get him up! Come on!" He was
being pulled across the room towards the door. Then he
was being lifted. "Stand him up! Keep the matches lit!"
Lyle was being propped up like a toddler mid-tantrum,
body limp. "Open your eyes!"

Lyle's eyes had adjusted to the dark room after years
of working in one. He could make out their faces and
features well, much better than they could see with their
sad matches. The red light above spread a bloody hue
around the room.

"Did you take those photos out there?" Billy asked.

Lyle had never known the names of his subjects. And
he admitted to himself that meeting them took the magic
out of it, just a little. But there was also something exhil-
arating about being this close to one of them. He wished
he could take a picture with a wide lens and a slow shutter
speed in a bright light—to really get all the details: the
freckles on his nose, the scar above his lip, the patch of
unshaved hair on his cheek.

"I asked you a question!" Billy said, grabbing Lyle's
chin. "Ew, what the fuck is on your face?"

"This guy smells like piss and vomit," Trent said, from
behind him. Lyle guessed that's whose hands were prop-
ping him up like a puppet as he hung limply. It reminded
him of a game he used to play with his dad.

"Play dead!" his father would say, and then he'd drag
Lyle into his bedroom and into the closet. "Don't move.
Don't make a sound. Don't even breathe. If you win,
you get a big, big treat!" It was a game Lyle was good
at, and the sudden memory of his father's whispers made
him smile. The treat was usually something sweet. Like
ice cream.

"What's so funny?" Billy asked.

"Let's get out of here," Becky insisted.

Lyle stopped smiling. He had been so focused on the
Billy subject that he had forgotten there were other
subjects here. And Becky was his favorite. Lyle had been

watching her for months, had even taken to following her home sometimes, from a safe distance, of course. He didn't dare take her picture out in the world. Not yet, at least. But he wanted to take a picture of her, close up, every crease and crevice. Every divet and dimple. More than anything.

"Stop looking at her like that!" Billy said, punching Lyle in the stomach.

The retching started again. Lyle fell to his hands and knees and continued throwing up.

"Get up!" Billy ordered.

"I think we need to go to the police," Becky said.

"She's right," Carla added. "I just want to get out of here."

The girls were holding each other, tiptoeing their way closer to the door.

"We should go, man," Trent offered.

But Billy didn't move.

"Get up," Billy ordered.

Trembling from head to toe, Lyle imagined he looked utterly pathetic and helpless, like those women in his father's photographs. With wobbly legs, he stood up but kept his head down, afraid of being hit again.

"I asked you a question. Did you take those pictures?"

Lyle offered a solemn nod.

"What is wrong with you?"

Lyle shook his head.

"God, you're pathetic."

Lyle's eyes focused on the chemicals on the table. His irises shifted in and out of focus, as if he were turning a lens, adjusting it ever so slightly. The room was probably too dark for anyone but Lyle to see. He needed a weapon, some way to protect himself. Billy would probably kill him. If not, expose him. And then everyone would know what he had been doing.

And he couldn't let that happen.

Billy grabbed Lyle by the collar, but kept him at a distance. "If I ever see you —"

Lyle squirted the bottle of developer right into Billy's eyes. Billy screamed and jolted backwards. The girls screeched and jumped towards the wall. Lyle shut the red light off, covering them in darkness. Trent rushed forward, but not being able to see, tripped on the edge of the table and fell face-first.

What happened next felt like he was looking through a photo album: the images were crisp, but he was outside himself, above himself, looking on. As if he were someone else entirely.

One picture was of Lyle stomping on Trent's head until he stopped moving. Another was of Lyle stabbing Billy with the broken end of the tong. The third was him laying a motionless Billy next to Trent. The fourth was of Billy's unblinking eyes.

The fifth was of the girls in the corner, grasping each other, eyes wide, faces wet with tears, snot bubbling at their noses, lips trembling — just like the ones his father used to take.

Someone had found him then once, too.

An older lady with a black, red, and blue face had crawled into his closet. She shook violently and stifled a scream when she found him laid out like a corpse. He was only twelve years old then. Before his growth spurt, he could get very small. The long jackets helped cover most of his body, but he had peered out to see who had joind him. No one had ever hidden with him before.

"Sweetheart," the woman had said, with one blue eye and one shut eye. "I need y-your help, okay? I need you to r-r-run for h-help." The woman was in a tank top and shorts. Her legs were covered with strange symbols. Her hair was a matted mess. He thought she could use a bath. "Can you do that for me, s-sweetheart?"

It was the first time someone had called him sweetheart. Now that he thinks about it, it may have been the last time, too. She seemed nice. She had even smiled at him, though her teeth were bloody and her lips swollen. No one had ever asked him to do something so nicely. Lyle thought this might be part of the game, a new added level.

Now it was her turn to play dead while he snuck out. So he told her to lie down, be very quiet, don't move or say a word. Lyle stifled a giggle as she followed his instructions, all the while wondering where his father was.

Lyle found his father playing dead in the living room. So Lyle was extra quiet because he didn't want his father to lose the game either. The doorknob was covered in blood, and Lyle remembered having to use his shirt to unlock the door. But he was proud of how quickly he did it—surely his father would be proud. Lyle went next door to the neighbors who were "retired old hags," which was what his mother called them. "I'm playing a game with my dad and his friend. She says I have to ask for help," Lyle explained, all the while smiling, because he finally had someone to play with. But he didn't know his father would get in trouble and go to jail. She didn't explain that helping her would hurt him.

"I thought it was part of the game," Lyle had explained to his father after the arrest.

To which his father just smiled. But it was a lifeless smile—his eyes cold, his lips tense, his eyebrows furrowed. That was the last time Lyle saw him.

Lyle turned the red light back on, so he could see them better. The lighting wasn't perfect, but it would do. "I'm not going to hurt you, sweethearts," Lyle said, giving the girls a soft smile. One he knew they probably couldn't see very well. But maybe they could feel it.

"Please," Becky said, "Let us go."

Lyle considered it, but thought maybe they'd like to play with him instead.

"What if we play a game first?"

He grabbed the camera by the developing basin, added a new roll of film, and put the lens up to his eye. He had never been so close to a subject before, so close he could smell them and feel them. He wanted to be closer, as close as possible. And he needed a picture. One perfect picture.

"Now, stay perfectly still, be quiet, don't move . . ." he said, as he took picture after picture, until he couldn't even hear their screams and cries anymore.

All he heard was the satisfying *click* of the shutter.

15

WASTE NOT, WANT NOT
Fionna Cosgrove

IT'S A STINKER OF A DAY AT Sherwood Mall. Heat rises off the pavement as Bruce Springsteen's "Born in the USA" pumps out of the open windows of every other car. Crowds of shoppers, drenched from head to toe in red, white, and blue, file through the open doors where a recorded voice bellows, *"Fourth of July sale! Assert your independence in every one of our stores! Everything's discounted! Fill your bags, keep your cash!"*

I lean against the wooden panel of our Chevy wagon, sweat rolling down my spine. Dad's burrowed headfirst in the trunk, just his jean-clad butt hanging out.

"Need a hand?" I ask.

"Huh?" Dad calls back.

"Need a hand?" I say a little louder so my voice can travel over the hoarded pile of randomness that is *the trunk*.

When Dad emerges, his cheeks are red, and his fringe, matted with sweat, sticks to his forehead. "What, Chip?"

"I said, do you need a hand?"

"Oh, right." He wipes his brow with an equally sweaty hand. "No, that's okay. Your mother just tucked it all the way in the back, that's all."

I don't say anything, but apparently, I don't have to.

"What is it, Chip?" Dad asks.

I shake my head. "Nothing."

He waits, raising one eyebrow.

"It's just . . ." I look around at the chaos of the parking lot. No doubt the inside of the mall will be twice as bad. "Did we really need to come on today of all days . . . just to return a toaster?"

Dad looks from me to the backseat, where Mom is busy unclipping my baby sister. "Your mom insisted. It won't take long, all right?" He gives me a weak smile.

I nod, waiting until he dives back inside the trunk before mumbling, "Seems like it could've waited a day. We don't even eat that much toast."

Dad continues ferreting through the wagon, digging into all the life debris he stores back there. He's on the road a lot, and the car is basically his second home. I watch as he pushes aside a box full of folders and paperwork, a shopping bag filled with old books, a duffel full of clothes, and even a folded stroller Libby's refused to get into since she joined the family three weeks ago. As he dives farther in, his elbow knocks over a bag, and a faded blue dog's leash falls out. As it tumbles from the trunk, it drags with it a black collar with a small silver box attached.

I pick it up, turning the silver box over in my hand. Heat builds at the base of my neck. It's cool to the touch and heavy in my palm. I've seen one of these before. There's an ad on TV and an annoying jingle that goes with it.

"Rover's e-stop! Cut the bark! You bring the dog, we'll bring the spark!"

As the jingle repeats in my head, an image appears: a golden retriever with a big red tongue slaps against its jowls as it bounds towards me. It has a black collar around its neck, and a blue leash trails behind it. Then, just as quickly as it appears, it dissolves, hovering for a moment on the back of my eyelids before disappearing completely.

A woman shrieking nearby pulls me back to the parking lot.

"You little hooligans!" she yells as a herd of kids on bikes weave between cars and swerve around families. The kid at the front, a boy on a pale blue Skyway, flips the lady the bird as she clutches her toddler.

Dad peers out the trunk at the kids. "Idiots," he mumbles. He's shaking his head as he turns to me, but he spots the leash and, with a sharp gasp, snatches it from my hands. With a quick glance towards Mom, he tucks it back into the bag.

"What is that?" I ask him.

"Nothing, champ," he replies, swallowing a lump in his throat. "Just some old stuff I need to throw out." He buries himself back in the trunk. No more explanation. But I'm used to that lately. Mom and Dad have been weird the past few days. Whispered conversations that stop when I enter the room. Half-baked explanations when I ask what's going on. For the most part, it's Mom, but I can tell Dad's on edge, too. I've read that a new baby can do that.

Across the parking lot, a fresh wave of screeches echoes as the kid on the Skyway skids around another mom and her toddler. He maneuvers the bike like he's flying. There's something special about bikes. The way they make you feel. Like you were weightless.

I have a lime-green Mongoose at home. Got it just a few days ago. A wicked collection of steel and rubber. I couldn't wait to ride it. That's until the gears jammed, and I decided I'd take it apart to see why. I had it dismantled within the hour. Each piece was delicately laid on one of Dad's plastic painting tarps in the garage. Mom found me and the bike that evening. I thought she'd be impressed. She always said curiosity is the sign of a keen mind. But apparently that didn't stretch to reverse bike engineering. From the scream that echoed around the garage, you'd think she found me cooking a dead mouse in the exhaust pipe. Dad was on the road, but I heard them on the phone that night.

"It's happening again, Tim."

"C'mon Cherry, it's just a bike."

Behind me, Mom slams the backdoor as she straps Libby into the carrier fixed to her chest. "It's all right, honey," she whispers. She glances up, catching my eye for a moment before looking away.

Libby's fine hair ruffles in the warm breeze. She came out the spitting image of Mom. Blonde hair, fair skin, green eyes. Whereas I have Dad's genes. Black curly hair, a darker complexion, and solid brown peepers.

"There'll be air conditioning inside," I tell Libby, tickling the bottom of her chubby feet.

Mom flinches. A breath catches in her throat as she twists her body, pulling Libby just out of reach. She drapes a light muslin cloth over Libby's head, fastening it around the sides of the carrier. I feel like I haven't seen my little sister in days. Mom's been squirreling them both away in her bedroom.

"You okay, Mom?" I ask.

"Fine," she replies curtly.

"Here it is!" Dad finally declares, pulling out a slightly mangled cardboard box. He looks awkwardly from me to Mom, then wedges the box under his arm and reaches up for the hatch.

That's when the kid on the Skyway appears. "Happy Fourth, old timer!" he yells, zooming past and chucking a handful of snap caps at Dad's feet.

The caps burst against the cement, crackling at Dad's ankles, sending the ashy smell of burnt paper and chemicals into the air. Dad jerks backward and smacks his head on the wagon.

"Christ!" he yells. "Show a little respect!"

He gets even less of that when the rest of the pack zooms past, half of them flipping him off while the other half laughs like a pack of sugar-hyped hyenas.

"What on earth was that?" Mom asks.

We all watch as they cruise over to an elderly couple. The kids spin a few circles around them, then throw another handful. The couple narrowly avoid falling over each other as they burst at their heels.

"That's it," Dad says, thrusting the toaster box into my arms and taking off across the parking lot.

I watch as the old man raises his fist in the air while the woman next to him tries to hold him back. I shuffle the toaster from one arm to the other so I can shut the trunk, but something rolls around inside the box. The flaps of the box are closed, but there's a narrow gap running down the middle, and I spot a few stray wires poking out of the darkness. I grab a corner to take a look, but before I can open it, Mom's hand slaps down on the box.

"Don't do that!" she snaps.

I don't dare breathe, worried if I make even the slightest of moves, it'll send Mom's mood nuclear.

"Close the trunk, Chip," she instructs, grabbing the box from my arms and balancing it precariously in front of Lily, still snuggling into her chest. She barely looks back before taking off across the parking lot.

I close up the wagon, waiting until I hear the *click* of the locking mechanism before I step away. *Click.* I hear that click every night now. Mom put a lock on her bedroom door a few days ago and from my bed, right before I fall asleep, I hear it.

By the time I cross the parking lot, the hooligans have disappeared, and the old man's sunk to his knees, his trousers ripped across the kneecap. Dad's trying to help him up, while Mom attempts to calm the woman.

"Absolute pests," Dad says, steadying the elderly man on his feet. "I'm so sorry this happened to you."

"Those *fucking* punks!" the old man hisses, spit spraying through his wrinkled lips.

Mom's eyes widen, and Dad makes a choked coughing noise.

"Gareth," the older woman says, clutching the silver necklace around her neck. "Language, honey."

I smother a smile as Gareth throws out another few curse words that make Mom blush.

"They fucking were, Judy! And if I were twenty years younger, I'd track 'em down and fucking dismember them."

I'm still smirking when Mom's head moves almost imperceptibly my way.

"Gareth!" Judy hushes her partner. "He's exaggerating," she quickly adds. "It's the war."

Gareth flinches, his body twitching as if he's reliving some of those memories.

Libby fusses in her carrier, and Mom begins to sway and pat as she talks. "Of course, we completely understand. Is there somewhere we can take you?"

"I don't need your bloody help," Gareth says, yanking his elbow from Dad's grip.

Libby fusses again, letting out a raspy cry, a gurgling noise that sounds more like a blocked drain than a baby.

The old man stops and looks at my muslin-cloaked baby sister. "What's wrong with 'er?"

"Excuse me?" Mom replies, wrapping an arm around Libby, still balancing the toaster in the other.

"Nothing," Dad interjects coolly. "A cold, that's all. Look, that knee's gonna need some tending to. Maybe a suture or two."

Blood soaks the torn cotton of the man's trousers above his knee, where a gash the size of my little finger is splayed open. I watch as the blood seeps across his trousers. An odd sensation ripples in my head, and then, with a zap against my skull, I see a flash of Mom's fabric scissors and clumps of golden fur.

"It'll be fine!" The old man spits, tugging the edges of his trousers over the open wound. He hooks his arm through Judy's and leans his weight against her as they hobble towards the double doors of Sherwood.

I blink back the latest slideshow in my head.

Dad looks to Mom, who's still swaying back and forth.

"He's not our problem," Mom says, giving the box back to Dad. "And we're busy enough."

Dad drags in a slow inhale but concedes.

"Ernie's isn't far." Mom checks her watch. "If we hurry, we'll be able to get dinner at the food court afterward."

"Dinner . . . *afterward*?" Dad laughs weakly, lines along his forehead deepening. "Cher, you think we'll really be in the mood . . ."

Mom stares back coldly, not bothering to respond. Instead, she power walks across the parking lot, following the elderly couple inside the mall. Without a word, Dad and I follow.

The air conditioning inside the mall's a welcoming relief, though the assault from the overhead speakers is swift and brutal, with Whitney Houston's "How Will I Know" replacing Springsteen's patriotic rock ballad. White tiles line the lower levels of Sherwood, with white brick walls rising to neon lights zig-zagging across the ceiling. A woman leaving a tanning salon shoves past me, her skin glowing a weird green under the fluorescent lights. But it's the crowd of last-minute shoppers, their bags filled with flag merch, that snake between me and my parents that makes me pick up the pace. I catch up right before my parents turn the last corner, and the blaring bright blue lights of Ernie's Electronics appear.

Ernie's is a mammoth electronic store with all the latest gadgets. We visit at least once a month, sometimes more. Mom and Dad are obsessed with technology. "The way of the future" is one of Ernie's favorite sayings. As well as: "Waste not, want not!"

The front windows are painted with discounts of neon pinks and blues, with a star-spangled backdrop.

50% off all TVs! Buy one VCR, get the second FREE! All Vacuum's 25% off!

And the list goes on.

We weave through the lines of people bustling for their very own basement-priced hand mixer, and as I cop a stray elbow to the gut in someone's desperation for that half-priced TV, I wonder how Mom and Dad are going to get the toaster returned before closing.

But then Ernie appears.

Ernie's a short, broad man with enough extra flesh to see him through a few winters. Thinning on top, he uses what strays of curls are still growing to give himself the illusion of volume, but all it does is make him look like a post-electrocuted scientist. Ernie never bought into the suit-wearing salesman attire, preferring instead to wear his oil-stained blue coveralls. He told me once that it makes him more approachable to the average buyer.

"Who wants a toffee nose in a black suit pulling five hundred bucks outta ya pocket for a dishwasher? Nah, when people see this —" he'd flip the collar up on his coveralls, *"they know I could 'ave any appliance repaired in twenty minutes. You can't buy that kinda trust."*

Arms open, Ernie steps past half a dozen other customers to reach us. "Cherry! Tim! And little Libby!" He claps Mom and Dad on the shoulder and gives Libby a little rub on her back. "How's the little peach doing then?"

Mom lowers her voice, and I have to strain to catch the tail end of her answer. "It's going to be a long recovery."

Ernie gives a solemn nod, but before I can ask any questions, he immediately swallows me in a bear hug. "Ah, Chippy, mate," he says, his signature scent of gasoline and aftershave engulfing me.

"Hey, Ernie," I mumble through his bulging arms.

"How's it going, matey?" He squeezes me tight, moving right past comfort, but easing before we get to pain. "How's school? Learning anything new? Making any friends? You into sports yet? You got bigger? You feel bigger!" He steps back, sizing me up. "Yeah," he says with a slow nod. "Definitely bigger."

"Um." I look down at my same self and shrug. "Pretty much the same."

Ernie winks at me with a grin and he reminds of the fun uncle at Christmas that brings brandy instead of gravy.

"Business looks good, Ernie," I say.

With his hands on his hips, Ernie surveys his bustling kingdom. "Technology's coming in leaps and bounds lately. Business ain't going anywhere fast. These tech guys have a solution for everything!"

Mom inhales sharply.

Ernie holds out his hands. "All technology comes with teething issues, Cherry. You know that."

"Better than most," she says under her breath.

"Speaking of," Dad says. He opens one flap to show Ernie.

Ernie peeks inside briefly before he calmly, but quickly, closes it and takes the box. "All right, all right, all right," he sings with a nervous chuckle. "Best be doing this kinda business out back, don't ya think?"

"No repairs this time, Ernie," Mom says. "Strictly returns."

Ernie whistles. "Cherryyyyy, he says, stringing out her name as if it were made of twenty syllables instead of two. "We talked about this. Let's not get hasty. Let's chat in the back. These things are expensive, and you know what I always say. Waste not . . ." he looks at me, one eyebrow cocked.

" . . . want not," I finish for him.

Ernie throws me a wink before wrapping an arm around Mom and guiding her through the crowds of people towards a staff door at the back of the shop.

We pass through the pet section, and I spot the Rover box in its own display. A picture of a black labrador, its mouth open, pink tongue hanging out, the little silver box nestled at its throat. Heat creeps up my neck again, but I shake it off as I spot Mom and Dad already heading through the open door.

I dart around a few other customers and step into the hallway, right as I hear a familiar voice.

"What's that? An emergency button?" Gareth and Judy are standing next to a flustered looking salesman in the security section of the shop.

"He's just trying to help, love," Judy says. "It looks quite . . . fetching, really."

"Fetching?" Gareth spits the word out.

"It's simple," says the salesman. "The pendant hangs around your neck and if you need assistance, you press a button and help is on its way."

"A button?" Gareth's face turns an interesting shade of purple. "Do I look like I'm dead?"

"What?" the salesman stutters. "Um, no?"

"I don't need no fucking button to help me off the floor! I know what I'm doing, and I know what I want. I need a weapon, you ignorant piece of—"

Unfortunately I don't get to hear the rest of Gareth's colorful vocabulary as the door closes shut, blocking out the sounds of the shop.

I bite down another smile, then remember the blood blooming across the old man's kneecap. The busted arteries. The ripped skin. Another flurry of fizzing sparks crackles against my temples, and I see another flash of fur. This time it's peeled back, jagged cuts revealing bright red muscle, and a ribcage.

"Chip?" Dad's standing a few meters down the corridor, Mom and Ernie powering ahead.

My tongue feels like sandpaper as I try to form words. "Um, yeah, coming."

Dad waits until I start walking before he catches up to Mom and Ern.

The images appear in a flash but seem to seep into my body. They feel familiar, even leaving a metallic taste in my mouth. I swallow them down as I make my way down the corridor.

Ernie has a workshop out the back where he does all his repairs. I've been a few times before, always mesmerized by the futuristic maze of wires and electricity that appliances rely on.

A handful of offices branch off from the hallway, but eventually, it opens up to a workshop twice the size of our living room, with metal bench tops skirting the walls. All kinds of machinery and tools hang from the white walls, with a few TVs and washing machines in various stages of repair. Right in the back corner is Ernie's desk, a tornado of paperwork strewn across his computer.

"Come, come," Ernie tells Mom and Dad, ushering them over to his desk, where he places the toaster box. But when I go to follow, Ernie steps in front of me.

"Ah, not you, Chip. Just boring paperwork over here. But there is a Sega with your name on it!" He spins me around to a bench top across the room where a black console is plugged into a TV. The screen has a green border with a yellow rectangle and the words SAFARI HUNT printed across it.

"Newest release." He winks. "We get them a little earlier to test. It even comes with one of those." He points to a black plastic gun. "Point and shoot." He claps me on the back with a nudge. "Go for it, kid."

I head for the Sega, taking a seat on the stool in front of it. In the back corner, I see Ernie grab a folder. Reams of paper are stapled together and filed inside. He flips through it as Mom and Dad talk at him, keeping their voices low. Ernie has his salesman voice on, soothing each of their complaints as they fire at him.

In front of me, the game turns on: a stammering of punctuated blips and beeps signals it's about to start. The gun's lightweight and feels more like a toy you'd find in a cereal box than a weapon. There are no real instructions, but it seems pretty straightforward. Like Ernie said, point and shoot.

It takes a few goes, but as another duck flies across the screen, I point . . . and shoot. A giant cross appears on its body, and it falls to the grass, dissolving into pixelated nothingness. I take out another couple of ducks and a fish or two, a high score flashing at the top of the screen. But there's something about it that feels . . . wrong. Detached. After a few moments, I realize it's the blood. Or lack of. Everything bleeds. It's a circuit within every animal. Especially after being shot. Any damage to the body like that will open up the skin, peel back the muscle, and cause the veins to burst. Blood would flow. Another spark explodes against the side of my head, a heated blow that seems to weld the others together.

Then the flashes come in hard and fast, one after the other like jigsaw pieces.

Golden fur coated in crimson blood. Fabric scissors with pol-yp-sized nubs of flesh stuck to its blades. Red liquid coats my hands. Tarps lie on the garage floor. Fresh anatomy, categorized into functional groups. Liver. Intestines. Heart.

"We won't do another repair, Ernie!" Mom's voice explodes. "We tried that, and it's happening all over again!"

Electricity fills my body, snaps in my limbs, and crackles in my fingertips. It's confusing at first. The images that appear. But I sit, let them come, let them slot into place. Then it makes sense.

"Easy there, Cher," Ernie says. "It's easy to get this worked up after a new baby. Especially when you've been trying this long. The first one's always the hardest.'

"What?" Mom snaps. "You think this is some kind of post-pregnancy hysteria?"

"That's not what he's saying," Dad says. "Is it, Ern?"

"No, no, no," Ernie says. "I just mean, when you came to me a year ago, you said you couldn't conceive, you remember? Then Chip came into your life, and you felt safer on all of Tim's long journeys."

"Things changed," says Mom.

"Exactly! For everyone! Don't you get it, Cherry? This was a big change for him, too. And what we're seeing now is some kind of . . . leap of sorts."

Mom scoffs.

"Look, Cherry, it's natural with such an upheaval of changes to feel . . . unsettled."

"Unsettled?" Mom repeats, a tease of maniacal laughter lingering at the end of the word.

"Cherry—"

"You weren't there, Tim!" Mom says. "I was the one that found Libby and raced her to the ER. I was the one that found Max." She chokes on his name. "I was the one that had to bury our dog! What was left of him, anyway . . ."

Max. That was his name. The golden retriever with the red tongue. I put the plastic gun down and turn to watch the three of them arguing.

"And that was horrible," Ernie agrees. "And what happened to Libby? Absolutely unacceptable. But as I said before the repair, it all comes down to programming. Language matters. It's not his fault. It's something in the coding." He flips through the paperwork again, his finger skimming over the sentences.

"I don't care about *the coding!*" Mom yells. "I just want it over." She turns to Dad. "I can't live like this, Tim. Locking the door every night. Checking on Libby every five seconds. I need to feel safe again."

Ernie furiously whips through the folder in his hands.

Safe. I used to make her feel safe. Something hums in my head. Wires connecting. Circuits rejoining. It's me and Mom, sitting on the lounge. Dad's away again. We're reading The Secret Garden together. She loved doing that. The worn pages and the words weaving mystery and magic. Max is curled up at our feet, his paws twitching as he dreams. We used to read together all the time when Dad left. That was one thing she wanted. A love of books . . .

"A fondness for nature. Helpful in the kitchen." Ernie reads a list from the paperwork. "A penchant for protection." He lingers over this last item, pondering. But it's when he gets to the next one on Mom's wishlist that he clicks his fingers. "A curious mind!"

He turns to Mom and Dad.

"That's it! I was focused on finding anomalies. Imperfections. Errors in his initial code. But it's not an error! What he—" he makes the sign of the cross on his chest "did to Max was only because of his curious nature. It was the e-collar, right? That's what he said?"

Mom shivers, and I notice her eyes close.

"This is important, Cherry," Ernie presses. "What did he say?"

They've stopped lowering their voices now. The pace of the discussion, too furious for caution.

Dad nudges Mom when she doesn't answer. Her eyes flash open, and she shoots him an icy stare.

"Circuits," she says through gritted teeth. "He said he wanted to understand the circulation of the currents."

"Then that's where we start!" Ernie closes the file and pushes it aside, pulling a keyboard towards him.

I get off the stool and head silently for them, sliding a wrench off a nearby counter as I go.

"No." Mom keeps repeating the word, shaking her head. Libby fusses, her voice choked and constricted. "It's okay, Libby," Mom says, peeling back the muslin cloth.

A white patch covers the wound on Libby's neck, the tape peeling back around the edges. Speckles of red blood dot the bandage.

Libby would have been fine if Mom had been just a few minutes later. Sutured up and peacefully silent. But when she found Max, her next thought was Libby. It makes sense from a genetic standpoint. Mothers and their babies. Babies whose cries are biologically programmed to burrow beneath our skin. I saw it in Mom. Black circles sunk beneath her eyes, tendrils of red arteries burst along her irises. With Dad away so much, it only made sense that I help. And how better than to go straight to the source? Human voices are so complex, so complicated in their function. It had been a delight to research it. One more minute and I would have removed Libby's larynx completely.

"This time, the repair will work, Cherry," Ernie promises. "You have my money-back guarantee. I just need . . ." He picks up a small white cable from his computer and opens the flaps of the cardboard box.

"I said no!" Mom yells, smacking the box off the desk. It skids across the floor, landing on its side. The flaps open, and a circular lump of olive-colored flesh and black curls roll out, coming to a stop at my feet.

It's a peculiar feeling to see your head detached from your body. Wires stick out of the neck, the eyelids open, and the brown eyeballs inside lazily focus on the ceiling above.

There's a silence in the workshop that makes the gentle hum of electricity from the appliances sound like a jet engine.

When I pry my eyes from the disembodied head, Mom's stumbling to the other side of the warehouse, her arms wrapped tightly around Libby. Dad's running his hands through his hair, clawing at his scalp as he tries to find words to fit the situation. Ernie, however, doesn't miss a beat.

He rises from his chair. "Ah, Chip, not the best thing for you to see." I tighten my grip on the wrench. I don't want to hurt Ernie. I don't want to hurt anyone. I *never* wanted to hurt anyone. I just want to understand. Understand how electrical currents can run through a dog's body. Understand how a baby's cry can be silenced. Understand how the world around me works. But I can't do that if they *repair* me. Or worse, *return* me.

"When did you do it?" I ask Dad, nudging the head with my foot. It rolls over easily, rocking back and forth until it finds an equilibrium with the nose pressed into the floor. "I assume you replaced my *head*?"

Ernie's eyes narrow. "Wait, Chip . . . do you remember?"

I nod. "I was only doing what I was supposed to do," I say. "Be curious. Protect." My neck twitches, and I wince at the surge of electrical currents.

"Amazing," Ernie gapes.

Dad gives Ernie a sharp look.

"The programming should remain in his brain," Ernie explains, pointing to the head on the floor. "The primary processing unit. It's where data is stored, decision-making algorithms occur, and where all the programming is located. But, Chip, he . . . he looks like he's naturally decentralized. I wonder if his limbs have kept . . . muscle memory? Maybe his organs, or his heart, or his senses of some kind. It's like he's actually learning." Ernie looks me up and down, admiring his creation.

"Fascinating," Dad says less enthusiastically.

"When?" I ask Dad. "When did the *repair* happen?" The circuits in my body fire away, memories from the past year connecting. They're different from the implanted ones Ernie programmed. And reprogrammed. Grittier. More colorful. More . . . tangible. I can tell the ones that are fake. My fourth birthday. Going on a road trip when I was eight. Listening to my first album. They're all shiny. Flat. Like I'm watching a movie. But the real ones. The past year. I can touch them. They have substance. They have weight.

"When you were asleep," Dad says. "The night after it all happened. I rushed home from my work trip. Libby was still in the hospital. Cherry only came home for one night to bury Max, but she couldn't look at you. She stayed at the hospital. I called Ernie. He convinced us to give it another go. You'd never been . . . violent before. A misfire." He looks at Ernie. "Wouldn't happen again, he said."

Ernie shrugs, still grinning. I even hear a ghostly "Remarkable" come from his direction.

Dad winces as he glances down at my original head. He takes a moment to compose himself, then he looks me in the eye. "It was late when I got home. You were already asleep. You need to recharge every night, you see. Much like us, really. I thought it might be difficult, but it was actually pretty simple once I found the seam."

"The seam?"

He points gingerly at my neck.

I run my fingers from chin to collarbone. I feel nothing but skin at first. Soft, malleable *human* flesh. But then I feel it. A ridge halfway down my neck. I slide a finger between the rubbery folds and feel a cool rim of metal.

It all happens quickly after that.

My foot twitches.

The head rolls over.

Dad moves towards me, and I pull my arm back, the wrench positioned for a perfect blow to his temple. But it's Mom who strikes first.

Something crushes the left side of my skull. A ringing reverberates inside my head as I plummet to the ground. In the background, I hear Dad scream, and Ernie yells, "Not the face!"

My head hits the ground first, another thunderous *thud* echoing in my cranium. The ringing swims around my brain, and my body spasms.

"Cherry, what the fuck!" Dad shrieks. I can see him as I lie on the ground. He's pacing back and forth, shrieking over and over again. "What the fuck, Cherry!"

Ernie leans against his chair, arms folded in front of his chest. "That was unnecessary, Cherry."

A thick, acrid liquid seeps from the crushed side of my face, pooling around my head. Mom steps over me, the rubber sole of her black canvas shoes squelching in the puddle. She kicks the wrench from my hand, sending it skittering across the cement floor.

"You could have done some serious damage." Ernie grimaces. "He has his flaws, but he's a fine specimen. And the face!" He throws his hands up. "The face is the hardest thing to get right!"

I can feel the circuitry in my body twitching. The fragile network of wires misfiring.

"Cherry, fuck." Dad's eyes are wide as he stares at me, bleeding out before him.

Mom stands next to him, the hammer dropping from her hand. "Harden up, Tim." She pats Libby's back, who's now soundly sleeping.

His voice breaks as he whimpers, "That was our son."

"No," she says flatly. "It wasn't." She looks at Ernie. "We done here?"

Ernie runs a hand over his face, paying close attention to the stubbly growth of beard on his chin. "I mean, I guess so."

I try to call out for Dad, but something's not working. Most things aren't working. I can't control my legs anymore, and my hands feel ice cold. There's a series of snaps inside my head, and a few sparks burst out of the gaping hole in my face.

Mom doesn't look back as she grabs Dad by the wrist and drags him out of the workshop. I hear her determined footsteps as she storms down the hallway, the door slamming shut behind them.

Ernie kneels in front of me, a gentle smile on his face. "Hey Chippy," he says, tilting his head ninety degrees so he can look me in my eyes. "It's not your fault, kiddo. You're amazing. You understand me? They just don't get it. Teething issues, that's all. There's bound to be some collateral damage with innovation of this magnitude."

My body spasms as black lines crackle through my vision.

Ernie grimaces as hydraulic fluid and oil gurgle from my mouth.

The phone on Ernie's desk rings. He strokes my matted black curls before standing and heading to the phone.

"Yeah, it's Ern," he sighs into the receiver.

There's another crackle of my circuits as numbness spreads through my body.

"Hang on, hang on. Just slow down, Wilson. What does he want?" Ernie says. "We don't sell *weapons*. You show him the emergency buttons?"

The ringing dulls, and darkness encroaches. But as the oil-stained cement floors of Ernie's warehouse begin to disappear, I hear his last words.

"Well, I'll be," Ernie says. "No, no, we can help. Tell him I just got an unexpected delivery. Needs some fixing up, but I think I have exactly what he's looking for. After all, waste not . . ."

Want not. I finish.

16

BANANA SPLIT
Elisabeth Tuttle

THERE WAS SOMETHING IN Heather's eye. It had been there since she'd woken up. The stubborn smudge in the bottom left corner of her world just wouldn't go away. She rubbed at it for what must've been the dozenth time that day, and even the little bursts of light behind her eyelid from the pressure seemed different. Duller. That was nothing though. It was opening her eyes again and seeing that the smudge was still there that bothered her.

Her brows pinched together as she leaned forward and stared at herself in the mirror. Everything looked normal. Except for that damned *smudge*. She reached up to gently pull her eyelid down, trying to find the source of the little cloudy spot to no avail. Releasing the lid, she hesitated just for a moment before pressing her finger into the corner of her eye. The feeling of it, wet and a bit more firm than she expected, made her wince. Then came the slight sting as she dragged her fingertip along the lower curve of it, but she persisted. Not that there was a point to it. She didn't feel anything. There was no debris, no speck of last night's mascara that she hadn't totally removed. She couldn't even find an errant eyelash. Frustration made her push at the flesh just above where the smudge lingered in her vision.

She yelped when something pushed back.

Twice. Something was pulsing behind her eye in response.

"Nope," Heather shook her head and stepped back. This really wasn't the day for any weird shit. Her boss would have her head if she didn't show up. Going to the doctor to deal with whatever was stuck in her eye? Not a good enough excuse. Summer was already busy enough as it was, but today was going to be even worse. The line of impatient parents looking to appease eager children with an ice cream cone was already forming in her mind, wrapping around and around her consciousness. It was going to be a nightmare.

And she'd had her fair share of nightmares already. She'd chalked it up to dread over working the holiday—the disturbances that her mind had conjured up last night. That had to have been why her boss had been there. In their stupid uniform, nonetheless. She shuddered at the memory of what her traitorous brain had inflicted upon her, at the image of the sterile room and the way she'd been strapped down while her boss had hovered over her and his face had peeled away. Strips of flesh had loosened around his head and then rolled down with the drawn-out sound of something stretching until there was a thump on the floor when it all landed. She hadn't watched it all. She hadn't been able to stomach it. There had been too many . . . pieces. The flesh on his face had all stuck together with gluey strings until it fell enough that they snapped and hung limp. Seeing them dangling there and somehow moving in the stagnant air had been more than enough to get her to squeeze her eyes shut. Still, she remembered thinking that it had looked vaguely like a banana peeling, even in her dream. Heather liked bananas.

A banana would have been much better than what she'd seen.

When she'd finally opened her eyes, nagging but still mostly tolerable, Greg had been replaced by something that certainly had not been a harmless fruit. She hadn't wanted to look. It had been the sound that had made her curious. Clicks and whirs of something being assembled had demanded her attention, and she'd given it. What else was she supposed to have done while lying there? Her stomach rolled when she thought of how helpless she'd felt as the thing that had replaced Greg loomed over her with its sickly gray skin stretched too tight over a wide skull. The milky eyes that she'd known were trained on her had sat in deep hollows like a trio of lifeless marbles staring down at her. Worse than its face had been the hands and those spindly fingers that she could've sworn had been made to sneak into crevices and dig things out, and worse than its hands had been the device it had put onto one of them to make what she'd assumed had been its index finger elongate the digit further.

Worse still had been when that finger had started moving towards her eye and something had been wriggling on the tip of it.

Shaking her head again, she gripped the blue basin of the sink and took a deep breath as if that would be enough to calm the assault of nausea that the memories brought. She looked at her reflection again. She looked tired. She felt tired. The smudge in the corner was still there. "You'll adjust," Heather told herself. If she just said it enough, maybe it would end up being true. Then she could make it through today and deal with whatever this was tomorrow. Not that she had much of a choice anyway.

So, she abandoned her reflection. The mall wasn't far, but traffic around it was going to be a mess. Throughout the week, stores had been putting out signs for their big Independence Day sales and promising unheard-of savings. If that wasn't enough to draw the crowds in, the promise of the fireworks that evening would be. She'd never seen the point of the Fourth, but even she was looking forward to the fireworks. Hopefully, the crowd wouldn't be as bad during the show, and Greg would let her step outside to watch it.

She snatched her hat up from where she'd discarded it on her dresser the night before. Every shift, she tried to get away with not wearing it. It always messed up the carefully crafted wisps of hair that she'd sprayed in place high above her head. The previous manager couldn't have cared less if a strand fell into someone's order here and there. She supposed that was why he was the *previous* manager now. Ever since Greg had stepped in at the start of summer, she rarely managed to make it more than fifteen minutes into a shift before he was snapping at her to pull her hair back and get her hat on. That didn't mean she didn't stop trying. The thing was in terrible condition anyway. It was the same one she'd worn last year when she'd picked up the job while spending her summer break from college back home. Maybe if it fell apart, they wouldn't have a choice but to let her leave it off. After all, they were too cheap to even replace the equipment in the store when it started acting up. A popular food court attraction with money to burn, but why would they help their employees escape the screeching mobs of customers who acted like their hot fudge sundae taking an extra minute was the end of the world? Were they really going to bother with her hat at the end of the day?

That stupid hat was shoved into the bottom of her backpack. An extra change of clothes went on top of it. In a perfect world, they would be overstaffed, and someone would get asked to go home early. Heather would always take that opportunity, happily turning back into a regular person rather than just another cog in the machine. Chances were slim, but a little bit of hope never hurt anyone. When she made it downstairs to the kitchen, she paused at the bowl of fruit on the counter. Even if her stomach clenched unhappily in response to the thought of putting anything in it, she knew that she should eat something. She hadn't all day, and there was no telling when she'd actually get a break to refuel. Her hand hovered over the bowl. She finally settled on an apple, avoiding the bunch of bananas like the plague.

The bus was more crowded than usual. She would have walked. Most days, she did, but she wasn't about to trudge through the blazing afternoon sun just to arrive at work drenched in sweat and trapped with her own stench and only making more of it for the next eight hours. Instead, she preferred to be trapped with the stench of other people for the duration of the ride while preserving herself as best she could. Worst case scenario, the bottle of Poison that she carried everywhere could salvage most stinky situations. It had come to her aid more than once at work when she'd spilled something and had been forced to walk around reeking with the sour scent of sweet milk that had dried into a powdery stain on her red shirt.

Most everyone on board got off at the stop closest to the mall, leaking out of the bus like pus from a wound that was already infecting her day. Judging by the number of cars piled up in the lot, she'd been right about it being busy. Her hope of getting to go home early was already dwindling, but she held onto the possible chance of at least getting to see the fireworks later. She was missing parties for this, and she had to have something to look forward to. Even if she was stuck in the prison-like box of white bricks with those headache-inducing neon lights taunting her from above, she was choosing not to let the day be a wash right away. Heather soldiered on towards the food court. She rubbed her eye again. The smudge remained.

The scene that greeted her when she rounded the corner made her head fall back with a groan. People weren't even bothering to form a line. They seemed to think that simply forming a mob at the counter and forcing their way to the front was the proper way to do things. She stopped at the edge of it and peered through a gap in their shoulders to see what she was about to walk into. Becky was at one of the registers. She looked as tired as Heather felt. More so. That was a bad sign. Out of everyone she worked with, Becky was the one who always seemed to be genuinely enjoying herself and sometimes even managed to get Heather excited about being there. Today, she looked like she was ready to hurl all over the person ordering before dropping to the floor. Had it really been that bad of a day already? Sherwood had only been open for a few hours. Breaking the indomitable optimism of Becky in that short of a time seemed unlikely. Hell, it seemed downright impossible. If she was down, there was no hope for the rest of them.

Before she was too tempted to run away and risk the wrath of Greg, Heather steeled herself and slipped through the door to the back hallway. Instantly, she was drawn back into her nightmare. The bare walls and stale air reminded her of the room her monstrous interpretation of her boss had restrained her in. Her stomach twisted over itself. There was no way she was going to get that apple down. She didn't even want to try at this point. She could hear the faint buzz of the lights overhead as she forced herself to take a step, then another and another. Her own body seemed hesitant to listen to her like it was now dreading the day just as much as she was. When she finally made it to the door, all she could do was stare at it. The regal name of the store stared back at her. One of them was going to have to move. Heather didn't think it was going to be her. For a while, it wasn't.

The near trance she was in broke as the door swung open too quickly. She swore she could feel her bones shifting as she nearly jumped out of her skin at the sight of her clearly annoyed boss. Her hand shot up to her chest to make sure her heart was still in the right place.

"Jesus, Greg, you—"

"You were supposed to be on the clock four minutes ago." He interrupted her.

"What? But I—" Heather looked to the left for the clock on the wall. Her eyes widened when her tardiness was confirmed. She'd gotten off the bus with fifteen minutes to spare. It only took seven minutes to get from the bus stop to the door, and she'd just stopped to look at the crowd for a second. Where had all of that time gone? Surely, it hadn't taken her that long just to get down the damned hallway. And her showdown with the door couldn't have lasted that long either. But the clock didn't lie. For a moment, she considered blaming the busy mall or the traffic around it, but if needing to go to the doctor to get her eye checked wasn't a good enough excuse for her boss, she knew that neither of those would fly either. "I'm really sorry." She finally relented as she turned back to him. "It won't happen again."

Greg didn't answer. For a long few moments, he only looked at her with his watery blue eyes narrowed in examination. All she could do was look back at him. She didn't know what he was looking for, or what else he was expecting her to say.

Heather thought of bananas. She thought of things peeling and something squirming on the tips of too-long fingers and a face that was too small for the skull it was resting on. She thought of cloudy eyes and the smudge. She looked down at the concrete floor. The mall had gray skin, too. She wondered how many eyes it had. Something pulsed.

"Can I come in?" She asked a little too sharply in her eagerness for the interaction to be over and for something else to occupy her mind. The less she had to talk to him, the better, and she needed to escape that analyzing gaze. Still, her smile was what she hoped was apologetic when she dragged her unwilling eyes up to him once more. He was still her boss, even if he was looking at her like she was some kind of specimen under a microscope. The summer was already in full swing. If she got fired here, trying to find another job for the rest of her break was going to be hell. "I-it looks like Becky's swamped. Do you want me to take over for her?" She offered to smooth over how she'd snapped at him. Getting to work actually sounded like the better option for once. Being busy would keep her distracted, and having an unending line of customers meant fewer chances for Greg to talk to her.

Thankfully, he didn't say anything more. He just nodded once and stepped aside to allow her in. She squeezed herself through the space he left to avoid brushing past him. He'd already gotten under her skin in her subconscious. She really didn't need him touching it during her waking hours. Once she'd put some distance between them on her way to drop her stuff and clock in, she relaxed a bit. His gaze was still on her, though. She could feel it sitting heavy on the back of her head. "Make sure you put your hat on." He called from where he still stood by the door. Heather only nodded. She knew he would see it.

Four minutes late turned into seven by the time she'd pinned her hat in place and clocked in. There was some staring in the bathroom mirror between the two actions, a steadying breath here and there, and a few gulps of water from the tap in an attempt to settle her stomach. None of it helped. Her nerves were still raw as she approached the front of the store and tapped her coworker on the shoulder once she was in between customers. The way Becky didn't even flinch at the contact did nothing to ease her anxiety. Something was definitely off with her. Heather's brow furrowed. She tapped again with a bit more force this time.

"Beck?" There was no response. She shoved more than tapped. "Beck? Becky? Hello? Earth to Becky?"

Finally, the other girl turned. Slowly. She looked even more exhausted up close. "Heeeeeeey," she drawled out in a voice that sounded far too rough to belong to someone so chronically chipper. But she wasn't looking at Heather. Even though her dark eyes were trained up towards Heather's face, they weren't focused on anything. It was like Becky had only responded to the sound or the touch and didn't quite register that someone else was standing there. Heather couldn't decide which one was worse—Becky's blank stare or Greg's too-analytical one. Both of them made her feel like she needed to escape, but she liked Becky enough to at least worry about her.

"Are you okay?" Heather asked.

Watching Becky try to find the answer felt like watching someone try to start a car that didn't want to run. Her coworker's engine seemed to squeal in protest for a few seconds before it turned over. "I'm good." Becky eventually managed to get out. "Just tired. Didn't sleep well. Weird dreams,"

Quickly deciding that she very much did not want to examine that further in case her own weird dreams came up, Heather just nodded. "Cool, I'm taking over up here. I think Greg just wants you on the line. Maybe take a second before you go over there?" Becky didn't move. The next customer had pushed their way forward and asked to order. At least they were polite about it. For now. Heather took hold of Becky's shoulders and began directing her back to where a kid whose name she could never seem to remember was scrambling to assemble orders. At least customers wouldn't see her like that back there. "Beck, go work on orders."

The simpler words seemed to do the trick. Becky gave her a slow nod before continuing on the path she'd been set on. Heather watched her for a few seconds. The other girl picked up a cone without even looking at the next ticket and began filling it with vanilla soft serve. Hopefully, she remembered the order she'd taken . . . but Heather doubted it. She wasn't sure Becky even remembered where she was.

"It's fine." She mumbled, once again trying to speak something into existence. Stepping up to the register, she put on a smile and greeted her first customer of the day, but that smile fell as she went to punch in the order. She blinked. The keys were out of focus. No, everything was out of focus. The entire world was fuzzy save for that little stain still plaguing the edge of her vision. "I, um . . ." she felt her cheeks warming as she glanced up at the woman. She was fuzzy, too. She was a smudge. "I'm sorry, just one second. There's- the register's just —" Heather blinked again and again. She cleared her throat and closed her eyes, trying to refocus on the world instead of the churning in her stomach and the sudden ache settling between her eyes. Her breath trembled. Her head spun. No. No, something *in* her head spun. But there was no time for any of this. The woman was already trying to repeat her order as if that would help. She didn't need her boss seeing her act like this after she'd already arrived late, seeing her fall apart. She wasn't a banana.

When Heather opened her eyes, she was relieved to see the world in focus again. Her eyes flicked to the left, though. Was the smudge bigger than it had been a second ago?

"I'm so sorry. The register just wasn't responding." She lied. What else was she supposed to say? She couldn't exactly apologize for her eyes not working. Maybe she needed to ask about glasses tomorrow. Tomorrow. She reminded herself that she needed to deal with all of this tomorrow. There was someone in front of her today who she could tell was very quickly losing patience, and people behind that someone who'd already lost theirs. She smiled. "Can you give that to me again, please?"

Things went smoothly for a while. The register stayed in focus for hours. The smudge didn't have any sudden growth spurts. She fell into a rhythm, going through the motions with one person after the next. She was a cog in the machine again. She did her part, and that wasn't so bad for once. That was better than whatever else was going on, and it meant that she could ignore the way that Becky was moving too slowly and kept having to remake things. It meant that she could ignore Greg watching the two of them like a hawk from where he'd started expediting orders to make sure that they matched what Heather had put down on the ticket. Although, one or two of those even seemed to be wrong. She reminded herself that mistakes were always going to be made when things were so busy. Human error existed. The world was hardly going to end over someone getting chocolate sprinkles instead of rainbow. Everything got fixed. Greg just kept looking at her too much while he fixed it.

She swore those beady eyes were trying to dig their way into the back of her skull.

But at least the crew was mostly functional, and she was glad for the crowds really. They distracted her from the passage of time. More importantly, though, they distracted her from the growing churning in her stomach and the way that the pulse coming from somewhere in her brain kept trying to remind her that it was there. If she ignored it for long enough, maybe it would just go away. No doctor, no pulsing, no bananas, no smudges. She was quick to decide that was the best course of action anyway. Finding somewhere to go on a Sunday would be bad enough to begin with, and she wasn't going to let this spoil her entire weekend.

As the clock continued ticking, though, ignoring whatever the fuck was happening was starting to prove less and less effective. The pulses were starting to come closer together. The pressure was greater. They were starting to hurt, like someone was rolling a toy car across her eyes from behind, but they'd covered the tiny wheels in tinier needles. Her stomach was practically dancing at this point. She shifted from one foot to the other. Sweat was making her hair stick to the back of her neck and rolling down it until it got trapped at the small of her back beneath the red polyester, and she had half a mind to wonder if she was pregnant. Not that it was possible. Months had passed since that one hookup at school with —oh, she couldn't even remember his name. She'd been regular since then, too.

Still, it felt like the only possible explanation for whatever was happening to her. Heather was sure that pregnancy could explain away just about anything, especially the sudden suspicion that there was something inside of her making all of this happen. Something was crawling around beneath her skin and making a personal theme park of her insides. Is that what babies did? Did they make someone feel like their body wasn't their own? She ignored the next person who stepped forward in line and curled her hands into tight fists until her nails bit into her palms deep enough that it stung just to prove that she could. Just to prove that her body was her own. She wasn't convinced.

And the only thing to do was to keep working. It all seemed so pointless then. The job, the customers, the meager paychecks that covered a few new cassettes for her to listen to on the bus ride back to school, her stupid boss and the way he just wouldn't stop *looking* at her-

"Becky's going on break. Take over for her."

Now it was her turn to stare. She turned to Greg, and the world seemed to turn with her. Slowly, like it was trying to catch up. One of them wasn't moving at the right speed. Greg was out of focus. He hadn't caught up yet, but she could tell that he had that dumb look on his face again. There was some silent question that he was asking her. If he just asked it, she'd be able to answer, and he'd stop making her feel like he was the magnifying glass and she was the microscopic ant who was about to burn to a crisp in a mini solar death ray. She had bigger problems. She was possibly going to be a mother to something. Her own mother was going to kill her. She couldn't remember what Greg said. Sweat was making her uniform stick to her back. A child was screeching at his parents. It sounded like glass shattering, and the car was rolling over the back of her eyes. She wondered where it was going, where she was going. She didn't want to be here anymore.

"Jesus, what is up with you?" Greg came in to focus, and he looked like he actually wanted the answer to that question. Not out of concern, no, but out of curiosity. He should have been irritated. He should have been a boss who was dealing with an employee whose peel was coming undone, whose segments were falling apart at the seams. On any other day, that was exactly what he would have been. He hadn't been relaxed since he started, and today should have been worse, but Heather giggled at the way he looked like he was about to start taking notes on her. At least, she tried to giggle. She told her body to respond. She walked it through the steps, told it to breathe in and then clench the muscles in her belly to force that breath out, but her stubborn stomach seemed intent on just continuing to roll over and over and over.

She watched him say something else. An echo of it reached her a couple of seconds later. The sound was bloated. He said it again. She didn't understand why he was speaking like that. There was something vaguely familiar about whatever he was barking at her, but he wasn't saying it right, and she wasn't hearing it right. Maybe she had water in her ears. Maybe he had water in his throat. Someone had something in them that wasn't supposed to be there, and he just kept sticking those sounds together until it finally hit her.

"Heather." She repeated slowly. He was saying some bastardized version of her name. "Heather. Hea-therrr-rrr," Greg had said it a hundred times before. She didn't know why he was getting it so wrong now, but she said it a few more times so he'd get it right, even though it felt like she was dragging her voice from a pit of mud that had replaced her body. Someone had to tell him.

He didn't say it back to her. He didn't try to correct himself. That was rude. He only shook his head like she'd disappointed him, and that was so, *so* rude. She wanted to tell him as much. She would've if she could've wrapped her mind or her mouth around the words. They escaped both. Greg pointed deeper into the store. Her eyes followed the gesture. Becky was shuffling away from the soft serve station. Two and two came together, and Heather finally knew what he'd been trying to tell her. She was supposed to take over there. It was time for Becky's break. Hours had gone by. The fireworks were happening soon. Heather didn't want to miss them. Hopefully she could take her break once Becky got back. Becky pressed her hand to her forehead. Heather mirrored the gesture. Her skin was slick.

She wandered over to the machine, her mouth pulling into a frown that only deepened as she passed the line of toppings and saw the banana pieces that were going brown from sitting open to the air all day. Fighting the urge to gag and reaching for a cone was nearly impossible. Her arm flung out and hit the counter before going limp. Heather grunted. Her brows drew together in concentration as she dragged the limb where she wanted it, but her hand gripped too tightly around the cone she managed to grab and shattered it. She watched the pieces fall to the floor and squinted at something shimmering down there. It was silver and writhing in a tiny puddle, and finally forced that gag out. With her mind flashing back to her dream, she scrambled to distract it with another cone. She wanted to be a cog again, so she pulled the lever to dispense globs of snowy white soft serve, but she stalled on what to do next. Wide eyes were trained on the ice cream. It was smooth at first glance, but the longer she looked, the more tiny cracks and craters she saw. She thought it would be good to fill them with something.

Heather gagged again, her head throbbing along with the motion. Her stomach stilled for a blissful moment before it lurched. Something in her throat burned, and before she could comprehend what was happening, fluid spilled out of her mouth and blanketed her hand and the cone in it. Her face went slack, refusing to move in response to her terror as she watched a small army of those things from the floor crawl across her skin and the surface of the ice cream. They were like sprinkles if sprinkles were . . .

Maggots. She was full of silver maggots, but they weren't maggots. She could see that they had legs pushing them through the thick clumps of her bile. A sob was snuffed out somewhere between her lungs and her mouth. Her body defied her, even as she willed it to drop the cone and run, even as the shimmering mass of larvae began to burrow into the ice cream, and the cone was abruptly snatched from her hands. Only her eyes would move as she followed the cone to where Greg was covering it in more sprinkles. The rainbow kind. The kind that didn't move and weren't still tickling her hand. How could he not see the ones that were wrong? He was looking right at them and just covering them up instead of doing anything, and she wanted to scream while she watched the tainted treat get handed across the counter and put into a waiting hand. But she couldn't. She couldn't scream as the recipient disappeared back into the crowd of red, white, and blue clothing. She couldn't scream when Greg turned around and she caught his gaze and realized that he knew exactly what he'd just done. He lifted a brow in a dare for her to speak up and nodded when she didn't.

There was a sour taste lingering behind her teeth, and when she felt what she knew was one of those miniature horrors slithering across her tongue, another retch finally shocked Heather's body from paralysis. She seized the opportunity to peel out of there. At least, she tried to. Getting to the back door seemed to take years between heavy coughs and stumbling steps. Still slick with saliva and bile, her hand slipped across the smooth surface of the door when she tried to push it open. Greg was calling her name behind her, but he was still saying it wrong. He was getting louder. Whatever was happening to her was connected to him somehow, she was sure of it. She had to get away from him. She shoved against the door with everything she had and spilled out into the back hallway as another wave of shiny worms forced its way out of her.

Not all of them made it down to the floor. The ones that stuck to her lips seemed happy to stay there and crawl across her face. That sob finally came when she realized that they were moving up towards her eyes. *Pressure. More pressure. More smudges. More pressure.* Her stomach was tearing open, she was sure of it. She tried to call for help, but all that came out was more of her tiny tormentors. They moved up her throat as she forced her feet to continue moving, flooding into her mouth and skittering across her teeth until they made their way out and then back in through her eyes. They muffled her cries and clouded her vision, and dug their way past her eyelids, and there wasn't room for them. No, her head was so full. They had to stay in her stomach. There was no room.

Heather sniffled and sucked one of them up into her nostril. It kept crawling up. More followed. She thought she could feel their slippery little legs roaming over her skull. A mist of tears was getting trapped in her eyes by their bodies. They sat there and stung. She tried to blink and force them free, barely able to manage the motion through the swarm. Whether it worked or not, she couldn't tell. Tears rolling down her cheeks or legs crawling up them—the sensations were all fading together. Pain and pressure and the tearing skin around her eyeballs. They might not have been tears. It could have been blood. She could hardly even breathe at this point, getting little more than a few gasps of breath here and there past the horde and her own anxiety, and it was only the glimpses she caught of the red glow of the exit signs leading her way through Sherwood's back halls. Not gracefully. Walls seemed to pop up out of nowhere, only making themselves known when an errant hand or shoulder collided into them. She wasn't sure if her heart was pounding or if they'd invaded the muscle, and the wriggling mass of them was pushing and pulling it around erratically.

By the time she made it to what she could mostly make out as a door beyond the encroaching smudges, her stomach had quieted, but the pressure in her head was agonizing. Heather thought it might've been replaced by one of the patriotic balloons that the mall had put up for the weekend. Whoever had replaced it had just blown more and more air into it until it threatened to burst at the slightest touch.

She sagged into the cool metal with a grunt. There wasn't much energy left in her, but it was enough to catch the bar with her shoulder and push the door open. A wall of warm air hit her. She staggered from the air-conditioned hall out to the balmy summer evening. Squinting as if that would help her see what was around her, only the sour scent of rot helped her pinpoint that she'd made it back to the dumpsters. She had to widen her eyes again. They'd gotten more frantic when she'd squinted.

At least their clouding of her sight kept the dingy lights from hurting her throbbing head further, but there was a great boom from above that felt like a sledgehammer to her skull. A haze of blue flashed around the smudges. Then came another smaller explosion. Too sluggish for the panic she felt, she looked around only to hear another explosion, to see another flash. Cheering floated in from somewhere. Then it hit her. She was getting to see the fireworks, after all. And there were other people out here.

"Hel —" her voice cracked. Her throat was raw from vomiting, from coughing, from being a pathway to the things that were communing beneath her scalp. She tried to clear her throat and only gagged again. But she had to keep moving. She had to get away. She had to get help. She had to figure out what the fuck her boss had done to her and maybe drink an entire bottle of pesticide.

Shuffling forward, Heather lifted her hands in front of her to try to minimize the chance of colliding into anything in her near blindness. They didn't hit anything. It was her foot that did. Something squished beneath the tread of her sneaker. It squealed in protest. Heather tried to step back, but it was like trying to pull her shoe from a glob of chewed gum. Leaning down to wrap her hands around her thigh, she yanked and tumbled backward onto the pavement. The impact made her head roll, but it quieted the critters for just a moment. Long enough for her to catch a quick glimpse of what she'd stepped in.

Illuminated in the sickly warmth of the lights and the festive sparks of fireworks, she saw one of the things that were trying to make their homes behind her eyes. But this one was . . . bigger. Big enough that when she'd stepped on it, it had splattered. Thick, white ooze flowed from its crushed carapace. She wanted to gag. She thought that she should, but she couldn't. She just gaped at what she saw lying a few feet beyond the thing.

Becky.

Not that she could recognize her face. Not with the mass of silver bodies covering it. Heather knew that uniform, though. She knew her coworker's, her *friend's*, frizzy curls. She tried to call out to Becky. Nothing but a pathetic whimper came out, but it was enough to alert Becky's parasites. They paused their constriction around her head. One of them reared up, pulling half of its body into the air and stretching toward Heather.

No, that wasn't it. It was pushing through a gap. There was a sound like her mom mixing meatloaf. As more of it came into the light, she could see that this one wasn't just silver. There was a thin sheen of blood coating it. Pale bits of flesh were stuck between what must have been dozens of legs. The bits turned purple when a pair of fireworks detonated just a heartbeat apart above them all. All three of its eyes stayed pale as its head lolled in her direction, though. The fact that she could even see its eyes at all made the thing that much more abhorrent to her. And it was looking at her. And they were the same eyes that Greg'd had in her nightmare. And its body just kept coming. And when it finally freed itself from its knotted kin, there was a sharp crack that Heather decided was another firework. She didn't want to see Becky through the space it had left. She didn't want to see the way her empty eye socket had shattered from the inside out. She didn't want to see her torn skin and peek into her brain. Becky was still. Her friend was dead. The happiest person she knew, the little ray of sunshine who'd made customer service hell bearable was gone, and Heather knew that she was next.

She wished her own bugs would flood back to her eyes and obscure everything again. Unfortunately, the larger one seemed to make them want to flee, and they were worse coming out. Hers had grown, too, not as much as Becky's, but enough for her to feel it. They pushed their way from her eyes and her nose, stretching the passages until searing pain ran up her face as one of her nostrils tore. Heather sobbed. She choked on blood and snot and tears and the grown worms when they shoved back down her throat and filled her stomach. Her jaw ached from being forced open so far, her bones groaning in protest. She knew that she had to run. It hurt too much.

She tried to scream again. Fireworks muffled the sound. The crowd cheered for her ruin.

There was an unbearable pressure between her eyes. The world spun. She was watching the creature advancing, but . . . but she could also see her hand on the pavement. The pain didn't register beyond what she already felt until her two perspectives merged and silver legs came into view by her hand. Its jaws opened, all four of them expanding before it pounced. Something tugged at her eye socket. Her nerves lit up like the fireworks. She heard her own flesh tear and shrieked as it consumed her eyeball. Bile rose in her throat. She could feel the smaller ones rising with it. They spewed across her front in wet warmth.

The door opened behind her.

She didn't turn to look. She didn't see her boss watching her in resignation. Mercilessly, she didn't have time to lament her own end. The last thing Heather saw was those jaws going for her other eye. She was dead by the time they gnashed their way into her brain, and her face peeled open. Her body trembled as the larvae inside of her fed and grew, as the now massive one feasted on her exposed brain, but she didn't hear Greg speak into the small box he pulled from his pocket and tell someone on the other end that incubators were successful, but they could only host one clutch before dying.

"Anyway," Heather didn't hear Greg say as he turned to go back inside. "Busy night. Gotta split."

About the Editor

Caleb J. Pecue is the owner and editor for Terrorcore Publishing, which specializes in bringing back the vintage feel of the 80s. His short story, The Turning of a Card, was published in the second volume of Horrorscope, edited by Harriet Everend. Another of his short stories, One More Time for Old Time's Sake, is published in Gridiron Gates of Hell for charity. By day, he works at a university in Illinois, advising students; by night, he works to find short stories to publish and writes his own that he hopes to publish.

About the Contributors

Nadine Stewart is an author, poet, and media creator. She has always been an avid reader with a wild imagination. Born and raised in beautiful British Columbia, Canada, Nadine now resides in Washington State. Her short fiction has been published in several anthologies, including Terrorcore Publishing's Dolls in the Attic, and Doors of Darkness I, II & III, Voices From the Mausoleum's That Old House the Bathroom Anthology, Readings From Cursed Room 301 from Mad Axe Media, and the charity anthology Pretty Girls Make Graves, just to name a few. Her first curated project Curbside Curses: The Yardsale Anthology was published in June 2024 through House of the Macabre.

When she is not writing she is reading and promoting indie horror, designing book covers and book trailers, and crafting whatever new things have added to her mountains of unfinished craft projects.

AJ Danna is a member of the Horror Writers Association and has served as a show writer for The Queen Mary's Dark Harbor and Los Angeles Haunted Hayride, among other theme parks and attractions. AJ's work with Terrorcore Publishing encompasses both writing and narrating audiobooks. As an actor, AJ's projects have included interactive experiences for brands like *Stranger Things, Dungeons & Dragons, Batman,* and *Trick 'r Treat.* Outside of writing and acting, AJ enjoys collecting LEGO minifigures and playing pinball. You're invited to explore ajdanna.com.

Austin Hinderliter is a graphic designer by trade, holding a BFA and MFA in Graphic Design. His interest in 80s horror paperbacks, especially those with a skeleton on the cover, led to a vastly growing collection of vintage books. His stories take inspiration from past eras, so don't expect a cell phone in sight. His story, *The Night Hearse,* is published by Undertaker Books in the first volume of *Stories to Take to Your Grave.* He was also featured in *Doors of Darkness II: Trick or Treat.*

John Martin is a writer native to Indianapolis, Indiana. His horror stories have been published in a number of anthologies, including the recently released Twisted Horrors. When not writing, he enjoys meeting new people and trying new hobbies.

Reece G. Donnell is a native of the historic city of Derry, Northern Ireland. He first began writing professionally aged 27, writing journalistically online about the horror genre. This translated to a job in print for the world-renowned Scream Magazine, where he is still featured today. Reece was first published creatively in Terrorcore's *Doors of Darkness,* offering "There's Something Wrong With Barbara." He next contributed "The Candy Snatchers" to *Doors of Darkness II: Trick or Treat,* and is thrilled to be featured in this third anthology and hopes to work with Terrorcore for many years to come.

Billie Karras has previously been featured in *Fish Gather to Listen, Cult Horrotica magazine,* and *Doors of Darkness.* He lives in Phoenix, Arizona.

Adrian DeLeon is a Sacramento Valley native, where he currently writes and performs. You can find his previous work on The NoSleep Podcast. When not writing, he plays bass for Contemporary Girlfriend, a Queer-Fronted emo-rock band. He still lives in the Greater Sacramento region of California with his girlfriend, Brit, and their black cat.

Liam Ray III is a life-long member of the macabre with a heart for all things horror and Halloween. Alongside writing stageplays and screenplays, he works under the name Gory Rory as a composer, songwriter, sound designer, and sonic exorcist for film and theatre. With ghoulish gratitude to his friends, fiends, and family, this will be his first publication. He can be found mostly on the Slasher App @GoryRory, reluctantly on Instagram @goryroryiii, and intermittently in a graveyard near you.

G.D. Bowlin became entranced with tales of masks and mayhem when he watched Halloween II on cable TV at a sleepover in the late 90's. Since then he's written weird stuff for the stage, the page, and the screen. He's the author of the novels ROCK CITY and DEEP DARK.

Jason Harlow is Memphis, Tennessee-based author of all things horror. He works in the petroleum industry, but his real passion is learning more about the things that scare him most and sharing stories about those things with others. He cites R.L. Stine, Sinclair Smith, and Jon Athan as his biggest literary influences. His spooky-middle-grade-meets-extreme-horror anthology Spooky Stories to Haunt Your Dreams released in 2024. He can be reached via email at lifeafterdeathproductions@gmail.com.

AudraKate Gonzalez started writing horror stories when she ran out of Goosebumps books to read as a child. Her love for writing grew and now she has a BA in Creative Writing and is working on her MFA. Her YA/Horror Series, This is Noir, is available now wherever you buy your books. She lives in Ohio with her handsome husband, and her adorable furry bad boys, Zero and Scrappy Doo. When AudraKate isn't writing, you can find her reading, watching scary movies or sleeping.

Vincent St. Claire is a Minnesota based writer, artist, and musician. He self publishes a zine of illustrated horror stories called, "Little Terrors", but enjoys the challenge of writing for anthology submissions. When not writing his tales of terror, he enjoys cooking, bowling, and spending time with his cats. He can be found on Instagram @littleterrorszine and more works can be read on his substack https://littleterrorszine.substack.com.

William "Bill" MacFarland is a husband, father to two awesome twin daughters, teacher, and toy maker. A child with an overactive imagination, he grew up obsessed with horror, action figures, and all things strange. Nothing has changed. When he's not designing toys or teaching, Bill loves hanging out with his family, reading, and cruising the backroads of Ohio in search of spooky spots and mysterious monsters. Recently, Bill and his family opened a bookstore in a historic building—complete with secret passages. His toy designs are on Instagram: @basement_sludge And the bookstore here: @snapdragonbooksandgifts.

Vanessa Leonardo is a horror writer from Staten Island, New York with an MFA in Creative Writing from the New School. She currently lives with her wife in New Jersey. The writers that most influenced her were those she read as a young teen such as R.L. Stine, Stephen King, and V.C. Andrews. She loves anything spooky, scary or paranormal.

Fionna Cosgrove is an Australian author who's childhood consisted of The Twilight Zone, The X-Files and Are You Afraid of the Dark?, giving her, not only an ample amount of story fuel, but also a healthy respect for all things that go bump in the night. Fionna's short stories have been published in multiple magazines, anthologies, and podcasts, and has several middle grade horror novels to her name, including the spooky pick your path series Twisted Trails. When she's not writing, you can find Fionna following that black line in the pool, chasing her two minis, or convincing her husband to watch one more Bigfoot documentary. Find her on Instagram @are_you_afraid_of_the_books and www.fionnacosgrovewriter.com.

Elisabeth Tuttle is a lifelong fan of all things horrific and fantastic with a soft spot for nameless terrors. She can often be found haunting book stores, tattoo shops, and local metal shows. Banana Split joins her previous contribution to Doors of Darkness III's predecessor and continues her quest to make readers squirm.

www.ingramcontent.com/pod-product-compliance
Lightning Source LLC
Chambersburg PA
CBHW010932120626
46552CB00009B/3219